About the Author

The author, before retiring, had worked on numerous large civil engineering projects both here in the UK and overseas. Projects such as the *Channel Tunnel*, HS1, and, *Cross Rail,* which brought John into direct contact with some very colourful and interesting characters many with incredible stories to tell. The author has successfully woven together many of these stories as the basis for his writing, whilst managing to disguise their true identities and factual locations. John writes to provide readers with stories that will entertain by highlighting life's pleasures and by providing many memorable experiences.

The Emerald Wedding

J. R. Davis

The Emerald Wedding

Chimera

A CIP catalogue record for this title is
available from the British Library.

ISBN 978 1 915541 05 7

*Chimera is an imprint of
Pegasus Elliot Mackenzie Publishers Ltd.*
www. pegasuspublishers. com

This is a work of fiction. Names, characters, businesses, places, events and
incidents are either the product of the author's imagination or used in a
fictitious manner. Any resemblance to actual persons, living or dead, or actual
events is purely coincidental.

First Published in 2023

**Chimera
Sheraton House Castle Park
Cambridge England**

Printed & Bound in Great Britain

Chapter 1

A Well-earned Break

It was a bright, sunny day in May, when on a London bound train heading into Kings Cross, our main character, Joshua Foster (Josh) once again wonders why so many people must immediately get up and head for the doors as soon as they hear the announcement, "We will shortly be arriving at London Kings Cross. "

Josh on principle, always remained seated in defiance, as if making some kind of a one-man silent protest. Josh then spent the last few minutes of his journey observing his fellow passengers, now all jostling by as if there was some critical need to immediately escape the carriage. While the queue slowly snaked past him, Josh indulged in another one of his public space pastimes, 'people watching'. Smiling to himself, Josh wondered if the very large middle-aged lady, who somehow managed to squeeze into some very tight, pink tiger print leggings, believes they improve her image, or maybe she just doesn't own a full-length mirror. Or it could be she does own one but can only see the front view. Either way, wearing those she should never be allowed out in public. As part of this well-practised pastime, Josh tries to guess what each of these people might do for a living, and or what brings them into the city. With some people, it's relatively easy, as their earlier and very loud mobile phone conversations make it abundantly obvious. However, others like the elderly man standing in the now static queue, presents much more of a challenge. Waxed jacket, brown corduroy trousers, flat cap, stout walking boots, leather and canvass rucksack, Josh can't help wondering whether this man may have actually got on the wrong train. Bemused at his fellow passenger's behaviours, Josh reminds himself, this is really a very special day and then he relaxes back into an extremely happy frame of mind. That's because this is Thursday midday, and this is Josh's last day of work before he starts a three-week holiday. Feeling very pleased, Josh reminds himself, that he is off to Southern Ireland, to visit places that he had never been before, to meet people he had never met and to what is in a way, was his ancestral home, well that is, on his mother's side anyway.

Leaving the fast-emptying carriage, Josh nonchalantly follows his fellow passengers along the wide platform, trailing somewhere towards the rear of this migrating heard of impatient humans. Although there are people rushing past him, Josh is determined not to speed up and join in that nonessential rush to the barriers, after all, they are not the finishing post and there are no negative consequences for being the last one through. As Josh walks along, past that long line of stationary carriages, Josh automatically scans the crowds of busy rail travellers, on the off chance he may see someone he knows, or maybe spot someone famous, or even spot some very attractive female. Passing through the crowded concourse, heading for the underground, Josh contemplates the holiday ahead and how different his days will be from his usual busy all-consuming London lifestyle. Having never been to Southern Ireland, Josh knows this is going to be a very different holiday, one with no targets, no deadlines and no reports to compile. Well, that is apart from the one Josh has almost completed in his bag, which is, apart from the necessary second person read through, is ready to submit. Although most of Josh's work involves travelling round the country from one assignment to the next, Josh is actually based in Central London, where his employer's offices are located. His employer, Dunning & Partners, is a really good employer that Josh absolutely loves working for, born and raised on a farm in a very rural part of central England, living in London has been a life-changing delight for Josh and one that he has passionately embraced.

Josh's personal development has progressed steadily upwards, through the business, to the point, where Josh is now an extremely valued member of a uniquely specialised team. Josh and his small team of colleagues are collectively responsible for investigating, interrogating and verifying the intrinsic value as well as the potential prospects of various UK companies. These are generally companies that are currently either being acquired or disposed of, working on the behalf of and for various good paying clients. Luckily for Josh, he is employed by a long-established and highly reputable company. A company which provides a niche service, to the wider UK financial sector. Working for Dunning & Partners, had provided the ideal working environment for Josh to further develop his sixth sense for sniffing out the hidden aspects and for identifying the commonly overlooked angles. Josh's extremely natural interpersonal skills have enabled him to speak confidently to people on all levels and with a very canny business knowhow. This combined with Josh's broad depth of understanding as to what makes businesses profitable, had enabled him to progress up through the ranks, rising from lowly clerical assistant, through to the position of senior project manager. Although Josh loves his work and enjoys the comradery of his close-knit team, he was definitely looking forward to a well-earned, three-week break.

Leaving the concourse and stepping on the escalator, Josh watches the people travelling up on the other side and wonders where they are all going, old, young, short and the tall, all off to somewhere or other. As he approaches the ticket barriers, with his combined ticket in his hand, the same old thoughts go through Josh's head, *will this fucking thing work, or will I have to apologise to the person immediately behind me in order to let me back out again.* The underground barriers, always remind him of the starting gates at a race course, although these have much more clatter when they open. But Josh's luck is in today, the machine takes the ticket out of his hand, the barriers clatter open and the card appears on the other side, just as it should. After a short journey on the Northern Line and a leisurely change on to the Jubilee Line, Josh immediately engages in another one of his public space pastimes, and after randomly selecting the number eight, his game begins. This involves picking a number, in this case it means that the eighth female to enter his carriage, providing they appear to be aged between twenty and up to pensionable age, this person is by the rules of the game, destined to be his imaginary sexual partner. Taking note of each female entering through the carriage doors, Josh counts them off in his head. *Oh,* he thinks to himself. *Number five is quite nice, so is number six and even seven would be OK at a push.* However, when number eight walks through the doors, Josh immediately places his hand over his mouth, in order to hide his bemused, disappointed smile. Josh thinks to himself, *will you just look at her, what a miserable looking cow, having sex with her would be a very miserable punishment even for a condemned man. But never mind, maybe my perfect partner is in the next eight,* and so Josh starts the counting process all over again. With his bag down between his feet and feeling a little bored, Josh starts reading the adverts posted above the windows, visit London Zoo, visit Madam Tussauds, visit London Dungeons, Josh thinks, *I must have been a very busy boy, as I've done all those,* then looking further along see's visit Battersea Dog's Home. *Now there's somewhere I haven't been.* But then thinks, *it's not as I don't want to visit any dog's home, I just know I would be coming out with some scruffy little dog, that nobody else wants, it's not as I don't like dogs, because I do, but I have just too many commitment's, so sorry Josh, but you just have far too many to have a dog, or even a cat for that matter.* Josh then thinks, *I think Battersea Dogs Home, do cats as well, so I will definitely stay clear of that place, otherwise I know I would be a pet owner. It must be hard to work there, I wonder if they go home depressed, or do they finish up with a house full of cats and dogs.* But just then he hears that familiar screech of brakes that tells him they are approaching his station, which immediately breaks his chain of thoughts.

On reaching his destination, Josh exits the station into bright sunshine, thinking to himself, *I hope the weather stays like this for the next couple of weeks.* Although Josh reminds himself, *that it is the west coast of Ireland that I will be visiting, which historically gets the full Atlantic rains, that's why they call it the Emerald Isle. I've heard that everything there is wet, lush and green, because of the constant rain, the low clouds and heavy mists. Ah, but never mind.* Josh thinks, on the positive side, *if it does rain, at least I can spend lots more indoor time with my lovely Jessica.* Jessica Holmes had been Josh's steady girlfriend for a little over two years and they are both going over to Ireland together to attend Jessica's cousin's wedding. However, this would not be their first holiday together, but he could feel it was going to be very different from their previous holiday destinations, like the holidays they had taken in Spain, Portugal, France as well as ten wonderful and very memorable days spent in Bali.

Stepping from a busy street into a slightly dated, but ultra-classy, oak panelled, polished marble floored reception, Josh is immediately challenged by a very stern looking middle-aged, female security guard.

Who in a loud and complaining voice, the guard calls, "Excuse me sir, but you have not swiped in. "And adds, "Where is your ID card sir, I think you know it needs to be displayed at all times, whilst on these premises. "

Josh, putting his arm around her waist and pulling her towards him, smiles at her and replies, "What's the matter Rachael, don't you love me any more?"

Both of them now laughing, when Rachael asks, "Where the hell have you been then Josh, it's been so bloody quiet here without you around the place, like some, one-horse ghost town. "

"Well as a matter-of-fact Rachael, I have been up in there in wonderful Peterborough, industrially attempting to generate the company some money, so that we can eventually run away together and finally live out our dreams. "

To which Rachael responds, "And just what do you think my old man is going to say about that then?"

"Well for a start he's not invited, because that would just spoil the whole thing, I'm sorry but it's got to be just you and me. "

Both smiling, Rachael says, "Anyway, you still need to swipe in and behave yourself while in the company of a happily married woman. " Rachael then goes on to say, "Don't forget, we have all-seeing, CCTV here Josh, watching your every move and it's all being recorded for future reference. So just be aware, I have all the evidence I need, should I need to bring a sexual harassment case against you. "

To which Josh replies, "For a start, Steve's probably fast asleep up there in the CCTV room and the system will undoubtedly be down again, so I would certainly never rely on that pile of outdated junk for reliable evidence. " Josh then says, "Well if you're not going to run away with me, then we will just have to make out round your place. So call me and let me know when Barry's away and the coast is clear. "

"You cheeky monkey, " Rachael replies as the lift doors close and Josh slips out of her sight. As he goes up in the lift, Josh smiles and thinks to himself, *Rachael still hasn't seen my ID card and I never actually swiped in again, so she should be realising it any second now.* Josh thinks, *Rachael is so easily distracted, completely useless as a security guard, but is such a great person, I wonder when she will realise, that I've gone and done it again.*

On arrival on the third floor Josh enters the modern open-plan office, a light spacey area only broken by the odd pot plant and the many colourful room dividers. As Josh make his way through the office, he is greeted by a multitude of, "Hi ya Josh, how you going?" Which comes from so many different directions at once that Josh is now spinning as he walks, trying to respond to each of them in turn.

After ten days away from the office, Josh is now beginning to feel like he is actually back home again. Josh continues his way through the office, to a small group of private offices located at the far end of the third floor. As Josh approaches his work area, there are two ladies sitting at their desks with their backs to him.

Helen, a blonde-haired middle-aged lady, who spends most of her money on clothes and hair dressers, without turning round to look who it is, says, "Right Joshua Foster, before you go galloping off on your holidays you and I need to complete that Harman report. " She continued, "Sam here has already completed the accounts section and I've done the rest, but I still need your final summary and recommendations to finish it off. " Sam was slightly older than Helen and technically was the more senior of the two, but for the quiet life, was happy to let Helen run things. Then plugging another memory stick into her desktop said, "Oh, and by the way, the old man wants to see you in his office and he's in there now, so if I were you, I would go straight in there before he goes out again. Oh, and I need all of your receipts if you want your expenses to be paid into your account next month?"

As requested by Helen, Josh opens his bag and hands Helen a small black memory stick, saying, "It's all-in here sweetheart, but it will definitely need reading through before you go submitting it, you know what my spelling is like?" Josh then looking her straight in the eye, reassures Helen, saying, "Don't worry Helen, I will come back to you before I go, honestly, just as soon as I have seen the old man. " Josh now winking to Pat, the financial secretary, sitting next to Helen, who in response, wryly smiles back. The 'old man', is the office nickname given to the company's business director and Josh's immediate boss, Jed Shelly.

Josh knocks on the door of Mr Shelley's office and promptly walks in. "Helen said you needed to see me Jed, I hope everything is OK?"

"Err, yes Josh, but I need to bring you up to speed with what happened last Tuesday morning, so please, take a seat for a minute. " Jed then goes on to explain, "I am pleased to say, the Cheltenham report we submitted to Cumberland & Tarn, was very well received Josh and as a direct result, they have assured us, they will be passing all their future business through to us. " Looking rather pleased with himself, Jed continued, "As you know, they are big, they're extremely big Josh, so this will probably double our business throughout and will undoubtedly require us to take on more staff. So you had better start thinking how we can expand your department in order to handle it all. "

Josh, slightly taken aback by the good news, quickly replies, "I hope this won't impact on my holiday arrangements Jed, "?" said Josh now looking slightly worried.

"No, of course not, Josh, so don't you go worrying about that, but I would like you to keep your mobile phone switched on, just in case. Anyway, during Tuesday morning's board meeting, the partners decided not to lease out the second floor again this term, as the lease was coming to an end anyway, but we are going to keep it for our own use, so one good thing, we will not have to worry about office space.

"Not only that Josh, " Jed continued. "But the board has set aside a very generous contingency budget to get things moving. So as soon as you get back off holiday, we will need to sit down and produce a new business development plan for submission to the board. Oh, and the other good news for you is, you have been given a 25% pay rise, which will be backdated to the beginning of April, so as you can see, things are really looking good for us all. But don't you go worrying about the business, while you are away, as it will still be here when you get back. So please, you just go off and have a really good and well-earned break. But please just give the new business some thought whenever you have a spare minute and we can sort it when you get back. "

Josh, still a little shocked from Jed's revelations, replies, "Look, Jed, as you know, I have a bloody good, very hard-working team out there, who have all given me their 100% support, so what's in it for them?"

"That's already sorted Josh, they will all have a good bonus in their next month pay, so don't you worry, I can assure you they will all be very happy with the changes. Oh, and there will also be a few promotions kicking around as well, as there are a few new positions on the horizon too. So that's something else we need to discuss when you get back. Now, on another, but equally important subject, what are we doing about Maggie, you being gone for a couple of weeks, do you think that will throw up any problems, Josh?"

"No, " replied Josh. "Not at all, that's already sorted, Jed. I have asked Helen to check on her by phone at least once a day, being as Maggie gets on very well with Helen and Daniel, her old gardener, well he is going to work over the three weekends while I'm away, so she won't be alone on the weekends. "

"Oh, well done Josh that's really good news. Now, please go and sit down with Helen, finish whatever needs finishing and then you can get gone. "

"Right, I will do Jed and thanks for the good news. And don't worry, I will make sure I tidy things up here before I leave, and just in case I will keep my phone on while I'm away. " Then shaking Jed's hand, Josh says, "I will see you when I get back then Jed. " As Josh leaves Jed's office, his brain is now working overtime, trying to calculate how much additional salary he would be earning and on the downside trying to work out how much extra tax he will have to pay. Josh was still trying to get his head around the proposed changes and was a little predisposed, when he tried to review the Harman Report with Helen.

After completing the report, Josh then calls all of his team together in the breakout room, and explains their good news, reminding them, "That although I will be on holiday, please don't think you are going against Jed's instructions, if you need to contact me, my phone will be on. " Josh then goes on to say, "So please just call me, or just leave me a text, like I said my phone will be on. So if you have any problems at all, that is apart from the department's usual sexual problems, please just contact me. " Now all laughing, they happily drift back to their desks chattering and with somewhat lifted spirits. After completing everything with Helen and after saying goodbye to everyone, Josh strides out of the office a very happy and contented man. As he walks back through the third floor, Josh thinks, *old Jed, you know he's a really good boss, he knows the business really well, I have been so lucky working for him.* He then thinks, *I must really enjoy my job here, as I am not even out of the building yet and I am already missing the old place.*

While exiting through the reception, Josh is once again confronted by the now very disgruntled Rachael, saying, "You did it again, didn't you, you never swiped in again, Josh. " Rachael then goes on to say, "If ever there's a fire, or we have an evacuation exercise, me with no accurate records of who's in the building, well I could be in some very serious trouble. "

To which Josh replies while walking towards the highly polished revolving doors, which lead out of the building, "If ever we have a fire here Rachael, it will probably be that old card reader by the doors that started it. Look, it's even got smoke coming out of it now. " As a curious Rachael, now checking it out and looking very closely at the card reader vent, Josh slid quietly passed her, saying, "I wouldn't worry Rachael, we're fully insured, I will see you in few weeks' time and don't forget to miss me terribly while I'm gone my special little sweetheart. "

Maggie, the lady mentioned during Josh's meeting with Jed, is the mother of one of the company's senior partners and is more or less Josh's landlady. Over the two years Josh had lived in Maggie's flat, Maggie had become more of a close friend and to some degree his second mother. Maggie was actually Mrs Margret J Langley MBE, a retired barrister and the widow of the late George Langley MP. Maggie lives in a large, very beautiful family house on the edge of Greenwich Park. Maggie's Georgian style eight-bedroomed house stands within its own private gardens and anyone visiting this timeless house would probably think: *well it's like going back in time to the 1950s.*

Maggie, now in her late seventies, had a few months before Josh moved in, been violently set about and robbed in her own home, which had understandably left her extremely shaken. Her son, Michael, anxious to prevent any similar reoccurrence had created a self-contained flat, in what was, the old servant quarters. Maggie's son had also installed a modern CCTV system, as well as an intruder alert system and in addition, had set up a twenty-four-hour security monitoring contract.

As part of this security upgrade, Josh had been approached by her son, who had offered Josh the flat at a very reasonable all-in rent, providing Josh would help keep an eye on Maggie for him. Taking up the generous offer and in the process 'dropping right on his feet', Josh had happily agreed. In Greenwich, a large self-contained apartment, with beautiful garden to enjoy, well you couldn't get much better than that.

Josh had been living there for almost two years and over that period, had struck up a very close and friendly relationship with Maggie, who Josh treated as a confident and to some degree like a second mother. That is almost like his mother, because there is nothing that Maggie liked better than a good dirty joke, or some juicy gossip, which is something that Josh would never dare to share with his, Irish born, Catholic raised and rather strait-laced real mother.

Josh, Jessica and Maggie often spent quality time together, either sitting in the garden, or watching TV and had regular trips out, eating at many of their favourite restaurants. However, Rules restaurant, in Covent Garden, was Maggie's absolute favourite place to eat and was firmly at the top of their eating out list, when it came to treating themselves. All three of them, Maggie, Jessica and Josh, would regularly go to see the odd West End show, or whatever exhibition was on at the time. As Jessica also travelled with her job, and in her absence, Maggie had helped to keep Josh on the straight and narrow and to some degree, away from the majority of, but certainly not all of life's little temptations. Although Josh had plenty of long-established friends, work commitments and spending time with Jessica, had reduced his relationships to the occasional telephone conversation, or special events, such as weddings, christenings and the odd birthday party.

Walking from the office, making his way back to his flat, Josh called Jessica on his mobile to check whether the courier had collected her suitcase, as arranged. As he and Jessica were attending her cousin's wedding in County Galway, what with the wedding presents and one or two special occasion dresses, it was decided they would have their suitcases picked up and delivered to Josh's parent's house in Staffordshire. His girlfriend, Jessica Holmes was from a middle-class family, who lived near Epson racecourse. Jessica's dad, Gerald was a retired businessman and Jessica's mom Mary was now a part-timecollege lecturer after retiring from the Home Office.

After a long chat with Jessica, Josh then phoned his brother Sean. Sean had been contacted so many times over the last couple of weeks, with Josh repeatedly going over the very same old arrangements; it was now becoming painful for Sean to keep answering the same questions. So with just a hint of sarcasm in his voice, Sean once again confirmed that he would be picking them up from Lichfield Trent Valley Station, as agreed and he responded to each of Josh's question with a, "Yes, yes, Josh, " or a "No problem, Josh. "

Both Josh and his brother Sean, were two very good-looking young men, Sean being the eldest by fourteen months. Both had dark hair, and both had deep brown eyes. Sean was the slightly taller of the two, more of the outdoor type, heavily into horses and farming, while Josh, although he also rode extremely well, unlike Sean, had never been the competitive type, or liked the demanding rigors

24

associated with farming. They both shared a love of the countryside, fast cars and together had built, renovated and repaired many old tractors, cars as well as the odd motor cycle. Although Sean and Josh were very close, they differed in many ways, Sean being the deep thinker and was a little more reserved, while Josh was more spur of the moment, extrovert who was highly social. To some degree, Josh was a bit of a Jekyll and Hyde, in that at work he was thorough, professional, questioning and extremely conscientious, but while at play, he was cheeky and always out for some fun and excitement. Although Josh loved living in London, he also enjoyed being back home and seeing his old mates and drinking his favourite draught beer, Bank's Best Bitter.

While walking the remaining half mile to his flat, Josh got to wondering how he was going to pop the question to Jessica and although he was fairly confident that Jessica would agree to his marriage proposal, there still remained some trepidation on his part. It was not that Jessica was not suitable to be his wife, but because Josh had always valued his bachelor lifestyle and had certainly made the most of it, throughout his teenage years while living at home, then through university and more recently, through his early years in London. Josh had already had a number of girlfriends, but good as they were, none of them had really been that special to him although none of them had really restricted his freedom. Although Josh had bought the engagement ring several months earlier, he had not told anyone of his intentions, just in case Jessica turned him down, or he developed last minute cold feet. Once again, Josh mulled over the marriage process in his head, weighing up the pros and cons, as he had done many times before. In the end, Josh always came to the same conclusion: that he could not go on being a bachelor forever and certainly knew that he would never find anyone as compatible or as lovely as Jessica. But then he would think, would Jessica want to be tied down, after all she is an independent, professional woman, building her own career. Like Josh, Jessica had started in a fairly low-grade position, working for a leading London auction house. But over the years, through hard work had risen through the ranks and was now a senior valuer, travelling throughout the UK on behalf of her employer. Josh had meet Jessica, while they were working together on a project near Bristol, Jessica was there valuing some of the company's more unusual investment assets, while Josh had been busy assessing and auditing the rest of their business interests. As they both were both staying in the same hotel, they began eating their meals together, going for the odd walk and drinking in the bar. As the contract was coming to an end, Josh had taken Jessica's mobile number and soon after Josh had started meeting up with Jessica after work and on weekends. Both enjoyed each other's company, and as a result, their relationship had grown steadily from there on. Josh then wondered whether he should ask Jessica's parent's permission first, although it was rather an old-fashioned tradition, on the plus side, her father would be at her cousin's wedding, so that would present an ideal opportunity to approach him and ask. *Mm,* Josh concluded. *Better ask Jessica first, get that sorted and then I can worry about asking her parents.*

On reaching his flat and checking his post, Josh went straight round to see Maggie and on entering called out, "Put the kettle on Maggie, I'm back and I'm dying for a coffee. "

Maggie then walking out of her kitchen holding a package, replied, "Here, this came for you today, Josh and your suitcase was collected at lunchtime. And please let me correct you, it's not coffee time darling, its late afternoon, so it is gin and tonic time. "

Josh feeling corrected, exclaimed, "Oh, yes please, Maggie, a gin and tonic, I think that would definitely fit the bill, yes, come to think of it, that's exactly what I need. " As Josh opened the plain brown paper package and exclaimed, "I was starting to get worried that this may not arrive in time. " Then eagerly opening the package, said, "Oh yes, these are really sexy. " As he held up some items of black lacy underwear for Maggie to see. "How about these then Maggie?" he asked. "What do you think?" Josh then displayed each item one by one, asked, "Do you remember wearing these then Maggie?"As he now held up a suspender belt.

Unaffected by the sight of the lingerie, Maggie replied, "Never thought they were that sexy when I wore them, bloody uncomfortable, especially after ten hours in court. "

"Well Maggie, they certainly do the trick for me, why even a table leg would look sexy in these, " he said as he held up some black, lacy topped stockings. Settling back into Maggie's big comfy armchair and sipping at a rather large gin and tonic, Josh said to 'Randy', Maggie's big black cat, who was now taking up position on Josh's lap, "Watch the goods please, Randy, we don't want these damaged by your claws, now do we?" Josh then reminded Maggie that Helen, his secretary would be calling her on a regular basis and that he had put Helen's contact details into her mobile phone just in case. Josh told Maggie that if she had any concerns at all, to immediately give either him or Helen a call.

"Darling, " replied Maggie. "I am not completely fucking helpless and believe me, I will be perfectly fine while you're gone. " Maggie, now speaking like his mother, continued, "So don't you worry about me; you just make sure you have everything you need for this holiday of yours and stop troubling yourself about me. " Then picking up the gin bottle said, "Well I'm having another, are you joining me, Josh?" Josh now well into his second gin thought, *isn't it strange, I am sitting here, miles away from where I was born, enjoying the company of my good friend Maggie, who I would never have known and I am about to go on holiday to Ireland with a beautiful girl called Jessica Holmes and none of this would have happened, if I had not applied for that job at Dunning & Partners. I know I am a real lucky bastard and I just wonder where life will take me next?*

After spending an hour or so in Maggie's good company and after drinking three more gin and tonics, Josh was starting to get well into the holiday mood and although the room was moving slightly, he was finally feeling properly relaxed. After saying goodnight to Maggie and Randy the cat, Josh returned to his flat feeling at peace with the world and would spend the next twenty minutes double-checking his holiday arrangements, in readiness for the off. As Josh lay in bed that night, his head was full of Jed's good news, how much he enjoyed Maggie's no-nonsense conversations and imagined how sexy Jessica would look wearing that lacy black lingerie.

Chapter 2

Going Home

Six a. m. woken by his phone's alarm, Josh lay in bed, thinking about the day ahead. *This is it mate,* he thought. *It's over to Euston, meet up with Jessica, grab a bite to eat, get on the train, travel up home and see Mom and Dad.* Whist showering Josh thought, *I hope that brother of mine has washed the Range Rover and maybe cleaned the interior out, the inside was a little bit like a farmyard last time I drove it. I must ask him if we have breakdown cover for Ireland as well and whether the insurance is good for driving in Ireland, oh and if the cars GPS works OK in Ireland. But not to worry,* he thought. *We still have our mobile phones for back up if it doesn't work.* Josh then thought, *it will be nice to see Mom again, as I know she has been through the mill recently. Dad tells me that her chemotherapy has knocked her for six, but every time I speak to her on the phone, she always sounds very upbeat and sounds just the same as she always did. She's a tough old bird my mom, even if she was doubled up in pain, she would just shrug it off as being a bit of a cold, so it's really difficult to tell how well she really is.*

After breakfast Josh, once again checked the contents of his rucksack, now cleared of his work stuff, which had been unceremoniously dumped in the bottom of his wardrobe. As Josh tips his work stuff out, he said to himself, "You're certainly not wanted on voyage. " As Josh repacks his rucksack, he checks things off in his head as he goes through the process, he then pauses for a moment and opens an old tatty white envelope. Josh carefully takes out a well-handled black and white photograph depicting an old single storey farm house. Josh studies the photo, as he has done a hundred times before and says to himself, "This holiday I am going to find you, by hook or by crook, I will find you. And then I will get to see where Mom's family and my ancestors actually came from. " Stamped on the back of the photograph, is the faded details of the photographic studio that produced the print, the address being Pound Lane, Swinford, County Mayo. This old photograph, along with mom's maiden name of O'Brien, were the only clues he and his brother, had to go on. Although Josh's mother never talks about her childhood, or anything about living in Ireland, Josh knows from his dad that his mom just up and left, leaving her Irish family behind. Whenever he or his brother has questioned their mom about her family history, she would immediately change the subject and if they persisted in asking her, she would say 'stop prying' and then get angry with them. Josh's dad had once told Josh and Sean that his mom had left Ireland because of a family dispute and had never been back there or had even been in touch with them since the day she left. Dad went on to tell them that their mom had arrived in the UK with just £37 pounds to her name, a small suitcase and had just started her life all over again, right here in England. Josh's mom had trained as a nurse in Birmingham and had then been a nurse at Burton Upon Trent General Hospital for most of her working life. Mom had met their dad when he was visiting his injured dad, their granddad, who had been a patient on his mother's ward. Apparently, their granddad had been badly crushed by a cow and finished up with several broken ribs and a punctured lung. Josh carefully replaced the old photograph, back into its envelope and packed everything back into the bag. *Well, that's it,* he thought. *If it's not in this bag, I don't need it. I've got my wallet, I've got a few Euros, got my driving licence.* And then tapping the bag, as if to confirm it, said to himself and most importantly, "I have got the engagement ring. " After popping next door to say a last goodbye to Maggie, Josh was finally on his way. As he walked to the tube station, he called Jessica, just to check that she was also on the move and remind her they would meet up in the Doric Arch Pub in Euston.

When Josh got to the Doric Arch, he went up the stairs to the bar, as he had done many times before, although they didn't serve Bank's Best Bitter, this was still his favourite bar whenever he was travelling to or from Euston. It was not one of your top end restaurants, but Josh liked the atmosphere and the slightly shady look of the place, what you might call a proper old London pub. After a quick glance around, Josh settled at a table which had a view of both entrances, then sat, browsing through a free newspaper someone had kindly left behind and sat waiting for Jessica. After several minutes, Jessica arrived looking really happy and after greeting her with a kiss, Josh went up to the bar and ordered their breakfast. When he returned to the table, they talked about the coming wedding and their holiday, when their conversation was temporary broken by the arrival of their food.

"Bloody great stuff, " Josh said as he enthusiastically began to eat his full English breakfast.

"Have you not had breakfast this morning then Josh?" enquired Jessica.

"Yes, sweetheart I have, well sort of, but only a mouthful of toast and a quick sip of coffee, but that was just to tide me over until I got here. Now this is what you call a proper breakfast.

"Oh, " Josh said, as he shook more brown sauce all over his breakfast. "I had some good news yesterday. Old Jed called me into his office, as he does and amongst other things, told me, I have been given a pay rise and apparently it's being backdated, so I might be splashing out a bit more than anticipated on this holiday. " Drinking the last mouthful of his coffee, Josh tells Jessica, "Now please hurry up Jess, as our train leaves at seven minutes past the hour and I am not even sure which platform it leaves from. " Josh then leans over, fork in hand and helps himself to the sausage and the remaining mushroom that Jessica had left. Several minutes later they are seated on the train and Josh said, "I wish I had known earlier about my pay rise, else I would have paid the extra and we could have gone first class, but never mind, these seats will do just fine. "

During their one-and-a-half-hour journey north, Josh goes over their travel arrangements with Jessica and tells her how much he is looking forward to their holiday together. Josh then tells Jessica that he has a couple of nice surprises lined up for her, to which Jessica immediately asks, "Can you give me a little clue then, as I hate not knowing. "

To which Josh replies, "I know your little clues, one little clue, just leads to another little clue, until it's no longer a surprise, so sorry but no I won't. "

"Then you shouldn't have told me, should you, "replies Jessica, who then immediately asks. "Are you sure I will like these surprises Josh?"

To which Josh replies, "I hope so, else I would have been wasting my time wouldn't I? Now, stop prying, you will just have to wait and see what they are, so please stop asking, or you will go and spoil the whole thing. "

As they pass through Tamworth Station, Josh tells Jessica, "You would not think it, but Tamworth Assembly Rooms have hosted many of the top groups over the years, including the Beatles and the Rolling Stones. My uncle Terry lives near Tamworth and he saw many of the famous groups play live there, but I'm not sure whether the place is still going now. I have never been inside the Assembly Rooms, but I have driven past it a couple of times with Uncle Terry, that's why I know. It definitely looked nothing special from the outside, but I've not been past it lately, they may have even knocked it down by now. Like the Cavern Club in Liverpool, they knocked that down. I bet they regret doing that demolition job now though, but that's progress for you. "

To which Jessica replied, "No Josh, you are wrong the Cavern Club is still there, I know that for a fact, because a couple of my old university friends went there on a Beatles Tour. "

"Yes, " replied Josh. "But that's not the original Cavern Club where the Beatles actually played in, that was knocked down some years ago. That Cavern Club was a replacement, it's just one they set up for the tourist, anyway, get yourself ready Jess, we will be arriving at Lichfield Station in a minute. " As the announcement, 'We will shortly be arriving at Lichfield Trent Valley, ' comes over the intercom, Jessica immediately gathered her things, got up from her seat and was about to walk towards the exit, when Josh says, "Not yet Jess, there are a still a couple of miles to go. "

To which Jessica complained, "Why wait Josh, there are other passengers who are already by the doors. "

"Oh, bloody hell, " says Josh. "I hate getting up too early, it's a thing with me. "But then he reluctantly got up to join Jessica waiting by the door. Walking along the station platform Josh tells Jessica a little about the city of Lichfield, "The last person to be burnt alive at the stake, was in Lichfield's Market Square. There's a bronze plaque there, telling you all about it. " Josh then adds laughing, "And that was only five years ago, old habits die very slowly in Lichfield. " Walking out through the ticket office, Josh is very relieved to see the family's Range Rover, all clean and gleaming in the car park.

As Josh throws their bags in the back of the car, Sean gives Jessica a welcoming hug and a kiss. Sean asks Jessica if she has received the award yet. Looking slightly confused at Sean's comment, "What award?" asks Jessica.

"The one you get for suffering my brother's company for the last couple of years. But I must say Jessica, you seem to be looking very well on it. " All laughing, they climb aboard and head for the family home.

"Oh bro, " Josh says. "If you could pull into the BP garage on the way home, then I will fill her up, being as we have to be up, out and gone early in the morning, we have to be in Holyhead for seven-thirty. " A little later, while Josh fills up the car with fuel and pays at the petrol station-cum-coffee shop, Sean and Jessica catch up on what they have been up to since their last meeting, which was Christmas, five months earlier. Jessica was laughing along with Sean, when Josh came out of the shop with a bag full of shopping and says, "I knew he would have to buy something, he just can't help it" "Well, " said Josh getting back into the car, "Come on, tell me what are you two laughing at?"

"I said to Sean, you just watch, I know Josh will come out with a bag full of shopping; he always does and then out you come out of the door with a bag full of shopping. So, what did you get then?, "

"A couple of orange fruit drinks some crisps a few packs of fresh mango, two KitKats and a bag of peanuts. " Then putting them into the glove box said, "Just a few things for the journey tomorrow morning?"

Pulling into High View Farm, the family home, Josh says, "Looks like you had some new gates fitted then bro, wow, they look very nice. "

"Yes, " replied Sean. "Ayoung guy driving his dad's car ran into them late one Friday night. "

To which Josh remarks, "How the hell did he manage that, it's a dead straight piece of road?"

"No idea, " said Sean. "Abit of luck really the old ones were nearly falling apart. The lad's insurance paid for them, Uncle Terry made them for us and one of his lad's came and fitted them. Trouble was, " continued Sean. "It showed the other gate up and so we had to get Uncle Terry to make some new ones to match. "

"How is Uncle Terry?" asks Josh, Sean tells him that he's in Spain at the moment with his wife aunty Linda.

"They spend a lot of time over there now, " said Sean. "Uncle Terry playing golf and Aunty Linda, who's either lounging by the pool, or is out shopping. Cousin Mike is running the business now and apparently it's doing very well, by all accounts, Mike calls in for a coffee whenever he is passing. "

"Pity Mike's not here today, I would love to see him again, I wonder if he still plays rugby, he used to play for the county once Jess and if you saw the bruises he used to get on his face, you would definitely know it. "

As they pull up in the farmyard, two rather muddy looking collie dogs come running over to greet them, as Sean gets out first, he shoos them away, "We don't want you little buggers jumping up and getting our guests all dirty, now do we. Don't bother with the bags, Josh, " says Sean. "Just go straight inside, Mom's been very anxious to see you both. " Josh's family home is a rather large, plain brick built, three storey farm house, with a large cedar tree in the front garden.

As they enter the extremely large farmhouse kitchen, Josh's mom immediately greets them, giving Jessica a big hug, saying, "Jessica sweetheart, you get more beautiful every time I see you, now you go through into the lounge and relax, while I put the kettle on. "

"Where's Dad then, Sean?" asks Josh.

"He's walked round to see old Amos and take him some of Mom's cakes, Mom was baking all through yesterday on the strength of your visit. "

"How is old Amos?" asks Josh.

"I'm sorry to say, he's not getting around very well at all these days, he's still got a few beef cattle and some very old chickens, but I don't think they will be replaced when they go. "

"Where's the keys to the pickup Sean?" asks Josh. "I think I will just pop down and see Amos and then I can give Dad a lift back at the same time. "

"Oh, by the way" says Sean. "I have put your bag in your old room and Jessica's in the spare room. Mom has already reminded us, that until you two are married, it will

be separate beds in this house, you know what she is like.
"

Josh then pops his head into the lounge and informs his mom and Jessica, who are busy chatting, that he is just popping down to see Amos and to give Dad a lift back, to which his mom adds, "Well don't be too late getting back, lunch will be ready around one. " Josh's mom knows that once Josh gets down there with Amos and Dad, all sense of time would simply disappear.

Amos is their neighbouring farmer and long-time friend of the family and ever since his wife Sheila had died, several years earlier, his health had steadily gone downhill. Prior to her death, Sheila had been extremely ill for quite a few years and because Amos was busy caring for her and was struggling to cope, Josh's dad had rented most of Amos' land and he and Sean had helped Amos out almost on a daily basis. Their mom would never allow Josh or Sean to have a motorbike, when they were younger so they secretly kept a couple at Amos' place, along with air rifles, a pile of girly magazines and a few other non-permitted items. Although neither Josh or Sean now smoked, years back, they would sometimes partake in the odd cigarette along with a few large beers with Amos, whilst enjoying listening to his very colourful stories. Josh's dad knew about most of their little secrets and other minor sins and often used to say, "For God's sake, don't let your mother know, or she will kill me. "

Josh had rolled into Amos' yard, just as his dad was leaving and on seeing Josh, pushed Amos' kitchen door back open shouting through the open door, "Josh is here to see you Amos. "

As Josh and his dad entered the kitchen, Josh said, "Hello Amos, you old bugger, how are you keeping mate. "

Amos replied, "Where's that girlfriend of yours, you know, Jessica, is she here with you Josh?"

"No, " replied Josh. "Jessica is with Mom back at our house. "

"Bloody pity, because she's got the nicest arse, I have ever seen you lucky little bastard. Nice girl too, far too nice for you. Why aren't you two married yet? Because here am I, fighting off the grim reaper, barely clinging on to life, just so I can attend you and your Sean's weddings, before I drop down dead. And no matter what I say or do, I just can't get either of you pair down that fucking aisle. I tell you, you had better get a ring on that girl's finger right now Josh, otherwise some bugger else will, I tell you. Too slow to catch a fucking cold you two. Your Sean did have a girlfriend, you know that hoity-toity Anna, but now he's fucking even gone and lost her. Mind you, she weren't right for him anyway, so he's probably better off without her. Bit of a stuck-up snob, that lass, mores the pity. He needs to get another girl and bloody quick, as we don't want him going addled in his old age, now do we?"

After sharing an hour or so talking with Amos, Josh said, "We had better go now Dad, Mom will have dinner ready soon. "

As they got up to leave Amos said, "Tell your mom the cakes were lovely and that Edward is a lucky guy, having an angel that can cook. "

As they were leaving through the kitchen door, Josh happened to look down and saw several spent twelve bore shotgun cartridges by the step.

Then asked, "Who you been shooting at then Amos, has that VAT man been here again?"

"No, that fucking fox has been after my chickens again, I didn't manage to shoot the bastard thing. "Then laughing said, "But I managed to scare the living shit out of him, you should have seen him go. "

After saying their goodbyes, Josh and his dad set off for home. As they drove back, on their short return journey, his dad said, "You know your mom's not been very well at all Josh, as you know, she will never let on, but she has been real poorly son. So please make a fuss of her while you are here, because she really needs cheering up. And I know Amos was just winding you up and taking the piss, but he is right you know son, Jessica is a lovely girl, so better hang on to her son, she's a real gem that girl. "

Josh then changing the subject said, "I haven't seen Amos since Christmas Dad, but bloody hell, he's certainly deteriorated. " Josh then slipped into his recall mode, remembering how tough and strong Amos used to be when they were kids. How he could wrestle with difficult cattle, carry full sacks of grain, like it was nothing at all and give him a spade and he could out dig a JCB. Josh's dad then told Josh how his mother was concerned over Amos being down there, all alone down at Apple Tree Farm and how she has begged him to come and move in with us.

Then added, "But you know Amos, he wants to be where his memories of his Sheila are. I go down there every day and I half expect to find him dead on the floor, it's a real worry. So, what do you think of the new gates then, Josh?"

After arriving back, they all sat round the big table in the kitchen and ate lunch together. "Who's doing the milking tonight?" asked Josh.

"Old Toddy is coming in this evening and again in the morning. But we have a new piece of kit now Josh, you just drive it through the cattle pens and it automatically delivers the fodder straight into the feed trough. It saves a good couple of hours every day, it's got air conditioning and a computer that calculates the amount of feed delivered. It's also got built-in wi-fi, Bluetooth and a radio, we are now just waiting for the new robot to come and drive it, but until then it's Toddy's new toy. "

"How many cows are you milking now then?" asks Josh.

Sean replies, "215. , "

"Bloody hell, " says Josh. "I remember when we had just thirty-five and that was real hard work. "

Then Dad replied, "Well Josh, it's either get big, or get out, so we had to get big, mind you, I sometimes wonder if it's all worth it though. Every time it comes round to TB testing, I lie awake, night after night worrying until I get the results and then I start worrying about the next round of testing. I still remember the last foot-and-mouth outbreak; you know, there were quite a few suicides in the farming industry when that was going round. Then there was bovine spongiform encephalopathy, when the price of beef just dropped like a stone, you couldn't give the stuff away then, like I said Josh, I sometimes wonder if it's all really worth it. "

After their enormous lunch, Josh went with Sean to see his new foal.

"Long legs, short back and a dark bay to boot, looks like a real nice filly, that one Sean, "said Josh. Then while they were alone and well out of earshot, Josh said, "Old Amos tells me you've split with Anna. So what's going on bro, did you still want see her, or was it a mutual decision?"

"No, Josh, she's run off with some new guy from her work, I think she just got tired of waiting, what with me working on the farm all hours, then competing on the weekends, the odd trip to buy cattle and with the occasional agricultural show thrown in, she was not a happy bunny. Mom misses her, but as you know, Anna she was never into farming or horses, so I don't think it would ever have worked out anyway?" Sean then changing the subject said, "Oh while we're out, come and have a look at the old MGA now it's finished. " As soon as they walked into the workshop, Josh could see this was a quality product and had been finished to a very high standard.

"Wow, it looks brand new Sean and I love the red leather interior. " Josh then opening the bonnet and having a good look, says, "Bloody hell, you have put four port throttle bodies on it?"

"Not only that Josh, I've fitted a custom-made ECU, electronic ignition, a half race camshaft, a high-volume oil pump, oil cooler and lots more, I went the whole nine yards with this one. The stainless steel exhaust and manifold cost me over a grand. "

Josh now really impressed, asks, "Have you taken it out yet Sean?"

To which Sean replies, looking very pleased, "I've done about three K's in it and so far, it hasn't missed a beat. And believe me, Josh, it moves incredibly well and sounds like a dream, I'm really very pleased with it. " Sean then explains how the old Armstrong shock absorbers had been replaced with specially made wishbones with coil over shocks, how the front and rear brakes had been upgraded, how even the old cooling system had been upgraded.

"Christ Sean, is there anything original left, it's more like a new car?" As Josh's eyes scan around the workshop, he spots some very familiar spare parts and other mechanical remnants, which reminded him of the numerous projects he and Sean had worked on together, everything from outboard engines, agricultural machinery to racing cars. Just looking round, bought it all flooding back to him, their many successes and just a few bad failures. How they had bought cheap worn out and knackered items from the local implement sales, repaired them and sold them on for profit.

"Well, " Josh said. "I can see you have been busy and can only imagine how much hard work has been done, it's a real credit to you. I just love the red leather seats and trim. "

After a tour of the farm, Josh returned to the house and met up with Jessica and his mom. As Josh had never had a sister; and Josh's mom had always wanted a daughter, Jessica was the next best thing and whenever Jessica and his mom got together, it was obvious that they both enjoyed each other's company very much.

After an evening watching TV and indulging in family chit chat, Josh announced, "Well I am off to bed now, so don't you go staying up too long Jessica, we have to be up, dressed and out for five-thirty at the very latest, so good night everyone. " When Josh got to his old room, he remembered sitting at the built-in desk, doing his homework and could still see the small hole in the ceiling made when the safety valve from his model steam engine struck, when the boiler exploded. He even had the poster of Brigit Bardot, still on the wall, although it was extremely faded. Josh always knew he had had a wonderful childhood and appreciated all that his family had done for Sean and himself. Although Josh could never understand why his old room had never been cleared out, but then another part of him knew exactly why.

Chapter 3

Outward Journey

Josh was a little taken aback, when Jessica came down for breakfast, wearing a pair of dungarees and looking like she had just stepped out of some beauty salon. "Wow, Jess you look very well turned out, you're making me look really scruffy. "

"Well, " said Jessica as she gave a little twirl, "We are on holiday and I have been dying to wear these since I bought them, do they look all right?"

"Look all right, they look really great, it's a good job Amos is not around, because your bum looks really hot in those and here's me in an old pair of jeans and a really outdated sweat shirt, if we had more time, I would go back and change. " Now with their suitcases and bags loaded they had said their goodbyes and at last started out for Holyhead at exactly five-thirty a. m. A few miles into the journey, Josh realised he had been talking to himself, as Jessica was now sound asleep. It was very rare that Jessica would be awake, up and about that early in the morning and as interesting as Josh's conversation may have been the need to sleep had obviously got the better of her.

An hour or so later, Josh pulled into Betws-y-Coed in North Wales and when Jessica was woken by the lack of movement.

"Are we here then?" asks Jessica, still waking up and rubbing her eyes.

"No, " replied Josh. "I have just stopped for a coffee and toilet break, we have another hour or so yet, so do you fancy a bite to eat, while we are here?"

"No Josh, no food for me just coffee please, "replied Jessica. "So please, let's say no to breakfast, let's just get there, then we know we are all right for time. " After buying a couple of take away coffees, the second part of the journey to Holyhead, was mainly taken up by Jessica's mobile phone conversations. First with her mom, then with Hilary her work colleague followed by her cousin Caroline and then Josh's mom. Jessica's telephone conversations were only broken by the odd comment regarding the passing scenery, the weather, the wedding, or the behaviour of some very inconsiderate road users.

As they journeyed along the A5, Jessica started to tell Josh what his mom had told her the night before, after Josh had gone to bed. She had told Jessica a little about her life in Ireland, how she had lost her mom when she was thirteen, that she had one older brother and one younger brother. A few days before prior to leaving home, then aged twenty-two, her father had died very suddenly. On the day of the funeral, after the service, she had gone upstairs to her room, as she was naturally feeling very upset. Apparently, at some point she went back downstairs and as she approached the kitchen, she had overheard her brothers discussing how they were going to improve the farm now Dad had gone. Incensed at their callous attitude, she had burst in on them and shouted angrily, "Dad's barely cold in his grave and all you two can thing about is how you can change things. Well, I am already missing the best dad anyone could ever wish for and I would gladly give everything we own to have him back and if the farm is so bloody precious to you, you can shove it where the sun don't shine. " She had then immediately returned back to her room to cry it off. Later that night she quietly packed a few things, took the little money she had saved from her egg round and at four o' clock in morning had ridden her bike into town, caught the first bus out and made her way to Dublin.

Josh was shocked at hearing the story of his mother's plight and after taking it all in, Josh said, "So that's what happened is it, I wonder why she never told me? It sounds like she blew her top, but knowing my mom I can just imagine how mad she would have been. Bloody hell, so I have two selfish and callous uncles have I, I wonder if the farm is still going. Anyway, we can go see for ourselves this holiday. Mom must really have taken to you Jess, to tell you that, mind you she always wanted a daughter and to me it looks very much like you are her new adopted daughter. I'm just so glad she likes you. "Then for a while, Josh just sat there driving along, thinking over what his mother told Jessica.

They finally crossed over the Menai Bridge leaving mainland Wales behind and arrived on the island of Anglesey. "Well, we are almost there now Jess, just got to follow these signs for the Ferry Port and then we can have a bite to eat, "said Josh. "I wonder if there's much of a queue at the terminal?"

Arriving at the port, being as Josh had pre-booked, they were able to quickly obtain their boarding and loading paperwork as well as having a quick bite to eat and still with plenty of time to spare. After loading, they made their way up the steep narrow stairs leading from the vehicle decks below up to the public areas and upper decks. As Jessica negotiated the steep steps, Josh was now taking interest in Jessica's buttocks, which were now conveniently at eye level, Josh then remarked, "You know something sweetheart, I can see what Amos was on about now, yes you really do have a nice arse. "

Jessica, now tiring of the climb, turned, smiled and said, "Did he now? You just wait till I see that Amos, the cheeky old devil. "

Reaching the top of the stairs, they both stepped out onto deck and into bright sunshine. "Well, " said Josh. "This is the start of our beautiful, beautiful holiday together. " Josh and Jessica now headed to the stern area and Josh feeling a little more relaxed, leant out over the handrail to better observe the crew getting the ferry under way. Both now leaning over the handrail, Josh asked, "Did mom say anything about where they lived in Ireland?"

"Well, no she didn't, " replied Jessica. "I thought you already knew that, otherwise I would have asked her. "

"Never mind, " replied Josh, putting his arm around her and pulling her closer, said, "At least we know we are in the right country, eh Jess? Which reminds me, I'd better get a few more Euros when we reach Dublin, as I foolishly only bought a few with me. "

The boat was now well under way and Josh said, "I know you have been to Ireland before Jess, but this is my first visit and do you know, I am really looking forward to it. Sean has been over to Ireland quite a few times over the years, buying horses, and when I was talking to him yesterday, he said he really enjoyed all of his visits. Oh, and talking of Sean, I don't think you will be seeing much of Anna any more Jess, it looks like Anna and Sean have split up. "

"I know, your mom told me last night, " replied Jessica. "I think she secretly hoped Sean would find someone else. I never really knew Anna that well, she was always a little bit standoffish with me. "

"She was a bit standoffish with me Jess, in fact she was a bit standoffish with most people, "said Josh. "You know I am very pleased you and Mom are getting on so well, I think she needs another woman to talk to sometimes. But I can see, I shall have to keep my eye on you two, because if you two join forces, we guys may just have to behave ourselves a little more. "

Jessica carried on saying, "I can't wait to see Caroline and her parents again. I used to stay with them every year during the summer holidays, I had some great times with them in Galway Josh, it's a lovely county. I remember you got on really well with Caroline when she stayed with us in London and I just know you will get on with her mom and dad, as they are both really lovely people. You probably don't know it Josh, but the family suffered a tragic event several years back, when Michael, their only son, was killed in a motorcycle accident. Caroline's mom was very badly affected by it and has never really got over it. Michael was a very clever lad, who did very well at Latin at his old private school and then went on to Oxford University, studying languages. Although he was extremely academic, he was also quite the lad, always joking and he used to get up to all kinds of mischief. When I was around thirteen and staying with them in the holidays, I had a secret crush on him. Although Michael was always friendly towards me, he never once made any advances, which really pissed me off at the time. I used to dream he would come into my room during the dead of the night and take advantage of me, you know, the stuff school girls often dream about. But it was very sad when Michael died and I will never forget his mother sobbing at Michael's funeral, it was all a very upsetting experience. "

"Well let's not dwell on sad things, " said Josh. "We are on holiday now and I don't know about you Jess, but I am really looking forward to our stay in Limerick. A bit of shopping, a top hotel, a table booked in a French restaurant and a passionate night spent with a very beautiful girl. I wonder if I can buy some Euros at the hotel, or better still just use my cash card. "

"Me, " said Jessica laughing. "Well, I was thinking, more of a room service meal, wash my hair, paint my nails and just have an early night. "

By lunchtime they were driving into Limerick. "Thank God the GPS works OK over here, "said Josh. "Oh good, here's a sign to the hotel and wow, here's their underground car park. " As they walked from the car park and into the hotel, they could see that their accommodation was going to be to a very high standard, as the interior decoration was first class. As they walked along the ground floor corridor, they passed a large lounge bar and through some large glass doors they could see the pool and health suites. "This looks good, " said Josh, stopping briefly to read the menu posted outside the dining room. "Oh, look they do chateaubriand and that Irish beef is supposedly the best, I know we are eating out tonight Jess, but I think we should try this while we are here, don't you?"

Chapter 4

The Proposal

After checking in at the hotel's reception, they went straight up to their room. "Wow, look Josh, we have a balcony, with a view over the Rive Shannon, "said Jessica excitedly. "Oh, and the bathroom is gorgeous. " Just then her conversation with Josh, who was now out on the balcony, checking it out, was interrupted by a loud knock on their bedroom door. When Jessica opened it, there was a lady holding a large bouquet made up of long-stemmed red roses with white calla lilies and was tied with long red silk ribbons.

"Jessica Holmes?" asked the lady.

"Well yes, " replied Jessica. "Then these are for you darling. "Handing the flowers carefully over to Jessica. Slightly taken aback by the gift of flowers, she called out to Josh, who was now checking out the bathroom.

"Are these flowers from you, Josh?" Josh who was now closing the door. "Yes Jess, I decided I was going to spoil you rotten this holiday, I hope you like them?"

"Like them, I absolutely love them Josh, " replied Jessica. "They are so beautiful. I don't get flowers very often and I just adore red roses, thank you. I must give room service a call and see if they have a vase I can put them in. "

"Well don't get too comfortable Jess, I want to have a quick look around Limerick before we have to get ready for dinner, "said Josh, who was now out of curiosity checking what channels were available on the hotel's TV. Leaving the hotel, behind them they walked hand in hand, towards the city centre, located just over the bridge from their hotel. Part way over the bridge, they stopped to look down at the River Shannon flowing slowly under them.

"So that's the River Shannon is it, " said Josh. "I wonder if they do boat trips, it's a pity we are only here for one night, I would have like to have had a good look round, especially with this weather. "

"Maybe in the morning, " said Jessica. "I've been on the web and there are a couple of antique shops I would really like to see and we should have plenty of time, as it only a couple of hours to Caroline's. "

Josh now nodding his head in agreement added, "Well please don't go buying anything too big. I don't fancy spending two weeks carting a grandfather clock around. "

Later, as they walked through a shopping centre, Josh asks, "Jess, have you brought any high heels with you?"

"Yes I have, " replied Jessica. "But why do you want to know?"

"Oh, I just saw some in a shop window back there and I like you in high heels, I think they always look very feminine and you look very, very sexy in high heels, it's just amazing what high heels can do to a man. " Josh continued, "Same thing with long hair, perfume and skirts, I love to see a woman wearing a skirt or a dress, they always look very feminine as well. I reckon there are girls who never wear a skirt, or a dress, thinking they are too girly and then they wonder why none of the boys take any interest in them. "

Jessica still not really sure where Josh was coming from, just replied, "Hmm, so you like high heels do you, Josh?"

"So what colour are they Jess, these high heel shoes?" asked Josh.

"Well as a matter-of-fact, they are black patent leather, but why are you asking, just what are you up to?" asked Jessica.

"Just wondering, that's all, " replied Josh. Jessica knew Josh extremely well by now and could tell when he was up to something and so her brain was now busily engaged in trying to work out just what it could be.

"It's a nice place Limerick, I wonder if the limerick was named after this place, you know, there was a young man from, Devises, type limericks. " Then in one of his rambling, relaxed conversations added, "I used to know quite a few of those limericks, well now I can say with some conviction I've actually been there. "

As they made their way back towards the hotel, Josh reminded Jessica that their table was booked for eight and it was about a ten-minute walk from the bridge they were now walking back over, to get to the restaurant.

"Obviously I've never been there before, " said Josh. "But the write ups are all very good, so fingers crossed eh, Jess. " Josh went on to say, "I love French food when it's at its best and I have eaten some real good food in France, but I have also had some real crap meals over there as well. Do you know, the meal I remember as being the best French food I have ever eaten, it was in a small cafe in Calais, I think it was called Cafe Pont de Rhine. Anyway, it was very small and very unassuming cafe type place, located halfway over the bridge; yes it was mussels in garlic, cream and white wine sauce, with lots of freshly baked crusty bread, a very simple but nevertheless a superb meal. And then, if you remember, we had that French onion soup at that small cafe in the students' quarter in Paris, again a very simple dish, but it tasted out of this world. "

Jessica then replied, "I just remember how cold it was, I think we almost froze to death that weekend, but yes, we had a few good meals and if I remember, you were sea sick on the ferry coming back. " Then laughing she said, "I don't think any of the meals you ate there, actually made it back to England, most of it went over the ship's hand rails. "

"Oh yes I remember that return crossing, very well, yes it was like a nightmare, I was so relieved when we reached Dover, I was still feeling rough two days later. " Then reaching for Jessica's hand said, "It was a bloody good job I had you with me Jess, I think I would have died at sea otherwise. "

Now they had reached their hotel, they went up to their hotel room and Josh relaxed on the bed, while Jessica was busy unpacking things from one of the two large suitcases she had brought along. However, while she was kneeling down, Josh began studying her very closely, benefiting from her reflection in the floor to ceiling mirrored wardrobe. Josh then began thinking to himself; Jess's hair looks lovely; I like brunettes, especially if it's long and shiny, it always smells good too. Josh then concluded that Jess had a nice slim body, although her tits were not that big, they were very firm and were extremely pert. *Yes, I think they are probably the best tits I have ever seen, really nice nipples too.* Josh carried on watching as Jessica moved around the room, folding clothes and taking items in and out of the bathroom, Josh reminiscing over their two years of sexual exploits, thinking to himself, *she's got a very nice pussy too, smooth as silk and absolutely perfectly formed. Not only is she beautiful,* he thought. But having shared the last couple of years together, he loved everything about her, the way she was with him and imagined just how empty his life would be without her. Yes, Josh decided, *Jessica Holmes is definitely the girl for me; I just hope she feels the same way.*

A short while later, Jessica held up a black shiny evening dress, then gently hung it on the wardrobe door asking Josh, "Do you think this dress will do for tonight Josh?"

"It's perfect, just perfect, "replied Josh. "And I mean just absolutely perfect. " A short while after, whilst preparing to shower, Jessica placed a pair of tights, along with some fresh underwear, on the bed, ready to wear when she came back out. Josh was now desperately rummaging in his rucksack, eventually brought out the small package that was delivered just before he left, said, "No Jess, this is what you are wearing tonight sweetheart. "Handing her the package.

Opening it and removing the black lacy items one by one, Jessica exclaimed, "So, this is what the high heel business was all about, was it, you don't want much do you, you cheeky little devil and just what do I get, in exchange?"

"Ah Jess, a great big surprise, honestly, a beautiful, great big surprise, "answered Josh. "Just you wait and see, it's a very special surprise. "

"Well, it had just better be an extremely good surprise and not just the one I can see I will be getting tonight. " Now holding up a suspender belt and Jessica added, "Well I can tell you now, this is not going to be very comfortable wearing for a meal out Mr Joshua Foster. "

"No, I know, " replied Josh laughing. "Sorry Jess, but it's just got to be worn tonight, it's all part of the special evening I planned for you. Anyway, you will look stunning wearing that, I know you will, just absolutely stunning Jess. "

A little later and after showering, Josh emerged from the bathroom wearing the hotel dressing gown, to find Jessica sitting at the dressing table, putting on her make-up wearing the lingerie from the package.

"I am not very impressed with this excuse for a bra, " said Jessica, twisting the upper part of her torso, to display mostly exposed breasts. "I might as well not have one on at all, it's just straps; God knows what it will look like under my dress?"

However, Josh was now transfixed on the sight of Jessica wearing a quarter cup bra, black lacy top stockings and suspender belt, moved closer, smiling and gesturing a groping motion with his hands and saying, "Bloody hell Jess, I don't think I have ever seen a more beautiful sight in my life, you look like a dream sent from heaven. Christ, you look stunning. "As he moved up closer and with his hand closing in on her exposed breasts.

Twisting back, away from his hand, Jessica replied, "Well you will have to keep your groping hands to yourself, well at least till we get back from this restaurant of yours, won't you. "

A little later, Josh now dressed in his dinner jacket, dress shirt and bow tie, re-emerged from the bathroom, turned towards Jessica and asked, "How do I look Jess, does it look OK?"

"It's not very often we see you dressed to kill, Mr 007, " said Jessica laughing. Although she was not going to let Josh know it, but deep inside Jessica, seeing Josh dressed up and looking rather sexy, was looking forward to being made love to, but answered, "I must admit Commander Bond, you do scrub up very well. "

Josh looking very impressed with what he saw said, "I tell you what Jess, no joking, you look a thousand times better than any Bond girl I have ever seen. Now, how about a flash of stocking tops before we go?" At that Jessica slowly slid the hem of her dress up her leg, revealing a lacy stocking tops and a silky-smooth thigh.

"Are you interested in me then Mr Bond?" Jessica enquired, holding a sultry film star type pose.

"Bloody right I am, "replied Josh, as he walked over and gave her a long passionate kiss. "Now come on, let's go, we have a table booked, "said Josh slapping her on her bottom as he ushered Jessica out of the room. As they walked through the hotel, everyone smiled and spoke politely, and Josh, just knew they were setting the standard, for everyone else to envy. As they walked along the river, hand in hand in the evening sunshine, through the perfectly manicured gardens, Josh knew this was going to be a very special night.

On arrival at the restaurant, it was obvious by the reaction they received from the restaurant manager, that they did not get that many diners so elegantly dressed. The restaurant was cosy and busy, but not crowded. A few of the diners looked on with interest as they were guided through to a corner table with a view over the river. The waiter was especially on the ball; no waiting between courses, topping their glasses up every time the levels were lowered and constantly checking everything was to their liking. They both had sautéed scallops in a brandy and parsnip sauce for starters and Jessica had crunchy almond-crusted duck, while Josh went for the more expensive filet mignon.

Josh then said, "Bloody hell Jess, you should have had the beef, it's so well-cooked and tastes absolutely delicious. "Finally, they ordered the classic crepes suzette for two, cooked at the table and flamed with brandy.

After eating a superb meal and whilst drinking their brandies and coffee, Josh moved his chair closer to Jessica's and said, "I am going to say something very serious, which could prove difficult for me to get right. So please don't say anything at all until I have finished. " Now getting Jessica's full attention, Josh went on to say, "As you know, we have been together for two wonderful years and over that time you have become the most important person in my life. " Then looking straight into Jessica's eyes, said, "You have become the one woman in the world that I know I could no longer live without. That is why Jess, I am asking you, if you would please agree to marry me. I may not be the greatest catch in the world, and I know I can be a little selfish and sometimes very annoying, but I am dearly hoping you will accept my proposal of marriage and agree to be my lifetime partner?"

Although Jessica had hoped that one day Josh would eventually propose, this had taken her by complete surprise, never thinking for a minute that Josh would propose in such a romantic and serious manner, after all Josh normally made a joke out of everything.

After pausing for a second or two, Jessica leaned towards him a whispered in Josh's ear, "Yes I will gladly marry you and will be very happy to be your lifetime partner. "

After a long and very passionate kiss, Josh said, "Thank God for that, I was worried that you might do the sensible thing and say no. " Then reaching into his inside jacket pocket, Josh pulled out a small black ring case and from it took out an antique diamond ring, which he slowly slipped on to Jessica's finger.

"There you go, " said Josh. "That makes it officially binding now. " Josh then with a serious look said, "Now I know this may seem rather outdated and may sound a little corny, but as your dad will be a Caroline's house tomorrow, I would like to ask his permission for your hand in marriage. So please don't tell anyone we are engaged until I have spoken to your dad tomorrow. You never know, he might just say no. "

Jessica, happy and in a laughing voice, said, "I know Dad won't say no, in fact he will probably pay you to take me away. But I would just love to see the look on his face when you ask him. Mom and Dad both like you a lot and unlike other boyfriends they have met, I have never heard them say a bad word about you. In fact, Mom often tells of the time you patted her on her bum while she was walking out through the theatre door that time. "

"Oh yes, " said Josh. "I certainly remember that experience very well, it was like an automatic reflex, not thinking, you know a subconscious thing I would normally do with you. I felt really embarrassed by it at the time, I am sure I must have blushed when your mom turned towards me and sort of smiled at me. "

"Well Mom must have enjoyed it, Josh, as she has mentioned it quite a few times and always smiles, "Jessica said laughing.

Thankfully, it was a warm pleasant evening as they slowly made their way back to the hotel. Walking alongside the River Shannon made it all seem just a little magical, as they stopped to kiss along the way.

Back in the hotel, while riding up in the lift and looking at the ring, Jessica said, "I have suddenly realised why I recognise this ring, it was the one I admired and tried on when we were in Edinburgh at the Fringe. How the hell did you manage to buy it, without me knowing?"

"Well, it was easy Jess, I phoned them up when I got home, " replied Josh. "And they kindly shipped down by courier. It's the only ring I knew would fit you and which I knew you liked. "

"Well, the reason I didn't buy it at the time was because it was very expensive, " said Jessica. "I never dreamed I would ever see it again, let alone be given it. Thank you Josh, I don't know why you were worried that I may have said no, because I thought it was rather obvious that you were the one I loved and that I wanted to be with. "

Now back in their room, Jessica stands with her back to the door and with her hands behind her back, she slowly slid the dead lock across. Jessica next moved across to the bedside switches and turned the lights down low.

Jessica then turned to face Josh and in a phoney foreign accent said, "I suppose Commander Bond wants to fuck me now, yes?" And then starts to slowly unzip her dress. "Oh no you don't Jess, " said Josh zipping it back up again. "That's my job and one I have been waiting to do all night. " Josh then removed his jacket, untied his bow tie and now standing behind her, he turns Jessica to face the large wardrobe mirror. Whilst Josh was kissing Jessica's neck, with his two hands started to slowly raise the hem of Jessica's dress, until it exposed the lower half of her beautiful body. Jessica then felt one of Josh's hands glide gently towards her crotch, while his other hand was gently pushing her thighs apart. Now Jessica's legs were partially spread, she felt one of Josh's hands slide under her crotch and started gently caressing her lace covered vagina. In response, now feeling aroused, Jessica's slid her hand behind her back and fumbled her way to Josh's trouser zip. Slowly Jessica unzipped Josh's trousers and pushed her hand inside. Josh was now unzipping Jessica's dress which then gently draped down, exposing her partially covered breasts. He gently started to squeeze her nipples between his fingers, which by now were erect and looking to Josh to be extremely suckable. Josh then turned Jessica to face him and he began to gently mouth and sucks each of Jessica's nipples in turn, whilst at the same time squeezing her breasts. Jessica had now undone Josh's trousers and was slowly pulling them down his legs and to his ankles. As Jessica lowered her body, to reach Josh's ankles, Josh could no longer reach Jessica's breasts, so he caressed her hair. Josh, now standing upright watched Jessica now lowering his under pants to reveal his

64

extremely hard cock. Jessica held his cock, tightly gripping the shaft and then began to slowly lick and mouth the tip. Jessica now slowly moved her lips along the full length of his cock, occasionally turning her head upwards in order to observe Josh's face. Josh's eyes were now closed, and Josh was enjoying every second of the erotic pleasures he was experiencing.

After several minutes of Jessica giving him the kind of pleasure every man would die for, Josh gently lifted Jessica up from her knees and slowly removed her dress. Josh then quickly removed his remaining clothes and was now standing completely naked. Jessica still clad in her underwear and high heels, was lifted onto the bed and Josh spread her legs apart. Josh, now lying face down with his head between her thighs, began mouthing her crotch and sucking her vagina through her lacy briefs. After a few long pleasurable minutes, Josh carefully removed her briefs, trying not to snag them on her suspenders. Now Jessica's silky-smooth vagina was naked and available, Josh resumed his mouthing and licking, but could now enter the tip of his tongue into her waiting pussy and licked softly around her clitoris. Jessica, her eyes now closed, was lying back, and was enjoying each of the waves of pleasure that she was experiencing. Josh's arms were outstretched, and his fingers were gently gripping each of Jessica's nipples very tightly, almost to the point of pain, but then relaxing his grip when he could sense Jessicawas tense. At the same time, he sucked her clitoris hard then slowly relaxed his grip and repeatedly continued with his oral stimulations. By now, Josh could feel Jessica's writhing body motions, along with the occasional muted groan.

Josh's fingers were now spreading Jessica's labia enabling him to rub her clitoris in a gentle circular motion and occasionally pausing to push his fingers deep into her aroused vagina or to lick her with just the tip of his tongue. Although Jessica was now getting all the physical pleasure, Josh was happily experiencing strong psychological satisfaction from feeling Jessica's strengthening orgasms.

Feeling that he could no longer stand the wait, Josh climbed on to the bed beside Jessica face up. Jessica, now eager to get Josh's hard cock inside her now wanting vagina, climbed back on top of Josh, with her legs astride him. Leaning over him with one hand on Josh's chest, Jessica used her other hand to spread her labia open and then lower herself down onto Josh's hard penis.

Jessica then began sliding her moist vagina up and down the shaft of Josh's penis, moving rhythmically from the tip of his cock right down to his balls. Josh was now in sexual ecstasy, as he fondled her breasts, and gently squeezed her nipples. Both Jessica and Josh were enjoying, this erotic wonderful mind-blowing physical pleasure from each other and each of them was keen to give the other complete sexual satisfaction.

Slowly but surely, Jessica than started to make her way up along Josh's body until her vagina was positioned over Josh's eager and waiting mouth. Josh was now taking immense pleasure from mouthing and licking Jessica's fully excited vagina. Jessica, having now experienced several orgasms, shuffled back along Josh's body and positioned herself over Josh's full aroused penis. With one hand behind her back, Jessica reached down to guide Josh's hard penis into her wanting vagina and then slowly lowered herself down onto it. When Jessica had all of Josh's penis deep inside, she pinned Josh's arms to his side, with her outstretched arms, then used her arms to raise and lower herself. Jessica paused occasionally, to feel her vagina contracting on Josh's penis and she would lean forwards, enabling Josh to suck her nipples. Jessica steadily increased her rhythm until she was finally overwhelmed by her ultimate orgasm. Josh who had been anticipating this very moment, and using his outstretched arms, pulled Jessica down by her shoulders hard down onto his fully aroused penis and then held her there whilst his semen pulsed inside her. As the pleasure they had both experienced simultaneously, slowly subsided, Jessica relaxed into Josh's arms and they kissed each other, neither wanting to move.

Both Jessica and Josh were left feeling completely drained, whilst at the same time feeling completely and utterly satisfied. They lay side by side holding hands, Jessica moving only to kick off her high heels. Jessica removed her remaining underwear and reclined back into Josh's comfortable arms.

After a few minutes Josh broke the silence and said, "You know Jess, having sex with you is the most beautiful experience I have ever known. " He went on to say, "Some people, who have had near death experiences, say that they see all of their life flash in front of them in those last couple of minutes, before their life fades away. Well, if that's true Jess, tonight will certainly be up there, flashing past at my life end. " Josh now running his fingers over her naked body said, "You know I'm such a lucky bastard, because you have got to be the most beautiful, adorable and sexiest girl in the world. You are so deliciously intoxicating; I believe I could actually get drunk on you. " Josh, then added, "Sorry Jess, I know I am a bit of a pain, getting you to wear stockings, high heels and things, but it's something special with me. "

Jessica, then cupping his head, with her two hands in front of her face, said, "Joshua Foster, please get it into your head, I am always blown away having sex with you and I will wear whatever you want, I will do anything you want and believe me, you can do whatever you want to do. And if it means I get fucked like that, then believe me I'm up for it, every time. You may not realise it Josh, but I am still coming now. " Jessica's eyes then slowly closed, paused for a second, then smiled and said, "There you go, I am just having another one right now, just thinking about it. "After having a half-hour rest on the bed, they put their dressing gowns on, tidied the room and ordered two champagne brandy cocktails from room service. They both then sat out on the balcony enjoying their night cap and chatting about tomorrow's visit to Galway. After finishing their drinks, they returned to bed and fell asleep in each other arms. Both Jessica and Josh had an extremely sound night's sleep, anticipating tomorrows visit to Jessica's relations.

Chapter 5

The Meet up

At eight-thirty a. m. they were awoken by room service knocking on their door, breakfast was waiting to be delivered.

"This is room service, " said a voice from the other side of their door. "Can I bring your breakfast in?"

"Oh, yes please, " replied Josh.

Then after hearing a key try the lock, a voice from the outside said, "Sorry sir, but the latch appears to be on. "

"Oh sorry, " said Josh, leaping out of bed naked, then putting his dressing gown on, Josh now feeling slightly jangled, he opens and holds the door open, while breakfast was wheeled in on a trolley.

"Shall I leave it here sir?"

"Yes please, that will be just fine there, " replied Josh.

"Should you require anything else sir, please don't hesitate to call room service. " He then left closing the door behind him.

Josh, curious to see what had been delivered lifted each of the silver covers in turn. "Oh, good, there's bacon, sausage, eggs, mushrooms, tomatoes and toast. Oh, there's even more underneath. You know Jess, I bet this is so much better than eating down in the restaurant and it's probably a buffet service down there anyway. I don't think you realise, how pleased I am we've booked this hotel again for our last night, on our way home, I really like it here, don't you?" As they sat eating breakfast, Josh watching the local weather forecast on the TV said, "It looks like another good day, weather-wise, let's hope this good weather keeps up eh Jess. "Then adding, "Lookout Ireland we are here and looking for a good time. "

After breakfast, Jessica began to shower and was soon joined in the shower by Josh. "Fancy washing my back Jess, here, please try some of this, " said Josh handing her a bottle. "It's much, much better than that stuff you get from the wall dispenser. " Josh now squeezing shower gel all over Jessica's back. "I always use this, it's Molton Brown shower gel, it's the best shower soap going, and it smells really great. " Josh's method of washing Jessica's back was gradually but surely changing from that of being purely functional, to that of a more sensuous nature.

"Don't tell me you are feeling horny again, " said Jessica, as Josh gently pressed Jessica against the wall of the shower using his body.

"Of course I am, " replied Josh. "Now please don't talk silly, I am here in the shower with an extremely beautiful girl, who is naked and is now covered in my favourite soap. " Then pausing for a response said, "I just hope you are as well, because here, take a look at this. " Josh said as he turned his body to display his rock-hard penis, "It seems a damn shame to waste it, don't you

71

think?" And at that Josh began washing Jessica's body. First her breasts, occasionally pinching, her now very soapy nipples and then Josh moved to her hips and then to her beautiful, sexy bum. Josh then slid his soapy fingers down onto Jessica's crotch area and into her vagina. Both covered in soap, they writhed together, as they held each other close, feeling each other's body through contact with their own. One thing naturally led to another, Jessica now giving Josh oral sex, with water washing over her hair and down across her face, a situation that quickly led on to full sexual intercourse. After they had finished, Josh gave Jessica a long passionate kiss.

Jessica, looking very wet with her hair stuck to her face, complained, "I was being very careful not to get my hair wet and now look at me. "

"Sorry Jess, but seeing you all wet and soapy, was too much to resist, I just had to come in and join you. Anyway, I am pretty sure that must be the best shower I have ever had, good old Molton Brown. You know, I could do with one of those, every morning. "

To which Jessica replied laughing, "In your dreams Mr Joshua Foster, in your dreams. Now please Josh, will you just get out of here and let me finish my shower in peace. "

After checking out and settling their hotel bill, they made their way down to the hotel's underground car park.

"Do you know the postcode for this antiques place, Jess?" asked Josh.

"Why not just leave the car parked here and then drive straight to Caroline's when we have finished shopping. " Josh, looking up skywards, said, "Thank you God, for sending me not only a very beautiful looking woman, but one who's smart with it too. Thank you for sending Jessica Holmes to me. Oh, and if you don't mind God, I would really like to keep her from now on and forevermore. "

Locking the car and walking into town, was their first day as fiancés and somehow felt slightly different as they looked forward to shopping together. It was later, whilst in the second antique shop they visited, when Jessica's eyes were drawn to a small oil painting, hanging next to a collection of old, faded prints. Drawing closer to get a better look, she called out to the elderly lady shop keeper

"How much is this please?"

The old lady then came over, looked at the painting and replied, "That one is seventy-five euros darling, it's a lovely picture, isn't it?"

"I would buy it," replied Jessica. "But not at that price."

"Too expensive, do you think. All right then darling, I can maybe let it go for fifty euros, " said the old lady in response.

"No, " replied Jessica. "I know this artist's work quite well and the price you are giving me is far too low. I'll give you two hundred and fifty euros and not a penny less. "

The shop keeper, now taking a second look at the picture, said, "There you are look, the price is marked on the frame darling,", seventy-five euros, so you can take it for seventy-five, that would be at its marked price. "

Jessica, now with her stubborn look on, said in a very commanding tone, "There is no way I am going to rob you of two hundred euros, here is my Visa card, now please put it through at two hundred and fifty euros. " Adding, "I will not let you turn me into a crook for two hundred euro's." Seeing that Jessica was not going to change her mind, the shop keeper rang through the amount as Jessica had instructed.

As she wrapped the picture, the old lady leaned over towards Josh and said, "There are not that many honest people about these days, in fact there are very few indeed. I really like your young lady, you want to hang on to that one, young man, she's something very special that lady. "

"I intend to, " replied Josh, putting his finger on the knot as the old tied the string around the brown paper parcel.

As they walked out of the shop, closing the slightly sticking door behind them, Josh said, "That was something else Jess. It really was, now I know why I fell for you. Is it really worth two hundred and fifty euro's then?"

"Josh," replied Jessica. "I still feel a little guilty paying just two fifty, it could be worth, maybe five hundred, or even more in the right auction, but it's definitely worth well over two hundred and fifty euros. "

"Well, " said Josh, laughing. "I'm pretty sure that old lady will be telling someone about that unusual sale before the day is out, I would bet you any money. " As they walked back to the hotel, Josh said jokingly, "I kept steering you away from the grandfather clocks she had for sale as well as that old wooden propeller, standing in the corner."

Then Jessica, playing Josh at his own game, said in a serious voice, "What? She had a wooden propeller for sale, they are like gold, Josh. "Then immediately stopping and pulling Josh back towards the shop, started to laugh. "You know I should have bought it, just to see you carrying it back through town. "

As they left Limerick behind them, Josh exclaimed, "I will certainly hold some very fond memories of that town Jess, I just hope our stopover on our return journey turns out just as good. It's a nice place, Limerick, as you know, I have not seen that much of Ireland up to yet, but what little I have seen so far, I am really pleased with, so thank you very much Limerick. "

Driving along the M18 towards Galway, Josh remarked, "Beautiful countryside round here Jess, it certainly looks different to the M25, there are no bloody queues for a start. " As they pulled off the motorway on to a side road, Jessica gave Josh all the directions, being as she had travelled the route many times before and knew it extremely well.

After another twenty miles or so, Jessica said, "Slow down Josh, the turning we need is just around this bend on the right. " The lane they now turned into had cattle grids, was surrounded by lush pastureland, and was flanked on both sides by white parkland fencing.

"Is their house off this lane then, Jess?" asked Josh.

"No, " replied Jess. "This is not a lane Josh, this is their driveway. And just here, " said Jess laughing and pointing at a roadside drain. "This is where I fell of my bike, when I was twelve. I was taken to hospital for stitches and I still have the scar on my ankle to prove it. " Then smiling broadly said, "I have spent some very happy times here, some really wonderful, magical times. "

Jessica was now getting very excited as a large Georgian styled house came into view and Jessica said very excitedly, "Well this is it Josh, this is, Mainear Darach, or Oak House in English. " As they got closer, Jessica, now even more excited, said, "Look Josh, Mom and Dad are already here. I can see their car. " Then pointing through the windscreen, Jessica said, "Just follow the drive round to the left and park next to Dad's car. " As Josh parked next to Jessica's dad's Mercedes estate car, he could now see why Jessica had enjoyed her time here. The house really was impressive; the courtyard was paved with cobble and stone and was flanked on three sides, by brick-built stables and ivy-covered out buildings. Beyond the courtyard Josh could see a paved road that led out to what appeared to be a range of old and a few newer farm buildings.

"Come on Josh," said Jessica, now already half out of the car and eager to go. "Oh, look Josh, here is Caroline coming out to meet us. " Then waving to her and running over to meet, after a few hugs and hello's, they all made their way towards the house. "Nice place you have here

Caroline, " said Josh, ". "And I see you have some cattle.
"

"I am not sure how many cattle Dad has, but there is just over eight hundred acres in total, well maybe a little more if you include the woodland and a few of the rough ground areas, " replied Caroline. Although they had entered the house through a side door, it was evident that their lifestyle was anything but average. Josh could just imagine old sepia photographs being taken of past shooting parties, groups photos of the house staff. As they left the lobby and entered the main entrance hall they were met by both Caroline and Jessica's parents, smiling, and looking extremely pleased to see them.

"So, this is Joshua, is it Jess?" said their large friendly-looking host holding out his hand. "My name's Howard, very pleased to meet you Josh. I've been hearing a lot about you, young man, "said Howard, Caroline's dad, now firmly shaking hands with him.

"All good, I hope, " replied Josh.

Then leading a very smart looking lady towards Josh, Howard said, "And this is my lovely wife, Jane. " Howard was wearing a checked linen shirt and a light tweed waistcoat, looking every bit the gentleman squire. His wife Jane looked far more elegant, and anyone could see, that she must have been a real beauty in her younger years, but still remained a good looking woman.

Jessica and Josh were then greeted by Jessica's parents who said, with drinks in hand, "We are all out on the lawn Jessica, it's such a beautiful day, so when you have freshened up and put your bags away, come back and join us. "

At that Caroline said, "Come on, let me show to your rooms. " Still with a drink in her hand, Caroline led them back across the courtyard and up some outside stone steps and into the first floor of an old beautiful ivy-covered brick building. Opening the door and leading them through, Caroline said, "These used to be the old groom's quarters, but Dad had them converted to a guest suite. " Josh could immediately see that they were going to be very comfortable, as they were now standing in a beautifully restored self-contained flat, with its whitewashed stone walls, exposed oak beams, a large wood burning stove and an immaculate, highly polished antique dark oak floor.

"There's a kitchen through there, " said Caroline, then leading them into a beautiful en-suite bedroom. Caroline said, "I thought you two would feel more comfortable out here in the annex, on your own and just a little more independent. So when you are settled, " Caroline said, taking another drink from her glass, "Just come across to the house, my Richard should be here later, he's joining us all for dinner. "

After unloading the car and making themselves at home, Josh, while trying out the TV remote, said, "You know, I love your Caroline, she's such a great girl, but that Richard fellow of hers, well he's already getting right up my nose and I haven't even met him yet. "

Jessica, now slightly annoyed, at Josh's remarks said, "Well you just listen here Joshua Foster, I have some bad news for you, I took the liberty of inviting you to Richard's stag party on Tuesday night. So please don't go letting him know that. "And then added, "Anyway you had better get to like him, because he will be family soon. Oh yes, before I forget, the other girls and myself are all going into Dublin tomorrow, to the dress maker for our final fitting and to collect our dresses. Oh, and I think Caroline's dad wants to show you round the estate, while we're gone. "

Josh now looking a little happier said, "Now, I like Caroline's dad, he seems like a proper man's man. I'll look forward to that and if you are going to the shops, bring me something nice back. "

"Like what?" said Jessica looking somewhat puzzled and ignoring Josh's 'You know what I like, surprise me'.

Now over at the big house, *this is the life,* thought Josh, sitting out in the afternoon sunshine, beautiful garden setting, good company and a large gin and tonic. *What else could anyone really need.*

Later that evening, Josh spotted Jessica's dad out on the patio and seizing the moment, went out to join him.

"Ah, Mr Holmes, " said Josh. "Can I have just a minute of your time please?"

Mr Holmes, seeing the look on Josh's face and subsequently looking slightly apprehensive, answered, "Of course, you can Josh and will you please stop calling me Mr Holmes, you must call me Gerald, or better still, Gerry. "

"Well OK Mr Holmes, sorry, I mean Gerry, I know this may seem a little old-fashioned, But I am in love with your daughter, in fact very much indeed and last night I proposed to her. But well, I think it's very important that also I seek your approval sir. So Mr Holmes, with that in mind, could I please have your approval, to take your daughter's hand in marriage?"

Slightly taken aback by Josh's unexpected and very formal request, it was a second or two before Gerry could find any suitable response, eventually he replied, "Look Josh you really must start calling me Gerry. "And putting his arm around Josh's shoulder said, "You know Jessica is one in a million and that she means the world to me and her mother, but if you truly love her and as she loves you, I would be more than delighted if you two married. "

"Oh, there's one more thing Mr, oh, I mean Gerry, obviously we need you to let Mrs Holmes know, but Jessica and I didn't want to make our engagement public news, until after Caroline's wedding. You see Gerry, we didn't want to distract the focus from Caroline's wedding, or to steal any of the occasion. I think you will fully understand where we are coming from, eh, Gerry?" Now looking very extremely relieved that a very difficult episode was over, Josh said, "Thank you Gerry. "Then taking a large sigh, said, "Wow, thank you very much indeed Gerry, I can now tell my mom and family. "

At that, Gerry said, "Now come on back to the house with me and let's have another drink. " As they walked back, Gerry then added, "I know, normally we would be celebrating with champagne, but Mum's the word regarding this engagement, eh Josh, so how about a very large brandy instead?"

A short while later Josh found Jessica, in the kitchen with her mom, Mary and Caroline's mom, Jane, who were all very busy chatting while at the same time putting a buffet dinner together. Josh nonchalantly asked Jessica to join him outside in the garden for a minute and when they were safely out of earshot Josh excitedly told Jessica what he had said to her dad and what he had said in reply. Josh went on describe how he had explained about keeping the engagement a secret until after the wedding and how her dad fully agreed with the delayed announcement. After getting a special hug and a few long kisses, they both returned to the kitchen holding hands.

A little later that evening, Richard finally arrived and while they were all enjoying a few more predinner drinks, Richard and Caroline came over to them, when Caroline explained about tomorrow's final fitting for the dresses. As requested by Jessica, Josh, dutifully engaged in polite conversation with Richard and whenever Josh saw Jessica looking across to observe his behaviour, Josh would obligingly smile back, as much to say, 'see Jess, I am being really nice to Richard for you'.

Later that evening, Jessica's mom, Mary, came across to their accommodation and explained how delighted she was with their engagement and how difficult she was finding it to keep it a secret. Jessica then held her hand out, to show her mother the ring.

"Why, it's absolutely gorgeous Jessica, " said her mom.

"I know it is, " said Jessica. "I am dying to wear it full-on, but that will have to wait until after Caroline's wedding. "

Jessica's mom, now holding Josh's hands and kissing him on the cheek, whispered, "I was hoping this would happen, I think you know Jessica really cares for you Joshua. So please, just make sure you take good care of her for me?"

As Jessica's mom turned to leave, Josh replied, "Don't you worry about that Mrs Holmes, I promise I will always take really good care of her. "Then looking at Jessica, said, "Trust me Mary, I really will. " A few minutes later, Josh phoned his mother to tell her that he and Jessica were now formally engaged.

Josh's mom then asked to speak to Jessica, telling her how pleased she was that they were finally engaged and said to Jessica, "You must now call me Bridie, or even by my nickname Bob. " As she was sometimes known to her friends. That night they climbed into bed together, a very happy couple, happy to be in County Galway and eagerly looking forward to Caroline's wedding.

Chapter 6

The Barn Find

The next morning, in bright sunshine, they made their way across to the main house and had breakfast with the two families along with Caroline's chief bridesmaid, Valerie, who had only arrived just minutes before. You could say Valerie was rather on the tall side, with long black hair, piercing grey eyes and a slightly pallid, almost white complexion. Josh thought to himself, *she looks like a younger version of Crueller Deville,* but she seemed to be good friends with both Caroline and with her mother Jane. At around eight, Jessica, Caroline, both moms and Valerie set off to meet the other bridesmaid in Dublin city centre, all leaving in Jane Anson's car.

As they disappeared down the driveway, Mr Anson said, "Right then young Josh, tell me, what size riding boots you wear, because they all tell me that you ride well and so I thought this morning we could have a hack round the estate. And unless you have bought some riding boots with you, then you can gladly use some of ours. "

"Well, I normally wear size nine if you have them Howard?" replied Josh, who then added. "I wish I had known I would be riding, then I could have brought my own boots along, still never mind, maybe next time. "

Mr Anson, then replied laughing, "Well here's a good tip for you then young Josh, never ever come to Ireland without bringing your riding boots, a corkscrew, a bottle opener and oh yes, maybe a very large umbrella. " When they eventually got to the stables, Josh was now wearing a very dried out, stiff and extremely old pair of size ten boots.

Howard then said, looking very pleased, "Now you have your riding boots, you have got two choices of mount Josh, lively or steady?"

"Oh, lively every time please Mr Anson, as long as it's not an absolute maniac. I normally leave the maniac rides for my brother Sean; he always seems to enjoy a difficult mount, God in hell knows why, I think it must be the challenge. "

Two very fit looking horses were led out by a middle-aged lady, who said smiling, "Here they are Howard and as you can see they are both on their toes this morning and they are absolutely itching to go. "

"Oh good, it's a dark bay, " said Josh slapping it on the neck. "And it's a mare, I love bay mares. " Then talking to the horse said, "I think you and I are going to get on just fine. " Howard being that little bit older and slightly less agile, used a mounting block to mount a beautiful looking dapple grey, while the lady held it steady for him.

"Thank you, Hazel, " said Howard, who was now going round in very tight circles, trying to get his horse under control, who then added. "I think this might be a rather lively ride today. " After Josh had mounted, Howard turned in the saddle, and asked Josh, "Are you ready to go then Josh?"

"Yes I'm ready, so please lead on Howard, as you're the one who knows where we are actually going. "And at that they rode off together to tour the estate.

It was a beautiful morning, as they rode along chatting, about the estate, how long the family had lived in the area how they used to shoot here some years back. As Josh felt at home in the saddle, he thought to himself, *it's a beautiful day, the horses are fit, Howard seems like great company, I am out in the sunshine, surrounded by beautiful Irish countryside and I am breathing clean fresh air.* It amused Josh slightly to think that Jessica and her friends were in Dublin City, with all the traffic noise, probably rushing around, fretting over this or that; and to think they had apologised for leaving me back here to ride round this beautiful estate. This seemed like a much better deal to Josh, well apart from these bloody horrible riding boots. Whilst regularly wriggling his toes to try and ease the discomfort, Josh was beginning to think that he may have had two left boots, two odd boots which must have been stiffening up for a good many years. As they continued they rode through a beautiful large wood full of very mature oaks, which looked very picturesque with dappled green sun light shining through the canopy. Howard, said, "See these oaks Josh, these trees were planted over a hundred and fifty years ago specially for the boat building industry and do you know, they are not even ready yet. Now that's what you call forward planning, you probably will never see anything like it again Josh, believe me, the world's now run by accountants, bloody bean counters, who just want a quick profit and they wouldn't know forward planning if it fell on their economically programmed heads. Oh, I think I should have checked first, you're not an economist or financial planner or the like are you Josh?"

Now laughing at Howard's remarks, Josh replied, "No I am certainly not Howard, but unfortunately my work does bring me into contact with quite a few of them, but you are absolutely correct, most of them are purely profit motivated and can't see past the next balance sheet. " Howard then said, "We used to bring the kids down here for picnics in summers gone by, just like my parents used to do with me and it's very reassuring that it never seems to change. "

After they had been riding for a while, they came to a long flat field with a grassed headland running along the full length.

"Fancy a bit of a gallop then Josh?" But before Howard had finished his sentence, his horse, knowing exactly where she was and aware of just what happens in this field, took her head and with one giant leap was away. Josh, not wishing to be left behind, was now in hot pursuit and trying to desperately catch Howard up, but all the time while he was up in the stirrups, all he was thinking, was, *These fucking boots are really something else.*

As they neared the bottom of the field, the horses finally slowed to a canter, Howard called back, with a jerky voice, "I really don't know why I don't do this every day Josh, it certainly blows out a few of those old cobwebs?" Howard then added, "How long are you with us for Josh, perhaps we can do this again?" By now the horses were sweated up, but were happily rid of their hot blood, so once more relaxed and once again Josh and Howard were able to ride side by side.

"That's a Ballyogan mare, you're riding there, Josh, she's a pure thoroughbred, I was thinking of sending her to stud this time round. But the trouble is Josh, although I love breeding foals, I'm a terrible worrier, especially near foaling time. " Howard then added, "You see, I lost a lovely mare during foaling a few years back, and well, that horrible tragedy has really put me off breeding. The other problem is selling them on. You will probably understand Josh, but when you have bred them yourself, you feel morally responsibility for their future welfare, sort of like your children and so when it comes to selling, or moving them on, well it's like you're somehow abandoning them. No Josh, breeding foals has never been easy for me, well it tugs at my old heart strings. "

After an hour or so riding round the estate and stopping to look at various aspects of the estate, they returned back to the house and bedded down the horses. "Now this is what I miss, with living in London, Howard, the smell of the horses, horse sweat drying on your hands and the feeling of being fully alive when you are up there in the stirrups and looking out between two pricked ears. "

"Well you ride very well, " said Howard. "I wish our Caroline's Richard could ride, but as you probably know Josh, you either enjoy horses or you don't. And I'm afraid young Richard just won't go anywhere near them. Mind you, sometimes I wish I didn't love horses so much; horses can be a lot of trouble and they can represent a great deal of expense. I guess with respect to owning horses, they are a little bit like women, they can be very demanding and are known to be high maintenance, but we still love them, just the same. Now come on young Josh, let's go into the house and have a nice cup of coffee, " said Howard already five strides in front and heading for the lobby door. "And then, after coffee, I will show you round the farm side of the business." *At last,* thought a much-relived Josh. *I can finally get my poor feet out of these fucking horrible boots.*

Back at the house, while drinking their mugs of coffee, Josh looking through the big bay window of the drawing room, said, "I can see why they call it the Emerald Isle Howard, it looks very green. "

Then Howard moving to stand closer to Josh and looking out at the same view, said, "I sometimes forget how lucky we are to live here you know, I have lived here most of my life, apart from my time in that bloody boarding school and my short spell in the army. " Then after a few seconds pause, said, "But believe me Josh, I have some very happy memories living here, yes of some very happy times, but sadly some very dark ones too. " But you are absolutely right Josh; it is a very beautiful country and as you correctly say, it's a very green country. "

Being as Josh and Howard were both extremely knowledgeable regarding all things agricultural, they found it easy and interesting to discuss farming, including but not limited to, livestock, arable crops, dairy farming and the like. Both of them were really enjoying their walk round together and as they chatted away, their friendship grew that little bit stronger. During their walk, they rounded an old half-timbered barn and approached a large old brick building. Howard now opening a very large pair of very old wooden doors, explained that they were soon to have this building, which had been the old sawmill, completely stripped out and converted into an ultra-modern cheese and yogurt dairy.

As they walked through this long abandoned, barnlike building, Josh was amazed to see all the rusty derelict equipment, old tools, and woodwork machinery still in place, exactly where they had been left, where years ago they would have been used for the last time, maybe seventy years or earlier. Carefully making their way through the mill, Josh was amazed to see it was all still there, just left abandoned to rust away, complete with its overhead drive belts and rusty steel shafts, criss-crossing above their heads. There was old rip saw benches, now covered in a thick layer of dust, complete with old fallen feathers and cobwebs, together with many interesting items of old, long abandoned woodworking tools.

Howard explained to Josh, "The family stopped producing its own timber in about 1940 because of a shortage of labour, what with the second world war on, everything in short supply and of course, not forgetting Ireland's mass emigration. But in its heyday, it used to employ around ten or so people full-time, making all kinds of useful things. Now of course, all our forestry work is contracted out and we just buy in what timber we need. The contractors we use have all that specialised equipment, they use experienced personnel with certified qualifications, because that's what you need to have now, and I know it would not have been viable for us to keep it going any more. "

As they headed further through the abandoned sawmill, Josh spotted something, that immediately attracted his attention and in response, said, "What's this over there then Howard?"

Howard, who was now looking at a complete loss to answer, said, "I am not actually sure Josh, but the scrap dealer said he will clear it all away for us and well he will be clearing the whole area by the end of next month. "

As Josh got closer, he was slowly realising just what the group of abandoned items were. "Bloody hell, Howard, it looks like an old steam lorry. " Now recognising exactly what he was staring at, said, "Yes it's an old sentinel steam lorry. My God Howard. "Josh said, looking very excited at what he was now looking more closely at, "I tell you what Howard, if my brother Sean was here, well, he would be absolutely drooling over this. " Josh now looking extremely concerned said, "Please, whatever you do Howard, please, you can't scrap this, why it's an extremely important part of your family heritage, a valuable historical vehicle, that really must be saved. " Josh then added, "I know Sean would gladly buy it off you, rather than let it go for scrap. "

Now taking a little more interest in the cab's barely legible sign writing, Howard, said, "Oh my God, it's still got our old telephone number on the door, well what do you know, I haven't seen that telephone number for a very long, long time. Well Josh its down for scrap, so if your brother actually wants it, tell him he had better get it out of here and collect it before the scrap man takes it away. " Walking around the various parts scattered about, Josh could see that the chassis had been stripped of its wheels; the cab had been removed and was stored nearby, probably, in order to expose then now rusty old upright boiler. But it looked like all the main components were all still there. Finding the chassis plate and after rubbing the dirt away with his hand, Josh could now read it was a 1931 Super Sentinel, six-ton steam lorry.

"Would you mind if I took a few photos Howard? I just know Sean would be really interested in buying this off you and if he doesn't I certainly will. "

"No problem Josh, I didn't know it was anything special. " But Howard, now slowly realising that it could be an important item to save, said, "Thanks to you telling me what it is and now that I am aware what it is, I would sooner it be saved Josh and you're right, it can't go to the scrap man. " Josh now excitedly darting around, took several photographs of the old lorry parts and sent them off to his brother, via his mobile phone. As they made their way back towards the house, Josh's phone began ringing, then Josh looking at the screen, before placing it to his ear, said, "It's my brother Sean, Howard; I knew he would be back to me on this one. " Josh was on the phone with Sean for several minutes, explaining what they had found.

He then handed his phone over to Howard and the conversations continued. When Howard eventually said, "OK then Sean, that sounds good to me, I will see you after our family wedding. "

After ringing off and handing the phone back to Josh, they continued on their tour of the farm and were now getting on like long-lost brothers.

"After lunch, I have to go into town, " said Howard. "and just pop into my solicitors to sign some papers and if you want to come along for the ride, we could go for a drink, as there's a very good bar there called Mad O' Riley's. "

"That certainly sounds good to me, " replied Josh. "I have always wanted to frequent a traditional Irish bar. "

"Well, you will definitely like this one then Josh, as they don't come any more traditionally Irish than this one."

After a quick lunch, they drove into to town, parked outside Howard's solicitors, while Howard popped in and quickly signed his documents.

On returning Howard, said, "Right then young Josh, now that's over with, I will show you a proper old Irish bar. "

It was only a short walk to the bar and as soon as Josh entered, he immediately felt at home and commented to Howard, "What a great place, I really like it. " There were old paving stones on the floor and oak beams supporting the ceiling and almost like a centre piece was a large soot blackened fireplace. The bar ran all along the whole of back wall and had an old blunderbuss hanging in the centre of the large oak beam that ran across the room over the bar. On the walls were old pictures of Swinford as it would have looked many years earlier. *Yes,* thought Josh. *Howard was just spot on, it definitely has tons of atmosphere.*

When they reached the bar Howard said, "What are you drinking then young Josh? Can I get you a pint of Guinness?"

"I'm awfully sorry, Howard, " replied Josh. "I don't want to sound ungrateful, or appear unsociable, but I really don't like Guinness, I find it a little too heavy, more like a pudding than a drink. " And now pointing randomly to one of the unfamiliar beer pulls, Josh said, "But I will have one of those please Howard. " As the landlord passed over their drinks, Josh started to explain how Guinness was first made in England. He related the story of how a small brewer had gone to buy some malt and was offered some black looking malt that had been left roasting to long and had almost burnt. As the story continued, other conversations in the bar noticeably diminished to a whisper and very soon they were all listening to Josh's story with much interest. Josh continued to explain that the brewer was far from wealthy and so willingly bought the bargain malt. Back at his North London brewery, the brewer used the blackened malt and after brewing with it, finished up with a very dark brew, what we now would recognise as Guinness. He continued to explain how it was for many years brewed at Guinness's Park Royal Brewery, in North London and at some point later, the brewing was transferred to Dublin. Josh continued to explain how lorry tankers then delivered beer from Ireland, back to their Park Royal plant, for sale in England, However, the beer bottled in London was in fact sold back to Ireland for many years after, so the English bottled beer was a well-travelled drink. Josh had now got almost everyone in the bar's undivided attention and some drinkers had even moved closer in order to better hear Josh's unfolding story.

Josh continued to tell that although all the beer is now all bottled in Ireland, some of the old English bottles were still in circulation and due to their rarity, they were now being sold to collectors for hundreds of euro's each. Josh went on to tell, that there were some collectors who purposely travelled around Ireland, eagerly buying bottled Guinness on the off chance they might just find one of these very valuable English bottles. Josh then asked the landlord if he sold bottled Guinness and in response the landlord, pointing to a lower shelf, confirming that he did.

Josh then asked him if he ever checked his bottles to see if he had any of these very rare English bottles and the landlord replied, "Well no, not really, no I don't, I never knew they might be valuable and what's more, I wouldn't know what to look for anyway. "

"Well, " Josh explained. "Youcan tell the difference by the embossed writing on the bottom of the bottles. " Now collecting a couple of bottles from the shelf, the landlord, holding one in each hand, turned them upside down to check.

Now closely studying the bottom of the bottles, the landlord asked, "So how do I know which are the English bottles and which are Irish bottles. "To which Josh replied with a wry smile spreading across his face, "The Irish bottles are all clearly marked *open other end.* "

Josh now had everyone in the bar laughing, especially the landlord, who still holding two upturned bottles, said, "Well young man, you certainly got me there all right, that was real good crack son. " The landlord then added, while still laughing, "You got me well and truly there, young man and because of that you can have the next round of drinks on me. "

After a couple more drinks they said goodbye to everyone in the bar and as they left, people were patting Josh on the back and some were even shaking his hand. Eventually they managed to escape from the bar, which was still at full chatter as they walked away.

All the way back to the house they chatted and joked, and Howard said, "Josh I have to say, I really enjoyed today and although I know you only came over for the wedding, you and Jessica really must come and stay with us again. " Howard then added, "And the sooner the better. "

To which Josh replied, "Thank you for your kind invitation Howard, you know I've had a great time too. I've really enjoyed today, and I can assure you, that Jessica and I will definitely be taking you up on your kind offer. " Josh then added, "And I definitely will bring my own boots next time. "

As they pulled into the courtyard, Howard said, "Well it looks like they are back, young Josh, I suppose we will have to hear all about their busy day, when we get back in the house. I hope it all went well, as Jane has put her heart and soul into this wedding?"

Josh then said, "I bet both, your wife and Jessica's mom, were real stunners when they were younger, because they still look very attractive now?" Josh, then added, "I think I am beginning to see just where Caroline and Jessica, got their good looks from, because all four of them are good lookers. "

Then Howard, looking slightly more serious said, "It's a pity, you never knew Jane before Michael's death Josh, she was so full of life and always cheerfully happy. Michael's death certainly changed her from the way she was before, it's such a pity. I try my very best to make her happy, but it's all uphill work now Josh, just such a pity. I am just hoping this wedding might bring Jane's old self back again, I really hope so. "

When they walked back into the house, there were boxes and packages everywhere. "Ah, you are back, are you, " said Howard's wife Jane. "I hope you two had a good day, because we certainly did, didn't we girls?" Jane continued in a happy sounding voice, "The dresses are absolutely beautiful, the flowers are now finalised, the caterers are sorted, so all I have to do now, is let the photographer know exactly what we require from them and then fingers crossed, we are all ready to go. "

After dinner Jessica and Josh returned to their room and while Josh was searching for the TV remote Jessica, holding a large pink carrier bag, said, "Now this time I have a surprise for you Josh. "

To which Josh immediately responded, "Just what have you got for me then Jess, just what do I need that comes in a flowery pink carrier bag. "

Jessica replied, "Well if you are a very good boy, I might just show you later tonight. "

Just then there was a knock on the door and a voice the other side of the door saying, "It's me, Caroline, can I come in. " Jessica immediately let her in when Caroline said "Well Jess it's Josh I have really come to see. "

As they all walked into the kitchen and sat down round the table, Jessica said, "Well tell me, just what has Josh been up to now then Caroline?"

"Oh, he's, well nothing's wrong Jess, in fact quite the opposite. " Caroline then went on to explain, that although her mom had taken it badly when Michael died, it was Dad who has never really got over it. Caroline went on to explain, that her mom, apart from Michael's birthday and the odd reminder, seemed to be coping fairly well.

However, it's Dad, who didn't seem to suffer so badly initially, but who has never quite been the same, or had really gotten over Michael's death.

"Well tonight, both mom and I both noticed that Dad was just like his old self, laughing and telling us all about his day out with Josh. So, thank you Josh, thank you for helping to cheer Dad up for us. "

Josh, now looking a little confused, said, "Just a minute Caroline, firstly you don't have to thank me for spending a great time with your dad, it was my pleasure. Furthermore, it wasn't done as any rehabilitation exercise, or as a doing Howard a big favour, it was just your dad and I having a bloody good day out together. Believe me, I really enjoyed your dad's company and I look forward to doing it again. So please don't go thanking me, your dad is just one great guy to be with. In fact, we got on so well, that when I got back, I was planning to take Howard and the family on a day out to the races. That is sometime just after the wedding, probably while you and Richard are away on your honeymoon. "

Then wanting to explain in more detail, Josh said, "I was thinking that all six of us, could spend a day at Limerick Races. "

Caroline then went on to say, "Well Josh, we could not believe that Dad had actually been out riding, as it's only a handful of times he has ridden this year. Which is really sad, as he used to ride out almost every day, right up until the day Michael died, so it was so good to hear that Dad had been out riding again. So, thank you Josh, he hasn't stopped talking about it. "

Jessica then said, "I think everyone knows that Josh has always been a very sociable kind of guy, who thankfully makes friends very easily. I am just pleased to know Uncle Howard enjoyed his company. "

Caroline then added, "And a day at the races, that's a great idea, I used to love going to Tipperary Races, especially on a sunny day, so please leave that one to me Jessica, I know the people who run it. It's just a pity Richard and I won't be coming with you. But never mind, on the plus side, we will be enjoying our sunny honeymoon somewhere in the Caribbean Islands. "

After Caroline had gone, Josh took a shower, was in his dressing gown and with a can of beer in his hand, said with a questioning look on his face, "So come on then Jess, what's this surprise you have for me?"

Jessica then replied smiling, "But first I am going to get my own back on you, by making you wait until I have had my shower. Oh, and you can get me one of those ring pull tins of gin and tonic out of the cooler please, I fancy trying one of those. " A short time later, Jessica emerged from the bathroom wearing a fifty's style dress, complete with net underskirts. It certainly looked the part and it made Jessica look like she had just walked of the filmset of some 1950s movie. Josh was immediately taken aback, as it automatically reminded him of some of the Bardot films he had enjoyed so much as a young man. The dress had a scooped neckline, perfectly showing off her smooth shoulders, with its charcoal black background, dotted with pink and white orchid like flowers and with just a hint of lace showing itself from under the hem, Josh was literally stopped in his tracks.

Up until this point, Josh had been lying on the bed talking to Sean on his mobile phone, but on seeing Jess, said, "Sorry brother, but Jess has just got me a surprise, so I've got to go mate, so bye-bye, I will speak to you tomorrow. " Now turning his full attention towards Jess, Josh said, "Wow two really beautiful surprises in one night, things in my life are definitely looking up. "

"So, what's the other surprise then Josh?" Jessica asked, now giving a bit of a swirl, to show off the dress.

"Well, mom phoned while you were in the shower and told me she has just had the all clear from the hospital. Thankfully, the treatment has been receiving has worked and apparently there's not even a trace in the test, I am so happy Jess it really was the best news I could have had. "

"Oh that's absolutely wonderful news, that's a big weight lifted off everybody's mind, " said Jessica. "Everyone, especially me. I am so pleased to hear that, she's such a lovely lady, I must ring her tonight. I bet your dad's pleased, I know it was getting to him and although he didn't say much, I know Sean will be over the moon. "

"And not only that Jess, but Sean's just told me he had spoken to your uncle Howard earlier tonight and Howard has agreed to sell the steam lorry, so Sean is now really a very happy man. Honestly, Jess, I don't think I could ever be any happier. All this good news following our engagement, as Mom would say, it must have been written in the stars. So tell me, you sexy-looking dream girl, where the hell did you manage to find such a beautiful dress, honestly Jess you look like a film star, no I stand corrected, you look every inch the most beautiful girl in the world, which you most certainly are. "

Still swishing the skirt, Jessica explained that she had seen the dress in a retro fashion shop window in Dublin and had told the girls she had been invited to a fifties style party, later in the year.

"And I said when I saw it in the window, that dress there would be ideal. As soon as I saw it, I thought of you and while I was in there, I got some tan-coloured seamed stockings and some white 50s style lingerie, including your favourite, a suspender belt. " Now looking happier than a butcher's dog, Josh walked across the room and locked the door, then closed all the curtains. Josh then picked up the coffee table from the lounge and carried it through into the bedroom.

"Joshua Foster, " Jessica asked, hands on her hips, looking very confused, "Just what the hell are you going to do with that?"

Now giving her a kiss on the cheek, as he moved past her carrying the table, Josh answered "It's for you to stand on sweetheart, I think it's time to indulge in a little intimate exploration, don't you?" Josh, dimmed the lights, selected some moody music, and helped Jess to climb up on to the table, saying as he lifted her, "I hope you are up for this Jess, because I certainly am. "

Jessica now wobbling slightly on her very high stiletto heels, said, "Well Josh, I will let you into a little secret, I have never done anything like this before either, but it's looking like a very interesting first. "

Josh, producing one of his ties said, "Apparently you get maximum satisfaction if you're blind folded, so here goes. "And then he carefully wrapped one of his ties around her head, covering Jessica's eyes. "Now just you relax Jess and enjoy all the sensations, of this erotic journey I'm hopefully going to take you on. "

Jessica now blindfolded was a hundred percent concentrating on this new sexual journey and was eagerly anticipating new, if not slightly unusual pleasures. Jessica was now starting to become slightly aroused, as she felt the hem of her dress, along with several layers of the net petticoats being slowly lifted. Jessica could feel Josh's warm breath against the skin on top of her thighs and at the same time was aware that Josh's hand was now sliding up the inside of her leg and was beginning to fondle her crotch. She could feel Josh's lips moving up and down the back of her legs, which made the hair on the back of her neck tingle. Josh, now pushed a hand against the inside of her left foot, indicating that she was to part her legs. Gingerly, she moved her feet apart, still feeling a little unsteady in her high heels and worried that she may even lose her balance and could fall. Jessica now felt Josh's other hand on her as it gently moved the crotch of her panties to one side. At this point Jessica tensed slightly, anticipating that Josh's fingers would now be touching her.

Just as Jessica had anticipated, Josh's fingers now began to slowly massage her moist clitoris, and then occasionally he would stop the massaging movements, only to push his finger deep inside her. Just as Jessica was enjoying Josh's penetrations, he would slowly withdraw and start the massaging motions once more. After a few minutes, Josh became aware that Jessica's breathing was becoming much shallower and at the same time, her breathing was becoming more rapid. Jessica's body movements now indicated to Josh that Jessica was now becoming sexually aroused and that she appeared eager for sexual intercourse to begin. Just as Josh's sensual stimulations were getting Jessica to the point of no return, Josh stopped and very delicately lifted the crutch of her panties back over her vagina.

Josh then rose to his feet and began to slowly undo the zip on the back of Jessica's dress, allowing the neckline to fall away from her breasts. Josh then gently sliding his hand inside the cup of her bra, lifted out each breast in turn and at the same time folding the front of her bra cups down, resulting in two perfectly exposed nipples. Moving around to the front of Jessica, Josh then began sucking Jessica's nipples, while carefully lowering her dress and the net petticoats down to Jessica's feet. As Josh lifted each foot to remove her dress, Jessica put one of her hands onto Josh's shoulder in order to steady herself. The dress now removed was moved to one side, which resulted in Jessica standing in just her white underwear. Josh slowly began to remove Jessica's briefs and again Jessica had to steady herself by holding Josh's shoulder, as he removed each leg in turn. Jessica could feel Josh's hair touching against her stomach as Josh began to lick Jessica's now very sensitive vagina and in response, Jessica guided Josh's head with her two, now slightly trembling hands. Once again, Josh would cease the oral stimulations, so that he could move his fingers in and out of Jessica's soft vagina and continued to gently massage her clitoris. Jessica, after enjoying this very pleasurable and erotic stimulation, was aware that Josh was once again changing position and after a moment or two, could feel her long hair being lifted from her shoulders. Jessica could now feel Josh's breath on her sensitive neck, which Josh now began to softly kiss. Jessica and Josh were now both fully aroused to the point where, sex would be extremely welcomed.

Jessica, now undoing the blindfold, whispered, "Mm that was so bloody lovely, it was almost too sexy, so believe me Josh, I really do need your cock inside me. "

With the blindfold removed, it was a few seconds before Jessica regained her eyesight and as Josh helped her down from the table, Jessica whispered in his ear, "Well, I will tell you one thing Joshua Foster, you can certainly do that again. That has got to have been the best erotic foreplay ever. " Jessica then steadied herself by holding Josh's hands as she slowly lowered to her knees. Swishing her hair to one side, Jessica moved her opening mouth on to Josh's hard, waiting penis. Now it was Josh's turn to be fully turned on. After several minutes Josh said, "I think you should stop that now Jess, otherwise I may be coming sooner than you would like. "

In response, Jessica rose back to her feet and firmly gripping Josh's cock, led him over towards the bed.

As they climbed onto the bed, Josh said, "Wow, Jess that has really turned me on, at one point I was actually trembling, the more I sensed you getting aroused, the more I became aroused. And you're right; we definitely will enjoy that again and I think, maybe sooner, rather than later. You know Jess, in the beginning, with you standing on the coffee table blindfolded, it felt just a little perverted, but that guilty feeling soon passed once I got into it. Now come here my beautiful Jessica and let me fuck you, because God only knows, I feel extremely horny now. "

Once they were on the bed, Josh moved Jessica into his second favourite sexual position, Jessica now on her hands and knees across the bed, with her knees just on the edge of the bed. Josh positioned himself, behind her, so that he could fuck her from the back. Josh knew that he could not have fucked Jessica in his favourite position, that is with Jessica on top, because he was just too sexually aroused and would probably have come, straight away.

After several minutes of fucking and after an almighty strong orgasm, they both relaxed back into bed and after kissing Jessica Josh said, "Thank you for buying the dress, I don't know what it cost, but believe me Jess, it was worth every single penny, or should I say euro. " Josh then said, "Maybe we could visit that shop on our way home, if you can remember where it was Jess. "

Jessica now pointing across to the pink carrier bag sitting on a nearby chair, said, "The name of the shop is on the bag Josh, along with their contact details. " Jessica then added, "You know Josh, I have always loved 1950/60s fashions and I think they are currently due for a bit of a renaissance, as they are certainly getting more popular and the shop was really busy. " Jessica then added, "Yes, I think we need to go back there again, as there were one or two other things I would have like to have looked at, had I had more time. "

Josh then leaning out of bed, with Jessica still in his arms, first turned the music off and then as he was switching off the lights, said, "I have got another little surprise tomorrow night for you Jess. "

To which Jessica replied laughing, "I don't think I could take many more of your little surprises yet Josh, my body is still trembling from that last one. "

Chapter 7

The Stag Party

The next morning after breakfast, Jessica went with Caroline to look at the church and then into town to finalise which wedding cars they would be using. So while they were gone and being as the weather was good, Josh and Howard decided on another ride.

While they were out riding Howard said, "I told Jane what you said yesterday, about Jane and Mary, both being good lookers and do you know what Josh, I think you now have a friend for life. And of course, making Jane happy certainly makes for a much happier life for me. " After being quiet for a minute or two, whilst deep in thought, Howard said in an enquiring manner, "You don't happen to partake in sailing do you Josh, because, we have our boat down in Galway Harbour and I could really do with taking her out for an hour or two. Sadly, I have not been near it for months, it's just moored up there doing nothing and although I can and have handled her single handed, it's much more enjoyable sailing with company. " Howard then continued, "We used to sail a lot when Michael was alive, but I don't seem to have the same interest in it now. " Then after another minute or so in thought, Howard said,

"Which is a pity really, as she's a lovely boat and I'm not even sure whether the engine would even start now?"

"Well Howard, " replied Josh. "I am pleased to say, I have sailed quite a few times and I actually completed my RYA crew training some years back, but it's my brother Sean, who's the real sailor in the family, he even took his yacht master's and has sailed down to the Med and back a few times. " Josh, after another minute, said, "He's a very cleaver guy that brother of mine, he even holds a PPL, err, Private Pilot's Licence. Yes, Howard he's some smart lad that brother of mine. I tell you what Howard, why don't we all have a day's sailing, that's providing the weathers right, because I'm a bit of a fine weather sailor me? How far away from here is it to the boat, perhaps we could go down later today and check her over?"

After their usual mad gallop and a steady hack back through the lanes and as they were riding back towards the house, Howard said, "I spoke to Sean for some time last night, you know, about him collecting that old steam lorry and he sounds like a nice guy. Now you must remind him, that when he comes over to collect it, he must stay here with us here at Mainear Darach. And then we can get some of my lads to give him a hand to physically get the thing out. " Howard then continued, "And that way, when he's here, we can all help him to get the thing loaded up. Maybe Sean could get some sailing in while he is here, there are some great places to sail. "

Josh then said, "It's funny at home, we always used to say, if it breathes, moves, flies or floats, then our Sean will love it. So, I don't think for a moment we would have any problem talking him into a day's sailing. "

Later that afternoon, Howard, Josh, Gerry along with the girls all went down to the boat, in order to check her over.

"Bloody hell Howard, she is absolutely beautiful and I can see why you say it is good sailing round here and it looks like you have a great mooring. " After collecting the keys and opening everything up, the girls had a bit of a clean-up in the galley along with the cabin areas, while Howard and Josh went to check out the engine. Luckily, the boat had two batteries, one for the engine and lights, while the other supplied the ancillary circuits and luckily both had been kept sufficiently charged by the boat's built-in solar panels. After checking the engine oil, fuel and flushing out the sea water cocks, it was time to start up the engine. Spinning the engine over and throwing the decompressor lever, all on board cheered as the engine burst into life and a big cloud of white smoke rose into the sky.

"Thank God for that, "sighed Howard. "I think we need to flush out and refill the freshwater tank, as that water has been in there for quite some time and maybe get a new bottle of gas from the ship's chandlers over there on the corner. " After a couple of hours, the boat was ready to sail. Coffee was served in the galley, as they powered their way out of the harbour and out into open water. Ten minutes later, Howard said, "I won't raise the sails during today's little trip, but I think it would be easier to just motor out for a mile or so. " Howard, looking rather pleased said, "I would hate to think what the old girl's keel looks like. There must be so many barnacles on her, it's a wonder we are making any headway at all. " For the hour or so they were out, everyone on board seemed very happily enjoying the pleasures of sailing in what are such beautiful waters as well as enjoying each other's good company.

"We really must do this again, " said Jane, looking extremely happy. "I can't remember the last time I went out on her, such a pity really as she is like a little home from home. "

As they sailed back towards their mooring, Howard, looking up at the rigging and while deep in concentration said, "I really must get John at the marina, to lift her out of the water and get the antifouling reapplied. And while he is at it, I will get him to check the sails over as well. Oh and the boats emergency flares and these old life jacket inspections are probably out of date as well. " Howard then stopped mid-sentence and said, "Come to think about it, I think I will get John to check the whole boat over, better safe than sorry. "

Jessica reminded Josh that it was Richard's stag party tonight and they can't stay too much longer as the minibus was picking Josh up at eight p. m. Reluctantly, the group re-secured everything on the boat, double-checked the mooring, dropped off the keys into the marina office, before heading back for home. On the way back, they stopped at the local fish and chip shop and after much indecision on the girls' part, they were finally able to place their order.

During their journey home, Howard said, "Now you have semi-retired Gerry, you and Mary should come over more often, after all we have all those empty rooms, so there's no problem there and Jane and I always enjoy your company. That would be just like old times, eh, Mary?"

Upon arriving back at the house, they all sat round the big kitchen table eating cod and chips and happily chatted about the upcoming wedding. They enthusiastically talked about their planned day at the races and they also discussed some fine weather sailing.

Jessica then said, "Oh I've got a DVD, I thought we could all watch tonight, I know you have all probably seen it before, but I just love watching *Four Weddings and a Funeral.* " At that Josh made his excuses and left to get ready for the dreaded stag night. Although Josh was generally first in line for a good night out, especially if it included a party, but he sensed that this one would probably fail to meet his idea of a good night out. After showering and getting dressed, he returned to the house where he was confronted by a concerned looking Jessica.

After moving Josh out of everyone else's earshot, Jessica said, "Now please Josh, don't you go acting antisocial with Richard and please don't go doing, or saying anything stupid, as I know what you are like when you're out on the town. "

To which Josh immediately replied, "You already know that I am not looking forwards to this so-called stag night, in fact I think I would sooner stay here with you and watch that bloody awful *Four Weddings and a Funeral* and God knows I never liked that bloody film anyway. "

At that point, they heard the minibus pull up outside and Jessica then giving him a kiss goodbye, said, "Well then off you go and try to look just a little bit happy about going. "

As Josh climbed into the minibus there was already a couple of passengers inside who were strangers to him and to break the ice Josh said, in a friendly voice, "Hello everyone, I'm Josh and I'm a guest of Richard's, over from England for the wedding. " The four passengers already in the minibus returned their hello's and introduced themselves by name. Luckily, although he did not know it at the time, Josh had sat next to John, who was a neighbour of Caroline's and unlike the three others, did not seem to be part of Richard's usual click. As they picked up other people at various locations, it was now very evident to Josh, that they were all long time and very close friends of Richard. That is except for John, all the others appeared to be the kind of people Josh would not normally enjoy associating with especially on a night out. When they arrived at a smart-looking country hotel for drinks, Richard along with one or two others were already there to meet and greet them. The hotel was one of those off the main road places, which stood in its own grounds and was part of a large country club and golf complex.

"Don't worry about paying for any drinks, " said Richard. "I have put some up money behind the bar, so come on through to the bar and have a drink or two on me. " Once in the bar, after everyone had a drink in their hand, Richard announced to the group, "Your attention please, at around eleven o'clock the minibus will pick us all up again from here and take us to Great Times Night Club in the town. " Richard in a very loud voice then said, "I have instructed the minibus driver to pick us up from Great Times at one-thirty. So please have a good night and enjoy yourselves. If anyone is not there at one-thirty, we can only presume you have made your own way home, or maybe you have struck lucky, with someone of the opposite sex. Anyway, I am telling you all this information now, while I am still of sound mind, because later on, I will probably be completely pissed. " While his friends all laughed in response, Josh just pretended to laugh along with them, but wasn't able to raise a natural laugh. However, other hotel guests drinking in bar looked on and did not appear to be so happy with the party's raised voices and loud cheering. Being as most of Richard's guests seemed to be enjoying themselves, Josh thought, *is it me, am I the odd one out here.* But then after studying his situation thought, *no thank God it's them.* And then smiled to himself, relieved in the fact that he was not in any way losing it.

As Josh had already chatted to John on the minibus and as he seemed to be of similar mind, he naturally gravitated towards John. While talking to John who explained to Josh that he worked as an economist for an Irish newspaper group, it was now evident to them both that the level of boisterousness was gradually increasing, up to a point where it was beginning to be an embarrassment. By ten p. m. the hotel manager had already been over a couple of times to complain about the noise and their rowdy behaviour and to remind the group there were other guests that they needed to consider. Although on both occasions they apologised profusely to the manager, within minutes, the group had reverted back to their childlike behaviours and were again creating some very annoying disturbances. It seemed like a gift from God, when the minibus returned, and everyone left the hotel and very noisily climbed back on board the minibus. During the thirty-minute journey to the night club, Josh was very impressed by the driver's high levels of self-control, as some of his passengers engaged in play fighting and were generally acting like complete twats.

When they arrived at the night club, on reaching the club entrance, one of Richard's stag party guests, was immediately recognised as a trouble maker by one of the doormen and was refused entry on the grounds that he had been previously removed for causing trouble and for possibly taking drugs. Richard immediately stepped in and with his arm around the doorman's shoulder, pleaded with him, insisting that his best man could never be left out from a stag night, he appealed for him on his behalf. Eventually, after Richard had given his word, promising that he would ensure Declan wouldn't cause any trouble at all, he managed by the skin of his teeth to fix the problem. When eventually they were all inside, things seemed to get a little better, some were dancing, and others were chatting at the bar. Josh was at last beginning to enjoy the party and was just very slightly, starting to get into the old party mood. That was until a couple of trays of Irish car bombs arrived at the table. Amidst much yelling and shouting there was a challenge thrown between two of the group, as to who could finish their tray off first. Josh was wondering what these creamy looking alcoholic drinks were and why anyone would want to drink so many as to make themselves ill. After a couple more of these mindless contests, two more trays arrived, and Josh was challenged to compete by another one of Richard's guests. After much jeering and a few insults, the challenge was thankfully taken up by Declan. By now the music was at full blast, Richard's friend were becoming slightly annoying and Josh was beginning to wish he was somewhere else.

A short while later, John, seeing that Josh was no longer enjoying the party asked if Josh would be interested in sharing the cost of a taxi home, because as previously agreed with Richard, he needed to leave early because of other next morning commitments. It was then that both Josh and John quietly said their goodbyes, why everyone was fully engrossed in yet another car bomb contest and they quietly crept out. On the way out of the club, Josh recognised Valerie, Caroline's chief bridesmaid coming in with a group of her friends and after saying hello, apologised for having to leave so early.

Josh, now eager to leave said, "It's a pity I am leaving early, else we could have maybe had a dance or two together. " Inside his head, Josh was thinking, *please God, help me to escape from here and there is no way I would want to dance with Crueller.*

This is when one of Valerie's friends, who being just a little the worst for drink, said to Valerie, "Well who's this then Val, tell me just where have you been hiding this one?" Valerie's friend was now putting her arm around Josh, said, looking straight into Josh's face, "If you play your cards right, you gorgeous handsome man, you could have me tonight. "

Josh, now smiling back, but not wishing to take up the offer and whilst at the same time was moving progressively towards the door, said, "Perhaps another time sweetheart, I am so sorry but I really must go, our taxi is waiting. " After retrieving their coats, they eventually stepped out into the fresh night air, when Josh said, "Thank fuck for that, eh John, I think I must be getting old, because that was sheer hell in there. "

"It was for me too, " said John, "Why fuck your hearing up and get yourself into a complete drunken state in the name of having a good time, is completely beyond me. " John then added, "There's a taxi rank round the corner, so come on let's go, before anyone comes out looking for us. " When Josh got back to Mainear Darach, the house was in darkness and although he had done his very best to be quiet, the dogs had already heard him and were barking loudly from inside one of the stable blocks. After successfully negotiating the darkened stone stairs, Josh was finally inside his peacefully quiet accommodation. Although Josh was ready for bed, he was also feeling a little hungry and for a few minutes sitting in the kitchen, in the dark, eating a large bag of cheese and onion crisps. Josh quietly removed his shoes and thought to himself, *oh that feels much better*. He then headed very quietly into the bedroom. After quietly undressing, Josh slid slowly into bed alongside Jessica, who was soundly asleep. As Josh lay in bed, still hearing that buzz you get from prolonged exposure to loud music, he thought to himself, *thank fuck that's over with. Ah well, I will just put that one down to carrying out a guest's duty.* Then imagining what the others were doing back at the night club, thought, *I know some of those guys are going to be so fucking ill tomorrow, so much for Irish car bombs.* He then thought, *just thank fuck you're not one of them.* Josh then turned onto his side facing Jessica, listened to her breathing for a few moments, smiled, then closed his eyes and fell asleep.

Chapter 8

Kissing the Stone

The next morning Josh was woken, by Jessica coming into the room carrying a tray with two coffees and two plates of buttered toast.

"Good morning 'Mr Night Howler' and what time did you get in last night then?" asked Jessica.

"Must have been around two, " replied Josh. "But I am not really sure. Anyway, I am so bloody pleased that's over with, if it wasn't for another like-minded guest named John, who's good company, thankfully made the whole experience almost tolerable, else I would probably have been back here by ten o'clock. " Josh then added, "You know how I always thought Richard was a complete arse. Well after meeting some of his friends, more especially his old school mates, I think I know where he gets it from. " Now eating a slice of toast, he said, "Well, I mean, Caroline seems such a clever girl, after all she's a qualified vet for fuck's sake, good looking, good sense of humour, intelligent, in fact an above normal and a rational thinking human being. " Then after starting on the coffee, went on to say, "So how the hell she got paired up with that complete twat Richard is completely beyond me. Honestly,

Jess, you should have seen him, when he's out, he's a complete show-off as well as a self-centred, pompous, painful to observe, fucking idiot. " Josh, now sipping more coffee, continued, "Richard and his mates were like a bunch of school kids on their first holiday away from their parents, it was a complete embarrassment just being near them, let alone partying with them. I just know some of those guys are going to be really hung over this morning or may even have been admitted into the local A&E. The stupid sods had some sort of drinking contests, drinking these things called Irish car bombs. They were drinking trays full of the fucking things, it made me feel sick just watching them. And his best man, some guy called Declan, was another complete fucking idiot, I think he was even slightly worse than Richard. However, being in that night club, well it did me a big favour really Jess, as it made me realise I was far too old for clubbing and it and made me painfully aware that the generation gap had finally caught up with me. And do you know what, I am really glad it has, because it seems like I can no longer stay awake after midnight. But that's enough about last night's nightmare, how was your night, did your four-wedding thing go down all right?"

Later, as they sat drinking coffee with her parents and Caroline's family, Josh said to Howard, "How far is it to Blarney Castle from here then Howard?"

Howard replied, "It's motorway all the way Josh, back down onto the N18, then onto the N20 and it's just before you get to Cork. About two and a half hours away, it's not a bad run, not bad at all. But why are you going there, Josh?" asked Howard. Then starting to laugh said, "You're the one person I know who definitely doesn't need to kiss the Blarney Stone. " Then still laughing said, "Why it would be like getting the pope baptised. "

At that they all laughed, and agreed, with Howard, when Josh replied, "People have always told me I must have kissed the Blarney Stone, well hopefully after today I can say, yes, you're right, I have. "

Howard then said, "It's been a long time since I visited Blarney Castle, thinking back, Caroline was still in her pushchair, do you remember Jane?" Josh then asked Jessica's parents whether they had ever been.

"Well, no, " said Gerry. "No, I've heard of it, but I have never been there. "

At that Josh slapped both of his hands on the table and said, "Right, that settles it then, it's sorted, we can all go there together, so come on, no more messing about, let's all get ready to go. " After a few half-hearted excuses and offering up some lame reasons for not going, Josh said, "Come on you lot, I am not taking no for an answer on this one, I think it would do everyone a power of good to go out for the day. "

Half an hour later they were all climbing into two cars and were off, heading for Blarney Castle, Jessica's uncle, aunty and parents were in Howard's car, while Caroline was in with Josh and Jessica. As they drove along the N18, Josh asked Caroline how Richard was feeling.

"I am not sure, " said Caroline. "I tried phoning him this morning, but he hasn't picked up yet. "

To which Josh replied, "I am really not surprised, the amount of alcohol they were drinking last night, it's a wonder they are even still alive. "

"How was the night then Josh, " enquired Caroline. "Was it good?"

"I have to confess, "replied Josh. "I left rather early, I think I am getting a little too old for clubbing. But Richard and the others, seemed to be enjoying themselves. "

"How did you get back then?" asked Caroline. "Oh, I shared a taxi with one of your neighbours, John, a real nice guy, I think he works for a newspaper, as an economist, I think he said, "Caroline replied. "Oh that's John Mahoney, he's a real nice guy, our families have been friends for many years and John spends a lot of time away from home in connection with his job. I am pleased to say, John and his family will be at the wedding, so you will have someone there you actually know. "

As they neared Blarney Castle, it began to rain and Jessica said, "I don't think this is the best idea you have ever had Josh, it's looking a bit like that picnic you organised in Regent's Park. "

"That was a good picnic, well I enjoyed it, " said Josh. "Rain or no rain. Especially when Lucy slapped that stranger on his back, thinking it was Nigel. I don't know who jumped the most, Lucy or that poor stranger. Wasn't he a foreign visitor, either German or Dutch? Anyway look, the rain is stopping again now, " said Josh. "You just watch, it will be red hot sunshine when we get in there. "

The castle itself was all but a ruin, but the gardens were something special, it even had a poison garden, which Josh thought might have been used by the cafe to get rid of unwanted visitors. After touring the castle and enjoying the gardens, Josh finally kissed the Blarney Stone, which was almost impossible to reach and then insisting that both Jessica and Caroline kiss it too. The obligatory coffee and cake was eaten in the small castle cafe and they all left for the city of Cork. As they drove into Cork following Howard's car, Caroline explained that Cork was known as the culinary capital of Ireland and that there was always something interesting to eat in the English market. Josh was pleased that there was plenty of parking spaces and that they were able to park near to the others. As the group walked out of the car park, Jane said, "You can't come to Cork without visiting the English market, I come here every Christmas, and they always have something different, especially the different cheeses. " By now, just as Josh had predicted, the sun came out and they were able to tour the town in bright sunshine and without getting wet. Howard insisted that they visit the Franciscan Well Brewery, which proved to be as good as Howard said it was. Everyone seemed to enjoy a beer while sitting out in the now very sunny beer garden and Josh would have happily spent the rest of the day there, but for Jane insisting they visited the English market. As soon as they walked into the old market, Josh could see why

Jane was so insistent to shop there, as there were certainly some different foods to be had.

Josh sampled the local dish of drisheen, which was a slightly different take on black pudding, that's when Josh exclaimed, "I am sure this would go down very well in England, well at least to those who like eating black pudding. " With a little shopping here and there and coffee and cake at a small bakery-cum-restaurant in the town, before they knew it, it was time to leave for home.

On their way back home, they pulled into Howard's favourite Chinese restaurant and all sitting round a large circular table, chatted about life in general. As they slowly worked their way through what seemed like a hundred different dishes of food, all of which Howard had ordered, it wasn't long before they were discussing tomorrow's wedding arrangements. Mary explained how they would, along with Richard's parents, be dressing the church and carrying out a last-minute check on the reception seating plan.

As they walked back to the car, Caroline said, "You were right Josh; Richard was very ill last night, stupid man. I had been trying his phone all morning and when I phoned Richard's home, even his mom said she had been trying to call him too. Apparently, Richard should have gone into work for a couple of hours today, just to tidy a few loose ends, before we go on honeymoon, but his mom phoned them and told them he was ill, which wasn't a lie because as we know, he really was, albeit self-inflicted. Richard's mom said that his boss had told her, it must have been some party, as two more of his work colleagues were also off sick. "

When they got back to Mainear Darach, Josh said to them all, "Well, thank you all for coming to Cork with me today. I really do appreciate you coming on our little trip, you were all really, really wonderful company. "

Howard, then as quick as a flash said, "There you go Josh, that Blarney Stone is working already. " Everyone was still laughing at Howard's comment, when Howard, said, "Come on in, there's just time for a nightcap before we go to bed. " Eventually, Josh and Jessica left for their room, leaving everyone in a happy mood, all watching TV and drinking.

When Josh and Jessica got back to their room, Josh said, "Great news, Caroline has just handed me the key to the cottage, you know the one we have rented in Ballycroy. It seems Caroline knows the owners very well and they have told her they will have the heating on for us and the hot tub will be all ready for use when we get there on Sunday. Better see if there's a supermarket on the way there, Jess, because by the look of it, this cottage is in the middle of nowhere, so we had better start making a list. Just think, over a week together on our very own, with nothing to do, but enjoy each other's company. God knows, I am really looking forwards to it, time to relax. "

"Yes, me too, " said Jessica. "I hope it's got a washing machine; I have a mountain of washing to do, or better still, I wonder if there's a laundrette nearby?"

As normal, Josh was first in bed and sat up watching some rubbish programme on TV, while Jessica tidied up.

When Jessica finally got into bed, she kissed Josh on the cheek, saying, "Good night Josh. "

"You're not going to sleep just yet Jess, I've got another surprise for you, " said Josh, who was now cuddling up close and affectionately biting her neck. A few minutes later Josh had got his way and they were both fully engaged in fucking each other.

Later, as they lay there in each other's arms, talking of tomorrow's preparations, Josh said, "I know what you are going to say Jess, and although it seems like the wrong thing to say, but I just know this marriage won't last, you just wait and see. "

"Well, it's happening Josh, whether you like it or not, so you had better start getting used to it and for God's sake, please don't let anyone else hear you saying that. Now please let's just go to sleep, it's going to be a very busy day tomorrow and I do really need to sleep. "

Chapter 9

Wedding Preparations

It was Friday morning, at around eight a. m. when Jessica's mom knocked on their door, calling, "Jessica, it's me, your mom, your Aunty Jane and I are cooking breakfast this morning and it will be ready in around half an hour. "

Jessica replied, "OK thanks Mom, that's lovely, we will be over in a minute or two. " This was immediately followed by, "Come on Josh, we had better get up, it's going to be a busy day today and I have absolutely loads of things to do. " Jessica was showered and dressed before Josh had even got out of bed. Looking slightly annoyed, Jessica said, "Come on Josh, don't just lie there, they will be serving breakfast for us by now. " Jessica then using the remote control switched off the TV and Josh then reluctantly got out of bed.

Josh then walked into the bathroom singing, "I'm getting married in the morning. " When they finally got over to the kitchen Jane and Mary were busy cooking, while Howard was making some fresh coffee.

"Good morning, Jessica, good morning, young Josh. Do you two want coffee or tea?" asked Howard. Who then went on to say, "You're lucky, because we have some special coffee that Jane bought at the English market yesterday. It should be good, it bloody well cost enough. "

A little later while they were all enjoying their full English style breakfast, Josh said, "I really do like this coffee Mrs Hanson, it has a strong rich flavour. " Then Josh told the group, "Do you know, this coffee reminds me of the old coffee shop that used to be near to where I lived in Staffordshire. Pity but it's long gone now, I believe the old man who kept it unfortunately died, I think it might be an estate agent's now. But anyway, every Christmas the shop would have a long queue of people waiting to get in, it was that popular. The actual shop was like taking a trip back in time; the old guy who used to run it always wore an old-fashioned brown cow gown and was a really polite and quietly spoken old man. "

Then appearing to reminisce, Josh went on to say, "It was a wonderful little shop, there were sacks of different coffee beans and numerous ornate wooden glass fronted draws, all marked with the names of the different and exotic coffees. Sometimes if I close my eyes, I can almost remember those wonderful aromas which came from those old gas fired coffee roasters. " Then with his eyes closed and his nose in the air, Josh continued, "You know, those aromas have never really left me. " Josh then continued, "As I was saying, it was almost Christmas and I was in the queue behind this middle-aged lady in a big fur coat; you could tell she was well-off, as her fingers were covered in rings and her clothes looked very expensive. When she got to the front of the queue, she said to the old man serving,

'I would like one of those Victorian styled storage tins please, one of those you have in the window, the large one please, the one with the old-time street scenes on it. ' When the old man took it out from the window and placed it in front of her, he said, 'I am sorry to inform you, but these are very expensive madam, they are all hand painted you see. '

"'Oh, ' she said. 'Don't you go worrying about the price, that one will do fine, so I will take it now, " said the lady, her eyes now scanning along the rows of different coffee draws and then said, 'But I will need some coffee to go in it. ' The lady then asked 'What is the best, most expensive coffee you have here, because I will need something special, as it's to be a very important Christmas present. '

"'Well, ' replied to old man. 'It's this, it is the best one here. 'Now pointing to a small wooden box. 'But I am afraid to tell you it is very expensive and to fill a tin like that, would probably cost around £100, if not more. 'Now looking at her face and waiting for her reaction to the price. But by now of course, everyone in the shop was listening to their conversation, me included.

"'Oh, that's fine, " said the lady. 'I will take some of those then. '

"It was at this point when the old man starting off towards this special coffee, suddenly stopped and said turning towards the woman, 'I think I should warn you before I sell you this coffee. That this particular type of coffee, you may no longer want when I tell you about its origins. ' The old man went on to say, 'This particular coffee is made from beans, that were fed to a special species of cat and after they have passed through the cat's digestive system, the beans are recovered from the faeces, before being cleaned and finally roasted. '

"The lady then, not at all flustered by this information, replied, 'Oh that's all right, so it will be just coming out of one arsehole and going into another, it's for my husband. ' And at that moment everyone in the shop burst into laughter and what made it even funnier was the look on the old shopkeeper's face. He was always very prim and proper, in fact, the complete gentleman and he was visibly taken aback by the ladies' language. "

By now everyone at the breakfast table was laughing at Josh's story. As the laughter slowly died down, Mary, who was now closely looking at the writing on the coffee packet, in all seriousness said, "This is not that same coffee, is it Jane?" Which got everyone starting to laugh again.

After everyone had finished eating and were busy watching Josh in amazement, who was now eating yet another one of the sausages Jane had bought from the English market.

Jane smiling towards Josh said, "I think I know the way to your heart Josh. "

To which Jessica quickly added, "Oh there is another way Aunty, but that particular information is probably unsuitable for discussion at the breakfast table. " Everyone then started laughing again.

As Jane and Mary were clearing the plates away, Howard said to Josh, "I spoke to Sean again yesterday, Josh and he's coming over here next Tuesday to look at that steam lorry and thank God, I have now talked him into to staying here with us for a few days. " Then smiling to face Josh said, "I just hope he is as entertaining as you are Josh, I really do. Like I have already told you, you are welcome to stay here anytime you like, it's a pleasure having your company, you certainly know how to make everyone laugh. " Then smiling said, "Why Josh, you are like a breath of fresh air. Oh, and I told the scrap dealer that the lorry was no longer included, and sounding very disappointed, he just replied, 'Oh. ' So, I think he realised he was not going to make as much money out of the deal as he originally thought. Anyway, he now knows that someone else is taking it away. "

After breakfast, everyone helped to load the cars and following Jane's impromptu reminder of the plan of action for the day was, they all set off for the church. The church was in a beautiful location, set back from a quiet country lane with two very large cedar trees providing a beautiful, shaded area over the church yard. Luckily, there was a large car parking area on the opposite side of the lane, surrounded on three sides by old, ivy-covered brick walls. As they crossed the road and approached the church, Josh said to Jessica, "I don't think I have ever seen a church as beautiful as this one, it's absolutely gorgeous. " Josh, although he was not in the least bit religious, did sense that there was something special about the place, one that almost made him feel just a little spiritual. When they entered the church, the flower lady was already there and was busy opening boxes upon boxes of flowers and there was greenery all over the place. Caroline and her mother were straight into assisting her by telling her where the different flowers were going to go. While they were busy with the flowers, Josh took time to look up at the vaulted ceiling and at the large stained glass windows, when he was joined by Howard and Gerry.

"What do you think of it then Josh?" asked Howard. "I was just thinking, how much this church would have actually cost to build back then and how very few people there would have been to pay for it all. I am amazed by it, as life back then would have been difficult enough to survive, so how they would have managed to find the money to build this, well I just don't know? It's quite humbling to think how many people would have been christened, married and buried here over the years. It certainly serves to remind us how short our lives really are and although people's lives start and eventually end, places like this just carry on through time serving yet another generation."

While they were looking at the pipe organ, the priest came over to talk with them. "Hello Mr Holmes, " said the priest. And looking at Josh, said, "And who might this be, Mr Holmes, I know it's not the groom, as I know Richard very well, but this young man, well I think he must be new to the parish. "

After their introductions, Josh said, "I was just looking at your lovely church and the workmanship that went in to building it, it's absolutely beautiful. "

"If you want to, " said the priest. "I will show our very unique and somewhat special crypt and believe me, I think you will find it to be very interesting. " They watched as the priest walked up to some dark oak wall panelling where there was an almost hidden small panelled door, which the priest opened and reaching inside, to switch on the light. As he started to descend the steep stone steps, with everyone following, he added "I don't go down here very often, but it is the oldest part of the church. " When they reached the bottom of the stairs, they could see the very ornate stone vaulted ceiling, when the priest, now pointing at some old stone wall carvings on the far wall, said, "This stone carving is thought to be much older than the rest of the church and some experts tell us they have French origins, which no one has ever been able to explain. " The priest then added, "No one really knows how they got here, or why they are here, or even if they are French, so it's another one of history's long forgotten mysteries. "

Josh now taking a closer look, said, "It's a pity we don't have a time machine, so we could go back in time and revisit history as it actually happened, as that would be something else"

The priest, now looking at Josh in agreement, said, "I am so pleased there are other people who think similar to me. I have always thought the very same thing, but thinking again, it wouldn't it spoil many of life's little mysteries, "The priest now smiling broadly said, "Ah yes, using a time machine, I wonder if they have one on eBay? As they seem to have everything else you may need on offer. "

When they returned back up to the main part of the church, they were all amazed to see the immediate difference the flowers had made. All along the aisle and on the end of the pews, were now decorated with greenery and dotted with white flowers. The altar had now several beautiful displays mounted on tall black and very impressive wrought iron stands. There seemed to be flower arrangements everywhere one could be placed, there were flower displays even in the vestry.

"Wow, " said Howard. "You guys have certainly been busy, is there anything we can do to help?"

"Yes" said Jane. "If someone can pick up the litter and if someone could brush the floor for us, that would be extremely useful. " After a couple more hours, Caroline, her mother, along with Jessica, Jessica's mother and the flower lady, took one last look round and agreed, they were finally all done. The flower lady then explained that she would return to the church first thing tomorrow morning to place the more delicate displays and give it a final check over. After that she would bring the bouquets and gentlemen's buttonholes to the house and with a cheery, "See you all-in the morning, " she was gone.

"Well, " said Caroline. "Hasn't she made a wonderful job of the flowers, I never dreamed they would ever look this good, wow, I am really pleased, isn't she good?" After saying goodbye to the priest, everyone then left for the hotel.

On arrival at the hotel, the manager asked if they would like coffees while they go over the final arrangements, which everyone agreed would be very welcomed. While drinking their coffees the manager brought over the menu, for one last check and proceeded to go through the final seating plan. On completion, everyone's attention had now shifted to the reception area and dining room.

"Well, " said the manager, now walking slightly ahead of the group. "I think you are going to be very lucky with the weather, I've just been listening to the latest weather forecast and by all accounts it's going to be sunny and warm. " The hotel manager while showing them round, commented on the flower arrangements that the flower lady had already completed and told them that her arrangements were so good he had arranged for photographs to be taken of them, so they could be used in their next brochure. Finally, they looked in at the marquee, where the guests would be moving into after their meal, for the live band and late-night disco.

Jane now happy that everything was as she wanted, she said, "You don't know how relieved I am, I was losing sleep worrying about the wedding reception being right. "

As they made their way back to Mainear Darach, Gerald said, "Well Jane, you've certainly done a first-class job of the wedding arrangements. " Gerald then went on to say, "You know you should really think about taking it up as a profession, there are lots of people who charge an absolute fortune for organising weddings and I'm sure they could never have done it any better than you have. You should be very proud of yourself. "

"Yes, " added Caroline. "You have really done a first-class job Mom. " Then squeezing Jane's hand, Caroline said, "Thank you Mom, I really do appreciate having the best mom in the world, you really are. "

That evening they all sat in the garden, feeling very pleased with the wedding arrangements, and were happily having a few drinks before turning in, as tomorrow was going to be that very special day. "Well, it's an early start in the morning, "said Howard, pouring himself another large brandy. "Let's, hope the weather people are correct, but remember we are on the west coast of Ireland and you can never be too sure. "

At that, everyone, complained, "Oh shut up Howard and please stop, you could be tempting fate. "

When Josh and Jessica eventually got back to their room, Josh went to the kitchen and came out carrying two cans of beer and the biggest bag of crisps Jessica had ever seen.

While they sat and watched TV, Josh said, "You know, I can't help this feeling of foreboding I have with regards to Caroline's wedding. I felt it so strong when I was in the church this morning. I hope that everything goes well tomorrow, I really do. "

After a dig in the ribs from Jessica, who again said, "Please don't go saying things like that Josh, I am telling you, nothing will go wrong, so please stop saying anything bad. " Then Jessica added, "And don't forget we are staying at the hotel tomorrow night and you need to take our bags over with you tomorrow morning. So, you had better do it first thing, before everything gets too busy. Now please, just shut up and give me a cuddle. "

Chapter 10

Wedding Day

When the alarm went off on Saturday morning at six a. m. Jessica jumped out of bed and immediately started preparing to shower. Josh could not quite believe his eyes, as he was normally the first one to be up and out, while Jessica usually took several minutes to fully wake up.

"This must be a special day Jess, " Josh shouted through to Jessica, who was now in the bathroom.

"Why is that?" replied Jessica.

"Well, " said Josh. "I have never seen you moving so fast this early in a morning before. "

Later, as they crossed the courtyard together, Jessica said, "Now I am going to be very busy this morning. "And right then a little grey coloured smart car pulled into the courtyard. "Oh, here's the hairdresser, now don't forget the ceremony is at eleven, so please be there and ready at the church by ten-thirty, oh, and don't forget to take our bags to the hotel first. " On entering the house, they were soon joined by the hairdresser. After saying their hellos, Jessica and the hairdresser made their way up to Caroline's bedroom, while Josh headed straight for the kitchen.

In the kitchen, Howard and Gerry were busy on their knees, trying to screw together some kind of metal frame. "So, what's this then, " asked Josh, now busy putting some slices of bread into the toaster.

"It's a wedding cake stand Josh, the bloody thing only came this morning, so I need to get it put together quickly as I can and get it straight up to the hotel. "

Then looking rather flustered, Howard said, "That's if we can ever get the bloody thing together. "

Josh, now studying the instructions, while eating his first slice of toast said, "You have the wrong screws there Gerry, it should have the one's with a square head, because when they are in there, pointing out from the joint, the head won't turn, because it will be captive, see what I mean?" Josh held up one of the correct screws to show him what he meant. Pretty soon, all three of them were on the floor, putting this very complicated stand together, when Josh said, "Don't worry about getting it to the hotel, as I have to drop our bags off there this morning, so it's no problem at all. So please, just leave it there and I will take it over, after I have eaten breakfast. "

As the three of them sat at the table and ate breakfast, there were people constantly arriving who had to be let in, first the lady from the flower shop, with five large cardboard boxes, then the DPD delivery driver who had a few more boxes and then the photographer and his wife turned up. They were soon followed by Valerie, the chief bridesmaid, who was quickly followed by Richard's sister, Emma.

"Well, " said Howard, returning to the table for the umpteenth time. "This is like working in some goods inwards department this morning. " Just then the doorbell went for the make-up lady, who was quickly followed by the manicurist. Howard, by now was looking slightly jangled, to say the least, as he returned to the table, sat down, and laughed, saying, "I hope they realise this is a very old house, with so many people now up there, I am worried the old floor joists may give way under the strain."

Gerry then said, "I think I should just pop up and see if they need coffee or tea, after all they are all guests. "

To, which Howard replied, "Please Gerry, don't make them too bloody comfortable up there, or make them any heavier than they already are. Please just spare a thought for my poor old floor joists. "

An hour later, Josh was at the hotel reception area, with their two overnight bags and a very ornate metal cake stand. *Bloody hell,* thought Josh. *I would hate to think what this is costing, but that's what weddings are these days, very expensive.* After collecting the room keys and handing the cake stand over to a very confused-looking receptionist, Josh then made his way to room 206. As soon as Josh entered the room, he was impressed with the view from the window. He could see the white marquee erected on the lawns below and people busy carrying tables and chairs, as well as cases upon cases of wine. Seeing all this activity, Josh thought to himself, *This wedding must be costing Howard an absolute fortune, I wonder if ours will cost this much, I bloody hope not.* Then shaking his head, thought, *No I really don't think so, it's all just too much trouble.* He then, thought, *If I am right and this wedding is going to fail, like I think it will, then it will all be an awful lot of waste of time, trouble and expense.*

As instructed, dead on ten-thirty, Josh was at the church, dressed in his morning suit and looking every bit like some handsome celebrity. Not quite sure what to do, Josh entered the church cautiously, when he noticed that there were already people seated who were ready for the service to begin.

Just then a smartly dressed middle-aged lady asked, "Are you bride or groom sir?"

"Er bride," replied Josh.

"And are you on your own sir?" asked the lady.

"Er yes, well no, " said Josh. "My partner is one of the bridesmaids. "

"Then you will need to sit on the second-row back sir, on the left-hand side, "said the lady pointing to the exact location.

"Oh, thank you, " said Josh. "But I think I will spend a few more minutes outside in the sunshine while I still have some time to spare, but at least I know where to sit now, so thank you. " Back outside, Josh smiled as he thought of the old adage, he had used so many times before, 'Like a spare prick at a wedding' well that's certainly fits this morning, he smiled to himself.

Just then someone said, "What are you smiling at then Josh?" When Josh turned, he could see it was John, his friend from the stag party, along with his beautiful partner.

"This is my wife Suzy and Suzy this is Josh, the one who escaped with me from Richard's stag party. So, come on then Josh, just what were you smiling at?"

"Well, John, "said Josh. "Please excuse my language, but we have a saying in the midlands 'Like a spare prick at a wedding', and that's exactly what I am this morning, being as Jessica's one of the bridesmaids and I'm on my own. So, feel like I am that proverbial, spare prick. So, there you have it John, until after the service, I am here on my own. "

Suzy then asked, "Where are you seated Josh?" Suzy was immaculately dressed and looked every inch a wedding guest, even down the hat she was wearing and the dress gloves she was carrying.

"Well, " Josh replied. "Apparently, I am second row back on the bride's side. "

Just then the organist started playing, and John said, "If we go in now, at least we can listen to a little Bach, while we wait. "

"Right on, " said Josh. "Please, after you two. "

Although there was a great deal of muted chatter in the church, the volume suddenly increased as Richard, Declan and his parents entered the church, and everyone turned to see. Most of those gathered on the right side of the aisle waved and smiled at them as they made their way to the altar. By 10. 50 everyone was seated and there was a great deal of chatter and polite smiling as they impatiently waited for the bride to arrive. Josh looking around him, thought, *It must be pretty universal, old ladies with small cameras, mothers trying to keep their children under control and husbands feeling uncomfortable wearing stiff new shirts.*

At eleven o'clock exactly, the organ broke loudly into the *Arrival of the Queen of Sheba,* when everyone immediately stood up and turned to see Caroline being led by Howard walking slowly down the aisle. As they passed, Josh got eye contact with Jessica who, without turning to face Josh, just smiled, which was Jessica's way of saying hello.

It was evident to Josh, that Caroline's dress must have cost some serious money, as it fitted her perfectly with the silver lace, overlaying the bodice, it literally shone in coloured sunlight streaming through the stained glass windows. Josh was quite taken aback by how beautiful and elegant Caroline looked with her long train, flowing down the few steps leading up to the altar. When Caroline reached the altar, she took up her place next to Richard and Howard left her side to stand next to Jane. The priest welcomed everyone one and explained the special nature and purpose of the marriage ceremony. However, just before the priest began the actual ceremony, Caroline quietly whispered to the priest, asking whether she could say a few words before the marriage ceremony started.

"Well, " said the priest. "It is a little unusual, but yes, I can't see why not, please, go ahead Jessica. " and waving her forward with his out stretched hand, stood back in order to give Caroline the floor.

"Well, " said Caroline in a clear unwavering voice. "First of all, I would like to thank my parents for arranging for this ceremony to happen. I would also like to thank the lady who supplied these beautiful flowers and the hotel for accommodating our reception. " Then pausing for a short while as if to get her breath, with everyone smiling and hanging on her every word, Caroline then said in a very clear and carrying voice, "But most of all I would like to sincerely thank Valerie, my long-time friend and who today is here as my chief bridesmaid, and I have learnt, spent the stag night in bed with my groom Richard, has shown me, just in the nick of time, what a complete untrustworthy philandering bastard Richard really is and if he thinks I am still going to marry him, after that, he is very much mistaken. " And at that Caroline hit Richard full-on in the face with her bouquet, lifted her skirt and ran back down the aisle and out of the church.

For a few seconds, the church was in complete silence, no one spoke, and no one was quite sure what they had just witnessed. Howard, now in hot pursuit quickly followed Caroline out of the church and everyone was left slightly shocked. Apart from the priest whispering something privately to Richard, who stood with a blood running from his nose, had now been joined by his concerned mother, no one was speaking or making any sound at all.

After what seemed like a silent eternity, but which in reality was just a few minutes, Howard came back up to the altar and addressed the stunned congregation.

"Well, " said Howard. "I think you may have already gathered, but it would appear that the wedding is permanently off. " At this point Richard, with his face still bleeding profusely, was led away to the vestry. Howard, then continued saying, "I know this is not what any of us expected today, but the reception is all paid for, the food is being prepared, there is a band ready to play and there is money behind the bar for drinks. So could you please accept my sincere apologies and if you could make your way the reception and although we have all been somewhat shocked by this unexpected turn of events, could you please all enjoy whatever part of the day you can? Again, I must apologise, but unfortunately these things can happen, so please carry on as best you can, and I will hopefully join you all at the hotel a little later, thank you. "

As Howard walked back down the aisle, followed closely by the priest, the chatter immediately started. You could see that people were shocked by the outcome and no one quite knew what to do. The strangest thing of all was the photographer, who all through this commotion had continued clicking away taking photos and was constantly diving around in order to get the best angles. By now all of Richard's and Caroline's relatives were leaving in relative silence and looking very confused.

"Well, " said Josh to Suzy and John. "I am really impressed with Caroline that takes real balls to do that. And through all that, she never lost her cool or looked even slightly out of control. " Josh then added, "That's another experience that will flash before my eyes when I die. I really feel sorry for Richard's parents, but it was, as we know, completely outside of their control. But what a girl, our Caroline was, eh John?"

When Josh got outside the church, he could see there were small groups of family and friends, obviously discussing this unusual show-stopping event and many of them were already on their mobile phones, probably informing others of the extraordinary experience they had all just witnessed. When Josh reached the car park, he was not really sure whether to go to the reception as planned, or stay on the car park and wait there for Jessica. In order to find out what to do, Josh called Jessica, who immediately on answering asked Josh where he was.

As soon as Josh told her he was in the church car park, Jessica said, "Please Josh, just wait there. "Before then ringing off. It was about ten minutes later when, Jessica still in her bridesmaid dress, jumped into the car beside him and said, "Right we must go straight to the hotel. " Then after calming down, Jessica said, "What a sneaky little bastard, that Valerie is, apparently, they have been shagging each other on and off for several months. Sounds very much like Caroline and Richard are finished for good, apparently someone told her about them first thing this morning. Poor Caroline, she has just phoned me and told me she is on her way to our rented cottage and her mom is collecting her bags from the hotel and is taking them over to her. "

Josh, now driving to the hotel said, "I tell you something Jess, your cousin Caroline, has got some balls. From what I could gather listening to everyone, chatting about it afterwards, almost everyone thought Caroline did the right thing. But what a complete fuck up eh, after all Jane and Howard's hard work? I wonder what that fucking idiot Richard is doing at this moment. Well apart from bleeding that is, that was some smack in the face. Thinking about it, I wonder what that good friend of hers Valerie is doing right now, she must be feeling really embarrassed? Perhaps you wouldn't have noticed Jess, but while it was all that commotion was going on, that Valerie just stood there staring and the ground, stunned and expressionless. What a really good friend Valerie turned out to be, eh Jess?"

Jessica then said, "The first thing I need to do is get out of this dress, so park near the reception. " Then Jessica suddenly froze and said, "You have got the key to the room haven't you Josh?"

"Of course I have, and I have put the bags in the room, now please just relax a little, please realise that what happened today is now just history and was probably for the best anyway. At least this way she won't have to go through that inevitable divorce shit, will she? Anyway, as you know, I never liked that fucking idiot Richard, he was nothing but a complete twat. Marriage to that idiot Richard would have been a tragic mistake for anyone, so it's a good job Caroline didn't actually marry him, but it was a real close call. "

When they arrived at the hotel, they went straight through to their room and as they passed through the reception area, they could see through a partially open kitchen door, the hotel staff being rebriefed. "Looks like they all know it's off then, " said Josh opening the door to the lift. Finally entering their room, Josh asked, "So what happens now?"

Jessica now changing into another dress said, "Well, Uncle Howard is going to get the guests, well those who turn up, to have a few drinks in the bar and then a little later get them all seated in the restaurant, when he is going to bring everyone up to date with events. Well to those who hopefully turn up, but I am not sure whether many of Richard's side will turn up though. The good news is they have taken Richard to A&E to get his nose stitched and I just hope it was very fucking painful for him, "said Jessica who was finally starting to relax.

Josh still feeling at little sorry for her, gave Jessica a big hug and said, "Anyway sweetheart if it's any consolation, you looked really beautiful in that dress. Oh, and who was the other bridesmaid Jess, I didn't recognise her at all?"

"That was Richard's sister, Megan, I felt really sorry for Megan, all she kept doing was apologising for Richard's behaviour, she's a lovely girl, not like her bloody brother. "

"So, what happened to Valerie then?"

"Well, the last I saw of her, " said Jessica, "she was arguing in the vestry with Richard's mother, who was calling her all the names under the sun. There," said Jessica, smoothing out her skirt, "that's me dressed, now come on Josh, let's go down to the bar, I am absolutely dying for a stiff drink. Oh, by the way," Jessica added, "I must say, you looked really smart, everyone was asking who you were, and I was very tempted to say, 'Oh that's my fiancé, Josh.'She then said, "I am not really sure how we can tell Caroline now, it might seem like very inappropriate timing if we do it before she is over her very cruel let down?"

On the way down to the bar, Josh said, "Do you know what the funny thing was Jess, that crazy photographer was still taking photos, he was there diving from one position to the next, while it was all going on. All the way through, unbelievable, just like things like that happen all the time. " After a short pause Josh said, "You know, I would really love to see those photos when they are ready, I wonder if we will ever get to see them?"

When they entered the bar, they were surprised to see just how many people had done as Howard had requested them to do and were happily drinking and socialising. Jessica said hello to the one or two people she knew and then found an empty table.

After the waiter had taken their order, Jessica said to Josh, "I am so pleased that people have actually turned up here, it would have been a terrible shame for all that food go to waste. Let's hope they stay for the entertainment later. " Jessica then said, "Mind you, it will seem very strange having a reception without the bride and groom, I wonder if they will still leave the top table in place?"

Then looking concerned Jessica said, "I cannot help worrying about Caroline, I wonder how she is? I tried phoning her, but understandably she is not answering her phone. I just hope that bastard Richard is suffering. And by the way Josh, I hate to admit it, but you were absolutely right, that Richard is a complete and utter twat. " Just then the drinks arrived, and the conversation was temporarily silenced until the waiter had left them alone again.

"What do you think they will do with all the wedding presents, Jess?" asked Josh. "I saw them all stacked up as we walked through. And can I say something that might just annoy you Jess. Well, a part of me was rather pleased when Caroline walked out on him. And l will tell you why Jess, I knew Caroline was a vet, but when she told me, you know, when we were in Cork, that she was large animal vet. That's when I realised, Caroline would make an ideal partner for our Sean, he could really do with someone like Caroline. She likes horses, she works with livestock and obviously knows, farming. " Now smiling at Jess, Josh said, "And above all, she would make an absolutely great sister-in-law. Who knows we could even have a double wedding, to boot, eh Jess?"

"*Oh* please, Joshua Foster, " Jessica said using her serious voice. "Now don't you go trying to fix that up, anyway she's never even meet Sean, let alone wanting to marry him. So, stop those silly thoughts right now, only you could come up with something like that and just three hours after Caroline's heartbreak of a wedding. "

"I won't say any more, " said Josh. "But Sean is coming over on Tuesday, so she might meet him then?" Just as they were trying to attract the waiter's attention, for more drinks, Howard walked in and after saying hello to a few of the guests, and came over and joined them.

"Well, "said Howard. "God knows what happens now? It's all been just like an extremely bad dream and believe me Jessica, my mind is still spinning from it. "

"Well, " said Josh. "The waiter's here now, so let's all have a drink and try and make something worthwhile out of whatever is left of the day. "

A little later while sipping a very large brandy, Howard said, "I have had Richard's parents on the phone to me, they were obviously very upset and kept repeatedly apologising. I told them, 'This was completely outside of your control. ' And I told them, 'Please understand, I don't want this to in anyway affect our long-standing friendship. ' I said to them the best thing they can do is to come to the reception, join in with the planned events, which will positively demonstrate that we are all still and will continue to be very close friends. Now, " said Howard, finishing off his brandy. "I really must do my duty and mingle, oh, and please keep your eye out for Jane, as apparently she is on her way back here. Oh, and Gerry and Mary will be here in a minute as well, so please keep your eyes peeled for me. "And at that Howard headed off towards the bar.

Later in the evening, inside the marquee, the band played, and people danced, while others sat round and watched. Josh managed to drag Jessica on to the dance floor and she was fine with the fast-moving music but was very reluctant to waltz. Josh, not wishing to miss out, danced the quick step with Jane and the tango with Mary. It was pleasing to see that everyone there were trying make the best of what had been a very difficult day.

When Josh eventually returned from the dance floor, Howard said, "Just where the hell did you learn to dance like that Josh, you looked really professional?" Howard then added, "I think we all need to book some dancing lessons eh, Jane?"

"I'll look on the web tomorrow, "said Josh. "There must be a dance studio somewhere around here, we can use?" Later on, and after a few more drinks, Josh managed to get Jessica back onto the floor and after a couple of awkward dances, she began to enjoy the experience. It was around one-thirty when Jessica and Josh returned to their room.

Just as they were going to sleep, Josh said, "Well Jess, that's another memory that will flash before my eyes when I die. "

"Josh, please don't keep talking about dying, we have an awful lot of living to share yet, a lot more. So please stop it. "

Chapter 11

The Cottage

As agreed, the night before, Josh, Jessica and the other three families all meet up at nine in the hotel restaurant for breakfast.

While they were eating, Howard said, "Well here's some good news for you. "

"What's that?" asked Jane. "We could certainly do with some. "

Howard then said, "The hotel wants to buy that bloody cake stand and what's more, we have lots and lots of wedding cake to eat. " Howard's little bit of humour certainly did manage to lighten the atmosphere slightly and over breakfast, things gradually got back to some sort of normality.

After loading the wedding presents and all the other bits and pieces into Howard's car, Jessica and Josh said their goodbyes to everyone and headed off to their holiday cottage.

Jessica, while entering the destination into the satnav, said, "It's a good job we have the post code for this place, as we probably would have some real difficulty finding it. "

"Well, " said Josh. "You had better put a supermarket in their as well, Jess, as we definitely need to go there first, else we won't have anything to eat. Oh, and don't forget to ask Caroline if she needs anything, "added Josh.

"That's OK, " said Jessica. "I spoke to Caroline earlier and she's now using one of the farm's mobile phones, as she wanted to avoid speaking to Richard, so I have her new number now. Caroline told me she has got her own phone with her and it seems she's had a quite a few missed calls from Richard. And would you believe it, she has even a couple from that cheeky bastard, Valerie?" Now busy searching the web on her mobile, Jessica, said, "Oh good, there's a supermarket on the way, however it's just slightly off our route, so I'll enter that destination first. " Jessica then spent the next thirty minutes talking to Caroline, telling her who said what, who went to the reception and although Caroline had already spoken to her parents, Caroline really needed to hear it from Jessica, just how well they were taking it. Josh interrupted their conversation, to ask Caroline if she had a bikini with her, because if not, they could get her one from the supermarket.

"What sort of question is that?" asked Jessica.

"Well, she will need one for the hot tub, won't she? Because that's where I intend to be later on this morning and you two can then chat away to your hearts' content?" Josh then emphasised, "In the hot tub. "

As they were on speaker, Caroline shouted, "No I haven't got my bikini with me Josh, so you had better get me one while you're in there. Oh, and better get a very big bottle of gin as well while you are at it, as there's nothing better than a couple of large gins to wash your cares away. And believe me, I certainly have one or two cares to wash away!"

As they walked out of the supermarket, pushing a very loaded trolley, Josh said, "Whatever you do Jess, make sure Caroline is still around when Sean gets here on Tuesday. "

Jessica's immediate response was, "Now I've already told you Josh, don't go trying to match make. It's just not the right time. "

"Get right back on the saddle Jess, that's the best thing to do after a fall. Trust me Jess, this is the best thing we can do. Just make sure that you keep Caroline around until Tuesday night and I will do the rest. "

"Look Josh, "replied Jessica. "They may not even like each other and even if Caroline did like Sean, it's just too soon after that bloody wedding fiasco, so please stop it, stop it right now. "

"Like I said Jess, she needs to get right back on the saddle, the sooner the better and trust me there's no time like present. "

As they pulled up outside the cottage, Caroline came out of the front door to meet them. "Wow" said Josh. "The cottage looks absolutely ideal, I wonder if it's got Satellite TV?" Jessica was straight out of the car to meet Caroline and with their arms wrapped tightly around each other they walked into the cottage together.

"How are you feeling now Caroline?" asked Jessica.

To which Caroline replied, "I feel very lucky, really, it was much better to find out, even at the last minute, then finding out after the wedding. It's not what I wanted to happen, but fuck Richard and come to think of it fuck that two-faced bitch Valerie as well. Anyway, " continued Caroline. "That's all in the past, so please let's all talk about something else instead. Anyway, where's my bikini and my bottle of gin then Josh, I'm also dying to try that hot tub out, it looks very sexy. I was looking at it this morning before you got here and it looked so inviting, with all that hot water swilling round, I was almost tempted to go skinny dipping. " When they got into the kitchen, Jessica was surprised to see there was plenty of food already there.

"I've got a load of shopping in the car, " said Jessica. "But I see you have got plenty in already. " Then opening cupboards, Jessica was looking very surprised, to see just how much food was already there.

"Well, you know my mom, "said Caroline. "She had it delivered. But don't worry Jess, I will be gone tomorrow."

"Oh no you won't, "said both Josh and Jessica at the same time. "You are staying here with us for a few days, there's a spare bedroom and it will be good fun, just like old times, " said Jessica. "And we need to organise that racing day next Thursday, " said Josh. "Oh and better organise it for an extra one please Caroline, Sean, my brother, as he will be over here as well. Josh then went on to say "I hope you two are hungry, because I've got three nice big fillet steaks and some frozen chips, so I will be making tea tonight, girls. Now if you will excuse me, I am going to try out that beautiful bubbling hot tub. "

Josh had the hot tub all to himself until an hour or so later when the girls came out and jumped in with him.

Soon all three were happily chatting and drinking gin, when they heard Caroline's mom calling, "Darling, where are you?"

"We are all out here, " they shouted. "We are outside in the hot tub. "

When Caroline's mother came out through the back door, she called out, "I hope you are all decent, is it safe to come out?"

"Yes mom, " Caroline's replied. "Can you bring that bottle of gin off the kitchen table out with you and better bring yourself another glass out too. "

To the rear of the cottage there was a small patio area, completely surrounded on all sides with flowering shrubs in large pots, which were covered in hundreds of small fairy lights.

"Oh, this is very nice darlings, " said Jane as she sat herself down on the small bench next to the hot tub. After pouring herself a large drink and with a glass in her hand, Jane said, "You know darling, that bloody Richard has been round to the house looking for you a couple of times. In the end, your dad went out and told him, 'I think you're wasting your time Richard. ' He then said to him, 'Caroline does not want to see you Richard, so just stay away please and let us all get over it. '" She then added, dipping her hand into the water, "I think he got the message, because, thankfully, we haven't seen him since. "Then changing the subject slightly Jane said, "You know Howard keeps talking about buying one of these hot tubs, I didn't know the water was this warm, it feels lovely. And by the way Josh, Howard's been speaking to Sean and he should be arriving here about six-thirty on Tuesday evening. I thought maybe we could all go out for a Chinese on the evening, you know how much Howard enjoys his Chinese food? So now that untrustworthy Richard has been chased away, when are you coming back home to us Caroline?"

Jessica, quickly responded, "Caroline is staying here with us for a couple of days Aunty, it's all sorted and don't forget we are all going to the races on Thursday. So, can you please remind my mom and dad? Oh, and next time you come, bring a swimsuit, as this is good for at least six people and tell Uncle Howard to bring his along too. "

Jane immediately replied smiling, "Well you must have heard that expression, 'there's an elephant in the room'? Well, it will be more like, 'there's a hippo in the hot tub'. But what a superb idea darling, mind you, God only knows where my swimsuit is, can't even think when I used it last?" A short while later, as Jane was leaving, she said, "Josh be a darling for me, I have a few more groceries in the car, oh and a few bottles of champagne left over from the reception. "

That evening all three of them ate steak and drank champagne, talking until the early hours. When Josh and

Jessica eventually climbed into bed, Jessica said in a quiet, concerned voice, "I hope you are not too annoyed with me inviting Caroline to stay with us?"

"Not in the slightest, sweetheart, "whispered Josh. "I think it's a good idea of yours, me getting to know my future sister-in-law a little better. And anyway, I really enjoy Caroline's company, she's really good fun, I'm so glad she didn't marry that twat Richard. "

Jessica then said, "Will you please stop saying that Caroline is going to marry Sean, it won't happen just because it suits you, you know, it's a matter of the heart, Josh and she might not even like Sean, so please just stop it. "

Josh now pulling Jessica over to his side of the bed and lifting her on top of him, whispered, "We had better go very quietly tonight Jess, we don't want to make Caroline jealous, do we?"

As Jessica was just about to say, 'no, not tonight, ' she felt Josh's warm penis beneath her and in response, moving herself over it, whispered, "You're a cheeky bastard Joshua Foster, you really are. "

Chapter 12

Finding Family

The next morning the sun was shining, and Josh was up and out of bed very early, leaving Jessica and Caroline to sleep off some of the drink they had consumed the previous night. After clearing away four empty champagne bottles, washing the dishes and empty glasses, Josh was now fully engrossed in doing something he really enjoyed: cooking breakfast. He had bacon, sausage, mushrooms, baked beans, and fried bread and was even keeping it all warm in the oven. The coffee was brewed, the brown sauce was on the table and everything was prepared for Josh's favourite breakfast, the full English.

He then went to Jessica and woke her saying, "Here's your coffee Jess, breakfast is already waiting, I've just got the eggs to fry, but I will cook those when you get to the table. So, could you get up and take Caroline's coffee in for me please. "

Reluctant to get out of bed, Jessica said, "Josh just knock on her door, for God's sake, let her know you have a coffee for her and take it in. "Josh, still a little hesitant, did as instructed and took Caroline's coffee in to her. With a, "Good morning Caroline here's your coffee sweetheart, your full English breakfast will be ready in five minutes, so please don't go back to sleep. "

Still half-asleep Caroline replied, "I am very impressed with you Josh, Jessica has certainly got you well-trained, hasn't she? What with steaks last night and a cooked breakfast this morning, I hope she realises that she's a very lucky girl. " Now taking her coffee from Josh, Caroline said, "Wow, a full English breakfast, well thank you very much Josh, I will be out soon, just give me a minute or two. "

A short while later, all three were sitting at the table eating breakfast and chatting away, when Josh said, "Caroline, do you know the Swinford area at all?"

Caroline now looking puzzled, replied, "I know Swinford, the town Josh, but there's not much around Swinford, lovely place, but nothing for the tourist, so why are you asking?"

"Well, I think that's where my mother was born, " replied Josh. "It's a bit of a family mystery really, but I would like to go there sometime today and have a bit of a look around, see if I can find the house. You never know I might just find it, but I've only got a photograph to go on. However, I'm pretty sure it's near Swinford somewhere. " Josh went on to say, "If you are not doing anything special today, I thought we could all go there and have a look for it, a bit later on perhaps?"

Jessica then said, "I don't think it would be fair on Caroline Josh, she probably has better things to do than go snooping round on the off chance someone might recognise the house in that photograph. "

Caroline then said, "I now have three weeks off work, with nothing planned, well that is, not any more Jessica. So yes, Josh, I would love to go snooping round Swinford with you, but you will have to give me a few minutes to shower and dress. Anyway, after what I drank with you two last night, I probably wouldn't be fit to drive anyway, so no problem Josh. "

An hour or so later, just as Josh had suggested, they were driving into Swinford, when Caroline who was sitting in the back said, "Drive down this street Josh and you can park anywhere along here. I don't think there will be anyone in the library, but we can maybe ask the parish priest, he might know, so let's try the church first, it's just over there, look. " Their luck was definitely in, as there were several people inside the church preparing for the day's service and one of the group was the priest. Caroline apologetically approached him and told him they were looking for a family named O'Brien and showed him the photograph.

"Well, " replied the priest. "There are several O'Brien families in this parish, but that does look a lot like the old O'Brien's farm, if I'm not mistaken. It's located about two miles south of the town, you won't be able to see it from the road, but there's a bus shelter directly opposite the farm's driveway. " After getting directions and thanking everyone, they set off to find Josh's old family home.

The directions the priest had given them, eventually lead them to a narrow gravel driveway opposite a bus stop, when Caroline said, "This must be it, Josh, opposite the bus shelter, so let's drive down there and take a look. "

"But there's a sign saying, 'Private Keep Out', "said Josh, looking a little uncertain.

"Oh, come on Josh, let's go for it, " said Caroline. "You will never know if it's here unless we go down and check it out. " Jessica in full agreement said, "I will remind you Josh, you were the one that started all this. "

As they drove dove down the uneven driveway, a very familiar view came into sight.

"This is it girls, "said Josh sounding very positive. "This is definitely it, this is my mom's old house, I'm bloody sure it is, but it now looks abandoned. " Josh then got out of the car and was standing by the car's open door, whilst holding the photograph between him and the old farm house. He said excitedly, "This is it all right. " And then he suddenly became aware there was a silver pickup truck driving down the track towards them and which then pulled up extremely close to the rear of their Range Rover.

"What the hell are you doing down here?" asked the angry-looking driver, as he approached them. "Can't you read: this is private property, " said the man, while at the same time speaking into a two-way radio.

"I am trying to find the house where my mother was born, the house in this photograph, " said Josh, who was now holding it up for the man to see.

"And who the fuck is your mother?" asked the man, who was not really interested in looking at the photograph.

"Her name is Bridie Foster, " replied Josh. "But her maiden name was O'Brien, Bridie O'Brien. "

Josh could see that the man was relaying the information to someone on the other end of the radio, when the man said, "Well I'm telling you, you will have to wait here, as the owner is coming down to speak to you. " As Josh's vehicle was pinned in by the pickup right up behind it, he was left with no alternative but to wait as instructed. While he was waiting, Josh bent down and spoke quietly to the girls sitting in the car, who were now looking just a little concerned.

"Apparently, "said Josh. "We are just waiting for someone to come down and speak to us. "

Caroline, not looking very bothered at all, said, "Well this is all very exciting, isn't it?"

"I knew we shouldn't have driven down here, it did say, 'private keep out', " said Jessica.

"Don't worry, " said Caroline laughing. "So what are they going to do, throw us all in jail?"

A short while later a second pickup truck arrived and parked behind the first pickup and an older man accompanied by another younger man got out. After talking to the first pickup's driver, the older man approached Josh and said, "My son tells me you are looking for the house your mother used to live in?"

"Yes, that's right, " said Josh, handing him the photograph to look at.

"And what's your mother's name?" asked the man, now after glancing at it, passed it over to the other two men.

"Bridie Foster, but her maiden name was O'Brien, Bridie O'Brien. "

"Well, " said the man. Turning to the other two men and now starting to smile said, "Then you had both better say hello to your cousin. "

Josh could see the older man was looking very pleased, with tears starting to fill his eyes, when he put out his hand and said, "Well it's beginning to look like, I'm your Uncle Padriag then and these two lads here are your cousins, Martin and Thomas. " Turning his head towards the two men, the older man said, "Well don't just stand there, come on over and say hello. "

Now shaking the old man's hand Josh said, "Well I am very pleased to meet you sir, my name is Joshua and I have an older brother back home named Sean. "

The old man now looking even more tearful said, "Tell me, how is Bridie, is she well, me and your uncle Patrick, have been trying to find her for years? Is she living here in Ireland?" Then turning to his two sons said, "Well come on, phone your Uncle Pat and tell him to come to our house, as quick as he can, tell him it's very urgent. Well now don't just stand there, Martin, do it now and then shift these trucks out of the way. "

Leaning down into the open car door, Josh's uncle Padraig said, "And who are these two beauties then, Josh?"

In reply Josh said, "This is Jessica, my fiancée and this is Caroline, Jessica's cousin. "

After introducing himself Padraig said, "Well, if you can turn your car around Josh and then you can follow us up to the new house and hopefully your Uncle Patrick will be already there. " Then laughing said, "You know, I think this is going to floor him. " Then looking very pleased with the situation, Padraig said, I just can't wait to tell Pat the good news. "

After turning the cars round, Josh followed the pickups to a large more modern house about half a mile away. The house was set back into some woodland and had a very impressive doorway with white columns with some large potted plants on the steps.

As they pulled into the farmyard, located to the side of the house, Caroline said, "You said, my fiancée, just when exactly did you two get engaged and if you are engaged, why the hell wasn't I told about it?"

"Well, I'm sorry, "said Jessica. "We didn't want to announce it till after your wedding, as we didn't want to steal any of the limelight. But we got engaged last Thursday night, when we were staying in Limerick. "

"Some limelight that was Jess, " said Caroline. "Even if you weren't going to announce it, you really should have told me; I need some good news. " Caroline, now looking extremely pleased said, "So that's another celebration we need to have then, it's a good job we have plenty of that champagne left over. " When they arrived at the O'Brien's house, they were all shown into the family kitchen and introduced to Padraig's wife, Angela and as they were talking, another older man walked in.

"So, what's this urgent situation then Padraig?" asked the man.

"Well, " said Padraig. "This young man here, is our Bridie's son Joshua. "

"Who is he?" asked the man, looking very confused and not really believing what Padraig had just said, "You remember our sister Bridie, well this is her son, Josh. "

Now suddenly realising what his brother was telling him Patrick said, "Oh thank God. " Now looking around the man asked, "So where is Bridie, is she here? It's been years of wondering, we've been through, wondering what became of our Bridie. "

After coffees and introductions, they sat at a large wooden table, with Josh's two cousins standing by the Aga, all wanting Josh to tell them all about his mother. Josh, still feeling a little cautious, told them that his mother had never told him what had happened for her to split with the family, but he had this old photograph, which had the studio's address on the back.

Now looking at the photograph, Josh's Uncle Pat said, "I remember this photograph being taken, yes, I remember that day very well. "

Josh continued, "My mother doesn't know I was coming here to look for you, I was over here to attend a wedding. And to be honest, I am not sure whether she will be pleased or not that I am telling you about her. " Josh went on to explain that Bridie had married his dad, who like them, was a farmer and told them he would contact his mother tonight and see if she was OK with it, and then only if she wanted him to, would he give them her contact details.

But on the positive side Josh said, "I now know I have two new uncles and two cousins, so I at least I can be in contact with you all from now on. But I'm sure you will agree, I must respect mom's wishes, I hope you understand?"

"Well, " said Padraig. "You know, you have more than just two cousins, you have five, two girls, Josie and Brenda and another boy, Joseph. " He then went on to explain, "The two daughters are married, living here in Ireland and your other cousin Joseph, well he lives in Hammersmith, West London. "

Josh, then explained that he also lives away from home in London but travelled around the UK with his job. He went on to explain that his job was investigating and assessing businesses that were either being purchased or sold. He informed them that his brother Sean worked on the family farm in England. Now feeling very much at home, Josh went on to explain that Sean would be coming over to Ireland in a day or so and that he would explain to him what had happened.

"Why not phone him now?" said Padraig. "Ask him to visit us while he is over here, we would all really love to meet him. So, he is named Sean, eh, " said Padraig. "Well, there you go, that was our dad's name. " Then looking serious, Padraig said, "Your mom really loved our dad, who would have been your granddad Sean. "And as he spoke, his voice stumbled with emotion saying, "Dad and Bridie, well, they were extremely close. And as our mom, bless her soul, had died some years earlier, your mom sort of took over running the house and everything. Understandably, when our dad died, it hit Bridie, really hard. Believe me Josh, we were all terribly shocked when we realised Bridie had gone and left home. She just up and left us without a word and leaving not any trace at all. At the time, we both foolishly thought Bridie would be back within a day or two, you know, when she had cooled off a little. But thinking on, we should have known better because Bridie was always a very strong-willed girl. Then when she had gone, we couldn't contact her, because we never knew where she had gone to. I tell you now Josh, me, and your Uncle Pat, were terribly upset over Dad's death as well, but like the silly young buggers we were back then, we both hid our sadness and despair, by talking big about the farm's new future. Your mom came in on us when we were discussing the farm's future and in floods of tears, well she verbally tore us to shreds, you know I had never heard your mother swear at all, until that day. "

As Padraig was speaking, everyone else in the room was silent and listening intently to every emotional word being said, with Patrick just nodding in agreement as they relived the situation.

"When you speak to Bridie tonight Josh, please let her know, that we have regretted that stupid conversation every day since she left. Tell her we had suffered a double loss first with Dad dying and then again when Bridie left us. " Patrick then went on to explain, that she had been left a third of their dad's estate, which they had kept in trust for her and that they had grown that money on for her, right up until this day.

"So, Josh, " Patrick said, looking him, straight in the eye. "Bridie owns a third of everything we now hold. Although our old house is no longer used, " said Padraig. "We never knocked it down, or reused it, all the time hoping that one day Bridie would return to take it. "

Josh, then watched by everyone there, called Sean on his mobile and explained where he was, told him of the circumstances, told him of his now very much extended family and asked Sean if he could speak to Mom and get her reaction. Sean confirmed he would be coming over on Tuesday and that he would do his very best to visit them while he was over. Josh then passed his phone over to Padraig, who had been eagerly listening and then watched on as Padraig and other family members spoke to his brother.

Later, they were shown round the farm, which now consisted of new purpose made buildings and concrete yards, this was not exactly what Josh was hoping to see. But later the family group, walked him down to the old house and after unlocking it, went inside to show Josh the room his mom was born in. Although it was looking slightly neglected, it was exactly how it had been left when his mom had left. He could see that his mom had a view over the surrounding countryside and that it would have taken in the morning sunshine. The large crucifix hanging on her bedroom wall, looked very similar to the one she had at home and it immediately linked his mother to this, the bedroom they were standing in. As they left down the steep stairs and passed through the old kitchen, with its now rather rusty range, again Josh could imagine his mother as a young woman, cooking the family meals. Josh's uncle Patrick then took Josh down to one of the old barns and inside of one, someone had erected a small garden shed. Unlocking and opening the door, Josh could see the metal shelving with many items stored under polythene sheeting. Carefully lifting the protective sheeting Patrick showed Josh how they had kept everything his mother had owned, right down to her old schoolbooks, clothes and even her church certificates. Stood between the shelves, again covered in a piece of age yellowed polythene sheeting, Patrick showed them his mom's old bike.

"We collected this from Swinford, the day after your mom left us and have kept it on the off chance Bridie would come back for it one day. " It was obvious to Josh that his mother had definitely been missed during her long absence and that they had kept alive their hopes, by keeping safe everything she had left behind. As they walked round the old farm building, some still being used to store the odd item of farm machinery and a couple being used to store fodder, they came across some tumbled down wooden chicken pens, now overgrown with nettles and brambles. Padraig was now leading the group and stopped to explain their history, "I am sad to say this doesn't look much now, but in its heyday, this was Bridie's pride and joy. " Then turning to face Josh and the others, Padraig proudly said, "Bridie was good with chickens, her and mom used to sell eggs in the village, and we had either chicken or duck for dinner every Sunday. " Then pausing for a second Padraig said, "Sometimes, when I drive down our lane, I can recall Bridie, coming home on her bike, on her way back from her egg round, with her old blue bag over her shoulder and a big smile on her face. " Then turning to lead them away, said, "We even kept her chickens till they all died, pausing for a moment, then continued, "But they all went one by one. Yes, Bridie loved her chickens, but we never kept chickens or any poultry at all after that. "

Then changing the subject Patrick said, "I don't know about all of you, but I could murder a cup of tea, so come on let's go back to the house. "

When they returned to the new house, Josh told them that his mother had been a nurse most of her working life, eventually progressing to senior matron, but had recently been very ill and had now retired. He explained that happily, she had now given the all-clear and although the treatment had gotten her down, she was now feeling much better and was almost back to her old self. After a tour of the farm garden, they all exchanged their telephone numbers, and as it was late afternoon going on evening, they finally left.

Driving back to the cottage, Josh said, "Well, that's another memory that will flash past me when I die. "He then added, "This trip to Ireland has certainly been something special for me. I just hope Mom's not going to be too angry now that I have met up with her Irish relatives. Anyway, it's done now and as they say, what's done can never be undone again. " All the way back to the cottage, the conversation was about the O'Brien family and the family's lost years.

When they arrived back at the cottage, Caroline said, "I am very sorry to say it, but I need to go back home tonight, it's not that I am not enjoying being with you guys, but I feel I am over it now. And anyway, I must start contacting everyone to apologise for the wedding, the wedding that that never was. Oh yes, and to find out what I should do with all those beautiful wedding presents?"

Josh quickly added, "We fully understand Caroline, but you do know where we are if you need us. " He then added, "I hope you realise that you don't have to go, because we have both really enjoyed your company and after all there's still that spare room if you change your mind. "

"No Josh, " Caroline replied. "Seriously, I need to get back to some sort of normality and anyway I have the sailing on Wednesday and the horse racing on Thursday to organise yet. So, I have plenty of things to keep my mind busy, oh, and of course, those well-intended wedding presents. I am not sure how I go about those, but either way it just must be done and I also need to speak to Farther Devlin, as he's probably still wondering what's going on?"

"Oh, and Caroline, please don't you forget to add Sean to the party list. And this may seem very inappropriate, but if there's any chance, I would just love to see the wedding photographs, " said Josh. Who then added, "You know I think I should probably invite my new uncles to the races as well, I would think they just might enjoy it? Oh, and please make a fuss over Sean for me, as he's always been a bit shy with people he doesn't really know that well. "And at that Caroline went inside to pack and a short while later, loaded her bags into her car. When she came in to say goodbye, Jessica said, "Now promise me if you have any problems, anything at all, you come straight back here, and please ignore Josh and the wedding photograph thing, I'm sorry but I think you know what he's like. "

Caroline laughing said, "Josh is not the only one who wants to see those photographs; I am dying to see them as well. " Caroline then gave Jessica a big hug and a kiss.

"So where's mine then?" said Josh. "or don't I count?"

"Of course, you do, " said Caroline. "I'm so sorry you didn't get the wedding you came here for Josh, but at least you haven't had a completely wasted journey, as I am pleased to say you got to know our family and that you found some more of your own. Now you just look after my favourite cousin and I will chase up those photos for you, " said Caroline, now giving Josh an even bigger hug and a longer kiss. She then got into her car and waving out the window, drove away.

As they walked back into the cottage together, Josh said, "Now, if I was you, I would be getting a just little bit worried, my gorgeous and very desirable Jess, because now I have you out here, miles away from anywhere, where no one can hear you and where I have you all to myself. "

Then, running ahead and laughing, Jessica said, "Huh, that doesn't worry me one little bit, because you will have to catch me first, won't you?"

Chapter 13

Hot Tub Days

Once back in the cottage, while heading towards the bedroom, Josh said enthusiastically, with a widening grin, while patting Jessica's bum, "Right then Jess, get your kit off sweetheart and get your arse into that hot tub, double quick, as I've been dying to try it out properly, ever since we arrived here. "

"Not as much as me, " said Jessica also wearing a big smile. "I have never been fucked in a hot tub before and I wondered what it would be like, every time I look at it. "

Josh now starting to get undressed, while hopping on one leg, desperately trying to get his foot released from his trouser leg, replied in a shaky voice, "Well hopefully you'll soon be finding out Jess. I think you should get some dry towels out while I go and fix us some drinks. " Josh now freed from his trousers, then broke into song, singing, 'I'm in the mood for love. " Entering the kitchen naked, Josh asked, "What would you like to drink, Jess? How about a nice champagne cocktail, because that's what I really fancy? I've been dying to open this bottle of champagne ever since we got it. " As the cottage was isolated and there was no way they could be seen or overheard, Josh put on some of his favourite classical piano music, poured out some very large champagne cocktails, placed them carefully down on the small table next to the tub and slid his naked body into the very inviting hot water.

"Oh God, this is absolute heaven, " said Josh. "What else could any man ever want, a champagne cocktail, a beautiful naked woman and a hot tub?"

Jessica moving Josh across with her foot said, "Well move over then if you want me in here with you. " After relaxing with a drink for a while, the focus soon shifted to their favourite pastime, each other.

Josh, looking slightly confused, but still smiling, said, "How the hell can am I going to go down on you, without drowning Jess, you know this might not be as easy as I first thought?"

"Well, we will have to give that some serious thought then hadn't we?" said Jessica now sitting on Josh's lap and up to her waist in hot water, while having her neck kissed said, "Oh God Josh, I think we are going to have to buy one of these, it feels like I am in heaven, oh that feels so good and as you know, I love having my neck kissed. "

A short while later, Josh was gratefully enjoying floating on his back, while Jessica was giving him beautiful oral sex. While Josh was enjoying this unusual pleasure, he said, "You know you're right Jess, we really do need to buy one of these, I could lie here like this forever, that is long as you are in here with me. I really think this is another memory will be flashing past when I die. Oh God this is so bloody relaxing, so I'm going to say it once again, I am really enjoying this Irish holiday so much, this is heaven. " As their passion increased, Jessica found the best position was floating on the edge of the tub, facedown with her arm folded on the side of the tub, while Josh fucked her from behind.

However, as Josh upped his rhythm to a faster pace, Jessica, said, "Josh, be careful, the water is going all over the sides and all over the towels. "

"Oh, don't worry about that, you just concentrate on this, because I'm about to, oh God. " As he came, Josh pulled Jess back hard on to him, with both of his hands gripping Jessica's hips tightly, Josh then murmured almost incoherently, "Oh fucking hell Jess, thank you, that felt so good. I think you must know by now, you are beginning to be like a drug to me, the more I have of you, the more I need you, this is absolutely crazy sweetheart, but wonderful too, all at the same time. "

After spending another half hour or so in the hot tub drinking and talking, with Jessica sitting between his knees with her head resting on his chest, Josh said, "You know Jess, we need to start thinking about our own wedding. "And after a long pause said, "It's going to be so hard living on my own again, after spending this wonderful time with you. You know, just eating with you, talking with you, sleeping with you and well, just being with you, I am absolutely dreading when we go back to being on our own again. "

"But we really need to start thinking about where we are going to live first Josh, " said Jessica. "I am not so concerned about the wedding, but we will need somewhere to live. "

After another long pause, Josh said, "I know I haven't mentioned this before Jess, but Granddad left Sean and me £60, 000 each and I have been putting about two thousand a month away. The last time I checked my balance and that was some time back, I had about £180, 000 saved and I have just been given a good pay rise, so I can't see any problem there. " Then sounding rather sensible, Josh said, "But where do we live Jess? Do we live in London, or out in the sticks somewhere and commute to work, you know, I've never really thought about it until now. " Then as if to emphasis the decision, turned Jessica's head to face him and said, "This is a very important decision to make, so we both need to give it some very serious thought. "

That evening Josh spent quite some time speaking to Sean and was very relieved to hear that his mom was not upset by him meeting her family, in fact on the contrary, she wanted Padraig to call her. When Josh called his mom, he was still a little worried what mood she would be in, but when he explained what had happened and more importantly what they had said about the night she left them, he could hear from the tone of her voice, she was almost in tears. Josh informed her that she was now an aunty to five more family members and that they were all very anxious to meet her and Dad. He also told her she owned one third of their estate and just as Josh expected she responded to the news with, "I don't need any part of it Josh, but I would dearly like to see my nieces and nephews. Your granddad would have just loved to see his grandchildren, such a pity he never met any of you, as I know he would have spoilt you all rotten. "

Josh then told her, "I have the contact numbers for both Padraig and Patrick. "And asked, "Shall I text their numbers to your phone mom?"

"No, please, not yet son, just give me a little time to get used to it all. Anyway, " said his mom. "How's that poor girl Caroline going on, Sean was telling me about the wedding, such a terrible thing to happen to her. "

"But I think it may have been a blessing in disguise mom, " replied Josh. "If you had ever met her, you would know, she was far too good for him, but. "Now pausing for a moment in thought, Josh said, "But I think she will be just ideal for our Sean though and I know you would just love her mom, you really would. "

"Now, now Josh, " his mom replied, using her voice of authority. "Please don't you go meddling in affairs of the heart son, God, nature and destiny will find a partner for Sean, believe me they always do. " In a happier voice, Josh's mom asked, "And how is my beautiful Jessica, I hope you are treating her well and you're not up to anything you shouldn't be?"

"No of course not mom, she's in the kitchen cooking tea, the place we're staying in is beautiful, you know, the more I see of Ireland, the more I love it. We aren't far from where you lived, " said Josh. "It's way out in the middle of nowhere though, it's called Ballycroy. "

"Well would you believe it son, what a coincidence, that's where your granddad and his brother, used to go fishing. That's my Uncle Noel, your granddad's brother, I think that would make him your great uncle, well he lived that way on, Ballycroy eh? When you get back, I will tell you all about it, now don't forget to tell Jessica to give me a call and I will speak to you soon son, bye-bye. "

"How was your mom Josh?" asked Jessica, as she came out of the kitchen carrying two hot drinks.

"I was a little taken aback by her not going mad at me, you know, I think she may even be pleased I contacted them. See Jess, it does sometimes pay to meddle, anyway she wants you to call her, " said Josh. "And you had better give your mom and dad a call as well. "

"Our dinner is nearly ready now, "said Jessica. "So no rush, I will call them all after we've eaten. "

"So what have we got then Jess, because it smells very good?" asked Josh.

"Just shepherd's pie, with oven chips and frozen peas, nothing that special I'm sorry to say. I just hope you are hungry, because I may have got a little bit carried away with the quantities. "

"Well, it sounds good to me sweetheart, "said Josh. "You know, I think I might give Maggie a call a little later and maybe find out how she's managing without me. "

The next morning, Jessica was woken by Josh talking to his brother Sean, "Oh you're awake are you Jess, I'm just talking to Sean, he's on the ferry and he is just leaving port. "

"I thought he was coming tomorrow?"

"No, " said Josh. "He managed to get an earlier ferry, it seems that Howard talked him into it, apparently he's very keen to go sailing and riding with him. " Josh then said to Sean "You know mate, Jess looks really good first thing in the morning, before she puts on her make-up. No joking Sean, I absolutely love her hair when it's all frizzy and wild, Oh Jess love, Sean says hello. "

Jessica shouted, "Good morning Sean and please take no notice of your brother, he's been like this ever since he kissed that bloody Blarney Stone. "

After speaking to Sean for several more minutes and after finally putting his phone down, Josh said, "So what are we doing today then Jess? The weather looks fairly good. "

To which Jessica replied, "I don't think we will be going anywhere until we have done some washing. I know there's a clothesline outside, I just hope there are some clothes pegs to go with it, now come and give me a nice cuddle before we have to get up. "

Later in the morning, with a clothesline full of drying clothes, Josh was on the phone again talking to Howard, when he shouted through to Jessica, "Howard said the boat's ready Jess, all checked over and ready to go and Caroline has sorted tickets for the races on Thursday. " Then Jessica heard Josh say, "No, not this morning Howard, but we will be there some time after lunch. "

When Jessica heard Josh say in a very loud voice, "I'm awfully sorry Howard, but I can't do anything this morning, I have all the laundry to finish first, but I am glad to say, I have nearly finished all our washing, so we will see you later. I just hope this weather holds out until my washing is all dry. "

As Josh rung off, Jessica came out of the kitchen looking a little cross and said, "You know, I never believed there was anything in that bloody Blarney Stone rubbish, but it certainly worked with you Joshua Foster. " Then, chasing Josh round the lounge, while try to whip him with a tea towel, Jessica said, "You lying little toad, now Uncle Howard will think I forced you into doing the laundry. Well, I tell you now, Joshua Foster you will be doing all the ironing. "

Later that afternoon as they pulled into Mainear Darach, Josh said, "Oh look Jess, Sean's already here, bloody hell he's come over in the MG, doesn't it look good?" The MG looked really impressive, especially with its hood down, almost like a new car. With its black paintwork and shining chrome, Josh could imagine some film star arriving at a film premier in it.

Josh was now three steps ahead of Jessica and was saying urgently, "Come on Jess, let's see how he is doing. " When they entered the house, they could see through the French windows everyone grouped together sitting out in the sunshine enjoying the garden and all looking extremely happy. Looking slightly anxious, Josh said, "Of course, I will need to introduce them all, as none of them will have actually met Sean before, not even your mom and dad. "

"Don't you worry about Sean, " replied Jessica. "Sean is quite capable of mixing in and as far as I can see, looks very comfortable in their company. "

As Jessica and Josh walked out of the French windows and onto the lawn, Jane said, "Oh here they are Sean. "As she walked over to greet them; and as she hugged Jessica, she whispered in her ear, "Isn't Sean good looking darling and so polite?" Which made Jessica smile.

"What's making you smile?" asked Josh.

"Well, I think my Aunty Jane has already been attracted to your Sean and Howard seems to be enjoying his company too. See Josh, Sean, is mixing very well, " Jessica said. "There you go Josh, I told you Sean wouldn't need any help. "

"How was the journey then Sean?" asked Josh. "I see you brought the MG over, so how did she go?"

Sean now giving Jessica a hug, replied, "The journey was fine, and the car ran really well. I had this guy in Holly Head Port, keep wanting to buy it off me, he kept following me round and his offers just kept going up and up. He said he wanted it for his wife's birthday. "

Caroline then joined in and said, "It's absolutely gorgeous, I love the red interior, is there any chance I could take it for a spin sometime, Sean?"

Sean laughed, "As long as you are insured and you have a valid driving licence, yes, of course you can, you are very welcome to take it out. Mind you, " added Sean.

"I'm afraid there's no power steering Caroline and it's a crash gear on first, so it may feel a little heavy to drive. "

"Just like my old Land Rover then, " replied Caroline. "That was the same, but I have to give it to you Sean, she looks absolutely beautiful. " Caroline then asked, "Why we don't make cars like that any more, it's beyond me, even though she is probably fifty years old, she still looks very modern and so very stylish. "

"What Land Rover did you have?" asked Sean.

"I've had a couple over the years, but the one I was referring to, was an old series two, "replied Caroline.

"Not a series two A, then?" asked Sean. "No definitely a series two. It had a two-litre diesel engine not the two and a quarter litre and it had the old square edged bonnet, not the rounded edge like the series two A. "

Josh who had been watching the two talking together, could see that Sean was already impressed with Caroline's knowledge of cars, and something inside his head, shouted, 'Yes I knew it, I can see he's actually starting to enjoy her company. ' Howard suggested they should all go into town after dinner to an authentic Irish bar for some proper Irish atmosphere. Later, when the men had all gone down to the old sawmill to look at the steam lorry, the ladies prepared dinner chatting away and discussing tomorrow's sailing.

Down at the sawmill, Sean looked over the steam lorry for the first time and immediately fell in love with what he saw.

"Are you really sure you still want to sell her Howard?" Sean asked. "As it's in really good condition and would be worth a lot more than I am paying you on the open market and the price when it's properly renovated, who knows?"

"Yes Sean, like I said, all I need is the building emptied so the builders can move in and if Josh hadn't have noticed it, well it would have gone for scrap anyway."

"OK then, " said Sean. "And to keep its provenance. I would like to keep the sign writing on the door, as its original, if that's OK with you Howard?"

"Yes, please do Sean, I was hoping you could, a little bit of family history there, "said Howard. Who then added, "You know I am now really looking forward to seeing it completed, I really am, I've never seen a steam lorry. "

"You know Josh, I think I will bring our old D800 flatbed over, " commented Sean. "But now looking at the amount of overengineering involved, giving it all that extra weight, I might need to make a couple of trips to get it all home? So, if it's all right with you Howard, I will get it all out of the mill on the first trip, take what I can and collect the rest on the second trip?"

Howard looking very pleased with the arrangement said, "Well, that's fine with me Sean, but there is one important condition attached to the deal"

"What's that?" asked Sean.

"On condition you stay here with Jane and I while it's all happening. "

"Are you really sure you will want me around the house when I am dirty and covered in grease and dust, "?" replied Sean.

"Absolutely, " said Howard putting his arm round Sean's shoulder. "Absolutely my good man. " As the four of them walked back towards the house Howard and Sean talked about farming.

"I love farming, "said Sean. "But unfortunately, as you know, it does have its ups and downs. What with the price of milk fluctuating, the constant worry about TB and other bovine nightmares, like foot-and-mouth which is always in the back of your mind? And of course, those crippling vet bills. And never knowing what the weather is going to do, or even what piece of critical equipment is going to breakdown next, I sometimes wonder why I even like farming at all? But then I see people working in the towns, commuting back and forwards to work every day, never breathing fresh air, or seeing something born, or experiencing the satisfaction of growing and harvesting your own crops, or even experiencing the satisfaction of seeing a full grain store. But that's life and as they say, it's each to his own, I suppose. So, what about you Howard, how do you feel about farming?"

"Me, I just do it out of habit now, Sean, we had our lovely son Michael, who I was hoping would take over the farm, but sadly he was tragically killed in a motorbike accident. Although Caroline is a vet; and even though she loves farming, I just can't see her taking it on, which is a real pity Sean, because the estate has been in the family for nearly two hundred years. I sometimes feel guilty that Jane and I only had two children. " Then Howard, obviously getting upset said, "Yes, losing Michael has literally torn our lives apart. I thought Richard, you know the philandering groom, might have given it a go, but that was a very long shot and now of course that is a big no way. So, you see Sean, I really don't know where it will go. But I can't let it get me down, as that will just get Jane down, so I just try to keep smiling through. " Then, snapping out of his downer, Howard said, in a much livelier tone, "But never mind, Sean, all being well, we will be sailing out of Galway Bay tomorrow, now that's something to be pleased about. "

While the men were out of the house and seizing the right moment, Jessica said in confidence to Caroline, "I think I should warn you Caroline, Josh is looking to get you hitched up with Sean. Believe me, he really means well, but now he's now got it in his mind that you and Sean are somehow going to hit it off and become a permanent couple. "

After a pausing for a while and smiling, Caroline said, "Although I've only known Sean for a couple of hours, but I must admit jess, I do like what I see. But thanks for warning me Jess, he's some guy your Josh, I see the way he fusses round you and if I could finish up with someone like Josh, believe me, I would be a very happy woman. Sean, hopefully will be staying with us for at least a couple of days, so let's just see what happens, eh Jess, but I must admit he is extremely attractive. "

At dinner that evening, Howard tapped his glass with a knife to get everyone's attention. He then went on to say, "It's good to have so many friends here at Mainear Darach, as this old house was never made for just two people to enjoy and it always seems to come alive on nights like this. I can see Jane looking at me thinking, now what the hell is he rambling on about? Well, I must say, having all of you here with us, really makes us very happy and please remember, while you are here, you must treat this house as if it were your second home. You are all very special people and are always welcome to stay here anytime and I really do mean that. I would also like to thank the ladies for preparing another delicious meal and being so lovely. So please enjoy yourselves. "And now holding up his glass Howard said, "Here's a toast to all of us; and to Mainear Darach. "And with one swallow, drank his glass dry. Howard then added, "And don't forget, we're all going sailing tomorrow, the weather forecast is good, the boat is all ready, and I know we are going to have an absolutely marvellous day. "That's when everyone realised that Howard was determined to make everyone's stay a time to remember, despite the wedding going down badly.

As they drove back to the cottage, Josh said, "I know Sean better than I know anyone and I can actually read his thoughts, you know Jess. And I am pretty sure Sean is beginning to warm towards your Caroline. " Feeling very pleased with himself, he then added, "I am sure if we can get them in the right situation, they will become very close indeed Jess. And like they say, out of attraction grows fondness and out of fondness grows love. "

At this Jessica looking sideway at Josh, asked, "And just who was supposed to have said that then Josh? Come on tell me who's famous quote that is, because I think it's something you just made up. "

"Well, to be honest it was mine Jess, like you guessed, I made it up. But do you know Jess, I can feel it in my bones, and I really hope tomorrow's sailing goes well for them? There is just one downside to all this you know. "

"Oh yes, " Jessica said. "And what's that then Josh, what's this downside?"

"Well, I enjoy sailing in flat calm waters, but I have been known to suffer very badly from sea sickness, you know the old Mal-de-Mare?"

As they pulled up to the cottage, Jessica could see there were two packages in the porch steps. "Oh look, " said Jessica. "We've had a delivery, surely they can't be for us?"

"Yes, they are, " said Josh. "These represent another of my little surprises Jess; I was beginning to think they might never get here, but thanks to good old eBay, they are here. "

After they parked up, they walked over towards the porch and Jessica said, "That one looks rather big, what the hell have you have bought now?"

Josh now handing Jessica the smaller one of the two packages to carry in and then struggling with the bigger one said, "I hope it's as good as advertised, I've wanted one of these for some time?"

"So, what the hell is it, Josh?" asked Jessica, watching very intently as Josh unwrapped the package.

"It's a fold up massage table Jess, no home should be without one, "said Josh now unzipping the carrying case. "Wow, " said Josh carefully unfolding its legs and flipping it upright. "Well, I'm very impressed with the quality and with this soft padding, I know it's not real leather, but I suppose it has to be wiped clean. Come on then Jess, open the other package and let's see what else they sent us. " Josh impatiently wanted to take over the unwrapping from Jessica, in order to speed the process up, but Jessica kept turning, putting her body between Josh and the package. As Jessica opened the package, she could see there were three plastic bottles of massage oils with three different aromas.

Jessica now smelling one of the bottles said, "Oh this one smells nice, it's called exotic mix. " Now looking Josh in the face, Jessica said, "I am absolutely dreading going back through customs with this lot, if ever they search our bags, I will just die on the spot. What with lacy lingerie and now a bloody massage table, it could be a real embarrassment. "

"Oh, now you're talking rubbish, " said Josh, who was now smelling the second bottle. "This one is vanilla, smells just like ice-cream, I wonder if it tastes like ice-cream?"

Jessica now looking at the massage table said, "How the hell are we going to fit all this in the car to go home?"

"Mmm, I'm not sure Jess, " said Josh smiling. "I think we may have to leave that old oil painting and that bridesmaid dress behind, to make space. " Then laughing loudly said, "Look I am pretty sure it will all fit in Jess, so no problem. But if it doesn't all fit in, " said Josh laughing. "We will just have to leave the massage table at your aunty's, or maybe your mom and dad could fit in their car?" At that, Josh had to quickly sidestep, in order to avoid another hard aimed elbow in the ribs.

"Don't you even think about it Joshua Foster, God only knows what Mom would think if she saw that, "Jessica said in her more serious voice.

"You know Jess, I seriously believe Mary would really go for session on this, if I offered her it, after all, I have heard your mom complaining of her bad back a couple of times and like you told me, she did enjoy having her bottom smacked that time, " said Josh now moving to the other side of the table for protection. "I think I should ask her tomorrow. But don't worry Jess being as it's your mom, I will make it absolutely clear to her, right from the very start. I will tell her I'm really sorry Mary, but there will be no happy ending for you this time, but maybe next time, " said Josh, now moving back, away from Jessica's clenched fist, which was now flying over the table in Josh's direction.

"Seriously Josh, " said Jessica. "What are you going to tell her if she sees that big case in the car?"

Josh now laughing so much he is having difficulty to speak, replied, "If she asks what it is, I will tell her that it's an authentic Irish wall papering table we picked up in one of your antique shops and that I'm taking back for my mom, because she's always wanted one. " Josh, now with tears running down his face with laughter, says, "Come on Jess, lighten up sweetheart. Don't worry, I'll put it at the very bottom when we load the car up, honestly it won't be a problem. So, can we have a truce now, please, as my ribs are now killing me, and all this laughing is making the pain even worse?"

Later that evening, Jessica came out of the shower and into the bedroom, to find Josh warming up the table's upper surface using her hair dryer.

"Just getting it warmed up for you, " said Josh, wearing nothing but a tee shirt. "Come on then Jess, hop on up, as it's your turn tonight, but please don't forget, it's my turn tomorrow night. " Josh had already turned down the lights, had the radio playing low and had even stood the oil bottles in a bowl of hot water, to warm them up. "OK, facedown please Jess, I think you may need to wash your hair again after this, as it could get very oily round here tonight. " Within minutes the mood had changed to one of quiet relaxation and impending pleasures, as Josh poured warm oil on to Jessica's back.

"Oh, God that feels nice, "said Jessica, as Josh began rubbing it over her back.

"No speaking please, " said Josh. "Your speaking could spoil the whole experience, just keep silent and relax into it. " Josh had partially covered Jessica's lower body with a large white towel, just like your expert masseur, but this quickly fell discarded on to the floor, not needed. Josh was feeling very happy as he now massaged Jessica's oily back from her thighs, right up to her neck. Josh then massaged each of her arms and then massaged her hands, finger by finger. At this point Jessica was starting to properly relax and was thinking how good it felt and thought, *Josh could be right, Mom probably would enjoy this.* But then Jessica came back to reality, thinking, *But not with Josh, but maybe I should buy her a professional massage table for her birthday, as it is very relaxing?*

Jessica's thoughts returned to the massage, as Josh was now very busy massaging her left leg. First, he gently massaged her foot, which Jessica especially enjoyed and rather hoped would last that little bit longer, enjoying the feeling of Josh's smooth oily hands soothing her feet was beginning to send her into a very relaxed state of sleep. However, as Josh moved up to her calf's and then up to her thighs, she became aware that her initial feelings of relaxation were now turning into those of a more sensual nature. Josh was now making long sweeping oily smooth strokes up the inside of her thighs and was purposely over reaching, ensuring that he touched her now very oily vagina on each stroke. Each time he reached the top of her leg, the contact became just a little more deliberate. Jessica was now starting to enjoy this occasional contact and was a little disappointed when Josh stopped, only to start all over again on the other leg. Josh, as usual, was enjoying the tease element of his massage as well as the erotic image of Jessica's oily wet body, which was now looking not only oily, but sexually inviting. After repeating the same massage on the right leg, Josh lifted and moved each leg in turn to the edge of the table, spreading her knees as wide as the table allowed. Josh, now feeling extremely horny himself, started to not only contact with her crotch, but was now slowly and purposely pushing his oily fingers into Jessica's vagina at the end of each sensual stroke. Josh was enjoying the sight of his finger's gliding without effort inside Jessica's beautifully formed body. Josh was taking the opportunity to explore Jessica's reactions to each of his erroneous movements, watching his finger slide in and out of her very oily vagina. Jessica was now eyes closed; completely focused on the pleasurable sensations she was experiencing and could feel several involuntary movements happening just slightly outside of her control. Josh could also feel his own body being taken over just by the pure delight of seeing Jessica's erotic body movements and he too was beginning to get massively turned on as he pushed his fingers deeper and firmer inside her now very responsive vagina. By now Jessica's breathing had become much faster and shallower, as she felt each orgasm flow through her now very aroused body. Josh was now starting to be a little too turned on to continue, so pouring more warm oil on to his hands retuned to massaging her back and neck and then signalled Jessica to turn over on to her back. Josh now stood near Jessica's head and with a little more oil applied, Josh began squeezing and massaging her breasts, paying special attention to her now very erect nipples. Josh could see from Jessica's facial expression that she was enjoying every sensuous movement of this massage as he now, once again began to slowly extending his hand stokes over her body to include her vagina. Josh's steady hand movements now had Jessica writhing her body upwards in time to Josh's probing fingers. Sensing that the time was right and feeling that he could not take any more of this mind-blowing pleasure, Josh moved near to her side and gently lifted both of her knees to the upright position and placed her feet together, while moving her knees apart. Josh then began a gentle circular motion with his oily fingers around Jessica's ultra-aroused clitoris and was at the same time observing her body movements in order to synchronise them with his hand movements. By now, Jessica was getting extremely excited and in response, her hand started to feel its way towards Josh's very erect penis. Seeing her enjoyment, Josh again began firmly moving his fingers in and out of Jessica's, smooth vagina. Jessica now thought, although this was all very sexy and was really turning her on, she needed to move things along and urgently wanted Josh inside her. Jessica then turned onto her side and with her hand moved Josh along the table until by moving her head to the edge of the table her mouth could finally reach his hard penis. Firmly placing her hand behind Josh's bum, Jessica pulled his body towards her and then literally sucked his penis deep into her mouth. At this moment Josh wanted to say something in response, but managed to fight it off, as he didn't want to break his self-imposed need for silence. Now that Jessica had Josh in the right position; she moved her hand to grip the shaft of his penis and tightly slid her gripped hand up and down its stiffened shaft, while sucking as hard as she possibly could. For Josh it was either stop Jessica right now, or ejaculate. However, not wanting to finish quite yet, Josh pulled his body back away from her and gently dragged Jessica down to the end of the table and lifting her ankles onto his shoulders pushed his penis deep inside her soft, warm body. After several deep thrusts, he felt Jessica's hands grip around behind his back and pull him tightly close to her. Although Josh would have liked to last out a little longer, he had reached the point of no return and fight the urge as he may, he finally felt that first pulsing spurt, followed by several more spine-tingling tremors, which took him to the heights of sexual ecstasy. After holding the position for a minute or two, to ensure that every ounce of pleasure was enjoyed, Josh lifted Jessica off the table and went to lay her on the bed.

"No, not on the bed Josh, " said Jessica, finally breaking her silence. "Otherwise how am I going to explain this scented oil all over the bed clothes? I think we both need to shower before we go anywhere else. " As Jessica stepped into the shower, her feet slipped almost from under her and after retaining her composure, she called out to Josh, "Be careful, this massage oil of yours is dangerous stuff, I feel a bit like *Bambi* on ice in here. "

Later as they both lay in bed, Jessica said, "I can't wait till it's my turn to get you on that table. I'm going to really tease you, just like you teased me, anyway, just feel me, I'm still trembling. You know I'm quite enjoying these little surprises of yours Josh and if you could bottle that kind of pleasure up and sell it, you would be a multimillionaire overnight. " Then laughing Jessica said, "You know, I think my mom might even buy some. I hate to admit Josh; but I'm so pleased you bought that massage table. I just hope I get my legs back working again before tomorrow's sailing. Because I tell you, they are somewhere else at the moment. "

As Josh switched off the lights, he said, "I know I keep saying it, but I'm really enjoying this holiday and well, just being here with you. You know every day of this holiday has been something special and with sailing tomorrow followed by horse racing on Thursday, I think we are really being spoilt and long may it last. "

Chapter 14

Sailing Day

The next morning, Jessica woke to the smell of bacon and the noise of Josh's cooking emanating from the kitchen. As she lay there contemplating getting out of bed, the door suddenly flung open, opened by a smiling Josh coming in with a breakfast tray.

"I hope you are hungry sweetheart?" said Josh, standing by the bed waiting for Jessica to sit up and take the tray off him. "I have just been listening to the weather forecast and it seems it's going to be a really nice day, so that's a big relief, I hate choppy water sailing. " Josh looking at the massage table said, "While you're eating that, I think I will clean this down and put it back in its case. "

Then Jessica in a startled voice said, "Bloody hell Josh, what are you doing? It's not even six o'clock yet, why the hell are we getting up this early? We don't have to be at Uncle Howard's house until nine o'clock, this is ridiculous. "

"Well, " Josh said still smiling. "I thought we could have an hour in the hot tub before we go Jess and I also want my breakfast to go down. " Then after short pause

Josh said, "Who knows and this way it will hopefully stay down. But you don't have to get up right away Jess, have another ten minutes in bed. "He switched on the bedroom TV. After cleaning and folding away the table, Josh went outside and dropping his dressing gown, climbed in the hot tub. Then after relaxing on his own for a few minutes, he started calling, "Come on Jess, come and join me it's bloody gorgeous in here. " A few minutes later a very naked Jessica tiptoed across the decking and slid gracefully into the hot bubbling water.

"You know Josh, " said Jessica. "I still don't know how that brain of yours actually works. "

"Oh, come on Jess, now you're in here, out here in the beautiful morning sunshine, don't you think it was worth the effort, life doesn't get any better than this, now does it?" Then leaning over her to get to the spa controls, Josh said, "I think I will put the power jets on full blast Jess, that should wake us up a bit, eh sweetheart?"

It was eight-forty-five, when they pulled in to Mainear Darach, and could see Sean and Caroline getting into Sean's MG, which then pulled up alongside them. Caroline was in the driving seat and rolled down the window to say, "Good morning, we are going ahead to sort everyone's lunch out, we put it up last night and I wanted to go the long way round, the insurance started this morning, so I really don't want to waste any of it. "

Shouting across Jessica said, "You just go carefully. "And at that moment, there was a loud exhaust roar, a small tyre squeal and the little MG had gone.

"There you go, " said Josh, looking very pleased with himself. "There, I told you they were going to hit it off. " Josh then added, "I just hope there's nothing too rich or sickly in that lunch. "

When they got the house, Howard was smiling cheerfully and holding out a yellow yachting jacket and said, "Sean left this for you Josh, he told me you both had one each, but he knew this one was yours, because your old vomit stains are still on it. "

By nine-forty-five they were all pulling into the marina. Howard was first out saying, "What a great day for sailing, oh, I love it. "

As Jane standing next to him just rolled her eyes, with a bemused expression, saying, "We were up at six this morning, it's like being married to a big kid sometimes, it really is. "

As they boarded the boat, Howard handed everyone a life jacket, saying, "They've all been inspected. "And pointing to a part of the lifejacket, said, "Please try not to get any water on this bit here, else they will automatically inflate. Oh, and whenever you're on deck, just remember to clip your safety lines on, we don't want anyone falling over board, now do we?"

Again, his wife Jane rolled her eye looking towards Howard and whispered to Jessica, "Well I can think of one, we wouldn't miss. " Sean and Howard took over running the boat and they eventually set off. Sean was at the helm and Howard was on the radio letting the harbour master know that the Irish Yacht 'Blow Me' was leaving the harbour and gave the number of persons on board and their destination and return ETA.

The sun was shining, the tide was going out and there was a moderate on coast westerly breeze as they passed a moored boat, Howard waved and shouted, across to four people eating breakfast, "Good morning it looks like another good day. "And as they waved back Howard said, "That's another good thing about sailing, everyone is very friendly. Smiling broadly as he went to join Sean, Howard said, "Got to do it right, serious stuff, sailing. " Once clear of the harbour, Caroline hoisted the main sail and set the jib.

As Caroline passed by them, Jessica whispered to Josh, "I haven't seen Caroline this happy for days. You probably don't know but Caroline used to sail this boat single handed and she and Uncle Howard won quite a few races with 'Blow Me' and before you say anything, all the jokes about the boat's name have already been done to death, so don't even go there. " Then laughing said, "Mind you, it was always very funny to hear the commentators pronounce it over the old tannoy system, you could see everyone smile when they heard it, I think that's why Uncle Howard named her. "

Once into open water Caroline took over the helm and the boat literally flew along. There was no doubt about it the coastline certainly looked beautiful and as they left the harbour behind them, they could see the houses on the shoreline, shining in the bright sun light. Just then Howard went back into the cabin, where most of the others were quietly seated drinking coffee, and said with a beaming smile, "Just like old times this eh, she's still got it, I don't know why we don't sail more often, I really don't. Out here in the fresh air, in this beautiful sunshine and with the smell of the sea, great feeling. " And at that Howard went back out on deck, shouting back as he left, "Caroline reckons with this wind we should reach Toremore before lunchtime. " Up until now, Josh had been sitting quietly with Jessica in the main saloon, hoping and praying that he would avoid the horrors of sea sickness. However, he was now feeling confident enough to venture out on deck to join Sean and Caroline in the cockpit.

"Hi guys, " said Josh. "How's it going out here? Jess and I thought we had better come a join you for a while. " Jessica could see that Sean and Caroline were getting on well and it was obvious that they were now very comfortable in each other's company.

Caroline then said, "Sean was saying he would teach me to fly. "And looking straight at Sean in the eyes added, "And I will definitely be taking him up on that offer. Sean tells me you both used to sail Josh, so why did you stop?" Caroline, asked with an enquiring smile.

Josh immediately replied, "I actually love sailing Caroline, I enjoy the skill of harnessing the wind and navigating your way around the ocean, but I am afraid my stomach doesn't. " Then Josh continued, "You see, sailing has made very me ill, on quite a few occasions, so it sort of put me off. I think I am probably more suited to luxury cruise liners, as that's now definitely more my style. " Josh then continued, "But she's a great boat Caroline and I must say you seem to be getting some good speed out of her. I have just been watching the tell tales on the main sail and they were right out there, so I can see you can sail well. "

Caroline then said, "Ah but did you know that Jessica used to sail as well Josh? She has even won one or two races with our Blow Me. She won a big one during Cowes Week, in the twenty-metre class, some years back, so I'm just surprised she hasn't taken over the helm yet. " Then smiling at Josh, Caroline said, "Back then we used to physically fight over who had the helm, hadn't we Jess. It's a real pity that we no longer sail her. I suppose it was university and then our job commitments that did it, since then we never seem to have found the time to sail her. "

Caroline, in her serious voice said, "Look Josh, if ever you or Sean feels like taking her out at any time, I am sure Dad would be more than pleased to lend her to you. " And now aiming her voice towards Josh, said, "She can sail really smooth if you want me to take it steady, so please let me know if you want me to keep her steady for you. " Caroline then added, "I do know what sea sickness is like, so please don't suffer in silence, just let me know. " By now Josh was starting to get his sea legs and was feeling a little more confident regarding sea sickness and was starting to enjoy the views and the clean fresh air you get coming off the Atlantic. Sitting on the saloon roof together, facing starboard, Josh and Jess could see the rugged coastline, literally shining green.

With his arm round Jessica's waist, Josh said, "Just look at that for a view, Jess, now I know that you sail, I think we should take up the offer and take her out some weekend. After a couple of hours of good sailing, the wind dropped slightly and instead of landing at Toremore as originally planned, they thought it better to turn early and in long outward loop to take the long way back to Galway. On the return leg, Josh even ate a couple of Mary's very tasty vol-au-vents and several of Jane's sausage rolls. Later when Josh knew he would soon be back on Terra Firmer, he even polished off the last of the trifle as well as a few strawberries. "Pushing your luck now, aren't you, " laughed Jessica as she joined Josh in finishing off the strawberries.

On the last part of the return leg, Josh, Jane and Jessica, along with her mom and dad, sat around the chart table as they talked about weddings.

Gerald looking at Mary, said, "Our wedding was a very quiet affair, wasn't it dear?" Then laughed saying, "We decided to spend most of the money on a good honeymoon instead, didn't we darling?" Jane just smiled back at him knowingly, while nodding in agreement.

Gerry then continued, "We had five lovely days in Paris, three days in Vienna and eight days in glorious Rome. And then we returned back to our half-renovated house. We had no hot water, no dining room window and no ceiling in the bathroom. My dad, bless his soul, thought we had gone absolutely mad and believed we should have spent the time and money on finishing off the renovations.

And he was probably right really, but we had such a wonderful time, didn't we Mary, one that I will never forget. And talking about house improvements Jessica, your mom wants me to put in a hot tub?" Then looking for feedback asked, "Have you spent much time in yours?" Gerry then added, "It would appear, that most people who buy one, spend loads of time in them initially, then after a month or so, when the novelty wears off, they hardly ever use them. I see there are lots of second-hand ones for sale, so maybe they are right. So now Mary and I are not quite sure whether to buy one or not?"

Just then Howard came in saying, "Come on you lot, come on out on deck, the sun's shining and we are about to pass the Aran Islands. You can't just sit in here all day, so come on out. Oh, and don't forget to clip on, you're all just too precious to lose. "

On the way into the harbour, Sean took the helm and Caroline was sat as close to him as she could possibly get, smiling chatting away like two old friends.

Indicating with his eyes, Josh whispered to Jessica, "Look at Caroline Jess, I think I am looking at my future sister-in-law. "Then Josh's conversation was instantly cut short by Jessica elbowing him in the ribs.

Back on shore and Josh was feeling very pleased with himself, in that he had not been seasick, the now reinspired Josh said, "Do you know Jess, I think the four of us should take her out one weekend. Maybe sail down to North Devon, you said a few months back you always wanted to eat at Rick Stein's restaurant. So what do you think?" As they all congregated on the marina car park ready to leave, they had a quick nose at some of the boats moored there.

"Oh, this one's from Galveston, Texas, " said Gerry. "She's a long way from home. "And as they walked along the quayside, they were amazed just how far some of the boats had come from.

When they got back to their cars, Howard said, "See that boat over there on that support platform, well that is one of the few remaining small boats, which helped to pluck our soldiers of the beach at Dunkirk, it's got special bronze plaque mounted by the helm. "

Later, and as everyone had previously agreed, they all stopped off at Mad O' Riley's Bar for a drink, on their way home.

A short while later, Josh and Jessica entered the bar and could see most of their group were already in there and had already been served with drinks.

When Josh reached the bar, he was immediately recognised by the landlord, who said jokingly, "Now I know for certain, you don't drink Guinness young man, so what's it going to be my good friend?" Then in a very loud voice the landlord said, "Everyone please take note, as this is the young man who made me look a complete fool, stupidly left holding two upside down Guinness bottles. And since that day, I now laugh every time I see one. Great crack that was young man, really great crack. " Then with an enquiring look, he leant forwards and moving closer, said quietly, "Have got any more stories like that?"

"Well, " said Josh, now raising his voice, "Tell me landlord; do you know what happened, when Buzz Aldrin visited Ireland some years back?"

Instantly picking up on Josh's question. "Well, no, " replied the landlord now realising this was the opening of another one of Josh's little stories. "No I never did hear about it. "

"Well apparently, " said Josh. "Some of Buzz's' ancestors were from here in Southern Ireland and that he and his wife were over here on holiday to look up some of the places where his ancestors had lived, "Josh continued. With most of the people in the bar now listening to Josh's new story, he continued, "Well, it was one lunchtime, when Buzz and his wife, were in some small village, I think it may have been in County Kerry, but I'm not exactly sure. Well anyway, they had stopped at this small rural bar for lunch. As soon as Buzz reached the bar, the landlord immediately recognised him, and in a very broad Irish accent said, 'I think I know you sir, why if I'm not mistaken, you're Buzz Aldrin, the world-famous astronaut?'

"'Well, that's right I am, ' replied Buzz. Looking slightly amazed.

"'Well of all of the bars in Ireland, fancy you walking in to this very bar, ' said the landlord.

"'Well sir, it must have been destiny, or maybe you had already heard about us, "Josh continued to tell them. "Buzz, now looking very curious at the landlord's remarks, said, 'Why what's so special about this particular bar?'

"To which the landlord replied, 'Why sir, I am pleased to inform you that this is the headquarters of the Irish space exploration initiative, so it is, to be true sir. ' Now looking extremely proud of the fact. 'And if you would care to follow me sir, ' said the landlord, now beckoning him to follow him out through the rear door. 'I will show our very latest space project. ' Outside in the middle of the bar's back yard was an enormous space rocket, shaped like a giant Guinness bottle. "

At this point the landlord, started laughing and pointing his finger at Josh and saying, "Oh, a giant Guinness bottle was it, oh I'm thinking, *here we go again.* " Josh continued to tell the tale, "Buzz, at first thought it rather absurd, but after checking it over could see it was the real thing. It had computer guidance systems, liquid fuelled propulsion rockets, a fully regenerative life-support system, in fact the space craft was now looking extremely credible.

"Buzz Aldrin, now looking very interested, said, 'Just where are you guys intending to go? Are you going for another moon shot?'

"To which the landlord immediately replied, 'No sir, you have already beaten us to that one. No sir, ' he said, now looking even more proud, 'No sir, we are actually going to the sun. '

"Buzz Aldrin, now looking even more confused, said 'Do you guys realise if you get within two million light years of the sun, you will just burn up?'

"'Ah yes, ' said the landlord. 'We're not stupid, we know that for sure sir, that's why we're going at night. '"

At this the whole bar was in laughter after listening to Josh's hilarious story.

The landlord slapped the bar loudly with his hand and said, "I don't know your name young man. "

At which point Josh replied, "It's Josh sir. "

The landlord then continued to say, "Well, young Josh, you are welcome to come in here anytime it takes your fancy, that's even if we are closed. Although I can tell by the accent you must be English, there must be some Irish blood in there somewhere. "

Josh then explained about his search and informed him that his mother was Irish, so technically he was 50% Irish blood and that furthermore he had two uncles who lived near to Swinford.

"What's the family name?" asked the landlord

Josh replied, "It's O'Brien sir. "

"What are their first names?" asked the now very interested landlord.

"Well, they are Padraig and Patrick, "replied Josh and on hearing that the landlord's face immediately changed, Josh said, "Why do you know them?"

Now looking completely overcome, the landlord said, "If your mother is named Bridie and if it is, she's my cousin. " Then grabbing Josh by the hand, almost in tears, he asked, "Where is Bridie, you know, I haven't seen her since she left home all those years back. She was a great girl; in fact, she was my favourite cousin and we all really missed Bridie when she left. I just wish my dad was still alive to hear this wonderful news; it almost broke his heart when Bridie left. He always thought the world of her, well, we all did. "

Josh now calling Sean over said, "This is Sean, my brother. "Then as he was about to introduce them, Josh said, "Sorry but I didn't get your name sir. "

"It's Aiden, Aiden Gallagher. "

"Right then, " said Josh to Sean. "This is your great uncle Aiden. "

"Bloody hell, "said Aiden, now shaking Sean's hand and not wanting to let go. "I just knew there was something special about this brother of yours. I must have sensed he was family. Now just wait here you two, till I get my sister round here. She's only a couple of doors away, so please don't go leaving here, until I bring her round. " And at that Aiden vanished through the front doors out on to the street.

Jessica and Caroline both wanted to know what was happening and just as Josh started to explain, Aiden returned dragging his poor sister Lizzie behind him.

"These are them, Lizzie, "said Aiden "These are Bridie O'Brien's two sons, over from England. "

Now wiping the water from her wet hands on her apron, Lizzie shook hands with Josh and looking him full in the face said, "Well Josh, I have to tell you, you look just like my old uncle. " Looking around the crowd, she then said, "So where's Bridie, is she here with you?"

To which Josh replied, "I'm sorry she's not with us, she's still back home in England. "

Lizzie, now shaking hands with Sean, who then said, "Sorry but like Josh said, our mom is still back in England."

Lizzie now looking very disappointed that her cousin Bridie was not with them said, "Well my name is Lizzie, your mom and me, we were very close friends and well I'm pleased to say, we went right through school together."

Just then Jessica stepped in and said, "I think I should maybe get her on the phone for you, I am sure she would love to talk to you?" For the next few moments, the bar went extremely quiet as Jessica explained to Josh's mom who she was with. After a brief conversation with Bridie, Jessica handed the phone over to Lizzie, saying, "It's Bridie and she wants to speak to you. "

For the next fifteen minutes Lizzie was in deep conversation, with tears streaming down her face, then Aiden managed to get the phone and the conversations continued.

Eventually Lizzie wrote down the number, said a very long goodbye and handed the phone back to Jessica, saying, "Thank you darling, that's just made an old lady very happy. "

Later that evening, when Josh and Jessica, eventually managed to escape from the bar and as they walked back to the car, Jessica said, "Well Joshua Foster, I will say one thing, there's never a dull moment whenever I am out with you. " And she then stopped to give Josh a big, long kiss, as a thank you.

As they drove back to the cottage, Josh said in a moment of panic, "Oh God, I forgot to invite Aiden and Lizzie to the races tomorrow. I remembered to invite Padraig and Patrick and thankfully they were really up for it. I wonder if I can get Aiden's number off the web? Bloody hell, in all that excitement I completely forgot, I wonder if Howard has Aiden's number?" As soon as they got to the cottage, Josh called Howard, who although it was late, luckily was still at the bar and who on Josh's behalf, invited Aiden, Lizzie and family to join them at the races. Josh, happy now that the invitation problem had been fixed, now turned his attention to the massage he had been promised.

Shouting to Jessica who was in the bathroom, Josh said, "I think it's got to be stockings, suspenders and high heels tonight; and don't worry, I will warm the oil up myself. " When Jessica eventually came back into the bedroom, she was a little taken aback to see scented candles lighting up the room and to hear soft music playing.

"So where were my candles then?" asked Jessica, wearing her dressing gown, which was barely covering what Josh had requested in the way of clothing. Josh had already erected the massage table, had heated the oil and was lying face down waiting, replied, "I only bought the candles today Jess, from the chandlers in Galway, I thought it would set the atmosphere. But never mind sweetheart, you can have candles tomorrow night. " As

Jessica started to pour the oil on Josh's back, her mobile phone started to ring.

"Leave the fucking thing, you can ring them back later, "said a slightly annoyed Josh. But by now Jessica had already answered it, unfortunately for Josh it was Jessica's mother, who was never one for short conversations. Josh's expectation was soon dashed when he heard Jessica say, "No Mom we were just sitting here watching the news on TV. " After twenty minutes Josh had climbed down off the table and was lying on the bed gesticulating to Jessica to hurry up. After thirty or so minutes Josh was in the kitchen opening a bag of crisps when he heard Jessica say, "Good night then Mom I will see you in the morning. "

"Thank fuck for that, " said Josh to himself, as he was climbing back onto the table and fearing he had lost some of his earlier enthusiasm. "I bet the oil's gone cold now, "said Josh now lying face down again. "I think you had better switch that phone off please Jess, as it will probably be Caroline or Jane next. " As Jessica slipped off her dressing gown and shook her hair loose and on seeing her looking extremely desirable, Josh was immediately back in the mood. Jessica then massaged Josh's oil covered back; all the time teasing Josh, by neatly stepping clear of Josh's groping hands.

When Jessica eventually turned Josh over onto his back, she could see that Josh was certainly back in the mood and pouring oil onto her hands said, "Right Joshua Foster, I am going to give you the best hand job, the like you have never experienced before. And true to her word

Jessica spent the next ten minutes, bringing Josh to the point of orgasm and at the critical moment switched back to massaging his very oily body. Then after teasingly removing her panties, Jessica climbed onto Josh saying, "I hope this table is good for two people?" Then with her stocking clad legs, straddled over Josh, Jessica then poured oil onto her hand and sensually rubbed it over her crotch region. Jessica then skilfully and deliberately slid her oily vagina all over Josh's body, spending a little extra time on his penis. All the time Josh was fondling her breasts and tweaking her erect nipples. After several minutes Jessica positioned herself over Josh's well-oiled penis and reaching down guided it into her oily smooth vagina.

"Oh, fucking hell, " said Josh, as Jessica worked herself up and down on Josh's penis. "Just laying here, watching your body sliding over me and feeling your vagina taking my cock, well, it feels so fucking good. " Josh then groaned and said, "Sorry but I can't hold it any longer. " Hearing that, Jessica deliberately worked even harder to make Josh cum inside her.

After sitting there for a few moments, Jessica climbed down and laughing said, "Same again tomorrow, sir?"

They both then showered together, being very careful not to slip on the now very slippery shower tray.

Before going to bed, Jessica started to fold the table away and clear up, when Josh came in and said, "Just leave it Jess. I can do it in the morning, just come to bed, I need to hold you. "

"But what if anyone see's it?" said Jessica sounding just a little concerned.

To which Josh replied, "Think about it Jess, we are miles from anyone, we can hear anyone coming up the gravel driveway, way before anyone even gets anywhere near our front door and at the end of the day, it's just an ordinary massage table, it's not stolen, it's not illegal, so just leave it where it is please and please just come to bed."

Chapter 15

A Grand Day Out

The next morning Jessica was awoken to, "Come on Jess, it's time to get up, else we are going to be late. I've made you boiled eggs, with soldiers, it's on the table waiting and it's getting cold, so come on, hurry up please. " At that Jessica quickly got out of bed, put on her dressing gown, and sat down at the kitchen table. It was at this point when Jessica noticed the time was 06. 16.

"Bloody hell Josh, you have done it again. You know we don't have to be at Caroline's until nine a. m. So why the hell are we up at this time in the morning?"

"No sweetheart it's eight a. m. and knowing that you will want to shower, get dressed up and be wanting to look good I woke you early, so look, now you have loads of time. See how good I am to you, see Jess I'm like your guardian angel. "

When they arrived at Caroline's everyone was ready there and waiting, Sean was taking the farm's telescopic handler down towards the timber mill. The farmhand, Peter, was following him, with their recently acquired brand new shiny New Holland tractor, towing their long low bed trailer. Jessica immediately went into the house, while Josh put on some very old rather large coveralls that Howard had kindly lent him.

Josh in a voice loud enough for them all to hear, shouted, "It's a bloody good job you don't run a gent's outfitters Howard, what with odd sized riding boots and now these oversized coveralls. Well, I think you would be out of business within a week, if not sooner?" Later when Josh was properly attired, in his old coveralls that were looking very greasy and faded, the group set off to clear a route out of the sawmill and to help Sean to get the Sentinel loaded onto the trailer. Putting the steam lorry on to the trailer was just a temporary measure in readiness for the final collection by Sean on his next visit. The others had now been joined by Chuck, who had just finished the milking, and was busy moving the general junk, clutter and other pieces of old machinery from the Sentinel's route out. Sean along with Josh, were busy fitting the rear hubs and wheels onto the axles. However, while they were trying to fit the rear hubs, they came across a problem, which immediately halted their progress.

"Which way does this spacer go on then Sean?" Josh asked, as he held up a rusty metal ring.

After they both studied the problem, for a minute or so Sean said, "Not to worry, I've got a full set of drawings on my laptop, back in my room, so I'll go back and fetch it. While I am gone, do you want to make a start on the front hubs, as that might save some time? But don't worry too much about fitting the brakes, Josh, as I'll be stripping it all down again, once I get it home. " At that, Sean left Josh and headed back towards the house.

On reaching the house, Sean took off his boots, washed the dirt from his hands and made his way upstairs to his room. This was when Sean, as he walked along the corridor that ran through to his room, heard a soft whimpering sound. Sean paused for a second to try and establish where the noise was coming from, but the noise then stopped. Curiosity then over, Sean continued his way to his room. However, after Sean had collected his laptop and was making his way back along the corridor, he once again he heard the same soft whimpering noise. This time Sean was able to follow the sound until it led him to a slightly open bedroom door. Not sure whether to investigate or not, Sean carefully looked in and from the doorway he could see Jane slumped over a bed sobbing. As Sean cautiously made his way into the semi-darkened room, which he could see had been Michael's old room and although Sean was thinking, *Perhaps this is not really any of my business and maybe it would be better if I just walked away.* But seeing Jane crying there, was just too much for him to walk away from.

As Sean got closer to Jane, in a very soft voice Sean said, "Are you OK Jane, I heard you from the corridor?"

Suddenly realising Sean was there in the room, Jane immediately jumped up and wiping her eyes murmured, "Yes, I'm fine Sean; I was just checking Michael's old room. But I am fine, thank you, I really am. " Looking around, in the darkened room, Sean could see photographs on the wall, shelves full of trophies and numerous items of motorcycle memorabilia.

Gently placing his hands on Jane's shoulder and turning her to face him, Sean said, "I think this sadness goes a little deeper than you are making out Jane. " Now pulling Jane close to his chest, Sean whispered, "I know this is really none of my business Jane, but I know torturing yourself like this is not good for you. Not only that, but this prolonged sadness making the rest of your family very sad as well. " Sean continued, "I think you know, that crying like this is never going to bring Michael back and before you say it, I know I could never even begin to understand the feeling of loss a mother has for her son, but I do know that prolonged grieving is never going to help. " Sean now holding her, continued, "Unfortunately Jane, I never met Michael, but from what I hear, he really loved life and although his death was a tragic waste of a young life, remember he died doing exactly what he loved doing. " Now trying to look Jane in the eye, Sean said, "I know your son would never have wanted you to suffer in this way, now, would he? What you probably don't realise is how much Howard and Caroline are grieving too, not just for Michael, but for their loss of a wife and mother.

"I have seen how Howard and Caroline, both fuss round you, trying their very best to cheer you up, but it's like they are permanently walking on broken glass, frightened they may trigger some memory that will cause you to feel pain. So, " said Sean, now lifting her chin to face him. "Now Jane, please stop all this sadness, it's time to draw a line under your grieving and let Howard, Caroline and everyone who loves you, start living their lives again. " Then walking Jane to the window, Sean drew back the curtains and said, "Look Jane, it's a beautiful sunny day, you're healthy and have many more years left to enjoy. So yes, keep all those happy memories alive, but you must stop this sadness for Michael's sake. " Now kissing Jane on her forehead, he took her hand and led her from the room saying, "Come on, let's go and show everyone the old Jane. " Then in a lighter voice, while closing the door behind them said, "I know there's still that fun loving Jane in there, so let's both go down and show them, that the old Jane is back again. " Seeing Jane wipe her tears and forcing a smile, Sean realised going into the room had been the right thing to do after all.

Eventually Sean got back to the timber mill, with his laptop already open, when Josh on seeing him said, "And where the fuck have you been? For Christ's sake Sean, while you have been fucking about, doing God only knows what, I have sorted it. That spacer is bevelled on one side to match the outer bearing, so it can only go one way. So, let's not waste any more time and give me a hand to get the wheels back on, well that is, provided we can find all the wheel nuts. "

After lunch the team managed to move the now rolling chassis out into the daylight, for the first time in around seventy years. By early afternoon they had completed their lorry removal, they had removed their work clothes, had washed their hands and were all now sitting at the kitchen table drinking coffee, when Caroline and Jessica walked in saying, "You lot been sitting here drinking coffee all day then?"

To which Howard immediately replied, "Bloody typical, you come back when all the hard work's finished. I think you lot must have been round the corner watching us, because your timing is absolutely perfect. "

Later that afternoon Caroline said to Sean, "I don't know what's come over Mom, but I heard her singing in her room earlier this afternoon and now she's even wearing her jewellery again?"

"Well, " said Sean. "It's a long story, so I will tell you later, when we are on our own. " Then Sean skilfully changed the subject, by saying, "I can't wait to get that beautiful old lorry home and start working on her. You know when I've finished with her renovation, she's going to look like new and I am absolutely dying to get her steamed up and then drive her down the road. "

That evening Caroline and Sean went out for a tour of the area and finished up at well-known restaurant. Caroline was not only feeling more comfortable with Sean, but while they were eating and chatting, she was beginning to learn a little more about him. By the end of the meal Caroline was beginning to think, Josh's attempt at matchmaking may not have been such a joke. While Sean was standing at the bar waiting to pay, Caroline was studying his looks and thought, *Well he certainly has what it takes in the looks department.* Luckily the restaurant car park was next to a popular woodland walk, which led in and round Dandies Pond and Caroline suggested, as it was nice evening, they should walk to the pond. As they walked both told each other about their ex-partners and compared their notes. When they reached the stile at the end of the wood, Sean went over first and then holding Caroline's hand helped her down the other side.

As Caroline climbed over, their faces came very close, when Sean said, "Do you think it would it be very wrong if I gave you a kiss?"

Caroline now staring Sean in the eye, said, "Of course not, in fact, I was thinking exactly the same thing. " For the next few minutes, they never moved from the stile, just kissing, and embracing each other.

Sean then said, "I don't know if you realise Caroline, but Josh has serious intentions of getting us two together and I know he means well, but well that's Josh for you. "

Caroline then replied, "I know very well what he is doing Sean, Jessica was telling me Josh believes we would be a perfect match, but like you say, that's Josh. "

As they made their way back to the car, they stopped several times to kiss, when Sean said, "Now knowing you a little better, I am beginning to think Josh may be right Caroline. "

Caroline then said, "You came along just at the right time Sean, I needed someone like you in my life, as I was beginning to think I was jinxed, when it came to finding someone suitable, but I don't want you to think it's just attraction on the rebound. "

"Same here Caroline, " said Sean. "I know it shouldn't be important, but you seem to like old cars, you sail well, and you know farming, so how about, going along with Josh's plot and just see if it works for us?" Now they were both interested in each other, they sat in the car, talking about their likes and dreams, until it was really late on.

"Oh God, look at the time, " said Caroline. "We really need to get back, before they send the search dogs out. " When they got back to Mainear Darach, they parked up and could see the lights were still on.

As they entered the house, they were immediately greeted by Jane, who said, "Oh thank God, you are safe, I was worried that you may have crashed that little car, but now you're both back I can go to bed relieved. " Jane seeing that their relationship seemed somehow a little closer, said with a smile, "Now darling, don't forget to lock up before you come up. "

The next morning, at the cottage, when Jessica woke, she could neither see nor hear Josh. The curiosity forced Jessica to get out of bed and look for him. As she ventured outside, she found Josh in the hot tub.

"Oh, here you are Josh, I wondered where you were."

"Well don't just stand there, Jess, get that dressing gown off and come and join me, it's so nice in here. "

"But what about the time? You know we have to be at Uncle Howard's by nine, "replied Jessica.

"Well, that's OK then Jess. "And looking at his watch, said, "It's just coming up to six and look and the sun's already shining. It's going to be a lovely warm day. Lots of friends around, a few drinks, a couple of races and another day spent with the most beautiful girl in the world. So, come in here and give me a kiss and make this beautiful sunny morning even brighter. "

"Yes OK, " replied Jessica. "But let me get a coffee first. "

"Oh, if you're going in the kitchen, can you bring me another coffee please, oh and could you bring me my mobile phone out with you, it's on charge by the kettle. " Then adding, "Thank you, sweetheart. "

A few minutes later, Jessica had joined Josh in the tub and now with a coffee in his hand Josh said, "You know Jess that was a great day we had yesterday, what with the sailing and with those crazy nights at Mad O' Riley's Bar, this holiday has already surpassed my wildest expectations. " Now holding Jessica's hand, Josh said, "But being with you twenty-four hours a day, has made me realise, how very special you really are to me. Every time I am with you, I look at you and think Joshua; you are one extremely lucky guy. " Then sitting Jessica on his lap, Josh kissed her on her lips and said, "I just wish this holiday could last forever, I really do. Why, just look what's happened over these last few days together Jess, we got engaged, I have found some long-lost relatives, we have been sailing. "

When Jessica, puts her hand over his mouth and said, "And you kissed the Blarney Stone and don't we all just know it. Now, just give me another kiss and let's get ready to go, nine o'clock soon rolls round, and Howard's got a minibus organised. "

When Josh came out of the bathroom, he was slightly taken aback, by the sight of Jessica wearing a very fetching white dress, covered with a large black flower pattern. With the wide black belt and her black stilettos, Josh thought she looked just like some wealthy film star, or royal heiress.

In response said, "You look stunning Jess, now what the hell can I wear to match that. They are all already hanging up, in the wardrobe; I picked them out for you last night, while you were asleep. "

As he closed the door of the cottage, Josh could not help feeling like they were going to another wedding, they both looked so smart. As Josh drove towards Mainear Darach, he kept glancing over in Jessica's direction and thinking, *Doesn't she look good, you lucky little bastard.*

When they arrived, Josh in his normal style, said, "Come on Jess, let's show them what you look like. " And grabbing her hand led her across to the house. When they got inside, they could see that everyone was dressed in their best outfits and after saying their hellos, Josh went over to speak to Sean.

Then Looking at Caroline, Josh, in a quiet voice said, "Tell you what bro, just look at Caroline, she really is some good-looking girl, isn't she?"

And was about to say more when Sean said, "You don't have to do the hard sell Josh, I can see she is. And as you may have noticed, we have been getting on really well.

But I am still just slightly worried that it may be a case of 'love on the rebound'. " Then lightening up a little, said, "But I sincerely hope not, because I am starting to get very attracted to her. "

In a more serious voice and while they were both looking in Caroline's direction Josh said, "Not only is she beautiful, but I know she is a very genuine girl, Sean and I don't think, even for a second it's not serious on her part, so just stick with it bro, I just know Caroline is genuinely interested. " Their conversation stopped when Jessica came back into the room accompanied by Jane and now Jessica was wearing a white large, brimmed hat, with a long black ribbon.

"Doesn't Jessica look really beautiful?" said Jane. "I've had that hat waiting for a special occasion for some time, but I must admit, it would never have looked that good on me. " Then added, "I suppose you realise Josh, that you're a very lucky man. "At that moment, the minibus arrived and after loading the coats and umbrellas, with Howard organising everyone, they all got into the bus. With Jessica sitting near the window and Josh sitting next to her they set off for the races.

Just a short way into the journey, Howard, sitting in front of them, turned and said, "Wasn't that was some night at Mad O' Riley's, you should have stayed Josh, we were there until after one o'clock this morning. "

"Sorry I missed it Howard. " Then laughing said, "But with all the washing, ironing and cleaning, I didn't get to bed till after one-thirty myself. " Then just as anticipated Josh felt Jessica's elbow dig painfully into his ribs.

Howard then went on to say, "You know, you certainly made a good impression on Aiden, he was talking about you and Sean all night. He was almost crying at one point, telling us about your mom, I hope I get to meet her sometime, as she sounds like some special woman. " He then added, "Now you must tell her when she comes over, she must stay with us, tell her I insist. " Now looking further back towards Caroline and Sean, he went on to say, in a much lower voice, "I think your Sean has been doing a power of good for our Caroline, I know that she came over all tough at the ceremony, but believe me it really did hit her hard. And to be perfectly honest, I never liked Richard that much, the poncy little bugger, but please don't tell anyone I said that. But never mind, Richard is history now. "

Being as Jessica did not catch all of Howard's conversation, Josh whispered it all back to her as they continued their journey.

Jessica in reply whispered back, "I know Caroline is really smitten on Sean and I know Aunty Jane likes him too, so please just leave them to it and don't meddle, it's really not needed Josh. " Then Jessica squeezed Josh's hand, to let him know she loved him and to show her affection.

As they drove into the racecourse car park, they could see it was going to be very popular place, as there was a row of coaches and literally hundreds of parked cars, with their windscreens glistening in the bright sunshine. When they got out of the minibus, everyone waited for the group to assemble before Caroline said, "OK now we are all here, just follow me and I will attempt to sort out our tickets out. " After Caroline had spoken to the gate staff, eventually everyone was through the gates and into the racecourse.

As they were walking towards the main area, they stopped for a moment to look at the large electronic information board, when Caroline called to everyone to get their attention, "Now today we have a competition, each person can bet up to fifty eurosand the person who finishes up with the most winnings, will win this 100-euro discount card. " Then smiling said, "Which can be redeemed at a large number of good restaurants. Oh, and to ensure there is no cheating, please keep your betting receipts, because I will need to see them. Dad here, has organised lunch at the Panoramic Restaurant for twelve-thirty. She then added, "Although the food is already paid for, you must pay for your own drinks. " As Caroline mentioned the free lunch everyone cheered, but when she mentioned they had to pay for their own drinks they laughingly booed. Caroline then said, "I have written my telephone number on the back of your admission tickets, so if you get into any trouble, get arrested, run out of money, or run away with some attractive stranger, then please give me a call. " Caroline still laughing then added, "I could really do with hearing some good gossip, so try not to keep it too clean. Now please go off and have a great time. Oh, and take a last look at my dad, while he still has a shirt on his back. "

Everyone gave Caroline a final cheer, before they all gradually dispersed into the crowd.

Josh, Sean, Caroline, and Jessica had agreed to stick together and as they made their way to the parade ring, Josh stopped as he thought someone was calling his name. He turned to see where the voices were coming from when he spotted Aiden, his wife, his sister, and her husband waving to get his attention. When Aiden finally caught up with them, still panting for breath, he said, "Thank goodness I found you, I saw Howard just now talking to one of the trainers, down by the stables and he said you were over this way. Anyway. "Aiden said, now breathing normally. "Well, I am pleased to say, this is my very tolerant and long-suffering wife, Jodie, this is Lizzie who you have already met, and this is her diamond of a husband Jackie, or Jackie Boy as he is more affectionately known. " After completing what seemed like an endless session of introductions and handshakes, the party finally moved off together heading towards the parade ring. From there the group moved to the bookmaker's ring and as they were studying the race card, Josh caught sight of Padraig and Patrick, along with their sons and daughters, his new cousins. Then, after another jovial session of introductions and even more shaking of hands, the party finally parted again as they all wanted to place their bets before the first race. As weather was good and as Sean had never met his newly found uncles and cousins, there was a great deal of catching up to do.

Josh, was now closely studying the horses being led round the parade ring, when Josh excitedly said, "That's the one, just look at the racing lines on his hind quarters, that's a very good sign of fitness and the angle of her scapular, well that's a perfect angle for a race horse, don't you think Caroline, as you must recognise good conformity in a horse when you see it. And not only that, she even looks fit and raring to go. " Josh then announced, "Well I tell you, that's where my money will be going, number eight 'Quantum Leap'. Yep, she's definitely the winner all right, so I think it's got to be twenty-five euroto win. " Josh then added looking very confident, "You certainly don't need to bet each way on a thoroughbred horse that looks as good as that, you just wait and see. "

As they watched the race, Jessica couldn't stop laughing when Quantum Leap came in trailing the field. "It must have been that perfect angle of scapular, " said Jessica sarcastically, "Or maybe those racing lines you saw, were just old stretch marks, eh Josh?"

"I tell you Jess, there's nothing wrong with that horse, it was that bloody useless jockey, constantly pulling her up. "Josh then added, "I bet that jockey or the horse owner had some money on the winner, believe me, it goes on a lot you know. " On the downside, by lunchtime Josh's fifty Euros had completely disappeared. However, much to Jessica's amusement, it didn't stop Josh trying to advise her on what horses to back. Unbeknown to Caroline, Howard and Aiden had managed to get most of the extended family booked into the Panoramic Restaurant for what turned out to be a very noisy and drawn-out lunch.

Later, as they all sat at their very long dining table, watching everyone drinking, eating, chatting and smiling, Josh said to Jessica, "Now this is what horse racing is really all about, having a good time with some very special friends, it's not about winning loads of money, it's about atmosphere, I just feel so very happy being here today."

Later in the afternoon, Josh managed to get Sean away on his own for a minute, while the ladies went off to powder their noses. As they leant over the railings looking out over the race course, Josh, putting his arm round Sean's shoulder said, "I bet you are really going to miss Caroline, when you go home tomorrow afternoon, eh Sean?"

"No not in the least, no I won't miss her at all," replied Sean, looking a little unmoved.

Josh, now looking extremely shocked at his unexpected response, asked, "Why ever not, I thought you two were hitting it off really well?"

Sean now starting to smile at Josh's shocked reaction, said, "It's because Caroline is coming back home with me, Mom has invited her back to stay with us for a few days."

Now looking a little more relieved, but still curious, Josh said, "So when was all that arranged then?"

To which Sean said, smiling, now almost laughing, "Since I spoke to Mom about ten minutes ago. Caroline is staying with us at home for a day or two and then she is driving mom back over here with her in the MG. Mom's staying with Howard and Jane; and Caroline is going to drive her round to meet up with her brothers and to visit her mom and dad's graves. " Sean then added, "I'm pretty sure it was speaking to Lizzie last night that help change Mom's mind. I know this might seem a little soppy Josh, but I have missed your company, since you left home, but thankfully I think I may have found someone to make life that little more complete. I think you probably know, but Caroline and I were fully aware of your little matchmaking scheme from the very start. But do you know Josh, both of us playing along with your scheming; well, it may have actually helped bring Caroline and I closer. " Sean, now giving Josh's shoulders a squeeze said, "Anyway Josh everything seems to be going very well between us and I'm sure most of it was down to you and that old Sentinel steam lorry. Now, come on, let's go back to the bar for one last drink before the bus arrives, as I think the girls will already be there waiting for us and holding our drinks I hope. "

After lots of hugging and many long goodbyes, the party finally got back into the minibus and were still waving to their friends, as the bus finally pulled away. On the way home amid all the laughing and chattering Caroline managed to get everyone's attention.

She then announced in a very loud voice, "I have finally worked out who has won our betting competition and so it is with a great of pleasure and may I add, with even greater surprise, I can confirm that the winner of the competition is my lovely Aunty Mary. "

Caroline, now trying to be heard over the cheering and friendly booing, then managed to shout out that Mary had won with a grand total of 527 Euros.

Mary in response was now waving her arm in the air holding a fist full of cash and in a slightly slurred voice, said, "Tomorrow night, for those who turn up in Mad O' Riley's bar, at least one round of drinks will be on me. " Mary was then completely drowned out by the loud hooping, laughing, and cheering.

Caroline then shouting over the noise, added, "And the 'Bookies Prize', our equivalent to the wooden spoon, goes to our good and very popular friend Joshua Foster, who breaking all previous records, managed to lose his whole fifty Euros by the end of the second race. " Now the whole bus was cheering as a very big wooden spoon, was passed from person to person until Gerry finally handed it over to Josh.

Jessica then said laughing, "If we ever come here again Josh, I think you need to team up with my mom, who as a non-rider and who knows absolutely nothing about the conformation of horses, does seem to know what's worth backing. " Josh, for once in his life was lost for words and in response, just smiled back, holding up and waving his big wooden spoon.

By the time the bus turned in to Mainear Darach, the noise had significantly died down and everyone was now eager to get into the house. As usual everyone gravitated to the kitchen and they all sat round the big kitchen table drinking black coffee. As everyone else was staying over and were not driving, Jessica had purposely limited her drinking, in order to safely drive Josh and herself back to the cottage.

It was a later in the evening when Caroline came downstairs carrying her suitcase, when a surprised Jane asked, "Oh darling, where on earth are you off to?"

"Well, Mom, " replied Caroline. "I'm going back with Sean. Sean's mother has invited me over to stay for a few days. Oh, and if all goes to plan, Sean's mom will be travelling back with me, while Sean drives the lorry over."

"Well, that's lovely darling, but you just be careful, as I've seen you driving that little car. Now are you sure you have everything you need?" And then smiling, Jane said, "I know you will take good care of her Sean, but please be careful and when you get back here, I will have the rooms all ready for you. "

A few minutes later the group walked across the courtyard to where Sean's car was parked and after a few hugs, the couple waved goodbyes and Caroline drove away. That's when Jane gripping Howard's hand said, "Oh I do hope Caroline drives carefully, she worries me at times. "

After dinner that evening, as they sat and watching TV, Josh could not help but notice Jane was almost sitting on Howard's lap, holding his hand and smiling up at him.

Howard now looking very relaxed, said, "Well, your Sean has only been gone an hour and do you know Josh I am already missing him. "

Then Jane added, "Sean's is such a lovely man and I think I'm missing him too. " And then after some thought added, "Oh and sadly when all you lovely people go home, life here at Mainear Darach, is going to be so very, very quiet. You know Howard, I think we should book ourselves on a cruise, we have not been on one for some years and I think a good cruise would do us both a power of good. " Then in a flash of inspiration, Jane said, "Come to think of it why don't we all go on a cruise, it would be such good fun. Just leave it with me, I'll get some catalogues and we can see what's going where and on what dates. " Then smiling at Howard said, "Yes it would be like a second honeymoon hey darling, yes, so let's go ahead and do it. "

After eating supper and talking about their memorable day at the races, Josh's wooden spoon was given pride of place, hung above the aga on the kitchen wall.

Before they left for the cottage, Jessica went to give Jane her beautiful hat back and was delighted when Jane said, "No Jessica, it's for you, because if I could look only half as good in it as you did, believe me I would keep it. But seeing you in it today darling and looking like you did, I realised, that hat must have been made especially for you. Oh, and I nearly forgot, if I bring my swim suit round, do you think I could try your hot tub?"

Quick to reply Josh said, "Jane you can use it whenever you like and don't worry about any swim suit. "And with a cheeky laugh Josh said, "Don't worry, we can all keep our eyes closed, well that is, Jessica can. "

After saying good night, to everyone Josh serenaded Jessica back to the car singing the *Kemptown Ladies* sings this song, do da, do da and when he finally climbed into the car Josh said, "Well Jess, that was another—"But before he could finish Jessica said, "Don't tell me that will flash before your eyes when you die. Well, " said Jessica, now starting up the car. "All I can say is that this dying experience of yours is going to be one hell of a long one. " Then still laughing as they pulled away, said, "I reckon so far, it should take at least two weeks. "

On the way back Josh said, "Christ Jess, what's on earth happened to Jane, she seemed to be in a really good mood? Oh, and that remind me, I must pat her on the arse before we go home. It just wouldn't be fair to smack one sister, without smacking the other, now would it?"

"Don't you even think about it Joshua Foster, " Jessica said. "Aunty is not like that. But I must agree with you, Aunty Jane seemed to be in a very good mood today, a bit more like her old self. But thinking about it, she seemed different last night as well, although I don't know what happened, but I am so pleased she's feeling happy again. "

Now safely back at the cottage and while Jessica was in the bedroom, Josh walked into join her opening another package.

"Now what's been delivered?" asked Jessica, getting ready to spend some quality time in the hot tub.

"Well, if you must know, it's some top-quality cotton rope Jess, just another little surprise for later on tonight, "replied Josh, now placing the package on the bedside table.

"What on earth do we need pink rope for?" asked Jessica. Then suddenly stopping mid-sentence and in a slightly concerned voice said, "Oh no, is that what I think it's for?"

"Well, there you go Jess, " said Josh. "Trying to spoil my little surprises again. Well, you will just have to wait and see, won't you sweetheart. " Then as earlier Josh suggested that they both made their way to their beckoning and very inviting hot tub.

After a while, Josh climbed out of the hot tub, leaving Jessica to relax, fully stretched and floating in that lovely hot water. Just as she was starting to totally relax, Josh reappeared holding a towel out, saying, "OK Jessica, I'm all ready now. "

"Ready for what?" asked Jessica.

"Jess will you please stop trying to spoil the surprise, with your prying questions. " As Jessica climbed out of the hot tub, Josh wrapped her in a big towel and after drying her, led her into the bedroom. Josh then jokingly said, "I've read the little booklet that came with the rope and after some practice I believe I sufficiently competent in tying most of the more specialised knots. The only thing is I don't seem to be able to undo them again. " Then laughing said, "But I am sure I will pick it up as we go along. " Now with Jessica laying naked on the bed and Josh, placing the small booklet that came with the rope, beside her, read a part of it out and while still smiling said, "First I have some

237

very important safety questions to ask you Jess. Do you or have you ever suffered with poor circulation, have you ever suffered from any form of thrombosis, or—"

And at that point Jessica was up, off the bed and was trying to get take the booklet from out of his hand, and said, "I think, by the sound of it, I should be giving this little surprise some very serious thought!" However, after Josh had turned out the lights, lit the scented candles and put on some relaxing music, Jessica started to get back in the mood again, albeit a little apprehensive at the sight of Josh coming towards her holding some lengths of brightly coloured pink cotton rope.

Josh now ready to tie Jessica up, said, "Jess, seriously, if this starts to freak you out sweetheart, please just let me know. " Then using several lengths of very soft cotton pink rope, he tied her left ankle to her left wrist and then did the same to her right ankle and wrist. Josh then passed a rope under the bed and tied one end around Jessica's left knee and after taking out the slack, secured the other end round her right knee.

Then after fumbling in his rucksack, came out holding a vibration wand and after plugging it into the wall socket, turned it on to a gentle hum, to test it was working, said, "Right Jess, now from here on I am aim to get you as horny as I possibly can and then after that I am going to fuck you while you are too helpless to resist my animal desires. " Josh then after blindfolding her, said, "Apparently, the feeling of helplessness will be a really big turn-on for you and is an important step in helping us to build up trust, or at least that's what states in the booklet. "

Josh then very softly began massaging Jessica's clitoris with the vibration wand and it was not long before he could see Jessica starting to respond. Josh could see her nipples becoming erect and her hands starting to clench tightly. After just a couple of minutes, he could see that Jessica was pulling away, indicating that she had had enough of the wand and switching it off, placed it to one side. After covering his fingers with the lubricant, Josh slid his fingers down along the full length of her labia and back to her clitoris, which he repeated gradually increasing the pressure, while at the same time increasing the speed of his hand movements. It was not long before he could feel Jessica pushing her herself onto Josh's fingers every time he reached the opening of her now sensitive vagina. Josh with his other hand now started massaging Jessica's breasts and gently squeezed her nipples. Seeing Jessica's face altering slightly with each movement of his hands and watching her body writhing in direct response to his sexual actions, was also having an erotic effect on Josh. Josh now started to push his fingers deeper into Jessica's very wet vagina and at the same time, began to gently bite on each of Jessica nipples.

It was at this critical point that Jessica's mobile phone began to ring; it was Caroline telling her they were now off the ferry and on their way to Sean's house.

Feeling slightly jangled, Josh said, "Oh that's good news, but I'm very sorry Caroline, but Jessica's a little bit

tied up at the moment, can I get her to call you back later?"
And then he immediately rung off. After a very long finger
massaging session, Josh once again switched on the
vibration wand and very precisely applied it to the tip of
Jessica's clitoris. The effect was almost spontaneous, as
her body went Into immediate tension and she started
quietly sighing. Pleased with the effect, Josh started to
apply a little more pressure and to move the wand in a
slight gyratory movement. He could see Jessica having a
strong orgasm and started to suck and gently bite her
nipple. Jessica's writhing body movements were now so
pronounced that Josh was finding it difficult to follow her
body movements, with the now very slippery vibrating
wand. Josh was now aware that his own heart rate had
increased considerably and that his erection was growing
so hard, it was almost painful, yet in a very pleasurable
way. Aware that his erroneous actions were taking
Jessica's pleasures to a peak, he spun her around until her
head was draped down over the side of the bed. Then
positioning himself over Jessica's face he let his penis
gently touch her cheek. Immediately Jessica turned her
head and took Josh's penis into her mouth and worked her
head as if to replicate intercourse. While Jessica was
enjoying stimulating Josh, he was busy with outstretched
arms massaging her beautifully aroused vagina. Now
feeling the need to lick Jessica's vagina, he spun Jessica
around again and climbing onto the bed started to lick and
suck Jessica's trembling vagina, while at the same time
pushing several fingers deep inside her. Climbing back off

the bed Josh undid the pink ropes and removed the blindfold.

Jessica now stretched her body and with a smile said, "Mmm, now that was a nice surprise, wow that was really sexy. " As Josh was now on the bed and about to fuck her, Jessica said, "No Josh, I want you to cum, while I am sucking, and I want it in my mouth. " Then after just a few more seconds, Josh reached his climax and ejaculated into Jessica's mouth. In order to maximise Josh's orgasm, Jessica then sucked as hard as she possibly could and then, while smiling cheekily, swallowed his cum. After resting for a minute or so, Jessica carefully inspected her ankles and wrists and after finding no visible marks said, "Oh, that's a relief, no marks, good then we can do that again, can't we? And for being very gentle and considerate, tomorrow night I think I am going to blow your mind. Now I had better call Caroline, I am just dying to know how they are doing. " As Josh went to pour them a couple of drinks, he could hear Jessica's conversations and overhearing most of it, was brought somewhat up to date with events.

Josh then climbed back into bed and was passing Jessica her drink, when she said, "Sometimes I wonder just what's going on in that mind of yours Joshua Foster, you really are something else. " Then giving him a big kiss, said, "But you know, I just wouldn't want you any other way, but how on earth did you know about cotton rope, have you been tying girls up before?"

241

"Oh yes of course, " said Josh starting to laugh. "We use them all the time in the office, the girls much prefer cotton rope than the ordinary rope, you see it's all about health and safety in the work place and reducing any risks to the workforce" and then he immediately got ready for his usual dig in the ribs.

The next morning Jessica and Josh had a late morning lie in, then, although it was raining outside, both of them slid into the hot tub for a nice long relax, before breakfast.

As the lay there, Jessica said, "It feels very strange, lying in here, all nice and warm with the cold rain running down my face. "And then she asked, "So what shall we do today then Josh?"

Josh, still busy massaging Jessica's shoulders said, "It's all sorted sweetheart, your Aunty Jane's coming about ten o'clock, to try out the tub, then we have dance lessons at four-thirty in Galway and after that we are meeting up with Uncle Padraig, Uncle Patrick and hopefully some of their family, later in Mad O' Riley's bar. Oh, and Howard, Gerry, Jane and your mom are joining us there. "

"You what?" said Jessica, now all of a sudden sounding very flustered. "What did you say? Aunty Jane is coming here at ten? Oh, why the fuck didn't you tell me sooner?" Now looking at her watch, she said, "It's ten past fucking nine now, oh fucking hell Josh. " And at that Jessica leapt out of the tub and ran into the cottage, leaving a trail of steaming water behind her. "So what's the problem, " shouted Josh. "She's just coming to try out the hot tub and we were already here in it. Oh, " then Josh

242

added, as he suddenly remembered. "And your Uncle Howard said he might come too. "

Then from the bedroom Jessica shouted, all in a panic, "Fucking hell, Josh, there are pink fucking ropes, vibrators and massage oils, all over the fucking place, there's a fucking massage table in the fucking hallway and you say what's the fucking problem? Oh, come on Josh, get real, now come in here and help me now, this very minute. And another thing, I don't even know where my bloody bikini top is, or even if I have bought it with me. Joshua Foster, please get out of there this minute and give me a hand, for fuck's sake. Aghh, why didn't you tell me earlier, if you ever do this to me again, I swear I will strangle you with your own fucking pink cotton rope. " Josh, then appears at the bedroom door, still nonchalantly drying himself, when Jessica screams, "And for fuck's sake, put your bloody swimming shorts on. "

Now frantically tidying things away, she said "Oh Josh, why the fuck didn't you tell me earlier? Oh God, I just hope they are running late. Now for fuck's sake, put that bloody massage table in the airing cupboard and have good check round please. " A short while later, panic over, they were both in their dressing gowns, wearing swimwear and everything likely to cause embarrassment had been hurriedly tidied away.

"Right, " said Jessica carrying an arm full of towels. "Right you can get back in the tub if you have too. Honestly Josh, I sometimes wonder where your fucking brain is, you just don't think and next time you make arrangements like that, tell me. "

At exactly ten, Jane and Howard arrived. "Not a bad little place you have here, " said Howard, now looking around and nodding agreeably. "

Would you like a hot drink or maybe something to eat, we are only just thinking about breakfast, we had a late lie in this morning, " said Jessica, only now feeling suitably relaxed again.

"No thank you darling, " said Jane. "But I really would like to take a proper look at your hot tub. " Jane then added, "You know I am really looking forward to trying it out. " Then she and Jessica both went outside to have a closer look at it. While they were outside, Howard and Josh sat on the settee talking, while Josh was recapping on yesterday's events, Howard, with puzzled look on his face, after putting his hand down the side of a cushion, pulled out a long length of pink cotton rope.

Now Howard, with a slight smile appearing across his face, said, "Well, well, what have we here then, is this yours then Josh?"

"Oh yes, " replied Josh. And now looking just a little embarrassed, said, "Oh yes that, well, I was just practising my knots after that wonderful sailing day we had, well it re-awakened my interest in sailing again. " Then taking it off Howard and putting in the coffee table draw, Josh added, "I was getting a bit rusty with my knots, especially that difficult sheep shank and I'm a little bit out of practice I'm afraid. So, I was just trying to catch up on them, it's a tricky old knot that sheep shank, but I think it's gradually coming back to me now. "

"Oh, I see, " replied Howard. "But it must be difficult using soft cotton rope eh, Josh? You know, that's a pretty unique type of rope you've been using there. "

When Jane and Jessica returned to the lounge, Jane asked, "So what have you two been talking about then?"

"Well, " replied Howard, with a slight smile. "Josh tells me he has been practising his knot tying skills, darling. "

"Oh, that's good. " said Jane. "It's been a long time since I did my RYA exam. And do you know, I think I may have forgotten them all by now, so maybe I'll have to practice with you Josh, I think I might really need it?" On hearing this Howard, sneakily put his hand over his mouth, in order to hide a now very wide smile.

Jessica, not really sure what had been going on, said, "Come through into the bedroom, Aunty, you can change in here. "

While they were both in the bedroom Howard said, "Jane tells me that Sean had a serious talk with her the other day. Although she wouldn't tell me exactly what was said, I can tell you Josh, I am very pleased to say, Jane has been a totally different person since. I don't know how Sean did it Josh, or what was said, but it bloody well worked. You know, he's something special , that brother of yours. "

Looking somewhat puzzled Josh replied, "Yes Howard, so everyone keeps telling me. "

After taking what seemed a long time to get changed, eventually Jane came back into the lounge, wearing a very low-cut white swimsuit and giving a twirl, said, "Well what do you think of it? I have had this in one of my wardrobes for ages, but this is the first time I have actually worn it. "

Josh immediately responded, "Well Jane, if I wasn't already spoken for, I think I might have been chasing you round that old hot tub, especially with you looking like that. You've certainly still got what it takes Jane, hasn't she Howard?" Jane then smiling at Josh said, "Don't tell me, but I think that might be that old Blarney Stone talking again, Josh. "

A little later, while all four of them were happily soaking in the tub, discussing everything and nothing, Jessica said, "Josh tells me he's booked us both in for some dancing lessons this afternoon. Somewhere in Galway and that we will all be meeting up later tonight in Mad O' Riley's Bar?"

Jane now looking at Howard and smiling, said, "We used to love dancing, didn't we Howard?"

"Well then, why don't you come with us and perhaps we could grab a meal somewhere before we go back to Aiden's bar?" said Josh now reaching for his phone, as if poised to immediately call the dance studio.

"Oh yes please come with us Aunty, " said Jessica. "I was a little worried about not knowing anyone there, so I would really love it if you and Uncle came along with us.

I wonder if Mom and Dad want to join us, I will give a call and find out. "

"OK, " said Howard. "You give the studio a ring Josh and I will sort out the restaurant booking. "

Jane went on to say, "Caroline called me this morning, Jessica, and she tells me she is really enjoying herself. Apparently Sean has booked some hotel in the Peak District, somewhere by a river. "

"That will be 'Dove Dale' Jane, " said Josh. "It's an absolutely gorgeous hotel, one that our whole family enjoys staying at and it's such a beautiful part of the Peak District. Believe me Jane, Caroline will absolutely love it there. "

"Yes, " replied Jane, "Dove Dale, yes that's the place and she tells me that they went riding together earlier this morning, so it sounds like she really is enjoying herself. And there I was, so very upset when the wedding went badly wrong, but do you know, I now actually think it may have been for the best. "

Josh then added, "I also spoke to Sean this morning and he tells me that Mom has really taken a shine to your Caroline and Dad already thinks the sun shines out of her—"Then pausing mid-sentence continued, "Yes Dad really likes her too. "

Jessica, who had just popped into the kitchen to phone her mom about the dancing, came back into the room looking very pleased and said, "Yes Mom and Dad are coming with us as well, they said they will go straight there and will meet at the dance studio. "

"Oh, that's wonderful news darling, " said Jane. "You know Mary used to be a very good dancer when she was younger and I bet you any money, that she still has it. "

Josh then said, "I was just about to tell Jane that I am pretty sure Sean will take Caroline out to visit some lovely parts of the Peak District, it's such a beautiful place and not very far from home. " Then looking at Jane, Josh said, "Well at least you can be certain that Sean will take good care of her and I can assure you that she is in very safe hands, Sean is 100% pure gentleman. "

To which Jane added, "Believe me Josh, I have no worries at all about Caroline being with Sean, why Sean has been like a gift from heaven and may I say, a gift that arrived at exactly the right time. " Jane then gave Howard's hand a squeeze and said with an exited voice, "Dancing together eh Howard, I am really looking forward to dancing again. " And looking at Howard, Jane said, "Oh and you had better decide where we are putting our hot tub, because I now know that I could spend real quality time in one of these. "

"Take it from me, " said Josh. "It's even better when you're naked, isn't it Jess?"

Jessica, was unusually lost for words and was blushing so profusely, that everyone started to laugh. That's when Jane added, "Exactly right Josh, just what I was thinking and with all those swirling jets of hot water, it must feel far better when you are in there as God intended. "

At three o'clock, they pulled into the dance studio car park, they were pleased to see that Mary and Gerry were already parked there and waving to them.

As they all met up and walked together heading for the dance studio, Howard said, "I think this is going to be very challenging for whoever is going to teach us, well more especially with regards to me, as I can't dance for toffee. "

As they neared the door, Gerry said, "It looks a little like our olds scout hut from when I was a kid, I'm fully expecting to see our old scout leader Mr Adams walk out at any moment. " Walking into the dance studio, they were immediately greeted by a tall middle-aged lady, who said, "Now you must all call me Gwen, the person who phoned, said you wanted to refresh yourselves on the waltz and quickstep, is that correct?"

"Well, yes, that's right, " said Josh. "It was me who you spoke to, my name is Josh, this is my fiancée Jessica, this is her mother Mary and her father Gerry—"

But before he had finished Jane said, "And I am Jane and this will be your main challenge, this my non dancing husband, Howard. " After a short practice session, during which Gwen had established who could already dance, who may be promising and who needed special attention. In order to concentrate her attention on the more needy, Gwen put Mary and Josh together, she then put Jane with Gerry and poor Jessica was put with her Uncle Howard.

Within minutes, Mary and Josh were away, dancing like two professionals, Jane and Gerry were picking it up very quickly, with Gerry repeatedly saying, "Yes it's all coming back to me now. " And Gwen obviously not one to be beaten, within thirty minutes even had Howard waltzing round almost, but not completely in time with the music. After a while Gwen changed them all back to their respective partners and good fun was had by all.

Everyone was really enjoying it all, when the music stopped and Gwen in a loud said, "I am pleased to say, you have all danced extremely well, but unfortunately your two-hour session has sadly come to an end. "

Howard, now wanting to carry on dancing, said, "Can we not pay for another session Gwen and maybe just carry on?"

"No I'm afraid not Howard, " replied Gwen. "You see, I have another group coming here in fifteen minutes time, but I am really pleased that you are wanting more and if you do really want to come again, please give me a call and I will gladly book you in for another session. "

Everyone then thanked Gwen for her well-appreciated coaching skills and Howard said, "Unfortunately the others are not local Gwen, but I can assure you that Jane and I will definitely be back again. "

As they walked out of the dance studio and into the car park, Howard said, "Do you know, I really enjoyed that, wasn't Gwen great? Well done for thinking of that Josh, because I would never have been here, enjoying all this, if you hadn't of suggested it, that was really good fun. " As Howard was the only one who knew where the restaurant was, they all followed Howard's car.

While Jessica and Josh were following, Jessica asked Josh, "What did Howard mean about practising knots?"

And almost laughing. Josh told her how Howard had found the pink rope, tucked down the side of the settee and how he had told him he had been practicing his sailing knots.

"But, " Josh said smiling. "I am pretty sure he had a bloody good idea what we had been up to though? But do you know, the funny thing is, Jess he knew immediately that it was cotton rope. You tell me, how the hell would Howard know that? Apparently, it's a pretty specialised rope that soft cotton rope. "

Jessica in response said, "I wish I had never asked you now. Oh, bloody hell, I don't think I will ever be able to look Uncle Howard in the eye again. " But thankfully, Jessica had soon forgotten about Howard's comments, as soon as they were all sitting in the restaurant together, enjoying each other's company, eating good food and enjoying the moment.

During the meal Josh told them about Amos and his late wife's dancing careers and repeated what Amos had once said, "That 'Jessica had the best arse he had ever seen and how he had told Josh to keep hold of that girl, as arses like that only come along once in a lifetime. '"

And then, while patting Jessica on the shoulder, added, "And do you know, old Amos was absolutely spot on. " That's when Josh suffered another hard elbow to his ribs.

Towards the end of the meal Josh went very quiet, to the point where Jessica whispered in his ear, "Are you all right Josh? As you have been unusually quiet. "

"Oh, yes Jess, I'm fine I was just trying to think of another Irish joke for tonight. Poor old Aiden will be expecting a good one from me. "

Then, after a second or two, suddenly back smiling once more said, "It's no longer a problem now Jess, because I have just remembered one. " He then chuckled to himself and said, "And thankfully it's a very good one. "

While Howard, Gerry and Josh rushed off to pay the bill, Jane leaned over to Jessica and said, "I think you must know that you've struck pure gold, with Joshua, isn't he a real joy to be with and such good fun, I just hope our Caroline and Sean hit it off?"

"Oh, I am pretty sure they will, " said Jessica with a knowing look. "In fact I would put money on it, Aunty. " Everyone had enjoyed the dancing, had eaten well and were now looking forward to another night in Mad O' Riley's Bar.

On arrival at Mad O' Riley's Bar, it would appear that the whole O' Brien and Gallagher clans had taken over the place. As soon as Josh and Jessica were spotted, it was yet another round of introductions and enthusiastic hand shaking. After managing to eventually get their drinks, Josh and Jessica mingled and chatted happily with everyone they met.

While Josh was talking to Howard, he said, "Howard you might find this a bit of a strange request. "And went on to explain how he had, without thinking one night had patted Mary's backside as they were leaving the theatre and how it had turned into a bit of a joke. Josh went on to explain how he had told Jessica, that it wouldn't be fair to pat one sister's backside without patting the other sister's backside as well. He explained how Jessica had warned him that she would kill him if ever he did. "So, " said Josh. "I would really like to wind Jess up, by patting Jane's backside, that is if it's all right with Jane. "

Howard immediately replied laughing, "I will ask her Josh, but I am absolutely sure that she will willingly agree. " And now starting to laugh even more, Howard said, "And if she isn't willing Josh, well you can just tie her up and do it can't you. And I will tell you now Josh, if ever you do, I know for a fact, Jane would definitely go for that. "

As short while later, and as predicted, Aiden approach Josh and said, "Josh my boy, I hope you have another little story for us tonight, because even the non-regulars are asking for them now?"

"Well, " said Josh "It's funny you should ask, but I am sorry to say that this one has very little content relating to Guinness. "

"Good man, I knew you would have one, " said Aiden. "Now I'll just get their attention. " Then ringing the bell and when the chatter had died down sufficiently, Aiden said, "If I can just have your attention for a moment please, Josh informs me he has another little story for us tonight.

" Then over a few noisy cheers and whistles, Aiden then went on to say, "If you want to get another drink before Josh starts, please get it now, as we won't be serving while Josh tells his story. "

Later, after ringing the bell for a second time, Aiden again addresses his customers saying, "Please give a big hand for our very welcomed visitor, Joshua Foster. Who I might add is fifty percent Irish and I am very pleased to say, is also one of my relatives. "

After a short round of applause, Josh, standing at the bar turned to face the crowd and said in a very loud voice, "Now this is quite a long story, so please make yourself comfortable and then I will begin. "

Josh then went on to tell the story of three middle-aged bachelors, an Englishman, a Scotsman and a Kerryman, who living in England, all met up every Thursday night in their local pub to partake in a few pints of Guinness'. Josh went on to tell how every year the three of them went on holiday together, and tonight it was Paddy's turn to decide where they were going for this approaching holiday.

"'Come on Paddy, ' asked Tommy. 'So where are we going this year for our holiday, it's your turn to decide. '

"'Well, ' said Paddy, with a slight hint of hesitation. 'I'm not sure whether you will agree or not with my suggestion. But I have always wanted to visit the Vatican, in Rome. But being as you are not all of the Catholic faith, I didn't know whether you would be interested or not. ' But to Paddy's relief, they both thought that was a really good idea.

"Jock the Scotsman said, 'My barber is Italian and he is always telling me what a wonderful country Italy is, so, yes, I would really like to visit Italy. '

"Then Tommy said, 'Rome that's a really good choice Paddy, the Vatican is in the city and I have always wanted to see the Colosseum, what a good suggestion. ' Now they are all-in agreement, later that month, they go ahead and book their Rome holiday.

"A couple of months later, after arriving in Rome, they tour the city, they eat in the best restaurants, they have a great day at the Colosseum and on Friday, the last full day of their holiday they take a guided tour around the Vatican. Everything is going well, when the three of them lose touch with their tour guide and with the rest of the group. Not really sure where they are, they find themselves walking through the pope's private apartments. They spent some little time looking at the paintings, wonderful ornaments and beautiful furniture, when they stumble across the pope, who is stone dead, lying face down on the floor.

"Quick as a flash, Tommy says, 'Come on lads, let's get out of here now, this is serious and it's best not to get involved. ' As they are hurrying back the way came in, they are stopped by several Vatican guards and as none of the guards could speak any English, they were held there until a senior cardinal finally arrived. The three men all explained that the pope's sad demise was not of their doing and that the pope was already dead on the floor when they found him. And to their relief, the cardinal said, 'I know. ' The cardinal then told them, 'You would never normally have found your way in there, only the guards, who would generally bar any unauthorised access, had left their posts to inform me of this tragedy. '

"'Thank the lord, ' said Paddy. 'So that means we are free to go then. '

"'Well, no, ' said the cardinal explaining that if news of the pope dying leaks out, before proper plans were in place, it could cause chaos throughout the Christian world and so until all the necessary arrangements were fully in place and they were then able release the news, the three of them will have to remain secured in the Vatican as their guests.

"As they are walking along the corridor that led out, Tommy explains to the cardinal that they were just three ordinary working men and if they failed to return to work on the following Monday, they will all probably be sacked and would finish up destitute. Reluctantly, the cardinal, after getting them all to swear an oath on the bible, swearing that they would not tell anyone of the pope's sad demise, until it was officially announced; he reluctantly allows them to leave.

"On the following Thursday, Jock, the Scotsman turns up at the pub as usual to find Tommy the Englishman behind the bar. 'What you doing behind there?' enquired Jock.

"'Well,' explained Tommy. 'I contacted Bet 365 and asked them what odds I could get on the pope dying before the end of the month. I then borrowed money on all of my credit cards, I remortgaged the house, emptied my bank account and gambled it all on the pope dying in the next two weeks.' And with a big smile Tommy said, 'I am pleased to tell you I am now a multimillionaire.' Seeing a new Bentley on the car park Tommy asks Jock, 'I wonder whose Bentley that is.'

"'Well as a matter-of-fact its mine Tommy,' replies Jock. 'Just like you, I borrowed money on my credit cards, remortgaged the house, emptied my savings and gambled it all with William Hill and just like you Tommy; I'm now a multimillionaire.' They were both celebrating with their glasses of Guinness, when Paddy walks in. Paddy immediately asks why Tommy is behind the bar and Tommy then explains his big win. Paddy then asks who owns the Bentley parked outside and Jock then explains his big win.

"Paddy then says, 'Well would you believe it, we all thought the very same thing, I borrowed money on my credit cards, I remortgaged the house, emptied my savings and gambled it all with Quinn Bet on the pope.'

"Tommy now handing Paddy a free pint of Guinness, said, 'So how much did you win then Paddy?'

"Who replied with a smile, 'Fuck all, Tommy. I had a double with the archbishop of Canterbury.'"

At this the bar erupted in laughter and when Aiden leaned over towards Josh, he said, "Josh, that's the best one yet, my boy. A double with the archbishop of Canterbury, oh my God, " laughed Aiden. "Well would you believe it. " Aiden still laughing said to Josh, "Please don't ever leave us Josh, because I have not heard this much laughter in this bar, since Patty Collin's knickers fell down, while she was singing *Molly Malone.* " And when returning to serve his customer, Aiden could still be heard muttering, "A double with the archbishop of Canterbury, well bless my soul, ha, ha, ha. "

When they got back to the cottage that night Josh was busy in the kitchen preparing tea, while Jessica was busy in the bedroom. When Josh called Jessica into the kitchen for tea, she came in looking just a little bit mischievous.

As she sat the table, Josh asked, "What have you been doing out there, Jess?"

"Oh, just getting ready for later, or had you forgot, it's my turn to tie some knots tonight?" said Jessica smiling.

"I suppose you've been reading that little booklet that came with the rope, haven't you?" asked Josh. "No, I don't need any rubbish booklet, " replied Jessica now smiling broadly. "I know my sheep shank from my running bowline. Don't forget Josh, " Jessica continued. "I completed my yacht master's and do you know what Josh, I'm really looking forward to using every one of those knots tonight. "

Josh now smiling, but looking slightly worried, said, "Err don't forget Jess, it's not meant to be any form of torture, it's for heightened sexual pleasure. "Now pausing to swallow his food, he then added, "And if you remember,

258

I was extremely gentle with you and all my knots were loose, so you could just slip out if you needed too. "

"That's right, " said Jessica smiling smugly. "And as hard as that may be, I will try and remember that Josh. But you know what I'm like when I get going, I can just get carried away. " As Josh was clearing up, he could hear Jessica moving things around in the bedroom and with his curiosity getting the better of him, looked in to see Jessica tying a length of pink rope to each of the massage table legs.

Now walking in to take a closer look, Josh asked, "am I getting a massage as well then Jess?"

Still busy arranging the ropes, Jessica replied, "Well yes, well sort of Josh, it's a special surprise really and you know how you hate me giving them away? Spoils the whole thing, that's what you always tell me. So you will just have to wait and see, won't you Josh? Now I am going to take a shower and when I come out of the bathroom, then you can take yours. "

A little later, when Josh had finished his shower, he went into the bedroom and could see that the candles were all lit and there was soft mood music was playing.

Jessica, wearing her dressing gown, pointing to the massage table said in a firm voice, "Right Josh, up you go, on the table and faceup on your back please, with your head this end. As he lay there naked, Jessica took a wrist and bound it using the already waiting rope. After doing the same with Josh's other wrist, Jessica moved on to secure his ankles. Josh now tied out in a cross position,

259

was wondering should he feel pleased with the situation, or should he be worried, unsure he was beginning to wonder what exactly would be happening next. Jessica then took off her dressing gown revealing the skimpy black lingerie that Josh had bought her at the beginning of their holiday, along with her black high heels. Josh, now seeing Jessica looking extremely desirable, started to feel just a little easier with the situation, although he still felt a little vulnerable being tied so securely.

Well that was until Jessica went to the wardrobe and bought out her blue canvas carryall.

As Jessica placed the bag next to the table, she said, in a very matter-of-fact voice, "See Josh, I have a bag as well, now what shall I bring out first?" Reaching into the bag, Jessica bought out a black leather riding crop and then immediately putting it back into the bag said, "Silly me, of course that's for later, when I've tied you face down. " Jessica then again reached into the bag and this time came out with a rather large box of matches and said, "Oh. "Now purposely holding the box where Josh could see them. "Sorry, silly me, these are for later too. " Putting them back in the bag Jessica then said, "Dear me Josh, I seem to be giving away all my little surprises and we all know how you like your little surprises, don't we, Josh?" Then returning them to the bag, Jessica said, "Ah, here we are. " Now holding a tall aerosol can, so that Josh could catch just a glimpse of it, said, "This is the stuff, this is what we need. " Then placing it on the table, near Josh's right leg, went back into the bag. "Ah, yes, " said Jessica, pulling a length of black cloth from it. "Now I will definitely need this. " By now Josh was feeling just a little concerned with Jessica's strange demeanour and to add to his concerns, he was now being blindfolded by a very focused Jessica, who was looking, every bit in charge.

"Just remember, Jess, this is fun bondage, " said a very nervous Josh. "It's not that BDSM stuff. " Josh then felt even more uneasy as Jessica failed to respond. This is when Josh was startled on hearing a very loud whooshing noise. "What the hell is that?" Josh asked in an even more nervous voice.

"Oh, that's just another surprise Josh, You know you really must stop asking all these questions, or you will spoil the surprises, won't you?" said Jessica, trying not to laugh. "Now then Josh, this may feel a little cold. "As she smothered whipped cream all over his chest. Josh, now feeling a little easier with the situation, started to relax a little. Jessica than began to lick the cream off, in a series of long deliberate licks. Then she proceeded to squirt cream onto Josh's naval, which Jessica again began to lick off. Then just as Josh was anticipating what was coming next, Jessica then suddenly stopped and said in a very panicky voice, "Oh fuck, I think Mom and Dad have just pulled up, wait here. "And then left the bedroom, closing the door behind her. Jessica, in a raised voice, while opening and closing the front door, said, "No please come on in Dad, I think Josh's in the shower. " She then quietly crept back into the bedroom and with her hand over her mouth to suppress the sound of her laughter, leaned over

Josh's ear and said laughing. "You know Josh, I am really enjoying this bondage thing very much indeed, how about you? See Josh, " Jessica said. "That was another of my little surprise for you, now where did I put those matches, " said Jessica, still trying not to laugh.

"Well, I think that should be enough of that, " said Jess, now feeling that she had more than got her own back. "So now I think it's time to get down to the more serious business of fucking. " That's when Josh felt Jessica's soft breasts and her long hair, brushing over his face and upper body. Although Josh was trying desperately to get one of Jessica's nipples into his mouth, Jessica was playing hard to get and was teasing him. But then Jessica skilfully manoeuvred a nipple into his mouth and Josh felt good again. A little later, Josh felt Jessica climbing onto the table and after a couple more squirts of cream lowered her crotch on to Josh's face, which was obligingly licked off by a very much happier Josh. Josh then felt a blast of cold cream as Jessica covered his penis in cream and then reassuringly felt her tongue gently licking it off. He was now thinking to himself, *Ah, a sixty-nine with cream, now that could really take off, maybe there's a market for fresh creamed pussy, or raspberry cock sundae.* But just seconds later his mind was instantly focused on oral pleasures. After several minutes of bliss, Josh could feel Jessica changing position. Jessica had now turned and was again straddling Josh, only this time she was facing him, when she untied the blindfold. After kissing Josh on the lips, Jessica, once again got hold of the spray cream and squirted a little on each nipple, before once again teasing Josh, by offering her breast to his open mouth and then moving away again. With Jess in total control, she eventually relented and allowed Josh to suck her nipples. At the same time Josh could feel Jessica's cream covered vagina pressing down on his penis. After lowering herself fully down onto Josh's penis, Jessica said in a sultry voice, "I hope you are feeling horny, because I feel like fucking you into the ground. " Starting slowly Jessica rocked forwards and back and closing her eyes, now concentrated on taking it up to the next level.

Within minutes, Jessica could feel Josh's body tense and heard him say, "Oh God I'm coming, oh, oh Jess don't stop. " Jessica felt Josh ejaculating deep inside her and leaning forward held his head in her hands and kissed him, Jessica now satisfied, gradually slowed down and finally stopped moving.

Jessica then climbed off the table and walking towards the bathroom, started removing her underwear. "Where are you going Jess?" asked Josh now half-covered in cream.

Jessica turning back and laughing said, "I don't know about you Josh, but I'm going, for a shower. "And at that vanished into the bathroom. After what seemed like ages, a fully showered Jessica came back into the room laughing loudly at the sight of Josh, spread eagled, naked and covered in florets of cream. Jessica was almost in hysterics as she struggled to untie the very secure knots. The situation was so hilarious, that now having freed Josh, who was now also laughing, Jessica had to close her eyes, as seeing Josh covered in cream, just started her laughing all over again. After finally releasing the last knots, Jessica, still laughing said, "Next time we do this Josh, I will make sure I have my camera ready I could then send a photo to Moon Pig and maybe have it made up into a Christmas card, as I just love unusual snow scenes. " Although Josh was smiling when he eventually emerged from the bathroom, looking all nice and clean, Jessica just knew she would be in trouble. And sure enough, when he managed to catch Jessica, he put her over his lap and smacked her a few times on her nice clean arse.

Climbing into bed, Jessica said to Josh, "I hope you realise that smacking me like that won't stop me doing it again Josh, in fact, it felt so good, I might do it again, as I really enjoyed being smacked like that. " Jessica, then still laughing, while climbing out the other side of the bed, away from Josh's reach, taunted Josh by presenting her bum, and saying, "If you can catch me, you can smack me. "

Later as they lay in bed talking, Josh said, "You know, you really had me worried with the riding crop and the matches. "

Jessica now laughing again, at the memory of it, said, "Yes I know I did, you should have seen your face, I had a job to keep my voice normal, as I could hardly breath. "

"Fucking brilliant, " Josh said. "Just brilliant. " Jessica then kissed Josh goodnight and it was sometime later, as Josh was trying to doze off, that he could still feel the bed trembling as Jessica was quietly laughing herself to sleep.

Chapter 16

Sightseeing

The next morning when Jessica woke, Josh was sitting up in bed, studying his laptop.

"What are you doing now?" asked Jessica, looking very sleepy.

"I am organising us a day out in the countryside. It rained all night, but today's forecast is warm and sunny, so I thought we could go up the road and take a look at the coastline, it's supposed to be really beautiful around here. I didn't realise it Jess, but there's a visitor's centre, not far from here and apparently there's a ninety-minute boat trip, from Westport, where you can see a seal colony and some lighthouse or other. It looks all right on the website and the boat serves food and drink. Ah yes and there's also a Gastro Pub nearby in Newport, which is also quite close to us as well. So, if that's OK with you Jess, I think that's our day sorted?" After a short pause Josh then said, in a more serious tone, "You know, I really think we should ask to see if your mom and dad want to come along. I sometimes feel we are not spending enough time with them, and after all, Jess, they are on holiday too. On second thoughts maybe we should invite Jane and Howard, I mean they have all been such bloody good company, don't you think Jess?"

"Well, I know Aunty Jane can't come, " said Jessica. "She has some urgent committee meeting in Dublin this morning, but Howard might be up for it? And yes, it would be a good opportunity for you to get to know my mom and dad a little more, now they are your potential family?" Jessica then added, "And of course they go back to Epson on Sunday, but that's if they want to come along of course?"

"Right then Jess, you had better contact them and see if they're interested. Oh, look Jess, " said Josh now positioning the screen to show her the photographs. "There's a peat bog as well. I have heard people talk about them, but I have never seen a proper Irish peat bog, so that could be interesting, don't you think?" Then, feeling more than pleased with himself, as he closed his laptop, he said, "Well come on then, find out if they want to come, it's far too nice a day to lay around in bed all day. "

A short time later, Jessica was on her phone talking to her mom, when Josh came back into the bedroom, eating a piece of toast. "So, what are we having for breakfast then Jess?"

"It looks like you already have yours, " said Jessica now trying to wrestle the second slice of toast from out of his other hand.

"Well, we have run out of bacon, so what about a sausage sandwich?" Then pausing and looking concerned, said, "We do have some brown sauce, don't we Jess? Well come on then, tell me who's coming with us?"

"Just as I thought, Aunty Jane is taking Uncle Howard with her into Dublin, and I think she said they are going to look at hot tubs while they are out. But Mom and Dad would love to come along, " said Jessica smiling. Who, now jumping out of bed added, "So you had better get my sausage sandwich cooked, then hadn't you, that's if we still have some bread left, you greedy little pig. "

When Gerald and Mary turned up, Gerry said, "Thank God for the old satnav, you're certainly hidden away down here, well off the beaten track. "

Josh, noticing that they were both dressed for walking said, "My word Gerry, when I saw you and Mary pass the window, I thought you were a couple of professional hill walkers. I'm really impressed with the gear you're wearing; I am afraid I am going to spoil the whole group image, with me wearing my old jeans and a tatty old M&S fleecy top. "

After coffee and a tour round the cottage, Gerry said, "What a great place you have here. "And looking out the back door, added, "With a nice big hot tub too, very nice."

Josh, who was never the best car passenger, picking up his car keys said, "Please let's all go in mine then, it's 4x4 so you never know, we might need it, especially in that old bog territory and not only that, but it looks very rural where we are going. " With Gerry in the front passenger seat and with Jessica and her mom in the back, they set off for Westport.

As they drove along, Josh said, in a raised voice so they could hear in the back, "I have found what looks like a good gastro pub for lunch. But I am only taking you there on the proviso, that you let me pay. " Now looking straight at Gerry, added, "What with you and Howard almost fighting to pay all the time, I was beginning to feel a bit like old *'Ebenezer Scrooge'.* "

"OK Josh, it's a deal, " said Gerry smiling, but then Gerry added proviso, "That is just so long as you keep your hands off my wife's backside. "

That's when Mary quickly said laughing, "Don't you dare agree to that one, Joshua Foster, there are all too few pleasures in this life without Gerry curbing all the good ones. "

As they drove into West Port, Mary said, "Isn't this a beautiful little town, wow, I could live here Gerry, it's so picturesque. "

"This little town is often referred to as Ireland's hidden secret, " said Josh. "I read it this morning on their website. " After they had parked up and walked towards the quayside, Josh said, "Well when you do move down here, make sure you have a nice spare room, because I think we might be visiting you on a regular basis, this place is absolutely lovely. " When they got to quayside, Jessica and her dad went along to the small kiosk type office, to check whether their tickets were ready to collect. While Mary and Josh were sitting in the sunshine waiting, Mary said, "I can see you two are getting on really well and although Jessica has always been a very happy girl, I don't think I have ever seen her as happy as this. "

"Not as happy as me Mary, " replied Josh. "Isn't Jessica the most beautiful girl in the world and a real delight to be with. " He then added, "Some time ago, my uncle Terry told me, in all seriousness, he said son, before you go marrying any girl, always take a good look at her mother first. " Now placing his hand on Mary's knee and looking her in the eye, said, "Well if that's true Mary, I think I have struck lucky with Jess. "

Now, feeling slightly embarrassed and breaking into laughter, Mary said, "Jessica warned me, that since you had kissed that Blarney Stone, you were quite something else. "

Just then Jessica and her dad returned and seeing them both laughing, Jessica asked, with an enquiring smile, "So what are you two laughing at then?"

"Oh nothing Jessica, " replied Mary. "It was just Josh making me laugh, that's all. "

"Right, " said Gerry. "The boat will be back in about ten minutes time and by all accounts, it stays here loading for another fifteen minutes before departing again. So come on, we have just enough time for a quick walk along this beautiful looking estuary. "

While Jessica was walking ahead with her dad, Josh was walking behind with Mary, when Josh asked, "So what was Jane like before Michael died, Mary?"

"It's very sad really, " replied Mary. "Jane used to be the life and sole of the party, she was always immaculately turned out and was probably the best mother going. She lived and died for Michael and Caroline. But since Michael died, well she has never been quite the same. Although, we did see the odd little glimpse of the old Jane break through every now and then. But I know, inside, Jane was still suffering. Maybe I shouldn't tell you this, but as you are now almost family and you probably won't be too surprised. Jane was under a psychiatrist for quite a few years and poor old Howard, well he has been an absolute gem. God only knows what would have become of Jane if Howard hadn't been around to help? Everyone loved young Michael, he was so like Jane, so full of life and always up to something, so it was a tragedy for all of us.

"When Caroline's marriage ceremony went terribly wrong last Friday, to be perfectly honest with you, I was more concerned with Jane than I was for Caroline. That's because I knew that Caroline is a very strong and extremely capable young lady. So, since then I have been trying my very best to keep Jane's spirits up. "

Josh then said, "Although I had met Caroline before, when she visited us in London, I think she was staying with you then. But when she stood up at that church altar and made that very controlled speech just before hitting that idiot Richard with her bouquet, I was both surprised and extremely impressed by her self-control. " Then he added, "I don't think I will ever forget that wedding Mary, I tell you, being there and watching on, it was like something out of a film, a sort of unreal situation. " Then after a short pause, Josh said, "I am still not really sure whether Caroline has either got over it very well or whether she is just very good at hiding it?" Josh then said, "I wish I could see inside Caroline's head, just to know how she's really handling it, because I am still not sure. "

Mary then added, that, "After speaking with Caroline, immediately following that bloody Richard fiasco, she told me that it may have been a blessing in disguise, as in the lead up to the wedding, their relationship had cooled a little. " With a sigh, Mary then added, "But only time will tell Josh, whether or not Caroline was deeply affected by it or not, I'm not sure, but knowing Caroline, I know she will get over it. "Mary then continued, "But you know, over the last couple of days, I have seen Jane back to her old self, and I think Caroline is happier that Richard has now gone. " Mary then said, "I think your Sean may have already stolen Caroline's heart, I know he has impressed Jane and although Jane won't tell me what happened, I am pretty sure Sean had something to do with turning Jane's life around. "

Then looking ahead, while smiling again, Mary said, "Just look at those two, Jessica always was a daddy's girl, I think that's where she gets her temperament from. "

Josh stopping in the middle of his stride, said, "That's it Mary, I think I've got it now, temperament from her dad and her good looks from her mom, eh, and believe me Mary, that is definitely not the Blarney Stone talking. "

All now safely aboard and settled, the pleasure boat pulled away from the jetty, when Jessica said, as not to be overheard, "What were you and Mom talking about?"

Then digging him in the ribs said, "I think I need to keep an eye on you two, I don't want Mom giving too many of my little secrets away, otherwise you might be asking for this ring back again. "

Then Josh, giving Jessica a friendly squeeze of the hand whispered, "Don't you ever worry about that Jess, please don't even think about it. "

Josh, then holding her hand up to show-off the ring, said, "Because this ring is for keeps Jess. " Although there was a fairly strong breeze, the boat trip was a real delight, as they saw plenty of wild seals and a first-class view of the isolated coastline.

Gerry went down to the snack bar and bought back four coffees and four rather large doughnuts. "Oh hell Dad, " said Jessica standing up to brush the sugar off her clothes. "You know I always finish up covered in jam when I eat these. "

"Yes that's right you did, I wonder if Mary has bought your old bib along, didn't it have a picture of *Sooty* on it. You probably don't know Josh, but as a child, Jessica had a real thing about *Sooty,* she had all the puppets, the pyjamas, she even had *Sooty* wallpaper in her bedroom. We even had to name our cat *Sooty,* and she was a tabby. Yes, she was a lovely child, " said Gerry smiling in thought.

"She still is lovely, " said Josh. "Wasn't there a dog puppet as well? You know I think the older guy's son is still appears on TV every now and then. Do you still watch it Jess?" asked Josh.

"OK, that's quite enough, " said Jessica. "I was about six years old and yes there was a dog puppet, who was called Sweep. "

"But you were lovely and always carried that stuffed *Sooty* toy with you wherever you went. I think your mom still has it Jess, " said Gerry smiling.

From there they walked through the town, looking in all the little shops and buying the odd post card. "I am keeping these post cards, " said Mary. "Just to remind me of our visit, it's such a lovely little town isn't it?" Touring the area and spending a wonderful morning together, they visited various local beauty spots and gradually made their way to Newport, where they parked up for lunch.

As they stood over the road from the red painted gastro pub, Jessica said, "Well it looks good from the outside, which is always a good sign. "

As they stepped inside Mary said, "Oh good it looks like a really nice place, but only tasting the food will tell, and to be honest I am absolutely starving. "

Then Jessica added, "I wonder if Jane and Howard know about this place?" Then pointing across the room said, "Shall we sit over there by the window and then we will have a good view of the town. "

After a superb meal, Josh said, "Tell you what, if this little pub was back in London, you would never get near it, let alone get through the door. Don't you just love traditional Irish bars, especially when they serve food as good as that. Well, Jess, now we know where it is, I think they will definitely be seeing us in here again, don't you?"

From Newport, they made their way to Ballycroy National Park, were they walked over some very wild countryside and walking along a series of raised wooden walkways, where Josh saw his first real Irish Bog.

"This certainly is wild round here, " said Mary, stepping over a small stream. "It's almost like we have the whole place to ourselves and those hills look completely untouched by time, I can imagine them looking like that thousands of years ago. "

On a whim, while in Ballycroy, Josh seeing the bus route posted up at a bus stop said, "Why not leave the car here and take the bus to Castlebar and back just for the ride, as I have never ridden in an Irish bus?" Pretty soon after waiting, the bus pulled up and along with two other people, they boarded the bus. The four of them enjoyed their ride to Castlebar and back, just chatting and enjoying the beautiful scenery.

Later as Josh was driving back to the cottage, he said, in a loud voice, so they all could hear, "That's another great day enjoyed, I hope you are stopping for tea, as I mistakenly bought far too much gammon from the village shop, I keep over buying, because it always looks so good. That's why I greedily bought six very thick slices, which Jess and I will never manage to eat by ourselves, so you would really be doing us a very big favour by helping us eat it. "

"Yes, thank you, that would be lovely, " said Gerry. But then adding, "Although I'm not sure if I could eat that much, as I am still feeling full after that delicious lunch. "

Jessica and her parents were happy sitting around the kitchen table chatting, as Josh was happily cooking their tea, when Josh said, "I'm sorry, but we haven't got any pineapple to go with it, but the good news is, we do have plenty of fresh eggs. Yes, I got a little carried away with buying eggs as well. The lady who owns the cottage sells them and they are real Irish running around the field eggs."

While they were eating Jessica said, "Well, you know I really enjoyed that day out, I had a really great time, so thank you both for coming it's such a pity you're going home on tomorrow, because, apart from the wedding episode, this has probably been the best holiday I have ever had. "

As Jessica and Josh stood on the step of their cottage waving them off, Jessica said, "Thanks Josh, I really appreciate you inviting them. "

To which Josh replied, "Look, I wasn't doing it as a favour for you Jess, I really do enjoy their company and that gastro pub, well, we really must go there again. "

That evening, as they were relaxing in front of the TV, Jessica said, "Just for curiosity, what were you and Mom talking about?"

"Well, if you must know, I was telling her about the massage table deal I got. " Then Josh quickly moved his rib cage out of Jessica's range, anticipating her injurious elbow. Later while Josh was finishing the washing up and clearing things away, Jessica came in wearing the black lingerie and holding a couple of lengths of pink rope. And with her mischievous look, said, "OK then lover boy, where do you want me?" Needless to say, the next hour or two was taken up by the kind of erotic pleasures you can only get with using very soft pink cotton rope.

Chapter 17

On the Ranges

The next morning, after drinking coffee and eating buttered toast while watching TV in bed, Josh and Jessica eventually got up and spent even more time relaxing in the hot tub.

"Well, " said Josh. "I hope you're in an adventurous mood today, because I have something totally different lined up. "

"So, what are we up to today then Josh?" asked Jessica. "I hope it's something we will both enjoy, " said Jessica, looking just a little doubtful.

"Well today Jess, " said Josh, sounding rather pleased with himself. "We are going rifle shooting. "

"Oh no, " said Jessica. "I am not going out shooting some poor defenceless animal, not for you or anybody. "

Josh quickly replied laughing, "No sweetheart, we are not shooting anything other than paper targets. We are going to a properly licenced rifle range and after some instruction; hopefully we will be firing a few rounds off on their outdoor ranges. So, what do you think about that then Jess? Becauseme, I just can't wait. Now that's something different, eh, Jess, another new experience for you, and who knows, you might even enjoy it? Anyway, it's all booked up for us, so we just need to turn up, receive our safety instruction and hopefully start shooting a few rounds off. "

Later that morning, as arranged by Josh, they arrived at the rifle ranges and could see from the number of cars in the car park, it was a very popular place. Arriving at the reception, Josh explained that they had booked for tuition, gun hire and some range time, and after completing a few registration documents, they were introduced to their instructor.

"My name is George, " said the friendly, red-faced middle-aged man. "And I am going to be your instructor for today. Now before we go near any guns, I need to show you this short video and then explain to you our very important safety rules. " After sitting with another elderly couple watching the gun safety video, George, along with another instructor came back and explained all the important, dos and don'ts. After picking up their rifles and ammunition, they all headed over to the ranges. During the walk over to the range area, Jessica asked George, whether there was much of a kick from these guns.

"Well not if you hold them correctly, " explained George. "But don't worry about it, as I will explain all that when I am setting you up. " Arriving at the range, there were clean rubber mats to lie down on and the shooting from area was covered under a low corrugated tin roof. After setting up the targets, George adjusted the strap to properly fit Jessica and after positioning her in the prone position, she loaded her gun with some trepidation and then gently squeezed the trigger, with a very loud crack.

"Well, " said George looking through his telescope at the target. "Keep that up young lady and we will have to put you in our ladies' competition team. " After firing all ten shots and scoring very a healthy sixty-two, Jessica was starting to enjoy this newfound sport. Then it was Josh's turn, however after only getting a couple actually on the target Josh was finding it a little more difficult, but he steadily improved until he finally got his eye in. Meanwhile, Jessica was finding it all very easy and was going from strength to strength. After firing off fifty shots, Jessica was disappointed to find she had used all of her ammunition.

George said, "If you want, I can order you another fifty rounds and I can get you a few more targets, as we still have plenty of range time. "

"Oh, yes please, George, " said a very eager Jessica. "It would be a pity not to, now that I am getting the hang of it and as we are already here. " While they were waiting, they looked at their targets and George seemed a little surprised, but very pleased with the consistency and accuracy of Jessica's shooting.

In response George said, "I have had people shooting for years, who have never had scores anywhere near as good as this. It's a pity you're not local Jessica, as I think we may have the making of a marksman here, I really do. " After watching Jessica fire of another fifty rounds, they all returned to the club house. It was when George took real delight in showing his fellow instructors Jessica's target scores. Everyone who saw her scores, recommended that Jessica seriously take up match shooting as a hobby, as she certainly had a natural underlying talent.

Sitting in the club's coffee shop and looking at her targets with some pride, Jessica said, "Thank you Josh for suggesting match shooting, you know I wasn't really sure if I would actually like it when we first got here. But now I've tried it, I found it really enjoyable and wasn't that instructor fellow George a nice guy? It's a pity we don't live near here, else we could join the club. " Jessica then added, "I must tell Caroline about this place, I am pretty sure, she would probably enjoy this shooting too. "

As they were both expected for tea and to say goodbye to Jessica's mom and dad at Mainear Darach, they drove straight over there from the rifle club. All through their journey, Jessica was talking about their shooting experience and how she would never have thought for a minute that she would have actually enjoyed it so much. Flushed with her success, Jessica was now seriously talking about going again.

"You know Josh, I think we should definitely look for a rifle range nearer to home when we get back to London, don't you? And maybe we could visit that one again before we return home, " said Jessica, now searching the web for rifle ranges on her phone. "You really do come up with some good ideas Josh, like the races and dancing, I think we should keep the dancing up as well, don't you?"

When they pulled up at Mainear Darach, Jessica was immediately out of the car and heading straight to the house, with all of her paper targets under her arm.

When they got into the house, Jane, Mary, Gerry and Howard were in the drawing room, relaxing with drinks. As soon as Howard saw them enter the room, in one of his happier smiles, said, "Here they are, our two little love birds. And what have you two been up to today then, wallowing in that hot tub, no doubt? Anyway, before you tell me, what are you two drinking, poor old Gerry is on the orange juice, aren't you, because he's doing the driving. " After sorting their drinks Howard said, "So come on then, just what have you been up to today?"

Jessica explained that they had been target shooting and passing round her targets, told them how exciting it all was, telling them, "It was something I would never have thought of doing. "Then looking at Josh, Jessica said, "But it was such good fun and all very exciting, I really don't know how Josh thinks all these things up. It's like I was saying to Josh, while we laying in the hot tub the other night, this holiday, has been so very special and not only that, but it just keeps getting better. "

"Oh, talking of hot tubs, " said Howard. "We ordered one for ourselves yesterday. "Then explaining how although it was second hand, it had been fully reconditioned and had all the extras, if fact just like new.

Jane then said, looking very excited, "The man is coming over tomorrow to see about fitting it in the orangery for us. As you know we never use the orangery any more, so it should be ideal. "

Gerry now studying Jessica's shooting scores said, "Wow, Jessica, you have scored seventy-two on this one, that's a really excellent score and over 100 metres too, I'm extremely impressed, well done girl. " Then added jokingly, "Better not fall out with our Jessica then Josh, else you really could be a dead man. So where are your scores then Josh. " Josh now looking a little matter-of-fact, replied, I think I left them in the car, Gerry, but to be honest, they weren't a patch on Jessica's, she was a proper Anne Oakley. We are going to see if we can make another booking before we go home. Are you and Jane interested in coming if we do, Howard?"

"What a good idea, " said Jessica. "Of course they want to come, don't you Uncle?"

"Well, yes, it sounds like good thing to try Jessica, so yes we're up for it. Oh, and what about some more dancing lessons, they were very enjoyable. "

"Well, there you go, " said Jessica. "Leave that one with me. "

Howard, still looking through Jessica's targets, then said, "When I was in the forces, well, my poor old weapons instructor, Sergeant Dean, well I'm sorry to say, he eventually gave up on me, he even sent me to get my eyes tested twice. But you know, he would have just loved you Jessica, yes he really would have been a happy man and considering this was your first session and you were using a club rifle, these are really very good scores. "

As they sat round the kitchen table having tea that afternoon, the mood grew a little more sombre at the thought of Mary and Gerry leaving for home.

Howard, with one of his more serious looks said, "Despite that bloody wedding, this has been a really wonderful couple of weeks, full of memories, I certainly will look back on this with great fondness. "

"Yes, " added Jane. "I have enjoyed everyone's company too and I am going to insist we all meet up here again and on a regular basis. " Then pausing in thought, Jane continued, "Or maybe we should all go on a cruise together, we keep saying we are going to go on one, but it never seems to happen. So if you would like to go, I will get a few catalogues and see if we can shortlist one for next winter?" Everyone agreed, a cruise would be just the thing and a very happy Jane immediately volunteered to do the organising.

After tea, Gerry's car was loaded up and everyone was outside to see them off. Jane was in floods of tears as she hugged her sister and almost had to be prised away from her, she was so upset that she would be leaving.

As their car drew away and went out of sight, the four of them walked back to the house, when Howard said, "Oh I never told you, we heard from Caroline earlier and they should be arriving back tomorrow lunchtime. I don't know what has gone on, but our Caroline tells us that she has a surprise for us. Now before you ask me what it is, I don't know, she won't tell us, but apparently, it's a very special surprise. We have the rooms all ready, and we are really looking forward to meeting your mom Josh. Sean tells me there would have been problems using your old lorry, so he has hired a slightly larger, more modern lorry instead, he said something about a problem with an operators licensing or something like that. Anyway, everyone there sounded very upbeat, so hopefully tomorrow we will find out what the big surprise is. "

Later that evening while they were all watching TV, Jessica answered her phone. "It's Mom and Dad, " she said. "Just letting us know they got safely on to the ferry and are half way over to Holy Head. "

While Jessica and Jane were in the kitchen making coffee, Howard said in a quiet voice, "Jane explained to me what Sean had said to her the other day. So when Sean gets here tomorrow, I'm telling him that he can have that steam lorry for nothing, I am not sure whether he has noticed yet, but I've already transferred all of the money he paid to me, back into his account. I tell you Josh, that your Sean owes me absolutely nothing, what he did with Jane, well, it has changed our lives. Oh, and what's more, he is going to be really happy when he knows that I have not only found the old registration documents, but I have found a whole file full of paperwork all pertaining to that truck. I've dug around and even found a few old family photographs, with the lorry in them, so don't tell him yet, I want to present him with the file when he gets here tomorrow. Now come and have a large brandy with me Josh, Jessica can drive you back. " Then as Howard handed Josh his brandy said, "I hope you realise Josh that if it wasn't for you coming here, none of this would have happened, so I am so very pleased you came. Now drink up son, there is plenty more where that came from. "

Just then Jane and Jessica came back with their coffees. "So you have moved onto the brandies already have you, "said Jane smiling. "Typical, just typical. Now I hope you two understand that the next few days are going to be absolutely hectic, what with meeting your family Josh, moving that lorry and with Caroline's mystery surprise. " Jane then looking very excited said, "Why this old house is going to be buzzing, absolutely buzzing again and I for one, well I am going to be thoroughly loving every minute, absolutely loving it. "

While Jessica was driving Josh back to the cottage, Josh said, "Earlier today, when you were blasting away with that rifle, do you know, I was genuinely proud of you. Not only did you look terrific, but you looked absolutely one hundred percent professional, like you had been shooting for years. I could almost feel you concentrating on every shot, and that wasn't just me either, I could see that George was also blown away by you. It's times like that, when I feel so very lucky, so lucky that you are in my life Jess. " Now changing the subject slightly, "I hope you are feeling horny Jess, because I am sitting here watching you drive me home, thinking I can't wait to get you into bed. "

Jessica then reaching out with her hand and feeling Josh's crotch, said, "You're not the only one, I could just pull over now and fuck you, no problem, so, you just wait till I get you home. "

When Jessica came out of the shower and into the bedroom, Josh was sitting in bed and holding a drink out for her, when he said, "What I would really like Jess, if you fancy it, is for me to just lay here while you fuck me."

Jessica putting a glass into his hand said, "OK Joshua Foster, that's a done deal, now just drink up and be prepared to get fucked. "

Jessica then pulled back the sheets, climbed on to Josh facing the foot of the bed and carefully positioning her vagina over Josh's mouth, then leaned forward and began mouthing his now extremely hard penis. As Josh moved his hands from behind his head and started to massage Jessica breasts.

Jessica, then stopped and in a very commanding voice said, "No Josh, I'm fucking you remember, so you can put them back where they were please. "

In reply, Josh said, "Believe me Jess, I just can't help it, I really need to touch you. "But then stopped mid-sentence, when Jessica carried on from where she had left off. After getting herself well and truly licked and giving Josh the best blow job ever, she moved down along his body and positioned herself over Josh's penis. Reaching back with one hand Jessica guided his penis into her vagina and said, "I hope you are enjoying this, because I am. " Then Jessica said, "Let me know when you're ready to cum and then I will fuck you dry. " And at that Jessica began slowly gyrating her hips, which moved up and down Josh's rock-hard penis.

After a short time, Josh could no longer keep his hands off her body and grabbing Jessica by the shoulders with both hands, pulled her down hard onto his penis and giving a soft grunt, said, "Oh, bloody hell yes, I'm coming Jess. " Minutes later, they were both laying in each other's arms, when Josh said, "I know I have said this before Jess, but you are the best thing that has ever happened to me. " Then giving Jessica a gentle hug and while stroking her smooth silky body, kissed her softly to sleep.

The next morning, Josh very gently picked up a still half-asleep Jessica out of their bed and carried her now laughing out to the hot tub. After gently lowering her into the water, Josh handed her a mug of coffee and then climbed in beside her. Josh then told her, "I lay there just looking at you after you fell asleep last night and do you know what Jess, you are even beautiful when you are asleep. " Josh then said, "I had a text from Sean this morning and they are on their way over here Jess. You know, I am just dying to know how Sean and Caroline are getting on together and it will be very interesting know how Mom is going to react to being back over here in Ireland again. I just hope Sean and Caroline are getting on well and at the risk of sounding completely selfish, I would love them to get married. " Then reaching for Jessica's hand, Josh said, "I know I have the best girl in the world Jess, but I also know that Caroline would be ideal for our Sean. " Then looking her in the eyes said, "Does that really sound so wrong Jess, am I being selfish, delusional, or just plain stupid?"

Jessica then replied, "I had a couple of texts from Caroline, yesterday. "And then carried on to say, "I don't really know what's happened, but I think your outrageous predictions might be coming to fruition Josh. But hey, we should know a little more by later on today, when they actually get here. Fingers crossed, everything is going well, eh, Josh? I can't wait to see them and to find out what this special surprise is. " Then lightening the mood Jessica said, "Well you know me Josh, I just love surprises, and especially the ones you give me when we are on our own. Now give me a kiss and then get my breakfast ready, double quick, before I get my gun out. "

Over breakfast, as they listened to the weather forecast Josh said, "Mmm that's not looking very good, heavy rain moving in from the west. I was thinking we could have taken Mom on that boat trip from Westport Harbour. "

"I don't think your mom will have the time Josh, she will want to meet everyone and go to the churchyard. I don't know what's going on Josh, "Jessica said looking at her phone. "But I have been getting these very cryptic messages from Caroline. She does this quite often, it's like she is purposely whetting my appetite, but I know from old, it's always something she is very happy about. " As they sat naked eating breakfast, Jessica said, "I am going to miss this place, it's so secluded and private, we could walk around like this all day. " A little later, Jessica, feeling a little impatient to find out and what Caroline and Sean had been up to, said with some urgency, "Come on Josh, hurry up and finish eating, while I do the washing up, we need to get dressed and get out, I want to get over to Aunty's house as I need to be there when they arrive. "

When they got to Mainear Darach, they saw Howard with Helen, the lady who looks after the horses for them, riding back towards the stables. Both of them looked happy and the horses looked very well, albeit a little on the wet and sweaty side.

When Josh and Jessica got out of the car, they shouted across, "Good morning and how was the ride?"

To which Howard replied, "Absolutely great, despite all this bloody rain. "While Helen, the groom, just smiled politely. "Please, don't stand there getting wet, go on in the house and I will join you there when we've finished with the horses. "

When Josh and Jessica got to the kitchen, Jane was looking really glamorous, which prompted Jessica to say, "Wow Aunty, you look really smart, now I feel scruffy seeing you looking so smart. "

"Nonsense darling, you will never know how much I envy your good looks. Eh Josh?"

"Very true Jane, " replied Josh. "But she always looks good to me. " Then looking Jane up and down very closely Josh said, "But Jessica's right Jane, you look a million dollars this morning. "

Then without any hesitation, Jessica added, "Be very careful aunty, else Josh will be smacking your bum again, especially wearing such a beautiful, knitted dress. "

"But darling, I've already told him, he can give me a smack, whenever he feels the need. "

And then breaking into a laugh Jane said, "And if this dress has that effect on men, I think I will be buying one or two more, eh Josh?"

"That's right Jane, this smacking thing, well it's now a sort of tradition, a tradition that must be properly maintained. Now before I go getting Howard jealous, is there any chance of a coffee?"

"Well, " said Jane, as she passed them their coffees. "I am pleased to say they are all off the ferry now; I have just had a text from Caroline. I can't wait for them to get here."

Just then Howard then came in shaking the rain from his coat and said, "Any chance of a coffee for me darling?"

"We were just saying how good Jane was looking in that dress, " said Josh.

"Of course, she looks good Josh, she would look gorgeous wearing an old sack, true beauty always shines through, " said Howard now putting his arm round her.

"I'm beginning to think you must have kissed that Blarney Stone as well darling, maybe you did it when I wasn't looking, eh Howard, " said Jane laughing.

A little later that morning, on hearing the air brakes of a lorry pulling up, Josh immediately looked out of the window to see Sean's six-wheeler lorry, closely followed by a little black MG.

"They are here, " said Josh and everyone immediately went outside to welcome them.

As Caroline helped Bridie out of the MG, Josh gave his mom a big hug and said, "Welcome back to lovely old Ireland Mom. "Followed by, "How was the journey?" But before his mom could answer, the heavens suddenly opened up and so they all hurried into the house.

Now inside, Bridie said laughing "Welcome back to Ireland indeed, well at least the weather is exactly as I remember it. " While brushing the rain drops from her coat, Bridie asked, "Now just let me look at my beautiful Jessica. "Then giving her a great big hug and a kiss, said, "You are such a lovely girl and I am ever so pleased Josh came to his senses and proposed and even more pleased that you agreed. "

Just then Sean came running in and said, "Hello everyone, it's really good to be back, the forecast said was going to be dry this afternoon, so let's hope they are right. " Sean then seeing Jane said, "Wow I like the dress Jane, it really suits you, doesn't it Howard?"

Bridie then said, "The weather was fine until we got to Dublin, but I must admit, Caroline and I have had a great time while travelling here and she has been telling me all about you all. "

After they all introduced themselves, Josh looking out of the door said, "Nice truck Sean, it looks brand new. What, is it a Scania? Nicer to drive than our old Ford, I bet. "

Sean in reply said, "It's so easy to drive and the driving position is really comfortable, it seems to be fitted with everything you can think of, I'm still discovering some of its special features even now. I hate to think what it must of cost to buy though, so I am being really careful not to do any damage to it. "

Now they were all in the kitchen, Caroline calling for everyone's attention said, "I think I should let you all know; Sean has proposed to me and I very happily accepted. I know some people will think it was maybe a little soon into our new relationship, but I think we both knew the first time we met, that this was the real thing. "

Everyone said how pleased they were, when Howard said, "I knew it, I just knew it, I saw how they looked at each other on the boat the other day and well I kind of realised it then. " Shaking Sean's hand, Howard said, "I was hoping this would happen, so welcome to our family Sean Foster. "Then laughing said, "Welcome to the mad house. " He then walked over to Bridie and taking her hand said, "I must thank you, Mrs Foster for raising two wonderful young men. " Then kissing her on the cheek said, "Welcome to Mainear Darach Bridie, please consider our house as your second home. " Then looking extremely happy said, "There you go Jane, I knew we should keep that wedding dress, so better get it down to the dry cleaners. " Then Howard, in a more serious voice, said, "I have ten bottles of 1946 champagne in the cellar I've been saving for a long time, I think this happy occasion calls for at least a couple of bottles, don't you?" Howard then suddenly vanished off down to the cellar to look for them. Jane showed Bridie up to her room, chatting as they went, while Josh trailed behind carrying her bags.

"Oh, what a beautiful room Mrs Anson, " Bridie exclaimed.

"Now, now none of that Mrs Anson stuff please Bridie, " said Jane. "Please call me Jane. "

"Shall I leave these bags here?" asked Josh, who then left to go downstairs and meet up with Sean.

As both Bridie and Jane sat on the small bedroom settee, that looked out from the large bay window, out over the gardens, Jane said, "I am so happy Caroline and Sean are together. I don't know if Caroline told you, but we lost our son Michael, who was killed in a motorcycle accident several years back. " Then, after pausing for a second or two, Jane continued to tell how she had been badly affected and had withdrawn into a miserable self-imposed, very sad existence. Jane then continued to explain how her own sadness had adversely affected the whole family. Taking Bridie's hand, Jane then told her how Sean had found her and within minutes, pointed out that what she was doing was wrong and how it was making everyone else sad.

"So, " said Jane. "You see, your Sean has been a real life saver for our family and then within just a couple of days he had captured our Caroline's heart. And looking back, " said Jane. "It all came about by your Joshua, coming here to attend Caroline's wedding, accompanying my favourite niece, Jessica. " Then rubbing Bridie's hand

Jane said, "So you might say, we owe our brighter future to the Foster family. "

Bridie pleasantly smiling with pride, replied, "Just seeing the four of them together Jane, makes me realise just how lucky I am. I have just come through a very dark period myself, when I was beginning to think my life was over. And now, just a week or two later, it looks like it's only just beginning. " Then squeezing Jane's hand, said, "Now come on Jane, our lives are good, things are on the up and look the rain's actually stopped. So come on Jane, let's go down and see what they are all up to. " As Jane led the way back downstairs, Bridie, said, "I tell you what Jane, I just wish I could look as good as you do, that dress it's absolutely gorgeous. "

As they entered the kitchen, Caroline said, "Come on Bridie, there's a tea waiting two sugars and a dash of milk and after you have drunk it, I need to run you round to see your old friend Lizzie, she's been dying to meet up with you again. "

As they drove over to meet Lizzie and Aiden, Bridie said, "It's funny, isn't it Caroline, I am really looking forward to seeing Lizzie again, but I am absolutely terrified of meeting my own family. "

"Well, " said Caroline. "I can tell you; they are going absolutely mad to see you again. I have had so many phone calls from Padraig, wanting to know what time you will be back, well quite honestly, he's been driving me mad with it. So don't you go worrying yourself over family, take it from me Bridie, you have been severely missed. "

When Caroline and Bridie arrived at Lizzie's house and just as they pulled on to her drive, the front door immediately opened and out came Lizzie smiling, but with tears running down her face. Their small house was built of stone, was in immaculate condition, set in a beautiful garden and had two beautiful flowering cherry trees.

Opening the passenger side door and after literally dragging Bridie out, Lizzie hugged her for quite a time, now with even more tears streaming down her face, said, "And where the hell have you been Bridie O'Brien, leaving me all this time, not one single word from you and me wondering how you were?" Then after a series of smaller sniffles, Lizzie said, "Never mind Bridie you're back home now. And I thank our good Lord, you have come back to me. " Bridie and Lizzie then walked into the house holding each other closely, while Aiden and Caroline followed them in. After entering the lounge, they both sat on the settee, still holding each other, Lizzie shouted through to the kitchen, "Chuck darling, put the kettle on and get that tray of cakes out, because we have some special visitors waiting in here. "

Bridie, looking puzzled asked, "So who is Chuck then Lizzie?"

"Oh, " said Lizzie. "He's my other half, he's originally from Cork, we met while we were working on the buses, but never mind about him for now, just tell me where the hell have you been. I met your two lovely lads. " And now touching Bridie's face, as if to make sure she was real, continued on to say, "And they are both fine looking lads you have their Bridie. Now, tell me where you went, you know I still think about you every third week in June, when we used to cut our hay. You must remember our hay making days, we used to be out in the bottom meadow working till it was dark, I sometimes wish we could go back to that time again. " Then getting back to her question, Lizzie said, "Come on then Bridie, after all these years of worrying, I just have to know, what happened to you?" For the next couple of hours, between sipping tea and eating cakes, Bridie explained where she went, how she met Edward and how she worked as a nurse. The more Bridie told Lizzie, the more it seemed Lizzie wanted to know. Chuck now finished in the kitchen, was finally introduced and the family photo album was brought out and lovingly discussed from front to back.

Eventually Aiden managed to say hello and chatted about their past together, Aiden then said, "You know, that you were my favourite cousin and when you upped and left, it took me quite some time to get over the loss. But never mind, you are back now, so come on Bridie, come over here and give me a hug. " Aiden then told her that there was welcome home party at his bar that night and that everyone would be there to welcome her back.

Bridie then said, "Our Sean has been telling me you have a bar in Swinford and that you were a very popular landlord, but then you always were the social one weren't you?"

Then in a more serious tone, said, "I think I should let you know Bridie, that Padraig and Patrick are very worried that you might still be angry with them, so please go easy on them. But bloody hell Bridie, it's really good to have you back. "

While Caroline and Bridie were at Lizzie's, Jessica and Jane were preparing the buffet for the welcome home party, while Howard, Sean and Josh were down at the mill, looking at tomorrow's jobs. Sean explained that they were lucky, because near where he lived, just a short distance down the A515, there was a really good steam society, where they had facilities that could overhaul, repair and retest the boiler for him. Sean then continued, "It looks like they like they were taking the boiler out, when the lorry project got abandoned, it may of course have failed its annual boiler inspection, so when I get it back home, I'll get the boiler straight up to them to see what needs doing. " Sean then said, "And regarding the cab, luckily I have a load of well-seasoned ash planks in the barn, so the cab frame shouldn't pose much of a problem at all. "

Josh then added, "I am hoping I might be able to pop up on the odd weekend and give you a hand with it. As I am beginning to think this is probably going to be the most interesting project you have ever tackled, " said Josh, sounding very eager to be a part of the action.

"I just wish I lived a little nearer, " said Howard. "Else I would love to help you with it as well, like Josh said, it sounds like a very interesting project. "

"That's no problem at all, " said Sean. "Because there's nothing to stop you and Jane coming to stay with us, in fact it would be really great, I would love to show the farm and some special parts of the area where we live."

When they eventually got back to the house the kitchen was covered in plates full of food, "Wow, sausage rolls, " said Howard, helping himself to one or two.

"You can keep your fingers off those, " said Jane, not expecting for a moment he would take any notice of her. Now stuffing a second sausage roll into his mouth, Howard leaving the kitchen for his study, said "Just you wait and see what I've found Sean. " Howard then reappeared a minute or two later carrying an old box file and the three of them sat at the table looking at its contents. "Christ Howard, " said Sean now looking extremely pleased. "You've found the original registration documents. I don't think you realise how much easier this will make putting the old girl back on the road and having this document, this means we can get the original registration number as well. " Sean, now looking ecstatically happy, said, "It just keeps getting better, you're a real star Howard. " Now, all three of them were randomly helping themselves to the prepared food, while at the same time, intensely studying the various items of historical information that Howard had found.

A short while later, Caroline and Bridie returned, chatting away happily as they entered the kitchen. "Oh, these look nice, " said Caroline, as she helped herself to a sausage roll. "Can I give you a hand?"

"Why, yes darling, you certainly can, " said Jane. "I have one very urgent and very important job for you, can you please keep these greedy men out of my kitchen?" Then while offering Bridie a chair, Jane asked, "Would you like a cup of tea Bridie? And please help yourself to a sausage roll. " Having got rid of the men out of the kitchen, the men had now gone outside to take a closer look at the shiny new lorry Sean had parked outside; the three ladies sat and chatted round the kitchen table.

Jane smiling said, "Funny isn't it, how a pile of rusty old metal and a few old tyres, can get three grown men extremely excited. "

When the men later returned, Sean was carrying a gold-coloured carrier bag and said, "I am so pleased you ladies are all here. "Then reaching into the bag removed five small packages, which he then handed out to the ladies. As Sean handed the fourth one to his mother, he said to them, "These small packages are engagement presents from Caroline and I. They are just small thank you gifts we bought, while we were visiting the Blue John Mine, up there in the Peak District. "

Each of the four ladies had been given a Blue John pendant on a gold chain.

Being the first one to open her package, Jane said, "Oh this is beautiful. "Then looking rather puzzled said, "But exactly what is Blue John?"

"Well, " said Sean. "It's probably the rarest stone there is, because there is only one Blue John Mine left in the world and that only works one small seam on a part-time basis. It's a pity, because it's a great place to visit, but sadly not that many people know of its existence. But it is a really special place to visit, "said Sean.

"Yes, it certainly is, " added Caroline. "There were 250 stone steps leading down into the cavern and perhaps more worrying, there are the same amount to climb out again. But it's well worth the effort, it was absolutely beautiful down there. "

Caroline then went on to explain how Sean had arranged for the guide to just take the two of them down, instead of the usual larger groups and when they got to the lowest part of the cavern, Sean had got down on one knee and asked Caroline to marry him.

Caroline then said "It was almost magical and something I will never, ever forget. Although it felt a little claustrophobic when we started down into the cave, I thought for a very panicky moment, we were going potholing, as it is a very narrow cavern, but that feeling just melted away when Sean proposed. "

"Oh darling, how romantic, " said Jane in her sentimental voice. "What a beautiful way to propose. "

"Yes, it certainly was, " said Caroline. "Even our lovely tour guide had a tear in his eye. But well I was just blown away with it all. "

Caroline, now gripping Sean's hand, added, "I know I have someone very special with Sean and that old Blue John Mine will always be a special place for me. " Sean then handed the fifth package to Jessica and asked if she would please pass it on to Mary for him. Bridie who had been listening with a smile said, "You probably won't know this Jane, but Edward and I always wanted a daughter. But God in his wisdom sent us two lovely boys. But now do I not only have two wonderful sons, but I now have two beautiful daughters as well. Who I might add, have already completely and utterly, stolen my heart. "

For a moment or two, no one spoke, all still taking in what they had been said. That was until Caroline's phone went off. "Hello, " answered Caroline. "Yes Aiden, yes we will all be coming over in about an hour's time. And Yes Aiden, we are all ready for a good night and yes, Josh will be telling another one of his stories. OK then Aiden, we will see you all very soon. " After changing clothes and carefully loading the food, they all set off for Mad O' Riley's Bar.

Chapter 18

Home Again

When they all walked into the bar, the room was already packed out with friendly faces and a great cheer went up as Bridie walked in. There were banners over the bar saying, 'Welcome Home Bridie' and posters made up of old family photos on the walls. Now in tears Bridie was met by Padraig and Patrick, who both put their arms around her, and hugged for quite some time. All three, now in tears stayed huddled as if trying to catch up on all those lost years, while family and friends just looked on smiling.

Aiden, now proudly holding his new radio microphone, announced, "Ladies and gentlemen, please put your hands together for the return of my favourite cousin, a very special family member our long-lost friend, Bridie Foster, AKA Bob. " As they all clapped and cheered, Aiden said, "Please give her a little room now, please let Bridie get into the place first, no need to crowd her, you have all night to speak to our Bridie. " He then said, "We also have two engagements to celebrate tonight. "Now even more cheering and clapping. Aiden then continued, "I am very pleased to announce that Jessica Holmes and Bridie's youngest son Joshua Foster, who some of you may recognise as our popular storyteller, and I am proud to say, is another relative of mine. Well Josh and the very lovely and extremely charming Jessica, are now officially engaged to be married. " And again, a big cheer went up. Aiden then said, "And not only that, but Caroline Anson, daughter of our good friends Howard and his good wife Jane Hanson, is engaged to marry Sean Foster, brother of Josh and another of Bridie's fine upstanding sons, and again I am very pleased to say is another relative of mine. Well, they are also officially engaged to be married. " Aiden, now standing on a step up, holding a glass of spirit up high in the air said, "I would like you all to raise your glasses and toast the return of our long time absent and much-loved Bridie. " After yet another big cheer, Aiden then said, "Now don't put your glasses down because I would like you to once again raise your glasses to our young and very lovely couples, Jessica and Joshua and Caroline and Sean. " Then after another big cheer, Aiden then said, holding a piece of paper up, "Now if I can just have your attention for a moment, I have two very important messages. " The bar went a little quieter, as Aiden said, "I am putting this list here, behind the bar, so if there is anyone who believes. " Aiden then paused to take another sip of his drink, which prompts a few to calls of, 'Come then Aiden, get on with it. ' Aiden then, after putting his drink back down said, "Like I was saying, anyone who believes they may not be able to walk home tonight, could they please write down their full postal addresses on this piece of paper. "Then pausing for a moment, said in a very loud voice, "Because the drinks are all free tonight. "Then, went up the biggest cheer of the night. Finally, when the cheers had died down a little, Aiden said, looking at Josh, "And I think, well I'm fairly sure, no I'm absolutely sure, after much public demand, that our resident storyteller, Josh. "Now putting his thumb up to Josh and getting a thumbs up back, Aiden then continued, "Will be giving us another of his now famous Guinness orientated stories. " Again, another big cheer went up. "Now everyone in the bar was smiling and still jostling to say hello to Bridie, who was now visibly overcome by her popularity. A little further back from the bar, Jessica and Caroline were busy showing off their engagement rings, while Jane was happily receiving numerous comments on how lovely she looked in her knitted dress.

Throughout that evening, everyone was in an extremely happy mood, as old acquaintances were renewed, and new relationships were made. Bridie was introduced to Padraig's and Patrick's extended families. Phone numbers were exchanged, and old friendships made stronger. After most of the food had been eaten, Aiden went back onto his step up and with microphone in hand said first in Gaelic and then in English, "My friends, as earlier announced, I am extremely pleased to introduce Joshua Foster. Who will be telling us another of his very humorous stories, so please put your hands together for that very welcomed friend of Mad O' Riley's Bar, Joshua Foster. " Again, a big cheer went up and friends were patting Josh on his back as he made his way up to the bar. Taking the microphone over from Aiden, Josh said, "First of all I would like, no I would love to say, what a great evening this is and what a good time we are all having. As you know I am only here in Swinford with my beautiful fiancée Jessica on holiday, but I honestly feel that I have lived here all of my life. There are very few things in life that make me sad, but I know that leaving you all behind here in Ireland, when we go home will be one of those very sad times. However, before I start tonight's little story, I would like to say, on the behalf of my family, a very big thank you, for making this the best welcome home party there could ever be. " With the whole bar cheering Josh, now waving his arms to quieten the noise said with a very serious look, "All of you. "Then pausing as if overcome, he continued, "Well I must say you are the best group of people I have ever had the pleasure to meet. "Amid a few more cheers continued, "And I mean that sincerely. " The bar now quietened as Josh continued in a more sombre voice, "And I mean that sincerely. " the room was now going very quiet as Josh continued, "And I believed in sincerity. "Then with his face turning to a smile, said, "I believe everyone should be sincere, whether they mean it or not. "

Now with everyone laughing, Josh said, "Well, tonight's little story is about our man called Paddy, who had been working overseas as a Tunneller in South America for six months and was making his way back home to Donegal. Anyway, when Paddy arrived back in

Dublin, rather than going home empty-handed, Paddy booked himself into a hotel for the night. This was so that Paddy could pay for the holiday in Rome he had booked at the travel agents, that's because his wife had always wanted to visit Rome. This also gave Paddy a little time for shopping for a few gifts to take home with him and to get his hair cut. The next morning, looking at himself in the mirror, Paddy decided he needed some new clothes and that he definitely did need a haircut. After paying for and picking up the tickets from the travel agents, Paddy went looking for a barber shop and as luck had it there was one in the same street as the travel agents, called Antonio's. When Paddy sat down in Antonio's barber chair, he was welcomed by the barber, speaking with an Italian accent. "Well would you believe it, " said Paddy. "Here's me just paid for our holiday in Italy and two minutes later I am here getting my hair cut by an Italian barber, well I'll be blowed. The barber then said with a slightly confused look, 'Why you wanna go to Italy, believe me it's a right shithole, why you think I moved over here then?'

"'Oh, dear, well bloody hell there's a problem, " said Paddy. 'Why is Italy not a good place to go then?'

"'No it's bloody well not, ' said the barber, who was now busy snipping away at Paddy's hair. Antonio, then asked Paddy, 'So where you going in Italy then?'

"'Well said Paddy, now sounding a little disappointed, well we are actually going to Rome. '

To which the barber said, 'Why you go to Rome, the worst bloody place to go in Italy is Rome. ' Then adding,

'It's a dirty place, so much traffic, so much bloody noise and what's more, there's no Guinness in Rome. '" At hearing Guinness, up went up another big cheer. Josh continued with his story, "Antonio then said, 'You just a save your money mate and stay right here, take it from me, it's a much better here than bloody Rome.

"The barber, still snipping away, then asked, 'So why you wanna go to Rome then?'

"'Well, ' said Paddy. 'It's my wife, she's always wanted to go to Rome and speak to the pope, apparently, he comes out of the Vatican and blesses the crowds in Vatican Square. The barber then tells Paddy that when the pope comes out on to his little balcony, he just waves his hand about, then says something in Latin, which nobody really understands, then he goes back inside, he don't talk to anyone. 'Oh, bloody hell, ' said Paddy, now looking extremely disappointed. 'I just paid all the money over and its non-returnable. I have paid for the hotel and everything. ' Antonio then asked Paddy which hotel they were staying at. 'Well, ' said Paddy now quickly looking at his paperwork. 'Oh here it is, it's the Hotel Delmar and we are booked in there from next Monday onwards. '

Antonio, now stopping in his tracks said, 'Not the Hotel Delmar, please you no stop there, it got rats as big as dogs and it's a right dump. I tell you sir I wouldn't stay there if they paid me to, it's a right dump. ' Later when Paddy left the barbers to go shopping, all the time he was thinking, what a mess he had made their holiday and was now dreading his Italian holiday.

"After Paddy and his wife had returned from their Roman holiday, Paddy while making his way back to the airport and before returning back to work, decide to get his hair cut before he left for South America. When he sat in the barber's chair, Antonio immediately recognised him and said, 'How the Italian holiday go, no good then eh. '

"'On the contrary, ' said Paddy. 'Me and the wife, well, we have holidayed all over the world and we never had a better holiday than we had in Italy. '

"Antonio now snipping away again said, 'What about Rome, it was a right shithole, eh. '

"'Wrong again, ' said Paddy. 'Why it's a really beautiful city, piazzas, fountains, churches, why it's a beautiful city, in fact it was so nice, we are going back there again next year. Oh, ' said Antonio. 'Itmust have changed a lot since I left back in 1950. '

"'Well, ' said Paddy. 'If I was you, I would be back there like shot, why it's a lovely place to live. '

"'Well, what about the Hotel De Marr, right dump eh?'

"'Well not at all, ' said Paddy. 'Apparently they had knocked the old one down and built a beautiful new one, it's the best hotel we have ever stayed in. '

"Antonio, now looking very confused and extremely apologetic, said, 'It looks like I give a load of bad advice, eh my friend. '

"'Well, ' said Paddy. 'You were right about the Vatican. Well when we got there, well there must have been ten thousand people in front of us, when the pope came out on to the balcony, it was just like you said. ' Which made Antonio feel just a little happier.

"'So, ' said Antonio. 'The missus never got to speak to the pope then, eh sir. '

"'Well actually she did, ' said Paddy and went to explain how they were both at the very back of the crowd. 'But, 'said Paddy. 'I kept getting very strong eye contact with the pope. ' Paddy went on to tell him that after the blessing of the crowd had finished, how the Vatican guards had cleared a route for the pope who came over to us and then spoke to them. Now standing back in astonishment, Antonio said, 'The pope, he spoke to you, so what did he say to you?'

"Paddy then turned to and said, 'the Pope said, 'Who the fuck cut your hair? Now don't tell me, I think I know, it's just got to be that useless little bastard Antonio. '"

At this the whole bar was in an uproar and even Bridie had to put her hand over her mouth to try and hide her slightly embarrassed smile.

Still laughing Aiden, took back the microphone and said, "Well there you go, I knew there would be a Guinness mentioned in there somewhere. Thank you, Josh. God only knows, what we are going to do when you leave us?" He then added still laughing, "Just wouldn't you love to have seen poor old Paddy's hair. " Then pointing to the back of the room said, "Now there's plenty more food to be eaten and believe it or not, we still have a little booze left. So come on my good friends it's party time. " Towards the end of the night, Aiden was back on his microphone and said to them all, "If you have been drinking and it's too far to walk, then please use Swinford Taxis, they are already paid for and they are ready and waiting for you outside, that's if you needed one. "

At the end of an unforgettable night and after many farewell hugs and kisses, Bridie's group finally left for Mainear Darach.

During their journey home, everyone was talking about their wonderful night out, when Bridie said, "You know I thought I was going to die without seeing my family again, so as you can see I have had the best time ever. Thank you all for bringing me here and thank you boys, for giving me two new daughters. Now, " said Bridie, holding up a bag. "Our Aiden gave me a couple of bottles of Poitín, so I think we should all have a glass or two before we go to bed. "

Jessica, who had been purposely staying sober, said, "What about me Bridie, I'm driving, and I have always wanted to try Poitín. "

"Well, " said Jane. "Just let me pop into the house and I will get you and Josh one of Howard's hip flasks. And you can drink it in the hot tub, later. "

When Jessica and Josh eventually got back to the cottage, they sat in bed, each sipping a very large glass of Poitín. After her first sip and holding the glass up to the light, Jessica said, "What the hell is in this Josh, do you know?"

Josh having almost finished his glass and with his hand moving towards Jessica's raised glass, said, "Sorry

Jess, I haven't got a clue sweetheart. But if you don't like it, I can finish it off for you?"

"Not a chance, no you bloody well won't, " replied Jessica' moving the glass out of his reach. "No this is all mine. " Within minutes Josh was fast asleep and snoring like a horse, leaving Jessica to switch everything off and try to sleep through his very loud snoring.

Chapter 19

The next morning Josh was awakened by his mobile phone, as he went to answer it, he could see he was alone. "Hello Josh speaking. "Now looking around to see where Jessica was. Then recognising the voice said, "Oh hello Sean, what's the problem?" Josh then said, "Well I was planning on being there at about eleven o'clock mate. " At this point Josh had now got out of bed and was heading into the kitchen. "OK then bro, I will let her know. See yah bro. " As Josh entered the kitchen, he could see Jessica ironing.

"Oh, good morning Mr Sleepy head, " said Jessica smiling. "I thought you were out for the day. "

"Why's that then Jess?"

"Well, " replied Jess. "It's nearly ten o'clock. "

Suddenly in panic mode, Josh said, "Oh hell, I was supposed to be at your uncle's house for eleven. Sean's just called and he told me to remind you bring a change of clothes, apparently because you and Caroline are out riding this morning"

This immediately resulted in both of them rushing to get ready and then rush out the cottage. As Josh was driving out from the cottage driveway, with a piece of toast in his hand, he said, "That was some night, eh Jess. When we have to go back home, you know I'm going to miss all this. But the worst part I am dreading, is being back on my own, what would you say to moving in with me and before you say it, I've already fixed it with Maggie and she loves the idea. "

"Well, " replied Jessica. "Thank God for that, I was almost in tears just thinking about it the other morning. "

Now leaning across and slapping Jessica on the knee, Josh said, "Now I am feeling happy again Jess, as I will now be going back to something I am looking forwards to, living with you. "

When they got to Mainear Darach they went straight into the kitchen where Caroline and Sean were finishing their breakfast.

"Good morning everyone, " said Josh, now picking a piece of toast up off Sean's plate.

"Have you not eaten then?" said Jane just putting things away.

"No, " said Josh. "Didn't have the time Jane, I was too busy doing the ironing and I completely forgot all about breakfast. "

"You lying little toad, " Jessica shouted. "Don't believe him Aunty, he got up late, after drinking too much alcohol last night. "

"Well, that makes two of them then, " said Jane. "Howard is still in bed and he's not feeling at all that healthy, darling. " Then Jane said smiling, "But wasn't it an excellent night?" Now putting the frying pan back on the range. She said, in a loud voice, "How about a bacon sandwich then Josh?" And now laughing Jane said, "I should imagine all of that ironing must have given you a real good appetite? What about you Jessica, are you hungry darling?"

"Oh, yes please, Aunty. You know Just lying there, watching Josh do all that ironing, has made me feel quite hungry. "

Where's Mom, Sean?" asked Josh.

"Well, you might know, " replied Sean. "She was up at six, made a cup of tea and went for a walk. She's outside on the patio now, sitting in the sunshine reading her book. So why don't you go out there and say hello? Oh, and tell her about your ironing, she will enjoy hearing that Josh, she won't believe it for a minute, but she will enjoy hearing you telling it to her. "

"Don't you dare Joshua Foster, " said Jessica. "And you, Sean Foster, stop encouraging him. You're very quiet this morning Caroline, " said Jessica. "Are you OK?"

Caroline slowly looking up replied, "Not really Jess, I think I had just a little too much to drink. But just give me a few minutes and we can go for that ride; I should be back in the correct world by then. " She then added, "Well, that is the ride will either kill me or cure me. "

Then as Jane handed Josh his bacon sandwich and with a pat on her backside Josh said, "Thanks Jane you're a real life saver, any chance of a coffee?" Now with a sandwich in hand Josh went out to see his mother. "Good morning Mom, how did you go on last night? That was some good night wasn't it?"

Bridie, now getting up and giving Josh a kiss said, "Wasn't it just, I really wish your dad could have been with us, as he would have loved it. But he had got a soil testing team coming out and with the milking, well you know what it's like. But next time I come over, he is definitely coming with me, even if I have to drag him here in chains, but you know your dad, when he does go out, he really enjoys it. Well son, if it wasn't for your Jessica inviting you to the wedding, I might have never seen all of my Irish family again. Oh, I've made my excuses to Caroline's mom, Jane. Oh and isn't she such a lovely lady. My brother Padraig will be picking me up and taking me to my old home for the day. Now tell me, where is that beautiful Jessica?" Now asked Bridie in a more serious tone, looking to see if they could be overheard, said, "Now you just look after that girl Joshua, believe me son, girls like Jessica are very few and far between. "

Now taking another bite of his sandwich replied, "She will be out with my coffee in a minute Mom, she's just waiting for Jane to make it for me. "

Now looking slightly annoyed Bridie said, "Well there you go again, now what have just told you. "

And at that moment Jessica appeared carrying Josh's coffee. "Is he being naughty again Bridie?" asked Jessica handing the cup to Josh. "Josh has just been telling everyone in there that he was late because he was doing the ironing. But I'm afraid it was just another one of his little stories, like the story he told last night. But you must know him better than me. "Then putting her arm round him said, "But I wouldn't want him any other way, because after all, that's our Josh, but I must warn you, that since he kissed that Blarney Stone, he's now even worse.

"But wasn't that some night at Aiden's?" said Jessica. "I don't think I have ever been to a happier gathering than that one, I was either crying or laughing. And your cousin Aiden, well what a star he is. I told him later that night, he should take up being a compere for a living, because he was a complete natural. Well, sorry but I must leave you, as I am off riding with Caroline, but hopefully I will see you all later, I just hope poor Caroline doesn't fall off. "

Then Josh said, "Oh Jess, if you're going into the kitchen. "Now handing Jessica a plate and empty cup. "Could you take these in for me?"

Bridie then said angrily, while at the same time trying to smack Josh's legs, but with little success, as Josh was just laughing and trying to dodge her slaps, "What have I just told you Joshua Foster, you had better treat that girl right and just remember this, you're not too big for me to smack. " Then picking up her book and handbag said, "Anyway I had better go inside and wait there, as your Uncle Padraig will be here any minute. " As they entered the kitchen, they could see that Padraig had already arrived and was sitting at the kitchen table drinking coffee with Jane.

"Good morning Bridie, " said Padraig smiling. "Now, tell me, wasn't that the best night ever? Your brother Patrick was coming with me this morning, but I'm afraid he's not feeling too well this morning. Not that it's anything too serious now. " Padraig added, "I think it may have been just a little too much of the drink I'm afraid. " Then looking across at Caroline, Padraig added, "And by the look of it he's not the only one, eh folks?"

Jane then said, "And there's another one upstairs Padraig and I think poor old Howard may be out for the day, as he looked a little green round the gills when I looked in on him a minute ago. But you're right darling that was some night. "

Padraig then added, "Linda my wife really liked that dress, you were wearing last night Jane and would like to know where you got from? And if you don't mind me saying Jane, it really did look good on you. "

Jane now feeling extremely pleased, said, "Well thank you Padraig, I bought it online, so please let Linda know that I will get Caroline to text the web address to you. " With that, Padraig and Bridie left for their old family home.

"Right, " said Sean. "Come on then Josh, we can bring that trailer up here and load it straight on to the lorry, I've bought a load of slings and strops with me, so there shouldn't be any problems there. And hopefully Peter should be already waiting for us down there, so best not to keep him waiting. "

When Josh and Sean arrived at the old timber mill, the big doors were already open, and they could hear Peter was busy clearing a route out.

"Good morning, " said Sean. "How did the milking go?"

"Oh, good morning Sean, yes, the milking went well, no excitement this morning thank God. Now, " said Peter. "If one of you can watch me back on to the draw bar, we can have this trailer out and away. "

After successfully coupling up the trailer, Sean said, "There's been a bit of a change of plan Peter, we are going to load the lorry up by the house now, where there's a little more space, because I am terrified that I might damage that hired lorry. Then when that's loaded, we can use the telescopic handler to reload the trailer down here. "

"OK boss, " said Peter. "I saw that new Scania lorry parked up there, nice looking truck, it looks brand new. "

"More's the pity it's not mine as I would love to own it, but it's on hire, " said Sean. "Like I said, it's hired that's why I thought it would be safer to load up there, I don't want to pay for any damage if I can help it. "

Then after checking the trailer, Josh said, "It's OK to go Peter, if you can take it up there. "

As they walked behind the trailer back towards the house, Sean said, "I checked my account last night and immediately noticed that Howard had transferred all the money I had paid him, back into my account. So, I raised the matter with Howard and he said, 'As it would have gone for scrap anyway, it seemed wrong to take my money for it. ' I tried reasoning with him Josh, but he insisted that I take it for free. So, Josh, have you got any ideas, you normally come up with all the solutions?"

"Well, the Sean, why don't you make Howard a joint owner, you know a partner in it, I think he would go for that?" Josh then added, "Isn't he a real nice guy our Howard, I don't think you would ever find a better partner than him, such lovely guy. "

After a little effort the rolling chassis was loaded on to the lorry and soundly secured. The partially stripped cab quickly followed and after a bit of temporary packing, using some of the timber Sean had brought over with him, the cab was also soundly secured on the lorry. Within two hours all the various parts of the steam lorry had been loaded, properly secured and it was ready to go.

After a final walk round the old sawmill, just to make sure they had collected everything, Sean secretly slipped Peter a fifty euro note and said, "Thank you Peter, you've done us a good job mate. Now please, whatever you do, don't mention this to Howard, as he doesn't need to know."

"OK boss, " replied Peter. "It was a pleasure, helping you, but where is Howard this morning, I would have put money on it he would have been down here for this, as he's been talking about nothing else for days. "

"Oh, " said Sean. "Well, we all had a good night at Mad O' Riley's Bar last night and I think Howard may have overdone it a little with the drink. "And then added, "But I wouldn't worry Peter, I think he will be OK in a few hours' time. Anyway, thanks again mate and hopefully I may see you again. "

Peter finally done, drove off as Sean and Josh walked back towards the house, Josh said, "You know I thought Howard might not be feeling too well this morning, he was really going for it last night. And I tell you what, Jane looked pretty good in that tight dress as well, isn't she just a star. It's just a pity I don't live nearer to here, because I am getting very fond of Howard and Jane's company and they are now both definitely on my favourite people list. "

As they neared the house, they saw Caroline, Jessica and Jane walking down towards them. When they met up, they said, "Oh we've just come to give you a hand. "

"No need" said Sean, "It's all loaded and ready to go."

"OK then, " said Josh. "As it's only one-thirty, so how about we all go to the rifle range?"

"Oh yes, " said Jessica, "We went there the other day, and we had a great time. " Before anyone could comment, Jessica said, "Leave it with me, I will phone them and arrange it. "

"Well, " said Caroline, now looking a lot more human. "It looks like we are all off to the rifle ranges, like it or not, whatever and wherever they are. "

When they all got back to the house, Jane got some sausages out of the fridge and said, "I don't know why, but I really fancy a sausage sandwich, does anyone want to join me?"

"Yes, please Jane, " said Josh.

"Me too, " said Sean.

Then Jane said, "Would you close the door please, I don't think Howard in his condition, would appreciate the smell of fried sausages. What about you Caroline? Do you think that stomach of yours can handle one yet?"

Then Josh added, "Sorry to be a pain, but do you have brown sauce, Jane, as I just love brown sauce especially on fried sausages"

"Yes, we do, no problem Josh, our Caroline loves brown sauce, darling. "

A short while later everyone was eating sausage sandwiches, when Jessica came in looking very happy, saying, "Right, it's all fixed, we are all booked in and the best news is we have George again. "

"Oh, that's lovely then darling, now tell me, do you want brown sauce on your sandwich, or we have tomato ketchup if you prefer it?"

An hour later they arrived at the rifle ranges, where a very eager Jessica excitedly led the way, explaining the virtues of target shooting as together they walked towards the reception. Because of the noise aspects, the firing ranges were set well away from any residential development and were located in a very rural backwater. Everything there looked immaculately maintained and the large tarmac surfaced car park was surrounded by flowering shrubs and ornamental trees. As they entered the reception, George was already there waiting for them and after a few introductions, George was helping them all to complete their registration forms.

As he checked the forms over, before handing them in, he asked, "Who's Caroline?"

"I am, " replied Caroline. "Don't tell me I made a mistake?"

"No, " said George. "You have put down you're a vet, you don't happen to do cattle, do you?"

"Well, yes, " said Caroline. "I am a large animal vet, why do you ask?" At that very moment, the conversation shifted from shooting to his small herd of bo riabhach cattle, which are a rare breed of Irish cattle.

"Then I need to rub shoulders with you young lady, " said George smiling. "As I might need a little technical information from you. " After a quick refresher, Jessica was away again and this time blasted her way through over a hundred rounds. The others eventually finished their fifty and all agreed that their visit had been a different and very interesting way to spend an afternoon.

When they got back to the club house and handed back the guns, George, looking slightly taken aback, said, "Well young Jessica, you've gone and done it again, just look at your scores. "

"Are they OK?" asked her Aunty Jane, not really understanding what George was going on about.

"Not just OK madam, " replied George. "These are marksman scores. Believe me and I am not being condescending in the least, nor am I exaggerating. " Then looking at Jessica, George said, "I think you need to join a rifle club young lady, you really do and when you have, I will probably be meeting up with you at Bisley next year."

Then Jane still not really understanding what it was all about, said, "This Bisley thing darling, is it good?"

"Good, " replied George. "It's one on the world's top shooting venues. "

Jane turning to Jessica said, "If this man is right then darling, you really must let me buy you one of these gun things for your engagement present."

Then looking rather pleased, added, "There you are darling, that's one engagement present sorted. I've just got Sean and Caroline's to go." When they all burst out laughing, Jane joined in with them, although she was not really sure what they all were laughing at.

Walking back to the car, still laughing, Josh putting his arm around Jane's waist and said, "Jane, please, please don't ever change, because you're a perfect star, a wonderfully perfect star."

"Well thank you darling, that's very nice of you to say so and you just watch me Josh, I will get Jessica one of those gun things, just you wait and see."

When they got back to Mainer Darach, they found Howard sitting in the kitchen looking a little bit worse for wear. "Hello darling," said Jane sounding extremely happy. "You should have come with us Howard, we have had an absolutely wonderful afternoon, shooting these rifle things. And Jessica, our clever niece, is going to Bisley next year to meet George, aren't you darling? Now," said Jane. "What are we all having for tea?"

"How about fish and chips?" said Josh, hoping that no one would object. Then before anyone could make any other suggestions, he asked, "Is everyone happy with fish and chips? Well, that's OK then, fish and chips it is. You take the orders please Jess and I will go and fetch them."

Later after they had all finished eating their fish and chips Sean said, "Did you actually look at Jessica's scores Josh, I've been looking at them while you were gone and that George fellow was right in what he said, you know, they were extremely good. I think George was right, when he said she should look at joining a club. " Sean then added, "Because you never know Josh; I could finish up with a famous marksman as a sister-in-law?"

Howard, now feeling a little better after he had eaten large portions of everything, said, "Sorry I wasn't there to help you this morning guys, but I see you got it all loaded up OK. "

"Don't you worry about that, " said Sean. "It loaded like a dream and it's all ready to go Howard. " Then looking out of the window, Sean said, "I must remember to set the tachograph when I leave in the morning, only I am not that used to using them. " Then in slightly louder voice said, "I still have over two hundred cows waiting for me back home Howard. "And then said, "But I am really going to miss being here with you and Jane. " Just then he saw Padraig and his mother pulling up outside. "Oh, Mom's back, I wonder how she went on?"

"I bet she will have had a wonderful time, " said Caroline. Now joining Sean by the window, and seeing her walking towards the house, added, "Well she looks happy enough and what's more, it looks like she has plenty of things to take home with her. " The curiosity was a little too much for Josh, who had now joined them by the window.

324

"Well don't just stand there watching her struggle, go out and help them, " said Jessica heading for the door. Now feeling just a little guilty, they all left with Jessica to help Bridie.

As they came back into the kitchen, all talking at once, Josh carrying a large carryall said, "I wonder what's in this bag, its bloody heavy enough, I think you may have to throw this one in the cab with you Sean?"

As Bridie came through the door accompanied by Padraig and with a big smile on her face, she said, "Hello everyone, what a day. " Now putting her handbag down by the chair and flopping down into the chair. "Well, I tell you, I must have walked miles. Padraig and Patrick, along with their lovely families, have taken me all over the old farm and took me inside the old house and when I got in there, I came over very emotional, when a million old memories, all came flooding back. And to answer your question Josh, I got all sorts of things in that bag, some of my old thing along with some old photos. "

By now Jane had boiled the kettle and was handing Bridie a cup of tea, saying, "We have saved you some fish and chips Bridie, as we didn't know whether you had eaten or not. "

"Oh, thank you Jane, you're very kind, but I don't think I need to eat for another week after what I have eaten today. I tell you Jane; they have all spoilt me rotten. " Then touching Padraig's hand, Bridie said, "And the best thing is, I have my two brothers back. "

"Look I really have to go now Bridie, " said Padraig. "But I will call on you tomorrow evening, just to check you got back OK. "

After waving goodbye to Padraig, Bridie then told them where she had been, who she had met and told them about her newly extended family. Later in the evening, they spent some time passing photos round and looking at some of Bridie's old, treasured possessions. Josh was very interested in a few of the photographs that showed his mother and uncles as children, as he had never before seen pictures of his mother as a child, and he found it all slightly strange to see.

At nine o'clock, Josh and Jessica said their long goodbyes to Caroline, Bridie and Sean, before leaving for the cottage.

As they drove back, Josh said, "It's our last night in the cottage tonight. "Then added "It's sad really, isn't it?"

"Ah yes, " said Jessica. "And this may be our last time in the hot tub. "

Josh then said, "Well the good news is, we've still got a bottle of the champagne left. Oh, and half a bottle of brandy. So, you know what that means Jess?"

"Yes, champagne cocktails in the hot tub. "

It was going very dark, as they lay in the hot tub. Josh with a drink in his hand said, "Look at those stars Jess. I'm living as near to Greenwich Observatory as anyone can get, but I've never seen stars as clear as these, too much light pollution I suppose?" Then casually stroking Jessica's naked body, said, "You know, this holiday is going to stay with me forever, it's been a bit like a dream, so many good things happening, never dreamt our holiday would be this good. " Now floating Jessica on to his lap and taking her into his arms, said, "But without you Jess, this holiday would have been nothing at all. Then kissing Jessica on her forehead, said, "Come on, finish your drink and let's go to bed. "

Jessica then looking into Josh's eyes, said, "And there are a few things I will never forget. "

"And what are those, Jess?" asked Josh.

"All those very intimate moments and all those sexual experiences we shared together. I think we both know Josh, that when we have been married for a few years and are maybe raising children, our sex lives will never be quite the same was on this holiday. But at least we can look back at this holiday. " And then bursting into laughter Jessica continued, "We can say, remember our Irish holiday Josh, when we almost fucked each other into the ground?" Then as Jessica climbed out of the hot tub, extending her hand to Josh she said, "Come on lover boy, let's go to bed, because I'm not quite fucked into the ground just yet. " That night there was no dressing up, no massage oils, no pink ropes, just a little sensuous foreplay and some slow intimate sex.

Chapter 20

Going Home

The next morning as it was their last day in the cottage it was all hands to tidying and cleaning and Jessica had gotten stuck right into it, while Josh was making breakfast.

"How many eggs do you want in your omelette Jess?" Josh called out to Jessica who was now in the lounge, hoovering up.

"How many eggs have we got left Josh?" she asked.

"About two dozen or maybe a few more, " said Josh peering into the fridge. Jessica's curiosity now drove her back in to the kitchen, to see for herself.

Looking into the fridge Jessica said, "Bloody hell Josh, look at all this food. There's enough here for another two weeks. "

"Well, I thought we could boil a few eggs and eat them on our way home, being as I really like hard boiled eggs, " said Josh now trying to block her view by closing the fridge door.

"Let me see in there, " said Jessica, now pulling the door wide open. As Jessica rummaged in the fridge she complained, "Look, there are three packs of unopened sausages, four sirloin steaks, at least a kilo of bacon and six bloody lobster tails. What the hell are doing with lobster tails?" Then, still in disbelief, Jessica said, "We will just have to leave some of this food at Aunty Jane's. " After cleaning the cottage from top to bottom and packing their clothes, they had just enough time for a last dip in the hot tub. As they lay there, Jessica said, "I spoke to Mom last night about moving in with you and she was worried that she wouldn't see me very often. So, I told her we would spend a weekend at Epsom every six weeks or so and she seemed a little happier with that. " Jessica then said, "I think we should do the same with your mom, as well. " Jessica was now waiting for a response.

"Epsom's not that difficult to get to and I do like being with Mary and Gerry, or maybe we could go away somewhere for the odd long weekend together, there's lots of places to go, "said Josh. "I told Sean we would go up and help him with the steam lorry every now and then, so problem solved, eh Jess?" Josh, now sounding a little more cheerful, said, "Maybe we could take your mom some boiled eggs, when we go round to see her, eh Jess? The one thought that's making me smile, " said Josh laughing. "Is how my mom is going to put us all in separate bedrooms on Friday night. I bet that's really got her scratching her head. "

After loading up the car and now with two carrier bags full of excess food and a massage table, it was looking a little full. When Josh returned from dropping the keys back and saying thank you to the owners of the cottage, they finally set off for Mainear Darach. When they arrived there, Josh carried the two carrier bags, full of food into the house. They found Jane and Howard in the old orangery.

"Come in and take a look, " said Howard. "It looks a lot bigger now it's cleared out, I didn't realise just how much junk there was in here. "

Then Jane looking very industrious in her new dungarees, said pointing out the different locations, "We are having new underfloor heating here, there's a wall mounted TV going up there for Howard, you know Howard, he just has to have his TV. " Then pointing to the old wooden framed windows. "There are new opaque double-glazing panels going here and like Howard said earlier, there's even room for a massage table over here, so what do you think Josh?" Jane now looking very excited said, "I cannot wait till it's all finished, oh and maybe a heated towel rail over here. "

Josh now smiling said, "Having a massage table, eh Jane?"

"Yes, " replied Jane. "It was seeing those bottles of massage oils in the cottage, that gave me the idea. So, my darlings, the next time you come to stay, we should have everything you could possibly need. "

As they all walked back to the kitchen, Howard said, "I was speaking to Caroline this morning and they got to your mom's OK. Apparently, they had already unloaded the Sentinel and have just dropped the hired lorry back off, somewhere near Derby. It's odd, Josh, but Caroline sounds like she is really getting into this steam lorry restoration thing and more importantly, she seems to be really enjoying herself. " Now putting his hand on Josh's shoulder, Howard said, "But you will see for yourself on Thursday, won't you?"

Now they are all back in the kitchen, Jane while washing her hands, asked, "Jessica darling, what's on earth is all this food doing on the table?"

"Oh, its food from what Josh over ordered, so I brought it all over from the cottage for you Aunty, " replied Jessica. "It would be difficult to take it all back with us, so we thought you might like it. "

Jane now peering into the bags, said, "Oh lobster tails, oh, I just love lobster tails, thank you darling, how thoughtful. "A short while later, that is, after they had all eaten their egg sandwiches, freshly made by Josh, they all walked slowly over to the car, where they said their sad goodbyes and then set off for Limerick.

As they drove into Limerick Josh said, "No satnav needed this time, eh Jess, I hope we get the same room? Oh, and I forgot to tell you, we are both booked into the hotel's spa tomorrow morning. I have booked us both an hour-long massage and you have a facial and nail sessions as well. "

"So, what are you doing while I have the facial and my nails done then?" asked Jessica.

Then moving his ribcage, a little further away from Jessica's elbow and starting to laugh, Josh replied, "Oh I think I might be going for the happy ending, I'm even taking those pink cotton ropes in with me. " They were both still laughing when they pulled into the hotel's underground car park and when Josh said, "It seems like years ago since we were here. And I booked us in to that same French restaurant tonight Jess, so you had better make sure that black lingerie is handy, eh, my beautiful, gorgeous, sexy sweetheart. "

When they checked in at the reception, Josh asked if they could have the same room that they had last time and could they order the same room service breakfast at around eight-thirty.

After a few clicks on her keyboard, the receptionist said, "There you go sir, that's the same room as before with room service breakfast for two at eight-thirty, and I see you are booked in the spa tomorrow morning. "

As she handed Josh the key card Josh said, "No need to tell us how to get there, I'm sure we can find our way again and thank you very much for changing the room, you have been extremely helpful. " A short while later and back in their old room Josh said to Jessica who was stretched out on the bed, "Don't get too comfortable Jess, it's gone half past three now and I thought we could have a quick walk round the shops before dinner. "

Jessica now sitting up and looking slightly confused, replied, "I thought we could go shopping in the morning, we have plenty of time. "

"Not if we are going to that retro clothes shop you went to in Dublin, we don't. So please come on Jess, let's get moving, " said Josh now eating yet another hardboiled egg and thinking, *Only another fifteen to go.* Once outside in the sunshine, holding hands, they were enjoying their short walk to the shopping centre. Once again, they crossed the bridge, stopping midway to look at the River Shannon flowing below and made their way into town.

"Just what are we shopping for?" asked Jessica.

"Nothing specific, " replied Josh. "Just thought a walk before dinner would do us both good. " But then passing the jewellers, Josh spotted a second-hand bracelet he liked the look of and stopping for a better look, said, "Look Jess, look at that bracelet on the second display up. I really like that, it's got that art deco look to it. " Then pulling her towards the door, Josh said, "Come on Jess, let me treat you to a bracelet. " Although Jessica was initially not that interested, once she had the bracelet on her wrist, she could see why Josh was so impressed with it. Jessica having put up only a token resistance was now walking out of the shop with a very stylish bracelet on her wrist. After a coffee and a walk around the shops, they headed back to the hotel.

Back in their room, with his usual, I'm in charge style; Josh said, "The table's booked for eight, so we need to leave the room at around seven-thirty, that gives us nearly two hours. " Josh then asked, "So what are you wearing tonight Jess, that black dress again?"

"No, I'm not, " said Jessica. "I have that dark shiny electric blue cocktail dress; I certainly don't want to be seen wearing the same dress twice. "

"Why not, " Josh said. "I'm wearing my 007 dinner jacket twice. "

"Yes, but it's different for a man and before you ask, yes the dress will cover the black lingerie. "

"Oh that's good, " said Josh. "So, you shower first Jess, then I will follow you. " Just then Jessica's phone rang. And with a, "Hello, Caroline. "Started a thirty-minute-long phone conversation.

"Bloody hell, you will see Caroline tomorrow, for God's sake, " said Josh now getting slightly impatient. "And if you keep talking now, then you will have nothing left to talk about. " At that moment Josh's phone started to ring. Josh was now lying on the bed, talking to Sean, but as if making a point their conversation only lasted for just a few minutes. "That was Sean on the phone, he was telling me that Howard and Jane are going to Mom's next week. Apparently, Jane wants to go down the Blue John Mine to see where Sean proposed to Caroline. "

"So, I had better phone the Blue John Mine up and tell them to get some extra stock in their gift shop, because knowing Jane, she will want to buy at least one of everything they have. And there's something else Josh, " said Jessica.

"What's that then Jess?"

"Well, " said Jessica. "It would appear that we are both sleeping in your old room. "

"Bloody hell, " said Josh. "Who would have thought it, well I'll be blowed. "

"Well possibly, " replied Jessica. "But only if you're very, very quiet. "

"Oh, sweetheart, " said Josh. "I bet that decision would have been a difficult one for Mom to make. "Then laughing said, "Well I wondered how she would fit us in, bloody brilliant. "

When Josh came out of the bathroom, drying himself, Jessica was sitting at the dressing table, putting on her make-up wearing Josh's favourite black lacy lingerie.

"Christ Jess, " said Josh. "I just love that lacy bra, it looks so sexy. "

"But this isn't really a bra Josh, it's not even half a bra, it's just straps and what's more, it's certainly not that comfortable to wear. Can't I just put it on when we get back, it just seems so pointless to me, " said Jessica.

"I don't think you fully understand the concept at work here Jess, " said Josh. "It's part of the mental build-up, you know, the thought of it, like the excitement you get unwrapping a present, even when you know exactly what's inside?"

"No, sorry Josh, " said Jessica. "I don't and if you dare eat another one of those bloody boiled eggs, then honestly, I am going to throw them all in the bin. Now, " said Jessica, putting her dress on. "Can you zip it up for me please and you had better hurry up, it's nearly quarter past, look. " After tying Josh's black bow tie, Jessica, gave Josh a quick kiss, stood back and said, "Well how do I look Josh?"

"Like a million dollars Jess. I think when I walk down through the hotel with you, all the men are going to think, *Will you just look at that lucky bastard, she is stunning.* " Now giving Jessica a kiss, Josh said, "And you know what

Jess, they will be exactly right, I am a very lucky man. So, let's go down there and show them what a happily engage couple looks like, " said Josh as he patted Jessica on her bum as she passed through the closing door.

When they got to the restaurant, they were immediately recognised by the manager, who said smiling, "It is so good to see you back again and may I say madam, you look absolutely beautiful. Please follow me to your table, I have especially reserved this one here by the window. " As the manager helped Jessica with her chair and handed her the menu, he said, "We have a new menu tonight and may I recommend the bouillabaisse, as our chef originates from the Marseille region and it is one of his speciality dishes. "

Later, after eating yet another superb meal and while holding hands over the table, Josh said, "As much as I love this place, I can't wait until we are back on our own again, you just look so attractive and very, very sexy, the anticipation it's almost driving me crazy. "

As they left the manager said, "I dearly hope we will see you here again, as it's so nice to see young people enjoying their food. As you probably know, we French just love good food lovers. "

"Well thank you for a wonderful meal, " said Jessica. "You are now our favourite Irish restaurant. "

When they got back to the room, there was a bottle of champagne and some chocolates waiting on the bedside table. "Are we drinking this before or after I get fucked by my adorable and very considerate fiancé, " asked Jessica, as she dimmed the lights.

Josh replied, "Well how about a very slow sexy striptease, followed by a little exhibitionism and then maybe you undress me, eh Jess?"

"Your wish is my command, " said Jessica. She then tuned the TV into a radio station that was playing late night music and finding some suitable music, began her slow striptease. Using the dressing table chair whilst teasing Josh by displaying, then covering her smooth sensuous body, it was only a matter of time before Josh, went over and started caressing and kissing her. Jessica now completely naked apart from her stockings, suspenders and high heels, then, started to undress Josh, who was enjoying watching Jessica sexily gyrating to the music. Now fully naked Josh carried Jessica over to the bed and pushing his face between her legs began giving Jessica some very intense oral stimulation. Being as the music now changed to a very fast tempo, Josh reached out grabbed the remote and switched it off. Then lifting both of Jessica's knee up and apart, began licking along both sides of her labia. A very relaxed Jessica, lay back a enjoyed every single second, knowing that Josh would soon be pushing his penis into her. As she lay there, enjoying the pleasure she was experiencing, she thought to herself, how some people can remain virgins, or spend a lifetime on their own, I just don't understand, to live without the pleasures of sex, is a life not really worth living. Then feeling so very alive, climbed on top of Josh and after looking down into Josh's eyes, said, "Being here alone with you, makes me realise, just how lucky I am. " Then leaning forward to kiss him with her long hair falling all over him, whispered, "I just want to stay just like this forever, with you inside me, I can feel every little movement you make, God I feel good. I don't think I could ever feel this happy with anyone else, my heart is just so full of you, well sometimes it's so strong, it almost frightens me. "

Josh then pulling her face closer to him said, "You know I'm yours Jess and I always will be and at moments like this, I realise how empty my life had been before I fell in love with you. "

"That's such a lovely thing to say Josh, I know you are mine. "Then slowly thrusting her hips, forwards and back, said, "I think I need to say thank you by making you come inside me. "And then very energetically moved her hips until she could feel him come. As they lay there holding each other, reluctant to move, they both realised that life was never going to be any better than this. Jessica then walked over to the coffee table opened the champagne, poured two large drinks, collected a few of the chocolates and returned to bed, putting a chocolate into her mouth gripping it in her teeth and so that Josh could bite the other half and kiss her at the same time. When all of the chocolates were eaten and all the champagne was finished, Jessica removed what remained of her lingerie and lay with her head on Josh's chest, with Josh gently stroking Jessica's hair.

A very relaxed Jessica, then said, "Don't you dare ever leave me Joshua Foster. "

Then leaning over Jessica's ear, Josh said, "I don't think I could survive without you now Jess. "Then starting to laugh said, "Because, how the hell am I ever going to find anyone who fucks me as good as you do. " Josh then immediately flinched, waiting for Jessica's to punch him in the ribs.

Chapter 21

Going Home

The next morning at exactly eight-thirty breakfast was delivered and was leisurely eaten while listening to music on the radio. "We must come here again, " said Josh. "And pretty soon we will find out what their spa facilities are like. There's nothing more relaxing than a good massage, so don't forget we are booked in for eleven-fifteen. Then we must be away from here for three. "

"Well, " said Jessica. "Why don't you take the bags down now, that would save some time? Anyway, we must check out by eleven. " When they arrived at the spa reception, they were given fresh dressing gowns and shown to the changing rooms. The spa was a touch of luxury to say the very least, with its stylish marble, glass and mood lighting. There was a central area, containing a series of small break out areas, all with cream leather soft furnishings and with modern art pictures on the down lit walls. After drinking their welcome coffees, their two lady masseurs came and after introducing themselves, took them each away for their massage. As Josh was being massaged and listening to that pan pipe music they always seem to play, he was remembering a massage he had on a cruise ship some years earlier and one he had in Bali, which was slightly eerie as the room looked extremely similar. Josh thought to himself as he lay enjoying the massage, not only do they all play the same background music, but they all must employ the same interior designers. Later after his massage, while Josh was waiting for Jessica, he phoned his brother, then Maggie and even he even called Jed.

When Jessica returned to the relaxation area, holding out her shiny new nails out in front of her for Josh to see and smiling, she said, "So what have you been up to then Josh, I know that smile?"

"I've just been talking to Sean and I was feeling very pleased knowing that he and Caroline were, well you know, extremely happy together. "

Then as they were walking towards the pool area, Jessica said, "Well come on Josh, a quick shower, dip in that beautiful swimming pool and we can then have lunch. I've just been looking at their lunchtime menu and it looks very good. "

Later in the restaurant, Josh was extremely pleased to see that they had one of his old favourites on the menu. "Looks like its muscle stew for starters then, " said a very pleased looking Josh. "Then maybe followed by lamb shank, although I'm almost too spoilt for choice here, so much on this menu that I like. So what are you having Jess, don't tell me, I bet you're having the king prawn salad and the chicken risotto. "

"Well, you're almost right, as I am having the prawns but I am then having the fennel and chicken pie. "

After checking out of the hotel and about to drive out of the car park, Josh said, "Can you find a car park near the retro fashion shop on the old satnav Jess? We can then do a little shopping in Dublin and definitely visit that retro clothes shop, oh and I need to get Dad something as well."

A couple of hours later they had arrived at the retro clothes shop and looking in the window Josh said, "Christ, I could spend some money in here Jess, come on let's see what they have inside. " Once inside the very smart middle-aged shop owner came across and immediately recognised Jessica.

"Oh, hello, it's so nice to see you back again, now how can I help you?" After trying on a couple of outfits and getting the thumbs up on both of them, they started looking the lingerie section.

"I feel like a kid in a sweet shop, " Josh said whispering in Jessica's ear. "Oh, you just must get one of these, along with two of those and I just love this. "

Needless to say, they came away carrying three large carrier bags and a box. Putting them in the car, Josh said, "It's a pity you can't try these on tonight Jess. "

"Oh no, " said Jessica. "Don't even think about it. I just want to know how the hell we are going to get it all back home. "

Looking very pleased with their purchases, Josh said, "Just think courier Jess, good old white van man, our friendly courier service, leave it with me. "

As the ferry pulled out of Dublin that evening, with Jessica and Josh stood on the rear upper deck watching Ireland fade steadily out of sight. With his arm round Jessica and kissing her neck Josh said, "Well, that was some unforgettable holiday Jess? Just think about it, I got engaged to a gorgeous girl, I found my mother's birthplace, I made a lot of new friends and I found Sean a partner. " Then feeling even more please with himself, Josh added, "That's not bad going in just a few short weeks. Three beautiful, unforgettable weeks, spent with my beautiful fiancée, now come on Jess, let's go inside and let me buy you a coffee. "

It was getting dark when they pulled into High View Farm, as Josh said laughing, "You know Jess, I'm just dying to hear how mom going to tell us where we are both sleeping in my old room. "

As they pulled up Sean and Caroline came out to greet them and the very first thing Sean said was, "Mom has told me to tell you that Jessica and you are in your old room. So, you can take your bags straight up there if you like. "

Then looking towards the house, Josh said, "Where is Mom then Sean?"

"Oh, " said Sean. "Dad and Mom are on their way back from Burton General Hospital, poor old Amos was taken into A&E on Wednesday, he's got a touch of pneumonia. "

"So why the hell did no one tell me?" said Josh, now looking slightly annoyed.

"Well, no one wanted to spoil your holiday, so we thought we would leave it until you got home. " Sean then added, "But when I spoke to Mom earlier, she had already spoken to a few of her old colleagues and it appears Amos is going to be all right. "

"Thank God for that, " said Josh. "He's been like a second dad to us and he's not actually that old, although I don't really know how old he is, but I certainly don't want him to go yet. " Sean continued to tell them that his mom had left Amos with a new fully loaded mobile phone and told Amos that like it or not he is moving in with them when he leaves hospital.

"You know Mom, once she gets something in her head and with that in mind, she has already had Uncle Terry round to see about converting the old coach house into a self-contained flat for him and plans to have a door put through leading from the drawing room. Either way, Mom is adamant that Amos comes back here and lives with us, where she can take better care of him. It's so strange that although Amos is always swearing, never does as she wants and with all of his cantankerous ways, Mom still thinks the world of him. We are all very pleased that Amos will be coming home again. "

Now in the house Josh takes their bags straight upstairs to his room, while Jessica catches up with Caroline in the kitchen. Being as Josh has Sean on his own, he asks him, "How are you getting on with Caroline then bro?"

"Well, " said Sean. "Don't ask me why, but I just know she's the one, I am so bloody sure this is it Josh, I am hoping Caroline will eventually become my future wife. In just a couple of weeks, she has literally taken over my life, I find myself just watching her, you know I just can't seem to take my eyes off her. Oh yes, Josh, Caroline is definitely the one. " Sean then added, "Thank God that you went to Ireland and found that old Sentinel, eh Josh. "

"Talking of the Sentinel, " said Josh. "How's it coming along?"

"Oh, great Josh, I will show you after dinner. And that's another thing, Caroline is a really good cook, I don't know if you remember, but Anna couldn't even boil an egg. Oh, and our dad has taken to her big time, yesterday he had one of the cow's down with a prolapsed calf bed and Caroline went down and helped him to sort it. " Dad said to me later, 'If you don't marry Caroline, I will bloody well shoot you, you will want your bloody head looking if you don't marry her. '"

"So, it's a win, win, eh Sean?" said Josh smugly smiling. Then as they headed for the kitchen, Josh thought to himself, *Didn't I just I know it, I bloody well knew it, yes you really did it again Joshua foster.* While Sean and Josh had been taking the bags upstairs, Jessica and Caroline had been having a parallel type of conversation down in the kitchen.

"How are getting on with Sean?" asked Jessica.

"It's like I have known him all my life, he is very calm, very gentle yet very strong and he's extremely understanding. I don't think there's a bad bone in his body Jess and he's such a gentleman. " Caroline then in a less enthusiastic tone, went on to say, "The only problem is Jess, I just can't bear the thought of being away from him, even for a minute. But to tell you the truth Jessica, I am also a little bit frightened though, as I have never felt like this in my life before. "

"Even with Richard?" asked Jessica.

"No Jess, never ever like this. Honestly, Jess, I would follow him anywhere, my feelings are so strong it actually worries me. "

Josh and Sean were walking into the kitchen together, when Josh said, "And what have you two been up to then?

"Never you mind, " replied Jessica. "Now look what Caroline has cooked for dinner. " It was very evident that Caroline had been busy with beef slowly roasting in the oven, vegetables all prepared and ready to go and more importantly the Yorkshire pudding batter, chilling in the fridge.

"I'm Just waiting for your mom and dad to show up before I put everything on, " said Caroline. Josh then asked if they had time to check out the Sentinel out down in the workshop.

"Well, yes no problem Josh, but as soon as you see your mom and dad, get back, " she said. "Then it will be ready after about a further twenty minutes. "

"Come on then bro, " said Josh. "Let's go and see how this old Sentinel is coming along. " When they got to the workshop and the lights came flickering on, Josh was taken aback by the progress they had already made. The chassis was almost stripped bare and now standing on four steel trestles, the axles and suspension had been removed, along with the engine and transmission unit. The workshop was cleared of all its usual clutter and all the components were neatly laid out, ready to be steam cleaned.

"Bloody hell bro, " said Josh, not quite believing his eyes. "Who's bloody army have you had in here to help you?"

"Well, " said Sean, "Dad had already cleared the workshop out ready, as well as part of the old Acos hay barn. " Sean continued to tell how Caroline had helped him strip the chassis down, photographing and cataloguing all the parts on her iPad. Sean then said laughing, "So it seems like you have lost your old job Josh, Caroline's taken over now. " Sean then went on to say, looking very proud, "It's surprising, Caroline is very knowledgeable and once started, she certainly goes for it. She even knew there were left and right-hand wheel nuts and she's a demon with the old impact wrench. Anyway, the boiler has gone off for reconditioning and I've been in touch with a guy from Worcestershire, who luckily for me owns the exact same model as this one. I tell you Josh, he sounds such a nice helpful guy and by the sounds of it, he is going to be a very useful contact. His name is Dennis Walker and what's more, he's coming up to have a look over her in a few days' time. " Sean now looking at the chassis with almost affection, said, "You spotting this old steam lorry, well and then getting me over there to look at it, is what introduced me to Caroline and this old girl here, well, she has changed my life in so many respects. " As they walked from the workshop, Sean looking back as he switched the lights off said, "I've told Jane and Howard, that I am naming her 'The Lady Jane' and it seems that Jane is really over the moon with the idea. "

Then Josh said, "I wish Howard and Jane lived nearer though, because I know I am going to be going over there on a regular basis, as I am missing them already, "

As they walked back to the house, they could see Dad's car was back. Sean said, "Another thing Josh, Mom has been a different woman since she went over to Ireland, I think Dad is still in disbelief of just how happy she is. " Sean then added, "And Mom is now driving again; she's even ordered herself a brand new, top of the range Discovery. " Putting his hand on Josh's shoulder said, "Yes Josh, it's really good to see Mom and Dad happy again. "

When they walked into the kitchen together Bridie was already in there hugging Jessica. "Ah, here you are Josh, now come and give your old mom a big kiss. Your uncle Padraig was asking if you got back OK, so I had better phone him and let him know you're all back home safe and sound. "

That evening they sat watching TV and chatting happily in the lounge when Josh said, "Oh I forgot to tell you earlier, that Jess and I are moving in together, we decided we would just have to live together from now on. "

"That's about the most sensible thing you have said, since you have been back, " said Josh's dad. Then laughing said, "Well apart from this new iPad you bought me. "

Sean then added, "And talking about sensible, don't forget he found me that old Sentinel and more importantly introduced me to Caroline. "

Then to everyone's surprise, Bridie said smiling, "Not only all those other sensible things, but Josh also found me two beautiful daughters and has given me my old family back again. And not only all that, but thanks to God above, they given me a brand-new start. " Then fetching a bottle out from the cupboard by her chair, Bridie, said, "What's more I have several bottles of Poitín, to celebrate with So if you can get me some glasses Edward, I think it's time we should all drink a toast to Joshua. " Everyone was feeling happy, as they drunk their Poitín and reminisced over their Irish experience. Dad was happily reading the instructions to his new iPad; Sean was sitting in their big old armchair cuddled up with Caroline on his lap while Josh and Jessica were reclining together on the settee. By bedtime the bottle was empty, everyone was extremely relaxed and Edward had photographed them all on his new toy.

That night while Jessica and Josh were in bed, what started as a cuddle, turned into a fondle, that turned into foreplay and before long Jessica was on top of Josh with both hands holding onto the headboard, desperately trying to stop it from banging against the wall. Happily, they managed to keep their lovemaking almost silent and

349

afterwards lay eyes closed talking very quietly, when Josh said in one of his more nostalgic moods, "You know Jess, when I was a teenager and growing up, I used to dream of having exciting sex with a beautiful girl in this bed. Well Jess, although it may have taken me a good few years, I finally got there in the end, so thank you Jess, that's another wish ticked off my bucket list. "

The next morning Josh was up early boxing up, cling filming and labelling their luggage along with those other bulky items, in readiness for the courier to collect them. Bridie, Jessica and Caroline were all in the kitchen laughing, while reminisced over Aiden's welcome party and all those wonderful things that had happened over there in Ireland.

A little later, Sean and his dad came in and dad said, "Well that's it, milking is finished until this evening, the store cattle are all done, so how about I treat you all to lunch at the Dog and Partridge in Tutbury? I think it's time to celebrate our good luck, being as we have two new daughters, Josh has got Jessica, Sean has got Caroline, I have a happy wife again and oh yes, I have a brand-new iPad. And if you could just give me a minute, or two, I will make our reservation using my shiny new iPad. Shall I tell them to expect us at about twelve-thirty?"

"I'm not sure, Dad, " said Josh looking just a little worried. "I've got the courier coming to collect our stuff, between ten and four. "

Then hearing a vehicle approach. "Then this should be him now then, " said Dad and before he could say any more Josh had gone to give the driver a hand loading his things up.

When Josh got back into the house, everyone had gone to change apart from his mom, who said in one of her quieter moods, "Do you know Josh, there were times I used to worry about you, as you were always up to something, as you know you were a proper naughty boy. But, " she then said now giving him a hug. "You have helped make my life such a happy one. "And she then gave Josh a kiss, saying, "Thank you for everything Josh, I needn't have worried at all, as you turned out really well."

When they left for lunch Caroline was driving the MG, with its top down, while Sean was sitting smiling away beside her, when Mr Foster, said, "Doesn't she just loves driving, she was driving our new fodder loader mixer this morning and was showing old Toddy how the built-in computer keypad worked. " He then added, laughing, "And I bet you any money, Caroline will be the first one to drive that old steam lorry, you just wait and see. " He then added, "It'sa pity you can't all live here with us, as I feel so happy when we are all here together, but never mind, that's life, one day, perhaps. "

As the Range Rover pulled into the Dog and Partridge car park, Bridie said, "I wonder if they have the piano player, playing here at lunchtimes, I love eating here while he plays that beautiful grand piano, so fingers crossed, eh?" When they walked in Bridie asked the waiter, "Is the pianist here today?"

"No, madam, " answered the waiter. "I am sorry to say he only plays on an evening and on a Sunday lunchtimes and evenings. "

"Oh, what a pity, but never mind we will have to come back again on an evening, won't we?" The Dog and Partridge was a favourite family pub, with a beautiful roomy and sunny restaurant, along with its old, blackened oak beam set into the ceiling.

When everyone had a drink Edward said, "Right then, here's a toast to us all, may we all have long and happy lives together. " What started out as just a lunch, turned into a real family party, everyone enjoyed the meal and well, just sharing a wonderful time with one another.

As they drove off the car park, Josh said, "See over there, Jess, well that's Tutbury Castle, or what's left of it. Mary Queen of Scots was kept prisoner there you know. It must have seemed like the middle of nowhere back then, some of the local historians still reckon there some of her hidden treasure buried round here somewhere. As Josh drove away from Tutbury, he pointed and said, "See that sign for Fauld Jess, well that was the site of one of Britain's biggest non-nuclear explosions, there's a great big depression in the ground where it happened. It's all fenced-off now, but you can see it from the fence line. It was an RAF underground munitions store, which went off during the war. "

Then laughing, Edward said, "I think we need to get one of those little microphones fitted, you know, like they

352

have on those tour buses, or better still have two, because I think Josh could wear one out within a week. "

Later that evening Sean and Caroline drove Jessica and Josh back down to Lichfield Trent Valley Station, when after a lot of long goodbyes, Jessica and Josh reluctantly caught the train back to Euston. As they sat together on the train, they reminisced about their wonderful holiday and looked forward to their future together.

Later, as they pulled into Euston Jessica, suddenly said, "Oh no, all my work clothes and most of my underwear, went with the courier. It's no good, " Jessica said, "I will just have to buy some more clothes, as soon as we get off the train, sorry but we will have to go shopping. " Twenty minutes later they were shopping in Oxford Street. "I need a suit for the office on Monday, then after work I will need to get back to Mom's and pick some more of my stuff up, "said Jessica, as she manoeuvred Josh into the entrance of a large departmental store. As they wondered through the ladies' section, Jessica pulled one or two suits off the rails and took them into the changing rooms, leaving Josh to wait. Within a few minutes, Jessica steps out wearing one of the two outfits and asks, "What do look think of this one then Josh?"

"Sorry I don't like it at all Jess, it's trouser suit. Do they do it with a matching skirt?" After getting the same response with the second outfit, they are back looking in the same section, this time looking at suits with a skirt. When Jessica steps out of the changing rooms, this time wearing a similar suit, but with a skirt, she gets the big thumbs up.

"Well, " said Jessica. "It's not something I would normally choose to wear for work, but it fits well. Oh but then I will need some tights. "

Josh then immediately replies, "No tights please Jess, it's stocking Jess, so no tights please, I think it has to be tan hold ups with that suit. " As she turns to go back into the changing room, the store lady supervising the changing rooms, said in a sympathetic voice, "Just like my husband, he hates tights as well. " Then laughing said, "I think it's a man thing, I really think it is. "

As if that wasn't bad enough, when they got to the lingerie section, Josh was there suggesting all of the most inappropriate items, prompting Jessica to say in a quiet voice, "These are for work Josh, not for the bedroom. " When they eventually left the store, with one new suit, two new blouses as well as over a dozen pairs of stockings and as many different pairs of briefs, they finally headed for Greenwich.

Riding back in the underground Josh said, "I've just remembered some of the benefits of living in the city Jess, late night shopping and loads of choices. "

"Yes, " said Jessica. "Way too many choices, especially when I have you with me. "

When they got back to Josh's flat, they immediately dumped their bags and went round to see Maggie.

Opening the door to Maggie's, house Josh shouted, "Hi ya Maggie, we're home. "

"Oh, come on through, I am in the kitchen, " replied a very pleased looking Maggie. "Now before we do anything Jessica, let me see your engagement ring. " After telling Jessica how lovely it was and how happy she was for them both, Maggie then led them through into the living room, saying, "Now this calls for a celebration drink, what would you like, how about a big gin and tonic?" After handing them their drinks, a very happy Maggie said, "Now Jessica, please tell me all about your holiday. " While Jessica and Maggie sat on the settee, with Jessica telling her all about the wedding, their engagement, Sean's engagement, and Josh's newfound family. Meanwhile, Josh sat listening on and smiling, while he was gently stroked Maggie's cat. That's when he thought to himself, *If there's a God above, I think it's about time you should thank him Josh.* While Maggie and Jessica were chatting, Josh secretly phoned his favourite Chinese restaurant and ordered them all a big takeaway. Jessica and Maggie were a little surprised when the doorbell rang, and Josh rushed out to answer it. When Josh then came back in carrying two carrier bags, saying, "It's Chinese food tonight. "

Jessica said, "But you never asked Maggie or I what we wanted. " Josh, now holding one of the three bags up said, "No need to ask because I know exactly what Maggie likes. "And then holding up the second bag, said, "In fact I know exactly what both of my favourite ladies like. "

Later as they sat in the conservatory, with the sun going down Maggie said looking at Jessica, "You will never know how pleased I was when Josh asked if you could stay here with him. I now have my two favourite friends living right next door. " And then walking back towards the drink cabinet Maggie said, "Now who wants to join me in another large gin?"

It was late when they both climbed into Josh's bed and Josh said, "Welcome to our new home Jess, I know we've had a long day, today, so tomorrow I think we should stay in bed till lunchtime?" Then, with a cheeky smile said, "And then we can fuck each other all morning.

"That sounds like an extremely good plan to me, " said Jessica as she switched off the bedside light.

Chapter 22

The next morning Jessica was gently woken by Josh kissing her neck and fondling her breasts. "Oh you're awake are you, sorry sweetheart, but I just couldn't resist it, you looked so lovely laying there. "

Jessica now turning to face him and kissing him on the lips said, "Please don't apologise, that's the nicest way you could ever wake me. " Now reaching down under the covers, said, "Joshua Foster, what is this beautiful thing I have in my hand, is it for me?"

Josh shuffling a little closer said, "Oh that feels really nice and yes, it's all yours Jess. "

Then slowly sinking under the covers Jessica said, "Well this is very nice, very nice indeed, I wonder what it tastes like?" After a while they moved into the sixty-nine position and spent a long time giving each other as much pleasure as they possibly could, which is something you may have already realised, they enjoy immensely.

Later as Jessica climbed on top of Josh, he said, "Look Jess, just because this is my favourite position, it doesn't mean you have to finish up like this every time, you know."

Then bending forwards, to kiss him, but with her hair getting in the way said, "Don't be silly Josh, this is one of my favourite positions too. " Then smiling said, "This way I feel I am in complete control, didn't you know that Josh, it's a girl thing?" Then cheekily Jessica said, "Now, are you ready to get fucked, because I need that beautiful thing of yours in just as far as it can go?" She then added with a laugh, "And apart from feeling good, well it's really great exercise as well. " Jessica then with her eyes closed and with the expression of intense pleasure on her face, once again took themselves to the height of sexual pleasure. Afterwards, they both just lay there, relaxing in each other's arms, enjoying their morning in bed.

After breakfast, Jessica unpacked their bags and loaded the washing machine, while Josh made space in his wardrobe and a few of the storage drawers. At the end of the exercise, Josh had a great pile of old clothes, surplus to requirements, which he placed in bin bags, ready for the charity shop.

"Right Jess, " Josh called. "I've now got some space for your clothes, just come and see if this is OK for you?"

When Jessica came in to see, she said, "Well it will have to do for now, but I really think we are going to need some more storage space. " When Jessica had hung up what few clothes she had, she smiled to herself, when she realised, that apart from her newly purchased work suits, the only other clothes she had bought back in her overnight bag, was a 50s style retro dress and a few other non-suitable for work items of clothing. When she finished putting her underwear away in her two newly obtained drawers, she smiled, when she realised, that both drawers looked a little like the returns bin at Anne Summers. By midday, they had more or less prepared workwise for the week ahead, when Josh said, "How about a walk down to Greenwich indoor market then Jess, we can get some food in and have a drink at this nice pub I know, and they have live music. I will ask Maggie if she wants to come. And I thought later we could maybe go for a walk in the park, or take a boat up the river, I always enjoy that and when we get back, have a relax in the garden. "

"No Josh, sorry, " said Jessica. "I just have to go home, over to Epson and get some more clothes, I really must. " Later that day, they headed over to Jessica's parents and on the way there Jessica chatted to Caroline and Josh chatted to Sean and then later on Josh spoke to Howard. When they got to Jessica's parents' house, Mary made them dinner and while they sat at the table, Jessica handed over a small package to her mother.

"What is it?" asked Mary.

"It's for you, Mom, it's an engagement gift from Sean and Caroline. "

As Mary removed the necklace from its small black case, then holding it up to her neck, while looking at herself in the mirror, Mary said, "Oh it's gorgeous. "

Jessica then said, "The stone is Blue John, Mom, they bought one for all of us, it's a reminder for when Sean proposed to Caroline, down at Blue John Mine. Apparently, Blue John stone is now very rare. "

"Sean's such a lovely man, now wasn't that a lovely thought. Now come on Jessica, let's get you some clothes sorted out. "And at that, they both left for Jessica's bedroom.

While they were upstairs, Josh and Gerry sat watching TV and chatting. Sounding rather pensive, Gerry said, "Do you know Josh, I've been dreading this, you know, with our Jessica leaving home. But I can see she's extremely happy and it was always going to happen one day. So please, you just make sure you take good care of her, as Jessica is all Mary and I have. "

Josh in reply said, "You don't have to worry about that Gerry, Jessica is extremely precious to me as well and I promise you, I will take very good care of her. "

Then as they carried on watching TV, Gerry said, "So what's this Blue John they are going on about then Josh? Because, I have never heard of it. " Josh then explained how it was mined in up in the Derbyshire Peak District and that visitors can go underground.

"Well, that is if you can manage the two hundred or more stone steps leading down. But it's well worth a visit Gerry, in fact, if you feel like going there, please let us know and we could go with you. " Josh then said, "Maybe we could all spend the weekend up there, because the Peak District is beautiful, it's my favourite part of the country. "

After a couple of minutes silently watching TV, Gerry said, "Yes Josh, I think we should do that, I'll have a word with Mary and let you know. " Both Gerry and Josh were slightly concerned when they heard loud banging on the stairs.

"You all right Mary?" shouted Gerry.

"No problem, " said Mary. "We're just getting this suitcase down, but it's rather heavy. "

Josh and Gerry immediately went to assist and when Josh saw the size and felt the weight of her suitcase, he said, "That's decided it Jess, I think it has to be a taxi back home then. "

As they were saying their goodbyes and the taxi pulled in, Jessica said, "I'll call you when I get home. "Then realising what she had said, "Well that is when I get to my other home. "

In the taxi home Josh said, "I feel a little sorry for your mom and dad, they are really going to miss you. " And then added, "Well I know I would if I were them. " That evening they sat in the garden with Maggie, telling her all about their wonderful holiday in Ireland.

As the evening was getting a little chilly and they were about to go in for the night Josh said, pointing to a corner of the patio, "You know Maggie, that would be an ideal place for a hot tub, I think I will get one if you don't object. " After a couple of hours putting clothes away and rearranging the bathroom, they eventually climbed into bed, set the alarm and went to sleep.

It was a bit of a shock to the system, when the alarm went off the next morning, being as they could have quite easily lay there together happily for another hour or so. While eating breakfast, Josh found himself with a new dilemma, a problem he had not properly considered, that of waiting for the bathroom. When eventually Jessica came out, she said smiling, "Oh were you waiting for me?

sorry I didn't realise. " When Josh came out of the bathroom, a fresh white shirt, newly pressed trousers and a very striking silk tie was laid out on the bed. When he was dressed in his new shirt and tie, Josh went to the wardrobe to collect his work stuff, but it was no longer there.

"Have you seen my work stuff, which was laying in the bottom of the wardrobe, Jess?" asked Josh.

"What that pile of old papers and rubbish, dumped in the bottom?" asked Jessica. "I put it in one of those bin bags in the spare room. " After ten minutes of franticly searching for it, he finally gathered it back up and put it back in his old rucksack. Josh now went to the small cloakroom just off the hallway and was now looking for his favourite work jacket. Fast giving up and in desperation he called out to Jessica, "Have you seen my work jacket?"

Immediately back came the reply, "If you mean that scruffy old anorak, I have hidden it, but I have left you that nice green coat the one that you never seem to wear. " Jessica then added, "I am not having you go into the office looking like a scruff. But don't worry, I have transferred everything from the pockets. "

Now in the kitchen with his nice green coat on and with his rucksack containing his work stuff and looking slightly different, Josh kissed Jessica goodbye and left for the office, calling out, "See you tonight Jess. "He closed the door.

At 08. 45, when Josh gets to the office reception, he was immediately confronted by Rachael, the security manageress, who in a very commanding voice says, "Right Mr Joshua Foster, you my friend, are going absolutely nowhere until you have swiped in. " After rummaging through his rucksack, Josh finally found his ID card and as instructed, reluctantly swipes his card.

"Sorry sir, " said Rachael, seeing a red light on the display. "But your card seems to have expired, so it will need resetting, that's as if it has not been used in over a six-week period, it automatically cancels out. "

Now looking a little concerned Josh says, "But I was here three weeks ago, I was here with you, you must remember, I was going on holiday, so it should be fine?"

Rachael now looking at her terminal screen says, "According to our records sir, you have neither swiped in or out for the last seven weeks. " Josh, feeling utterly beaten, was now having to fill a new card application form and was then given a temporary visitors card. Only then, was he finally able to get through security.

Rachael, now smiling broadly, said, "Oh, by the way, welcome back Josh, I really like the jacket, and may I say, you look really smart, yes Josh you're looking very cool. " As Josh made his way through the office everyone was welcoming him back and also commenting on how smart he looked.

When Josh got to his work area, Helen, in amazement, said, "Welcome back Joshua, my word you do look very business-like today, yes very smart indeed. " Then Helen said, "Doesn't he look smart today Sam?"

Throwing his bag under his desk, Josh goes straight into see Jed, who on seeing him said, "Welcome back Josh, pleased to see you are taking this company development seriously. You know, I've never seen you dressed this smart, well not since your first interview. " Jed went on to say, "When you have read your emails and sorted your team out, I want you to look through these CVs, there's a couple here, which look fairly promising. By the way, I believe congratulations are in order, Maggie told me, that at last you have seen common sense and have got engaged to that lovely Jessica So well done Josh, now don't forget those CVs. " That afternoon Josh spent several satisfying and very productive hours going through their business improvement plans with Jed.

And all through the day everyone of Josh's friends and colleagues, were commenting on how smart he looked and as Josh finally left through reception at the end of his busy day, a voice said, "Here you are Josh, don't forget this, it's your new ID card and may I say Josh, I really like your new look. "

Josh, realising that Rachael had well and truly got her own back and had even rubbed it in, laughing said, "Good night Rachael. " And now waving his new card, said, "See you in the morning sweetheart. " Whilst travelling home on the tube, Josh suddenly realised that his life had significantly improved, now that Jessica was sharing his life and that the change was certainly one for the better. On his way back home, Josh caught the odd glimpse of himself reflected in shop windows and he could see, he was definitely looking much smarter than the old Josh. When he got home, he could see the courier had been as all their luggage was in the hallway, taking a quick look, he could see that even the oil painting had got there in one piece.

After hanging his new green jacket up and throwing his rucksack to the back of the cloakroom, Josh headed straight for the kitchen. He was surprised to find that Jessica wasn't there and thought it was very strange as Jessica generally finished work earlier than he did. Josh now getting slightly worried, tried calling Jessica a couple of times, but with no response, his concerns now started to worry him. Filling the kettle, Josh thought to himself, *I hope Jess hasn't changed her mind and gone back home to live in Epson.* But just then he heard the door opening and Jessica calling out, "I'm home. "

"Oh yes, Maggie told me she had let the courier in, oh that's good news. " When Jessica came into the kitchen, Josh could see immediately where she had been.

Carrying several large bags, Jessica said, "I was looking through your clothes, yesterday and I could see that they were seriously letting you down, so I've been clothes shopping for you. " As Jessica showed Josh what she had bought him, it was not really registering, as Josh was just pleased to see Jessica home again.

"Did you see our things have come. " Jessica then said, "Oh and I went on eBay today and ordered a new flat pack wardrobe, it should be here for the weekend. Quicker we get that up the better, anyway, how was your day?" As they sat eating dinner, Jessica said, "I have to admit it Josh, I had so many lovely comments today, about the suit with the skirt I was wearing, so I stopped on the way home and got another one. Even my boss said how good I looked, and he never usually notices anything like that. Then looking at her feet Jessica said, "Oh yes and I got some new shoes to match as well. " Josh sat there just smiling, thinking, to himself, *Sweetheart you could buy what the hell you like, I am just happy that you're back here with me.*

That evening as they sat watching TV and chatting Josh said, "Thank you Jess. "

"What for?" asked Jessica

"Everything Jess, absolutely everything, " replied Josh.

Chapter 23

This is unfortunately where we have to leave Josh and Jessica, but obviously their lives go happily on.

A year later, there was a very special double wedding in Ireland. Needless to say, after the ceremony there were two new Mrs Fosters. Their joint honeymoon was taken on a cruise ship, accompanied by almost everyone they knew. After meeting at one of the ship's afternoon dance sessions, Maggie stuck up a strong friendship with a retired American Army Major. Howard and Jane got their hot tub and spent ten days touring the Peak District. Jessica and Josh joined a local gun club and as good as her word, Aunty Jane bought Jessica her first match rifle.

Eight months later Josh was given a partnership in Dunning & Partners and after training up three new members of his team, Josh rarely worked away from home. The steam lorry now named 'Lady Jane' was completely renovated and toured the various agricultural shows and steam rallies, normally driven by Howard Anson, accompanied by his new stoker/engineer Mrs Jane Anson. Sadly, old Amos developed a chest infection and passed away at a local hospice. Bridie and Edward Foster had been there at his bedside earlier that day, when Amos whispered to Bridie with a knowing smile, "I shall be dancing with Sheila again tonight. " In his will, Amos left the farm to Sean and Josh in equal shares. Within weeks of each other, both Jessica and Caroline were pregnant. The old oil painting Jessica bought in Limerick, was sold for an undisclosed amount and using some of the auction money Jessica purchased the yacht 'Blow Me' from her Uncle Howard. The yacht was eventually sailed down to the River Medway and was used most weekends and holidays.

A year later, Bridie's old family home near Swinford was renovated and became Bridie and Edward's holiday home. Mary and Gerry Holmes sold their house in Epsom and moved to a smaller house in the Derbyshire Peak district, soon after they fell in love with the area, following their trip to the Blue John Mine. Aiden kept up the story telling nights in Mad O' Riley's Bar and became a very sought after and well known, after dinner speaker and who's stories often featured on their local radio station.

Four years on, Josh and Jessica were the proud parents of twin girls and a baby boy. Josh had his Uncle Terry and his cousin renovated Amos' old house which then became Josh and Jessica's new family home. Josh commuted to London twice a week and often stayed overnight Maggie and her charming new army major partner. Sean and Caroline also became proud parents of two very good-looking boys and as agreed Sean took over the running of the Mainear Darach Estate as well as the family farm. Sean, as promised taught Caroline to fly and often commuted between the two farms using their newly acquired second-hand Cessna. Bridie and Edward, more or less, retired from farming and shared their time between High View Farm and their Swinford home, just enjoying the company of their grandchildren as well as the close friendship of their second family in Ireland.

It is with much pleasure I can report that fortune continued to smile on the Foster family and friends, but as they say, that could be another story.

THE END